Praise for
New York Times bestselling author
Brenda Jackson

"The only flaw of this first-rate, satisfyingly sexy tale is that it ends."
—*Publishers Weekly*, starred review,
on *Forged in Desire*

"[Jackson's] signature is to create full-sensory romances that deliver on the heat, and she duly delivers.... [S]ure to make any reader swoon."
—*RT Book Reviews* on *Forged in Desire*

"Leave it to Jackson to take sizzle and honor, wrap it in romance and come up with a first-rate tale."
—*RT Book Reviews* on *Temptation*

"Brenda Jackson is the queen of newly discovered love... If there's one thing Jackson knows how to do, it's how to pluck those heartstrings and stir up some seriously saucy drama."
—*BookPage* on *Inseparable*

"This deliciously sensual romance ramps up the emotional stakes and the action.... [S]exy and sizzling."
—*Library Journal* on *Intimate Seduction*

"Jackson does not disappoint...first-class page-turner."
—*RT Book Reviews* on *A Silken Thread*, 4½ stars,
Top Pick!

"Jackson is a master at writing."
—*Publishers Weekly* on *Sensual Confessions*

BRENDA JACKSON

BEST LAID PLANS

HQN™

HQN™

ISBN-13: 978-1-335-90069-2

Best Laid Plans

Copyright © 2018 by Brenda Streater Jackson

Recycling programs
for this product may
not exist in your area.

Printed in U.S.A.

To the man who will always and forever
be the love of my life and the wind beneath
my wings, Gerald Jackson, Sr.

Special thanks to LaSonde Jones, Dana Ross,
Aquanetta Powell and Samantha Miguez for naming
the newborn Madaris twins—Landon and London.

Special thanks to Joyce Snipes for naming
Ivy Chapman's perfume, Forever You.

To all my readers who waited patiently
for a new Madaris novel, this book is for you.

In memory of my fur baby Yorkie,
who passed away during the writing of this book.
Mookie, you are deeply missed.

I have found the one whom my soul loves.
—*Song of Solomon* 3:4

THE MADARIS FAMILY

Milton Madaris, Sr. and Felicia Laverne Lee Madaris

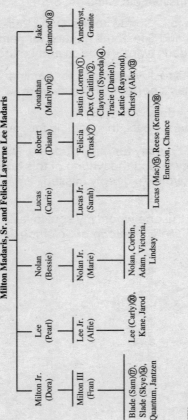

Milton Jr. (Dora)
- Milton III (Fran)
  - Blade (Sam)⑩, Slade (Skye)⑭, Quantum, Jantzen

Lee (Pearl)
- Lee Jr. (Alfie)
  - Lee (Carly)⑳, Kane, Jarod

Nolan (Bessie)
- Nolan Jr. (Marie)
  - Nolan, Corbin, Adam, Victoria, Lindsay

Lucas (Carrie)
- Lucas Jr. (Sarah)
  - Felicia (Trask)⑦
  - Lucas (Mac)⑮, Reese (Kenna)⑱, Emerson, Chance

Robert (Diana)

Jonathan (Marilyn)㉑
- Justin (Lorren)①, Dex (Caitlin)②, Clayton (Syneda)④, Tracie (Daniel), Kattie (Raymond), Christy (Alex)⑬

Jake (Diamond)⑧
- Amethyst, Granite

KEY:

( ) – denotes a spouse

○ and number – denotes title of book for that couple's story

① Tonight and Forever
② Whispered Promises
③ Cupid's Bow
④ Eternally Yours
⑤ One Special Moment
⑥ Fire and Desire
⑦ Truly Everlasting
⑧ Secret Love
⑨ True Love
⑩ Surrender
⑪ Strictly Business
⑫ The Midnight Hour
⑬ Unfinished Business
⑭ Slow Burn
⑮ Taste of Passion
⑯ Seduced by a Stranger
⑰ Sensual Confessions
⑱ Inseparable
⑳ Courting Justice
⑳ A Madaris Bride for Christmas
㉑ A Very Merry Romance

THE MADARIS FRIENDS

Maurice and Stella Grant

Angelique Hamilton Chenault

Kyle Garwood (Kimara)③

Trevor (Corinthians)⑥,
Regina (Mitch)⑪

Sterling Hamilton (Colby)⑤,
Nicholas Chenault (Shayla)⑨

Ashton Sinclair   Drake Warren   Trent Jordache   Nedwyn Lansing   Sheikh Rasheed Valdemon   DeAngelo Di Meglio
(Netherland)⑩   (Tori)⑫   (Brenna)⑨   (Diana)⑭   (Johari)⑯   (Peyton)⑲

KEY:

( ) – denotes a spouse

○ and number – denotes title of book for that couple's story

① Tonight and Forever	⑧ Secret Love
② Whispered Promises	⑨ True Love
③ Cupid's Bow	⑩ Surrender
④ Eternally Yours	⑪ Strictly Business
⑤ One Special Moment	⑫ The Midnight Hour
⑥ Fire and Desire	⑬ Unfinished Business
⑦ Truly Everlasting	⑭ Slow Burn

⑮ Taste of Passion
⑯ Seduced by a Stranger
⑰ Sensual Confessions
⑱ Inseparable
⑲ Courting Justice

PART ONE

"You often meet your fate on the road you take to avoid it."

—Jean de La Fontaine

PROLOGUE

Christmas Day

NOLAN MADARIS III took a sip of his beer while standing on the balcony of his condo. Leaning against the rail, he had a breathtaking view of the exclusive fifteen-story Madaris Building that was surrounded by a cluster of upscale shops, restaurants and a beautiful jogging park with a huge man-made pond. The condo where he lived was right across from the water.

The entire complex, including the condos, had been architecturally designed, engineered and constructed by the Madaris Construction Company that was owned by his cousins Blade and Slade. For the holidays the Madaris Building, surrounding shops, restaurants and jogging park were beautifully decorated with colorful, bright lights. It was hard to believe a new year was just a week away.

When Nolan had arrived home from his cousin Lee's wedding, he hadn't bothered to remove his tuxedo. Instead he'd headed straight for the refrigerator, grabbed a beer and proceeded to the balcony for a bit of mental relaxation. But all his mind could do was recall the moment his ninety-something-year-old great-grandmother, Felicia Laverne Madaris, had finally cornered him at the reception that evening. She was a notorious matchmaker, and he'd been avoiding her all night. Her success rate was too astounding to suit him—and she had calmly warned him that he was next.

He was just as determined not to be.

Nolan, his brother Corbin, and his cousins Reese and Lee had all been born within a fifteen-month period. They were as close as brothers and had been thick as thieves while growing up. Mama Laverne swore her goal was to marry them all off before she took her last breath. They all told her that wouldn't happen, but then the next thing they knew, Reese had married Kenna and today Lee married Carly.

What bothered Nolan more than anything about his great-grandmother setting her schemes on him was that she of all people knew what he'd gone through with Andrea Dunmire. Specifically, the hurt, pain and humiliation she had caused him. Not to mention her cunning, scheming and underhanded manipulations. Yes, it had been years ago and he had got over it, but there were some things you didn't forget. A woman ripping your heart out of your chest was one of them.

Andrea had meticulously plotted and carried out her plan while conspiring with her cousin to do so. He had learned a hard lesson he would never forget. As a result, he would not allow anyone—not even his great-grandmother—to manipulate him into doing anything he didn't want to do. If he wasn't on board, then to hell with it.

Nolan knew in his heart his great-grandmother's intentions were good. He could even believe that she might have a golden thumb where matchmaking was concerned. But his feelings about being manipulated and controlled by anyone, including Felicia Laverne Madaris, wouldn't change. He intended to resist, defy and oppose whatever trick, tactic or scheme her pretty little mind conjured up with every fiber of his being.

His cell phone rang. Recognizing the ringtone, he pulled it out of his pocket and answered, "Yes, Corbin?"

"Hey, man, I just wanted to check on you. We saw you tear out of here like the devil himself was after you. It's Christmas and we thought you would stay the night at Whispering Pines and continue to party like the rest of us."

Whispering Pines was their granduncle Jake's ranch. Nolan took another sip of his beer before saying, "I couldn't stay knowing Mama Laverne is already plotting my downfall. You wouldn't believe what she told me."

"We weren't standing far away and heard."

Nolan shook his head in frustration. "So now all of you know that Mama Laverne's friend's granddaughter is the woman she's picked out for me."

"Yes, and we got a name. Reese and I overheard Mama Laverne tell Grandaunt Marilyn that your future wife's name is Ivy Chapman."

"Like hell the woman is my future wife." Nolan had never met her and didn't intend to. "All this time I thought Mama Laverne was plotting to marry the woman's grand-daughter off to Lee. She set me up real good."

Corbin didn't say anything and Nolan was glad because for the moment he needed the silence. It didn't matter to him one iota that so far, every one of his cousins whose wives had been selected by his great-grandmother was madly in love with their spouses and saw her actions as a blessing and not a curse. What mattered was that she should not have interfered in the process. And what bothered him more than anything was knowing that he was next on her list. He didn't want her to find him a wife. When and if he was ready for marriage, he was certainly capable of finding one on his own.

"You've come up with a plan?" Corbin interrupted Nolan's thoughts to ask.

Nolan thought of the diabolical plan which his cousin Lee had put in place to counteract their great-grandmother's shenanigans and was guaranteed to outsmart Mama Laverne for sure. However, in the end, Lee's plan had backfired.

"No, why waste my time planning anything? I simply refuse to play the games Mama Laverne is intent on playing. What I'm going to do is ignore her foolishness and enjoy my life as the newest eligible Madaris bachelor."

He could say that since, at thirty-four, he was ten months older than Corbin, who would be next on their great-grandmother's hit list. "By the time I make my rounds, there won't be a single woman living in Houston who won't know I'm not marriage material. Especially one Miss Ivy Chapman," Nolan added.

Corbin chuckled. "That sounds like a plan to me."

"Not a plan. Just stating my intentions. I refuse to let Mama Laverne shove a wife that I don't want down my throat just because she thinks she can and that she should."

After ending the call with his brother, Nolan swallowed the last of his beer. Like he'd told Corbin, he didn't have a plan and wouldn't waste time coming up with one. What he intended to do was to have fun, as much fun as any single man could possibly have.

A huge smile touched his lips as he left the balcony. Walking into his condo, he headed for his bedroom. Quickly removing the tux, he changed into a pair of slacks and a pullover sweater. The night was still young and there was no reason for him not to go out and celebrate the holiday.

As he moved toward his front door, he started humming "Jingle Bells." *Let the fun begin.*

CHAPTER ONE

Fifteen months later...

NOLAN CLICKED OFF his mobile phone, satisfied with the call he'd just ended with Lee about his cousin's newest hotel, the Grand MD Paris. Construction of the huge megastructure had begun three weeks ago. Already it was being touted by the media as the hotel of the future and Nolan would have to agree.

This would be the third hotel Lee and his business partner, DeAngelo Di Meglio, had built. And knowing Lee and DeAngelo like he did, Nolan expected the Grand MD Paris to open its doors on time in two years with fanfare and the likes of a presidential inauguration.

Nolan's company, Madaris Innovations, would provide all the electronic and technology work for the Grand MD Paris; some would be the first of its kind anywhere. All high-tech and trend changing. It would be Nolan's first project of this caliber and he appreciated Lee and DeAngelo for giving him the opportunity.

After getting a master's degree at MIT, Nolan had begun working for Chenault Electronics at their Chicago office. Chenault Electronics was considered one of the top ten electronics companies in the world. The owner, Nicholas Chenault, was a family friend and had taken Nolan under his wing and had not only been his boss but his mentor as well. After eight years working for Chenault, Nolan had returned to Houston to start his own company.

Nolan leaned back in his chair. He had returned from spending two weeks in Paris just yesterday. In a way, he regretted being back in Houston. Before leaving, he had done everything in his power to become the life of every party, and his reputation as Houston's number one playboy had been cemented. In some circles, he'd been pegged as Mr. One-Night Stand since most of his dates were one-night stands. Now that he was back, that role had to be revived.

It hadn't taken him long to discover the life of a Casanova was pretty damn taxing and way too demanding. The nights of mindless, emotionless sex with women whose names he barely remembered wasn't all that it was cracked up to be. He only hoped that Ivy Chapman's grandmother and his great-grandmother were getting the message—he had no intentions of settling down anytime soon. At least not in the next twenty-five years or so.

Unfortunately, it seemed nothing was deterring Ivy Chapman.

Nolan picked up the envelope on top of the stack on his desk. He knew what it was and who it had come from. He recalled getting the first one three months ago and he had received several more since then. He wondered why Ivy Chapman was still sending him these little personal notes when he refused to acknowledge them. All of the notes said the same thing... *Nolan, I would love to meet you. Call me so it can be arranged. Here is my number...*

Nolan didn't give a royal flip what her phone number

was since he had no intentions of calling her. He would continue to ignore Miss Chapman and any correspondence she sent him. No matter what, he refused to give in to his great-grandmother's matchmaking shenanigans. He refused to be manipulated.

Tossing the envelope aside, he picked up his cell phone to call his family and let them know he was back. He had slept off jet lag most of yesterday and hadn't talked to anyone other than his cousin Reese and his brother Corbin. Reese and his wife, Kenna, were expecting their first baby in June and everyone was excited.

Nolan ended the call with his parents, stood and walked over to the window to look out. Like most of his relatives, he leased space in the Madaris Building. His electronics company was across the hall from Madaris Explorations, owned by his older cousin Dex.

He loved Houston in March, but it always brought out dicey weather. You had some warm days but there were days when winter refused to fade into the background while spring tried emerging. He was ready for warmer days and couldn't wait to spend time at the cottage he'd purchased last year on Tiki Island, which was on the Galveston Bay. He'd hired Ron Seamore as the property manager to handle the leasing of the cottage whenever he wasn't using it. So far it had turned out to be not only a great investment, but also a splendid getaway place whenever he needed a break from the demands of his job, life itself and yes, of course, the women who tried demanding his time.

The buzzer sounded and he walked back over to his desk. "Yes, Marlene?" Marlene was an older woman in her fifties who'd worked as his administrative assistant since he started the company three years ago.

"There's a woman here to see you, Mr. Madaris. She doesn't have an appointment and says it's important."

Nolan frowned, glancing at his watch. It wasn't even ten in the morning. Who would show up at his office without an appointment and at this hour? "Who is she?"

"A Miss Ivy Chapman."

He guessed she was tired of sending notes that went unanswered. Hadn't she heard around town what a scoundrel he was? The last man any woman should be interested in? So what was she doing here?

There was only one way to find out.

"Send her in, Marlene."

"Yes, Mr. Madaris."

Nolan had eased into his jacket and straightened his tie before his office door swung open. The first thing he saw was a huge bouquet of flowers that was bigger than the person carrying them. Why was the woman bringing him flowers? Did she honestly think a huge bouquet of flowers would work when her cute little notes hadn't?

He couldn't see the woman's face for the huge vase of flowers, and without saying a word, not even so much as a good morning, she plopped the monstrosity on his desk with a loud thump. It was a wonder the vase hadn't cracked. Hell, maybe it had. He could just imagine water spilling all over his desk.

Nolan looked from the flowers that were taking up entirely too much space on his desk to the woman who'd unceremoniously placed them there. He was not prepared for the beauty of the soft brown eyes behind a pair of thick-rimmed glasses or the perfect roundness of her face and the creamy cocoa coloring of her complexion. And he couldn't miss the fullness of her lips that were pursed tight in anger.

"I'm only going to warn you but this once, Nolan Madaris. Do not send me any more flowers. Doing so won't change a thing. I've decided to come tell you personally—the same thing I've repeatedly told your great-grandmother and my grandmother—there is no way I'd ever become involved with you. Ever."

Her words shocked him to the point that he could only stand there and stare at her. She'd crossed her arms over her chest and stared back. "Well?" she asked in a voice filled with annoyance when he continued to stare at her and say nothing. "Do I make myself clear?"

Finding his voice, Nolan said, "You most certainly do. However, there's a problem and I consider it a major one."

Those beautiful eyes were razor sharp and directed at him. "And just what problem is that?"

Now it was he who turned a cutting gaze on her. "I never sent you any flowers. Today or ever."

IVY CHAPMAN STARED at the man who had the gall to make such an outlandish statement. Of course he'd been sending her flowers. His name had been signed on every card. She'd got one bouquet after another over the past three months. And the card always said the same thing. *Ivy, I would love to meet you. Call me so it can be arranged. Here is my number...*

"What do you mean you didn't send me any flowers?"

Dark eyes filled with agitation bored into her. "Just what I said. I haven't sent you any flowers."

"Are you or are you not Nolan Madaris?" She asked the question, although she knew the answer. Over the past year his face had appeared often in the Houston newspapers as one of the city's most eligible bachelors.

"Yes, I'm Nolan Madaris. At least one of them. I'm the third. My father is the second and my grandfather is the first. However, I can say with a degree of certainty that they didn't send you any flowers either."

Ivy frowned. "Look at the card. If it didn't come from you, then who did it come from?"

The man had the nerve to scowl at her before snatching the envelope off the flowers and opening it. A frown spread across his lips before he glanced back at her. "Regardless of my name being on this card, I didn't send these flowers or any others you might have received, Miss Chapman. However, I might know who did, and it's probably the same person who's been sending me little notes from you."

Surprise lit her eyes. "What little notes? I haven't been sending you any notes."

"You haven't?" he asked, retrieving a small envelope from his desk and handing it to her. "Is this not from you?"

She took the envelope, opened it and pulled out the note card inside and read it. Moments later, she shifted her gaze back to him. "Certainly not."

He nodded. "I believe you. And just so you know, I've received several personal note cards over the past three months, supposedly from you. Just like you received those flowers, supposedly from me."

Ivy paused to collect herself. It was crystal clear they'd been played. "Who on earth would..." She stopped midsentence, when a person immediately came to mind. "My grandmother."

"And my great-grandmother," he said.

"Ms. Laverne?" she asked as her gaze moved to the wall on the other side of his desk where a huge portrait of the woman she knew to be Felicia Laverne Madaris hung.

"You know my great-grandmother?"

"Yes," Ivy said, returning her gaze to his. "She and my grandmother have been good friends for years. I'm told their friendship began when Nana got her first teaching job out of college."

He nodded. "You are aware they want to matchmake us?" he asked her.

Yes, she'd been aware of it but had chosen to ignore it. "Yes, but I never thought they would go this far."

"Well, obviously, they did," he said, throwing the card he'd been holding down on his desk. "I don't know about you, Miss Chapman, but I won't put up with this," he said in a tone filled with anger. "I refuse to be manipulated and will be dealing with my great-grandmother for her part in this."

Ivy felt so embarrassed by how she'd stormed into his office ready to give him hell. She should have known better. Men who looked like him didn't pursue women who looked like her. She was definitely not his type, if the tabloid pictures of him with his many, many women were anything to judge by. That fact should be obvious to his great-grandmother and her grandmother.

"I intend to deal with my grandmother as well. I just don't understand. Of all people, my grandmother knows the last thing I'd want is to be involved with a man like you."

His gaze narrowed. "And what exactly is 'a man like me'?"

Did he really want her to spell it out for him? In that case, she had no problem doing so. "Mr. Madaris, you have quite a reputation around town. There obviously isn't a commitment bone in your body. No woman in her right mind who's looking for a serious relationship would look your way."

He crossed his arms over his chest. A very broad, very firm, very fine-looking chest, she couldn't help but notice. "And are you looking for a serious relationship, Miss Chapman?"

"No, and of all people my grandmother should know that. Good day, Mr. Madaris. I apologize for bothering you."

She turned to leave with as much dignity as she could muster after such an embarrassing encounter. The reality of the situation was that they'd been played by two crafty old women. "Hey, wait a minute. And just what am I supposed to do with these flowers?"

Ivy turned back around, met his gaze and lifted her chin. She tried ignoring that dark penetrating gaze that seemed to see to the heart of her. "The same thing you can do with those cards that I didn't send. Trash them."

She paused and looked at the flowers. "On second thought, they are way too pretty to be trashed."

And they were. A huge assortment of white lilies, blue delphiniums, alstroemerias and yellow roses in a beautiful ceramic vase. "I suggest you drop them off at a hospital or nursing home. That's what I did with all the others. Or you can give them to your great-grandmother."

And with that, Ivy turned and walked out of his office.

CHAPTER TWO

Ivy Chapman HAD insulted him, and very few women did that. In fact, Nolan couldn't name one who ever had. He should feel delighted, downright overjoyed that his strategy had worked and she'd thought he was a two-bit womanizer. However, something was keeping him from being filled with over-the-top excitement. Probably the realization that he'd been conned by his great-grandmother.

He'd told Corbin over a year ago that he refused to come up with some elaborate plan to counteract his great-grandmother's shenanigans. There was no plan that could outsmart Felicia Laverne Madaris. Rather, he was simply going to enjoy life—and women—to the fullest. A strategy aimed at deterring the woman his great-grandmother had selected as his bride.

He figured sooner or later Miss Chapman would get wind of his womanizing ways and come to the conclusion that he was a man incapable of ever committing to any one woman. The most logical thing for her to do would be to put up as much resistance to a Madaris-Chapman match as he would be doing. That's why those notes had annoyed the hell out of him. It seemed no matter how many women he became involved with, she was determined not to go anywhere. Now he knew that hadn't been the case at all and his strategized efforts had worked.

So why was it bothering him that she was thinking the very thing he'd wanted her to think about him? Maybe his agitation was due to the mere fact that he found Miss Chapman attractive. She had nice features, including a gorgeous pair of eyes and nice-shaped lips. Both her eyes and lips could definitely captivate a man. His only question was why was she dressed so conservatively? And why would his great-grandmother assume, given his taste in women, that he would be interested in her?

He was used to beautiful women who considered themselves fashion divas. They not only dressed to impress but dressed to possess...namely a man's heart if given the chance. And he knew for a fact none would be caught wearing the buttoned-up-to-the-neck blouse and the long skirt Miss Chapman had worn. Nor would they have put a pair of low-heel pumps on their feet. Most women, for business or otherwise, wore stilettos to showcase their legs.

She hadn't been wearing any makeup. However, he thought she had beautiful skin without the use of any. He'd also noticed there hadn't been any polish on her fingernails, no rings on her fingers, no bracelets on her wrists and no necklace around her neck. But she had worn a pair of gold hoop earrings in her ears.

He couldn't help but be curious about Ivy Chapman. Was she a woman who didn't have a problem not being cut from the same cloth, and wasn't trying to impress anyone but herself? If that was the case, he found her rather unique.

But if that wasn't the case and she was nothing more

than an uptight, straitlaced businesswoman who was a man hater as well, then she was the type of woman he stayed away from. But regardless of what type of woman she was, he would stay as far away from her as he could, mainly because his great-grandmother assumed she was the perfect woman for him.

But still, his curiosity about her wouldn't go away and he decided he would Google her and find out more about her. He suddenly realized he looked like a damn fool sitting there with a huge vase of flowers staring him in the face while he gave Ivy Chapman far too much thought. It would be just his luck for one of his many relatives who worked in the building to show up and see the huge bouquet. He would never hear the last of it. Especially, if they got wind of the story behind them. He pushed the intercom button.

"Yes, Mr. Madaris?"

"Marlene, please step into my office and bring the rolling cart with you."

"Yes, sir."

Moments later his administrative assistant opened his office door and rolled the metal cart in as he'd instructed. "Take these flowers and have them delivered to one of the hospitals in the area." He refused to give them to Mama Laverne like Miss Chapman had suggested. His great-grandmother deserved a harsh scolding and not any flowers.

"All right."

After Marlene left his office, Nolan Googled Ivy Chapman. The photo on her website looked just as conservative as the real thing. Her hair was in that bun thing again and those same earrings were in her ears.

She owned a cybersecurity business, Cyber-Tech

Securities. And it was described as "a unique technology company, specializing in moving the twenty-first century into the twenty-second." She stated her occupation as a cybersecurity analyst. In other words, she was a legal hacker.

He had to admit she and her business were impressive. Cyber-Tech Securities was linked with some of the best in the business, including Intel and Texas Instruments. But what he'd found most impressive was that she'd begun her career with the government, working for the Department of Homeland Security.

He noted a wealth of community work and charity affiliations. She'd even established a college scholarship foundation named after her grandfather who, like her grandmother, had been a well-known educator in the city. Her foundation awarded numerous scholarships each year.

She was twenty-six, with a degree in technology engineering from MIT. Very remarkable, indeed. They had attended the same university. However, their paths would not have crossed due to the eight-year difference in their ages.

She'd only been in business for two years, but she'd been able to snag several lucrative contracts.

Nolan pushed back from the computer, impressed. More than impressed. She wasn't a plain Jane as he'd originally thought, but a techie. There was a difference, and someone like him who owned an electronics company and had been enamored with technology all his life understood the difference. To reach the level of success that Miss Chapman had and in such a short period of time meant she'd worked hard and pushed to the side anything she'd considered nonessential or frivolous.

Growing up, his life had been centered around computers, so his choice of a profession wasn't a surprise to anyone, especially not to his family. As a kid, he'd have rather spend time indoors messing around with computers than outdoors playing with other kids. He'd been the proverbial geek, with glasses and all. He hadn't minded since he'd been happy and everyone had pretty much left him alone, except when he and his cousins had gone to Mama Laverne's house, where she taught them to cook, or to Granduncle Jake's Whispering Pines, where he'd bonded with Corbin, Reese and Lee and, more important, discovered how important it was to have a social life.

He wondered if Ivy Chapman had a social life. Drawing in a deep breath, he figured that her social life or lack of one wasn't his concern. But the issue of his great-grandmother meddling in his affairs was. He glanced across the room to the wall where a huge portrait of said meddler hung.

Felicia Laverne Madaris was the matriarch of the family. Having borne seven sons, his grandfather Nolan being one of them, Mama Laverne had taken over the running of their ranch with her sons after her husband, Milton, died. All her sons were still alive except for Robert, who had been killed in the Vietnam War.

Mama Laverne had insisted that each of her grands and great-grands hang this particular portrait of her in their places of business and in plain view. She sat looking regal, dressed in her Sunday best with a huge dressy hat on her head, and she appeared to be looking directly at the viewer with those shrewd eyes and all-knowing smile. It was known by every member in the family that she liked giving orders, and she expected them to be carried out. Regardless. Well, he had news for her. He had no intention of allowing her to butt into his affairs. Namely, his romantic life or lack of one.

Nolan reached for his phone and then decided telecommunications with Mama Laverne wouldn't do. He needed to see his great-grandmother in person and look her in the eyes to make sure she had a clear understanding of where he stood and what he would not tolerate.

He stood and headed for the door. He would have it out with Mama Laverne once and for all.

"WHAT DO YOU mean Nolan Madaris isn't the person who was sending you those flowers?"

Ivy glanced across the desk at her best friend, Tessa Hargrove. She had left Nolan Madaris's office and come straight here, to Tessa's property management office. She and Tessa had been best friends since high school, and although they'd gone to different colleges, their close friendship had remained intact.

Their friendship surprised some people. While in school, Ivy had few friends and was considered a geek because of her deep love of science, math and computer technology. Unless they needed her tutoring services, she was ignored by her classmates...until Tessa transferred to the school in their junior year.

Tessa had been ignored as well but for a different reason. Because of Tessa's beauty, the other girls saw her as a threat and treated her as such. So, Tessa and Ivy, as different as night and day, had become the best of friends.

"It was so embarrassing," Ivy said, covering her face with her hands. "I practically stormed into his office, carrying that huge vase of flowers and told him not to send me any more. Only to discover he wasn't the one sending them. His great-grandmother was."

A confused expression appeared on Tessa's face. "His great-grandmother? I don't understand. Why?"

"As part of a matchmaking scheme. But what has me so angry is that my own grandmother was in on it."

"Ms. Helen?"

"Yes."

"How?"

"By practically doing the same. While Nolan's great-grandmother was sending me flowers, my own grand-mother was sending Nolan notes from me."

"Ms. Helen actually did that?" Tessa asked in a voice that clearly said she was having a hard time believing such a thing.

"Yes, Nana actually did that."

"What did the notes say?"

Ivy took a sip of coffee. "The same thing the card on the flowers said. That I would love for us to meet and the note was signed with my phone number."

"Yet he didn't call."

"Nor did I call him. I don't know why his great-grandmother and Nana think we make any sense as a couple. Maybe I shouldn't have, but I told him that because of his reputation around town as a woman-izer, there's no way I'd want to be linked with him."

Tessa's eyes widened. "You actually told him that?"

"Yes. But then he probably thought something simi-lar about me not being his type, but for a different rea-son. I'm sure he saw me as most men do, as a techie queen."

"You are not a techie queen."

"Most men think so and you know it." And until

Damien Fargo, she hadn't cared what they thought. She'd been fooled enough to think he was different. That he could see beyond her in-depth knowledge of scientific and digital technology and accept her for who she truly was. He'd pretended to and then, like every other guy, he'd proved he hadn't liked a woman with a brain; one who was smart enough to think for herself and who didn't hang on to a man's every word. In the end, he'd tried changing her into the woman he had wanted her to be. When that failed, he had dumped her for someone else.

"You know my opinion on what most men think about your love for science, math and technology. As far as I'm concerned, they only wish they could be as smart."

Ivy smiled. Tessa had always been her champion, lifting her up when others—especially men—tried putting her down. "Now, back to Ms. Helen. I just can't imagine her doing such a thing."

"Well, she did. I saw proof. He had one of those notes I supposedly sent him right on his desk. I read it. It was Nana's handwriting. He and I were set up."

Ivy sighed, rubbing one of the gold hoop earrings she wore between her fingers. "I thought about it on the drive here, wondering why Nana would do such a thing, and could only come up with one reason."

"And what's the reason?"

"She's getting older and unfortunately for her, Dad didn't settle down and marry until his late thirties. Nana was nearing sixty when I came along, her one and only grandchild. I guess she wants to live long enough for me to give her a great-grandchild."

Tessa nodded as if following her logic and agreeing

that had to be the reason as well. "What are you going to do?"

Ivy released a frustrated sigh. "I'm going to pay my grandmother a visit. She should be home soon from her exercise class. I was so mad when I left Nolan Madaris's office. You don't know how tempted I was to go straight to that gym and confront her. I came here instead to cool off."

"And I'm glad you did." Tessa then leaned toward her. "So tell me, Ivy. Is Nolan Madaris as handsome in person as he looks in the newspapers?"

Ivy shrugged. "I didn't notice."

"Liar."

A smile touched Ivy's lips because she had noticed, even when she hadn't wanted to. He'd looked so tall and commanding while standing behind his desk. What she'd almost found too distracting was the dark stubble on his jaw like he hadn't bothered to shave that morning. "Okay, I'm lying. I couldn't help but notice. And yes, he looks just as handsome in person. Doubly so. Too much for his own good if you ask me." No need to mention that he smelled good, too. Her senses had been filled with the subtle, masculine scent of his cologne the moment she'd walked into his office.

"My kind of man."

Ivy took a sip of her coffee thinking, yes, Nolan Madaris would be Tessa's kind of man, but he wouldn't be hers. Although she'd arrived at his office angry and ready to chew him out, her anger hadn't stopped her from noticing how good-looking he was. After all, techie or not, she was still a woman who could appreciate a handsome man when she saw one.

She figured Nolan Madaris was at least six-two or

six-three. And his skin was a stunning coppery brown.
Although his eyes had stared her down almost the entire
time, she thought the dark coloring of his pupils was
his most valued asset. He had that wow factor, which
was probably why he was so popular with women. And
she knew just the type of women he dated. The sleek,
sophisticated type, draped in jewelry with her hair perfectly styled. A woman whose mind was filled with
passion and romance instead of scientific knowledge
and data.

Ivy noticed Tessa was staring at her. "What?"

"If what you said earlier is true—about the reason
Ms. Helen wants you to hook up with Nolan Madaris,
and she's teamed up with his great-grandmother to make
it happen—I can't imagine her stopping now. Look how
long she's been trying to get the two of you together."

Ivy recalled that it had started right after her breakup
with Damien, nearly two years ago. Her grandmother
had come by her apartment the following day to find
her a total mess. Nana had told her to wipe the tears
from her eyes because Damien Fargo wasn't worth it.
Helen Chapman had then told her that she hadn't met
the man she would one day fall in love with and marry
but that his name was Nolan Madaris.

Of course Ivy had thought her grandmother was
joking, but when Nana kept dropping Nolan Madaris's
name at every turn, Ivy couldn't help wondering why
her grandmother could believe such a thing. The only
answer Nana would give her was that it was meant to
be. Well, she had news for her grandmother. It wasn't
meant to be.

Like most people living in Houston, Ivy knew of the
Madaris family. They were a large family, all highly

successful and wealthy. She had graduated from high school with Victoria Madaris, who'd been one of the popular girls. Unlike some of the other mean-spirited girls at school, Victoria had always been nice to her and Tessa and would speak to her when the other girls would not. For that reason, she'd always liked Victoria. And Victoria had even invited them to her huge party when they'd graduated from high school, but Tessa had been out of town visiting her grandmother that weekend and Ivy hadn't wanted to go alone.

Then there was the fact that the matriarch of the Madaris family, Nolan Madaris's great-grandmother, Felicia Laverne Madaris, was a good friend of her grandmother's. According to Nana, their friendship began over sixty years ago when Nana was fresh out of college. Her first teaching job was at one of the local elementary schools, and one of her first students was Ms. Laverne's oldest son, Milton Madaris Jr.

Nana remembered ten-year-old Milton as a holy terror of Long Pine Elementary School, and Ms. Laverne had to come to school quite often because of her son's misbehavior. Over the following years, Nana had also taught Milton's younger brothers Lee, Nolan and Luke, and they'd been just as much of a handful as Milton. Working together, Nana and Ms. Laverne had been able to turn those behaviors around somewhat.

A half hour later Ivy was pulling into her grandmother's driveway. Before getting out of the car, she sat there for a moment while memories flooded her mind. The huge two-story Victorian-style home had always been her refuge; a place she'd loved to visit and found comfort in doing so. Thanks to her grandmother and grandfather, there had been so much love radiating inside those walls. Love that she'd desperately needed.

Her parents had divorced when she was twelve and as far as she was concerned, it had been twelve years overdue. No child should have been exposed to such constant fussing and back-and-forth bickering as she had. There had been a fifteen-year difference in her parents' ages. It was a known fact that her father, Dr. Ivory Chapman, had enjoyed his life as a bachelor and highly respected physician, and hadn't been in a hurry to settle down and marry. When he'd decided to do so, he'd been in his late thirties and wanted a young wife—one who would easily bend to his will. He'd thought thirty-year-old Reba Andrews, a nurse at the hospital, would be the perfect woman. He'd discovered too late that Reba had no intentions of bending to anyone's will but her own.

Ivy had drowned out her parents' constant bickering with her books and her love for computers. She had also escaped the dysfunctional madness by coming to this house to visit her grandparents every chance she got. Both had been educators and had encouraged her to read. They had even converted her father's old bedroom into a library just for her. They'd also encouraged her love for technology and would take her to tech conventions every year. Her grandparents had shown her how a loving couple could live in harmony with each other and had tried shielding her from the ugliness they'd known she experienced at home.

After her parents' divorce, the real battle between her parents began with her caught in the middle of a custody battle. In the end, the judge awarded them joint custody. Six months of the year with each parent.

She was certain that neither truly wanted her, but had used her to get back at the other. Graduating from high school and leaving for college had been liberating and seeing her parents only during the holidays had suited her just fine.

As if Dr. Ivory Chapman hadn't learned his lesson the first time around, her sixty-five-year-old father was dating a younger woman. This time it was someone he'd met at a club. When she had talked to him last weekend, it was obvious he was quite smitten. He'd even told her he was thinking of marrying the thirty-two-year-old and retiring so they could become world travelers. He'd sounded happy and she'd told him she loved him and had wished him the best.

Her mother had remarried two years ago and moved to Florida. Ivy liked her stepfather, Harnett Clemmons, and whenever she visited them she saw how happy her mother was. She loved her parents and was glad they'd each found happiness, although with someone other than each other.

Her grandfather had died five years ago, and Ivy still missed his presence whenever she came here. Nana, who'd retired years ago after over forty-plus years as an educator in Houston's public school system, had been the one constant in Ivy's life, which made this conversation hard. Why would her grandmother do such an outrageous thing as send Nolan Madaris those notes? Only Nana could answer that question and explain her actions.

She got out of the car, walked to the door and, using her own key, let herself inside. Placing her purse on a table in the living room, she called out to her grandmother. She didn't get a response; however, she knew for certain she was home since her car was parked out front. Moving toward the kitchen, Ivy figured Nana was in the backyard tending to her garden.

Moments later she came upon her grandmother busily snipping away at her prized rosebushes. Without saying anything, Ivy just stared at her and all the love she could feel for any one person came flowing through.

They'd always had a close relationship, which made it difficult to get mad at her about anything. But this wasn't about just anything. This crossed the line. Nana usually gave Ivy advice only when asked. Ms. Laverne must have somehow convinced her sensible grandmother to take part in her schemes.

"Nana?"

Helen glanced up at her granddaughter and smiled. "Ivy? I wasn't expecting you until later."

She and her grandmother had made plans earlier in the week to have dinner later today and take in a movie. "Yes, but we need to talk."

"Oh? What about?"

"I think you know. I paid a visit to Nolan Madaris this morning to return his flowers, only to discover they hadn't come from him at all. And then imagine how I felt when he showed me a note I had supposedly written him."

Her grandmother smiled. "So, the two of you have finally met?"

"Yes, but that's not the issue here. Why did you let Ms. Laverne talk you into doing something so outlandish?"

Her grandmother shook her head. "Laverne didn't talk me into anything. It was both our idea and one we decided to execute. You and young Nolan were taking entirely too long to suit us."

Ivy tilted her head to stare at her grandmother, certain the woman was an impostor who'd taken over her nana's body. She recalled when Tessa and her family had discovered one of her elderly aunts had the first stage of dementia. One of the signs was changes in mood, personality or judgment. She could certainly attest to the fact that her eighty-year-old grandmother's actions were out of character.

"I am in my right mind, Ivy," her nana said, as if reading her mind.

Ivy drew in a slow, deep breath. "If that's true, then we definitely need to talk."

"I agree," Nana said, placing the snippers on a nearby table and tugging off her work gloves. "It's almost lunchtime. I made some chicken salad this morning. Go ahead and start on the sandwiches. I'll be there in a minute to make the tea."

Ivy nodded and turned to go back inside the house. Her grandmother was going to do more than make a pitcher of tea. She had a lot of explaining to do.

CHAPTER THREE

"So WHAT DO you plan to do?" Corbin asked his brother.

"For starters, pay Mama Laverne a visit. I'm on my way there now," Nolan said, getting off the interstate onto the ramp that would take him to what used to be the Madaris family homestead, Whispering Pines.

Years ago, the Madaris brothers had signed their shares of the ranch over to their youngest brother, Jake, keeping only an investment interest. That act of faith and show of confidence from the brothers had made Jake determined to make Whispering Pines succeed. And he had. It was listed as one of the largest working ranches in Texas and produced some of the highest-quality Texas longhorn cattle for the buying public.

"Good luck. Be prepared for her to twist things to the point where it will confuse your mind."

As far as Nolan was concerned there was nothing that could be twisted and nothing to be confused about. He and Ivy Chapman would not get together. Under no circumstances would he allow his great-grandmother to interfere in his life like she'd done the others. He didn't care about her success record. "There will be no confusion. I plan on letting her know where I stand on the matter and that I refuse to be a pawn in her game of nonsense," Nolan said.

"By the way, you never did say what you thought

about Ivy Chapman when you saw her today. Is she pretty?"

Corbin's question immediately made Ivy Chapman's image flare to life inside his brain. He vividly recalled how she'd unceremoniously placed those flowers on his desk. Before she'd learned the truth about the sender of them, she had looked mad, annoyed, fit to be tied. And pretty as sin. Then after finding out the truth, she appeared embarrassed, disconcerted and slightly humiliated—and still pretty as sin.

"Yes, she's pretty but that means nothing."

"It doesn't?"

"No. If you've seen one pretty woman, then you've seen them all."

"Hey, speak for yourself, Mr. One-Night Stand."

"Whatever. You just better hope I'm able to stop Mama Laverne in her tracks or, dear brother, you are next," he reminded Corbin.

Moments later, after ending his phone conversation with Corbin, Nolan drove through the gates of Whispering Pines. The twenty-four-hour security guard posted at the entrance had become a permanent fixture after his granduncle Jake Madaris married Hollywood actress Diamond Swain many years ago. The media and paparazzi had tried more than once to get on the private property and disrupt their lives.

He had checked with his parents to verify that his great-grandmother was here at Whispering Pines. Jake was Mama Laverne's youngest son and she stayed with him at least six months out of the year and rotated the other six months among her other five sons.

When Nolan brought his car to a stop in front of the sprawling hacienda-style ranch house, he was greeted by Jake's nine-year-old son, Granite. From all the pictures he'd seen of his granduncle Jake from when he'd been Granite's age, anyone could see that Granite Jacob Madaris was the spitting image of his father. Whereas his twelve-year-old sister, Amethyst, was the spitting image of Jake's wife, Diamond. Both Granite and Amethyst were tall for their ages, which couldn't be helped since Jake stood way over six feet tall and Diamond was barely short of six feet. Unless you knew Granite was only nine, you would assume he was much older because of his height.

Nolan still found it hard to believe that his ranching-loving granduncle, whom everyone thought would never remarry after a disastrous first marriage, had engaged in a secret love affair with Hollywood actress Diamond Swain for almost two years before Jake had finally announced it to the family. So far Jake and Diamond's marriage was one of the few Madaris weddings that Mama Laverne hadn't manipulated. His great-grandmother had been just as shocked as everyone else to learn about Jake and Diamond's marriage. That was one of the reasons Nolan considered Jake his hero. Anyone who could pull anything over on Mama Laverne deserved a medal.

"Hi, Nolan! You plan to stay awhile?" Granite asked after trotting over to meet him.

"No, just for a few hours," he said, grabbing Granite around the neck in a playful hug. "Where is everyone?"

Granite smiled up at him. "Dad's inside the house working on the ranch books and Mama Laverne is inside, too. But I don't know what's she's doing."

Probably busy tending to other people's business, Nolan thought.

"Mom and Amethyst left this morning to go shopping in Los Angeles, along with Syneda and Remi," Granite said. "They won't be back for a couple of days."

Syneda was the wife of his older cousin Clayton, and Remi—short for Remington—was their daughter. "Sounds like they'll be doing some serious shopping," Nolan said.

Granite chuckled. "They will. Mom said it's a mother-daughter trip, but she promised to bring me something back."

Nolan nodded. "How is school going?"

He knew both Granite and Amethyst were home-schooled by a private tutor. "School is great, but I'm glad it's spring break. We get two weeks instead of just one."

Nolan figured when you were homeschooled, your parents could make the rules. "You got a lot planned for those two weeks?"

Granite bobbed his head up and down grinning. "Yes. I've been helping Dad with roundup every morning. And he's going to take me to see Luke at his rodeo school for lessons next week."

Luke was his cousin who'd been a rodeo star and was now the owner of the Luke Madaris Rodeo School in Oklahoma. "Sounds like it's going to be a fun trip."

"It will be. Just me and Dad. No girls allowed."

Nolan was about to respond when the front door opened and there stood his granduncle Jake Madaris. He admired his granduncle, not just for outsmarting Mama Laverne with his marriage to Diamond, but simply for being an all-around wonderful granduncle who loved his family, especially all his nieces and nephews, and he showed it in everything he did. Jake was not only a dedicated rancher, but he was also a highly successful businessman and one hell of a financial adviser. Over the years, Jake had made a number of wise investments on behalf of the entire Madaris family. Even if Nolan never worked another day in his life, thanks to Jake he could live a very wealthy and prosperous lifestyle.

"Dad! Look who's here," Granite said with excitement in voice.

Jake Madaris smiled at his son. "I see. Nolan, what a nice surprise," Jake said, leaving the doorway to give his grandnephew a huge bear hug. "What brings you to Whispering Pines in the middle of a weekday?"

Nolan didn't hesitate in answering. "Mama Laverne."

Jake, Nolan noted, couldn't hide the humor in his eyes when he said, "Must be serious."

"It is."

There was no need to tell Jake anything. Everyone was still shaking their heads in amazement as to how Mama Laverne had outsmarted Lee and pulled off his marriage to Carly. And everyone knew that he was next on the list.

"Come on in. She's out back on the patio shelling peas."

"Thanks."

BY THE TIME Ivy was finishing up making the sandwiches, Nana entered the kitchen and said, "Today is a beautiful day. I hope there will be many more like it, don't you?"

"Yes." Ivy decided to keep her answer short. She really didn't have much to say by way of small talk until her grandmother explained a few things.

It didn't take long for Nana to make the tea. Ivy

put the plates with the sandwiches on the table. When she'd arrived, she hadn't thought about eating, but when Nana had mentioned she'd made some chicken salad, Ivy couldn't prevent her stomach from reminding her she'd missed breakfast. The reminder of why she'd done so brought everything, especially why she was here, back to the forefront.

She waited until Nana was seated and had said grace for the both of them before asking, "Nana, why would you think Nolan Madaris and I would make a good couple?"

"Because you will."

Ivy shook her head. "No, we won't. There is nothing about the man that interests me."

"Then you need to take a second look. I haven't seen him recently, but last time I looked he was stopping feminine hearts all over the place."

"Well, he won't be stopping mine. Nana, you read the newspapers like I do. I'm sure you're aware every time Nolan's name appears in print, which is quite a bit. Usually it's the society column detailing his latest conquest—usually a debutante or some sophisticated lady. I have enough sense to know I am not his type."

"Of course you are."

Ivy tried to rein in her temper that had never, ever been directed at her grandmother before. She bit into her sandwich and then took a sip of her tea before asking, "Do you think I'm so lacking that I can't find anyone on my own, Nana? That you have to invite men to call me?"

"No. And we're not talking about any man, Ivy. We are talking about a man who I believe will one day be your husband."

"He will *not* be my husband. Have you forgotten that I never, ever plan to get married?"

"We will see."

Ivy couldn't do anything but stare at her grandmother. She'd never known Helen Chapman to be so illogical. Deciding to try another tactic, she took her grandmother's hand and said in a softer tone, "Look at me, Nana. Nolan is used to dating real pretty girls. Girls with capital *G*s printed on their foreheads for *gorgeous*. I'm not chopped liver but I know my limitations."

"Do you?"

"Yes."

Nana pulled her hand away, picked up her sandwich and took a bite. Then she took a sip of her drink before saying, "The only limitations you have are the ones you place on yourself, Ivy. Regardless of what you think, you are pretty. You are gorgeous. Contrary to what you evidently believe, being smart and intelligent doesn't make you unattractive."

"Yes, but it makes me oblivious to stuff most women find important. Like their looks and clothes. I like who I am just fine."

"And you should. Earlier you asked if I thought you lack something and I told you no. What I didn't say was that I think because of that Damien fellow, you're denying yourself a chance to meet a nice guy. One who will think you're beautiful, both inside and out, and who you'd want to marry."

Ivy rolled her eyes. "Even if I was the least bit interested in ever getting married, which I am not, why would I want to marry a man like Nolan Madaris? A better question to ask is why would he want to marry a woman like me?"

"Because you were made for each other. Why can't you see that?"

"And why can't you see that we aren't and that I'm not his type?"

"Quite the contrary. Laverne and I think you and young Madaris are a perfect match."

A perfect match? She had to be kidding. "Nana, I want you to promise me that you will drop this whole thing. If you only knew how embarrassed I was after going into his office to give him those flowers back, only to discover he hadn't sent them at all. And then to find out he thought I'd been sending those notes to him. You can't imagine how humiliated I felt."

"There was no reason for you to feel humiliated about anything. Our goal was to finally get the two of you to meet and we were successful in doing that."

Ivy took a sip of her tea. Yes, they'd been successful in achieving that. But she had no intentions of seeing Nolan Madaris again and there was no doubt in her mind he had no intentions of ever looking her up either.

Ivy decided she would no longer argue that point with her grandmother because she could see it would be a total waste of her time. She figured when Nana and Ms. Laverne saw their antics had failed, they would soon realize that as well.

NOLAN FOUND HIS great-grandmother just where Jake said she would be. On the patio, shelling peas. She looked up the moment he stepped through the French doors, which as far as he was concerned, dispelled the notion that she had a hearing problem. Everyone knew Felicia Laverne Madaris heard just what she wanted to hear.

"Nolan, this is a surprise."

He doubted it. He had a feeling she'd been expecting him. "Hello, Mama Laverne." He walked over to her, leaned down and placed a kiss on her cheek. "I hope I'm not interrupting anything, but there's a reason for my visit."

She smiled up at him. "Is there?"

He shook his head, thinking she had the gall to look innocent. "Yes." He slid into an empty chair to face her. As soon as he sat down she shoved a handful of pea pods into his lap, directly onto his pair of Giorgio slacks.

"While you're here you might as well make yourself useful," she said.

He drew in a deep breath and began shelling peas. Doing so reminded him of years gone by when she'd made all her great-grandsons do this very thing, the day before their mandatory cooking class with her had started. At the time he'd resented learning how to cook, but now he appreciated her for caring enough to take the time to teach all of them. And there had been so many of his cousins learning at the same time. It had been about more than cooking, though, which he now saw. It had taught them how to get along not only as cousins but to form relationships that were, in most cases, closer than brothers.

To know Mama Laverne was to love her, although at the moment he wanted to strangle her. He would never actually harm a hair on her head. Not a single strand. Not this ninety-something-year-old woman whose hands were a lot older than his, yet moved with a quicker precision than his while shelling peas. Years of experience and a demand of discipline.

She was the reason all seven of her sons had grown up to be God-fearing men. Even after losing her husband, she hadn't given up. She had been there for her sons, their children and now her sons' grands. She was the glue that held the Madaris family together. She was the backbone. She had a heart of gold. She thought of others before she thought of herself...maybe too much at times. She was the epitome of a strong woman.

But did that give her the right to interfere in their lives like she'd been doing lately? Hell, it hadn't been lately; it stretched all the way back to his grandparents' generation. He knew the stories were more fact than fiction. Wasn't it time for her to stop the foolishness? Take a much-needed break? Did she not think they were capable of selecting their own mates if and when they desired one? And shouldn't it be when they were ready to make the move and not when she thought they were ready?

"So, I take it you got something to say, Nolan."

He glanced at her. Yes, he had a lot to say and would make sure that no matter how frustrated he was with her that he would give her all the respect she deserved. "You had no right to send Ivy Chapman flowers and let her think they were from me."

"They were from you. Eventually you'll get the bill. I told your aunt Sarah to hold off sending it until I told her to do so."

Nolan was too stunned to say anything for a moment. His aunt Sarah, his cousin Reese's mom, owned a florist shop in the Madaris Building. Mama Laverne had flowers sent for a full three months to a woman he didn't know and intended for him to pay for them.

Without saying anything, he placed the peas he'd

shelled into the container on the table and the remaining pods back in the pail they'd come out of. He stood, brushed off his slacks and began pacing the floor, reining in his escalating anger.

He wasn't certain how much time passed before he finally stopped and said, "No matter what you say or do, nothing will ever develop between me and Ivy Chapman."

"If you say so."

He frowned. "I not only say so, I mean so. She's not my type."

"You don't know your type."

"Excuse me?"

"I said you don't know your type, obviously. You thought Andrea Dunmire was your type and she proved you wrong."

"That was years ago, and I'd like to think I've matured enough to know what type of woman is good for me and what type woman is not. You know that old saying about learning from your mistakes. Well, trust me, I learned from mine."

He had been wrong in thinking Andrea was his chosen one. The one he thought he would spend the rest of his life with. That day she hadn't clicked off her cell phone as she'd thought and he had heard her conversation with her cousin, he had felt a deep pain in his heart when she'd said she was only putting up with him, his touches, his kisses and sex with him to give her cousin a clear path to Blade. And what was so sad was she hadn't denied anything when he'd confronted her. The pain of her betrayal and manipulations had been deep.

"How have you learned from your mistakes?" Mama Laverne asked him, cutting into his thoughts.

"By deciding never to give your heart to any woman again? That's not learning from your mistakes, Nolan, that's giving in to them."

He tried to hold his anger at bay but found it hard to do so. "Whatever way that I decide to handle my business, Mama Laverne, is my business."

"Whatever way you decide to handle your business is a moot point now that you and Ivy will be spending time together."

He shook his head. His great-grandmother was so sure that crazy scheme of hers had worked. He had no problem bursting her bubble. "I like my life just the way it is."

"You mean dating all those women around town? Trying to make Clayton's and Blade's past reputations as womanizers look like those of choirboys in comparison? Oh, I've heard all about you, Nolan. I read the papers, you know. I'm aware of each and every time the name Madaris shows up in print. I know you've become a skirt chaser of the worst kind. What you do is your business just as long as you're aware of one thing."

"Which is?"

"You're messing up my timeline."

Her timeline? Now he'd heard everything. "I'm sure Corbin will be glad to hear that."

"Corbin isn't next on the list."

Her words gave Nolan pause. "He's not?"

"No. I decided to skip over Corbin, Emerson, Chance and Adam for the time being. Victoria is next."

"Victoria?" he said in disbelief. She had to be kidding. Victoria, his twenty-six-year-old sister, was no more ready to be any man's wife than he was ready to be any woman's husband.

"Yes, Victoria."

Nolan couldn't believe this. He refused to believe this. He had to talk to someone. Hell, he needed to alert the entire family. Definitely warn Victoria. No one would agree to this. Victoria, who'd been named after their deceased paternal great-grandaunt, was the first female Madaris born in their generation. No one would agree to her being pushed into marriage. They would finally see that Mama Laverne had gone too far in her matchmaking schemes.

"Victoria won't be getting married," he said. As her oldest brother, he was protective of his sister. As were all his cousins and brothers. That protection went doubly so for his baby sister, Lindsay, who was attending college in Florida.

"Don't worry about Victoria, Nolan. The guy I have in mind will do right by her. Just like I believe in my heart that you will do right by Ivy."

Nolan had heard enough. Coming here had been a total waste of his time. He walked back over to his great-grandmother. He loved her to pieces but at that moment he was more frustrated and annoyed with her than ever for sticking her nose into his business. For trying to manipulate his life. "Mama Laverne, I'm only saying this once more," he said with as much respect as he could muster. "Ivy Chapman is not my type, and she made it pretty clear today that I'm not hers. There isn't—and never will there be—anything between us. Please stop concerning yourself with my love life or my lack of one."

With nothing else to say, Nolan turned and left. He ran into his granduncle Jake on his way out. "How did it go?"

Nolan shook his head. "She thinks she has her plans all laid out with no room for error. She even had the nerve to tell me in so many words that I was wasting her time because she needed to move on to Victoria."

A surprised look touched his granduncle's face. "Victoria? What happened to Corbin, Adam, Emerson and Chance? They're older than Victoria."

"She's skipping them to marry Victoria off. It's time for the family to step in and do something, Granduncle Jake."

"Something like what?"

Nolan shrugged massive shoulders. "I don't rightly know. I need to get away for a while and think about it. Friday morning I'm leaving for my place on Tiki Island and plan to be there a week. When I return I'm calling a family meeting."

CHAPTER FOUR

IVY MENTALLY AWAKENED from the ringing of her phone. Without opening her eyes, she reached for her cell phone on her nightstand. There was no doubt in her mind it was past the time she usually got out of bed, but when you were your own boss and worked from home, you had the luxury of sleeping late. Especially after putting in additional hours to finish a project from hell earlier than expected. And she planned to sleep the rest of the day since she didn't get into bed until daybreak.

"Hello," she said in a groggy voice.

"Congratulations!" a bubbly feminine voice said. "You've won a week for two on Tiki Island."

Ivy slowly opened one eye. They had to be kidding. She never won anything. Pulling herself up in bed, she pushed back the hair from her face. "I won?" she asked, hoping she was speaking with a live person and not a recording.

"Yes. You've won a week for two in a beautiful beach cottage."

"For two?"

"Yes, so you can include your husband, boyfriend or significant other," the bubbly woman said.

Ivy frowned. She had none of those, but she did have a best friend. It would be a great girls' trip if Tessa was available to go with her. More questions began flooding her mind, like how had she been selected? She didn't recall entering any type of contest. "How did I win?"

"Your name was selected from a list of customers who frequent Altamonte Dry Cleaners."

Ivy nodded, thinking that explained things. Since she hated ironing, she would drop her things by the cleaners every Thursday. "Is there a time frame that I have to take the week?"

"You can take it as soon as you like, but it must be taken within the next thirty days."

Thirty days? That wasn't much time, Ivy thought, rubbing a hand down her face. She would love to get away now before beginning her next project for Wonderbelly, a cyberware company in Boston. It would be nice to go somewhere and relax for seven days. If Tessa wasn't available on such short notice, then she could take her grandmother with her. But then she doubted she would get much rest if she did. Even after their little talk a few days ago, Nana was still tossing Nolan Madaris's name out whenever she got the chance. Take yesterday for instance. Nana had asked if she'd heard from him. Why would she hear from Nolan Madaris? Obviously, her grandmother refused to accept that the plan she and Ms. Laverne had concocted had backfired.

She truly hoped Tessa could go with her, but she would go alone if she had to. "Can I claim my prize and go to Tiki Island starting this week?"

"Yes. We can deliver the winning voucher to you or you can pick it up at our office."

"Where is your office?"

The woman quoted an address that was less than ten miles from where Ivy lived. "I'll stop by."

"All right. Everything you need to know will be in

the paperwork you'll receive with the winning voucher. Again, congratulations."

"Thanks."

Ivy couldn't help smiling when she hung up the phone. Seven days on Tiki Island was a dream come true. She'd heard rental property there was pretty expensive and couldn't wait to tell Tessa. She hoped her best friend would be able to join her.

She had reclaimed her comfortable position in bed when the phone rang again. Thinking it was the bubbly woman calling her back for some reason, she shifted in bed, grabbed her phone and said, "Is there something you forgot to tell me?"

There was a pause as if the person was surprised by her question. And then a masculine voice she remembered all too well said, "Yes. I'm sorry for how I treated you when we were together."

Ivy drew in a sharp breath not believing Damien Fargo had the audacity to call after all this time. "Too late for an apology now, Damien," she said and hung up.

"HELLO, NOLAN. I saw I missed a call from you."

"You missed several, Victoria," he said, frowning. "Where are you?"

"New Orleans. I flew here for a job interview and I've been busy preparing. What's up?"

Nolan's frown deepened. "New Orleans? You're thinking about moving to New Orleans?"

"If I get the job."

"Why? There're plenty of job opportunities here in Houston."

"Yes, but in New Orleans I won't have to worry

about being treated differently because my last name is Madaris."

Nolan didn't say anything, not sure he liked the idea of his sister taking a job in another town. Another state.

"And before you say anything, Nolan Madaris, remember you moved to Chicago after college."

"That's different."

His sister chuckled. "Always is when it comes to the guys in the family. I always get treated differently because I'm a female."

Her words reminded him why he'd called. "Well, there is one person who intends to treat you as an equal."

"Who?"

"Mama Laverne. I went to see her yesterday and she informed me that after she marries me off, instead of moving on to Corbin, Adam, Emerson or Chance, that you're next."

"Me?"

"Yes, but don't worry about it. I plan to call a family meeting to deal with her meddling."

"Hold up, Nolan, call one on your behalf if you're so inclined, but not mine. I have no problem with our great-grandmother finding a husband for me. It frees up my time in doing so because I know Mama Laverne is going to vet him to the nth degree."

Nolan couldn't believe what he was hearing. "You want a husband?"

"Not really, but if Mama Laverne says I'm next, then I'm not going to buck the idea. Hey, she has an astounding track record."

"That's not the point."

"Maybe for you it's not but for me it is, so if she wants to find a husband for me, let her at it. I have no

problem with it. I welcome her doing so. And if I were
you, I wouldn't buck her either. Lee tried and look what
happened. We all thought Lee would best her at her own
game and we were wrong. Besides, Lee is madly in love
with Carly. They are a perfect match. Remember that."

Nolan didn't need to remember anything. He'd just
returned from Paris, where he'd spent time with the
happy couple. It was obvious to everyone Lee adored his
wife, but like he'd told Victoria, that wasn't the point. If
she wanted Mama Laverne to control and manipulate
her life, then that was her business. However, he had no
intentions of letting her control and manipulate his. As
far as he was concerned Victoria had been duly warned.

A short while later Nolan ended the call with his sister, knowing he needed to get away more so than ever.
Although there was no need to call a family meeting
for his sister's sake, he still needed answers as to how
to handle his great-grandmother. Unlike his sister, he
wasn't satisfied to let Mama Laverne make decisions on
his life. Earlier, he'd got a call from his property manager to say his house on Tiki Island was ready for his
arrival. Marlene had cleared his calendar, which wasn't
hard to do since he'd originally planned to remain in
Paris for an additional week anyway.

He was about to head out and grab lunch when his
phone rang. He recognized the ringtone. He smiled as
he picked up the phone. "Hi, Gramma Bessie."

"Hi, Nolan, how are you doing?"

"Fine. What about you?"

"I'm doing fine as well. However, I need a favor."

"Anything for you, Gramma Bessie."

"Can you take me to visit your great-aunt Caroline?
All I need is to get dropped off there. Your granddaddy

will pick me up on Sunday evening." Caroline was his grandmother's sister who lived in Andrews.

"Sure. When?"

"Friday. We can leave that morning."

That's was the opposite direction from Tiki Island. If he dropped his grandmother off at his great-aunt Caroline's, that meant he wouldn't get to the island until late that evening. He sighed. "No problem. I'll take you." This was family after all.

DAMIEN FARGO LEANED back in his chair and snapped the pencil he'd been holding in half. Ivy intended to be difficult, which meant he had to come up with another plan.

"I hope you don't anticipate any problems."

He glanced at the man sitting across from his desk. For a moment, he'd forgotten about his presence. His mind had been reeling with the fact that Ivy Chapman had hung up on him. He'd figured she would still be upset. Most women would. But hadn't he begun the conversation with an apology?

He thought it best to give the man his undivided attention and answer his question. "No, I don't anticipate any problems. She might be a little mad with me now, but I know how to work her. She'll be putty in my hands again in no time."

The man nodded slowly. "See that she is."

CHAPTER FIVE

IVY STEPPED OUT onto the huge porch and stretched. She'd finally unpacked and was ready to relax. The porch swing looked inviting, and she could see herself sitting in it a lot during the next week while reading. This time it would be pleasure reading and not for business. In fact, she didn't want to think about business at all this week. She was here to enjoy herself and intended to do just that.

Tessa couldn't come with her since this was the weekend she was to go visit her aunt in Austin. More than once Ivy had taken the drive with Tessa to share the driving and for company. However, lately Tessa had found it a lot easier to fly. Her best friend had racked up a lot of frequent-flier miles doing so, especially now since her aunt was showing signs of dementia.

Ivy had felt a little bad about not inviting Nana, so she had called her a couple of days ago to see if perhaps she wanted to join her this week. However, Nana had made plans to join a group of senior ladies for a weekend trip to attend a gospel revival in Lake Charles, Louisiana. Her grandmother had been taking such trips for a couple of years now. At first Ivy had been concerned about a group of older women traveling alone together. The families of the other ladies voiced the same concern and decided to pool their moneys together and hired female chaperones to travel with the group. Nana and the ladies didn't like the idea of chaperones and often referred to the younger women as their traveling companions.

Ivy glanced around, deciding she liked the place. It was on a private road and secluded from the other homes. It looked just like a beach cottage with its wooden frame painted a pristine white. What she liked the most, besides the huge front porch, was the stone walkway that led to a private area of the Galveston Bay.

The inside of the house was gorgeous with its two bedrooms, both king-size suites with private baths. It was a split bedroom concept and both faced the ocean with floor-to-ceiling windows. There were marble floors throughout, with a cozy living room and an eat-in kitchen with a wide breakfast bar.

When she'd arrived that morning, a huge gift basket that included bottles of wines, an assortment of cheeses, bread, fruits, chocolate and snacks had sat on a table in the living room with a welcome note. She had parked her car inside the detached garage, which made it easier to bring in her luggage, as well as the items she had stopped by the grocery store for and purchased. She wasn't a big eater, so the food should be enough to last the week she would be here. Other than eat, sleep, read and drink wine, she didn't plan to do much of anything else. It was time off she otherwise would not have taken if she hadn't won this trip and for that reason, she intended to get the most out of it.

And she intended to put that call from Damien out of her mind. She couldn't believe he'd called after all this time…and to apologize. It was too late for that now. His leaving Houston and moving to New York had been best for the both of them. Her feelings had been raw and she couldn't imagine them in the same city and running into each other. She'd been given time to get over him and she had. Whoever said "Out of sight and out of mind" knew exactly what they'd been talking about.

Refusing to let thoughts of Damien ruin her week here at the cottage, she moved across the porch to sit on the swing. She smiled, thinking how nice it was here. Even the weather was agreeable. Since this was March the weather was still cool. Too cool for her to think about taking a swim today. However, the good news was that forecasters had predicted the coming days would be nice and sunny. She figured all those students on spring break whose destination was the beach next week would appreciate that.

The first thing she'd done after arriving and unpacking had been to take a nap. Now she was up, well rested and ready to explore what would be her private place on the island. Getting up from the swing, she stretched before going inside the house. After grabbing a light jacket, she moved toward the kitchen. Moments later she was outside and happily walking toward the bay.

It was late evening when Nolan pulled into the drive. He could have arrived sooner, but when he'd got to his great-aunt Caroline's house, he decided to hang out with a few of his cousins that he hadn't seen in a while. Then there was the fact that his great-aunt had cooked a mouthwatering meal as well as his favorite dessert of peach cobbler since she'd known he was coming.

Deciding not to put his car in the garage for the time being, he got out of it and looked around. He loved coming here and had known he'd wanted to buy it the first time the Realtor had shown it to him. Less than an hour's drive from Houston, it was one of those places he could get to in a reasonable time. He often regretted having decided to list it as a rental because it wasn't always available for him to use whenever he wanted. Instead of getting into his SUV and driving here on Friday nights and staying the entire weekend whenever he felt like it, now he had to check with his property manager to make sure no one had rented it.

At least he'd got here before dark. He intended to build a fire in the pit, pour a glass of scotch and chill for a minute. He had talked to Corbin during the drive here and his brother hadn't been surprised with Victoria's attitude. The women in the family seemed to be more accepting of Mama Laverne's interference in their lives than the men. It was apparent that Victoria had it in her head Mama Laverne would hook her up with a love match made in heaven.

Entering the house, he lifted a brow when he saw the huge basket sitting on a table in the living room. That was thoughtful of Ron to do that and he wondered if it was something his property manager had begun doing for all renters. If so, such a kindhearted gesture would definitely have renters returning.

Nolan walked over to the basket, grabbed an apple, rubbed it against the thigh of his jeans and then bit into it. It was good. Sweet and juicy, just the way he liked his apples. Leaving the living room, he went into the kitchen and saw a can of coffee, bags of chips and a case of bottled water on the counter.

When Nolan opened the refrigerator he discovered it fully stocked as well. He smiled, thinking his property manager had definitely outdone himself. Was he vying for more than just the 15 percent cut he was getting?

Ron's contract was up for renewal in a couple of months. Was that the reason he'd gone out of the way to make sure Nolan had everything he needed? Bread, eggs, butter, milk… Although he wasn't sure why Ron had purchased the 2 percent kind. But he had redeemed himself with the wine coolers.

Nolan smiled while thinking not only would his property manager's contract get renewed, but the man might even get a raise on top of it. Tossing the last of the apple in the trash, he grabbed a bottle of water and had taken a huge swig when suddenly the back door opened and someone gasped. He swung around and nearly choked on the water.

The one woman he hadn't expected to see for a long time, if ever, was standing before him. Ivy Chapman. And from the expression on her face it was quite obvious that she was just as shocked to see him as he was to see her. He tried not to notice how different she looked now compared to a few days ago. Her hair was no longer tied in a knot on her head, but flowed wildly around her shoulders in thick yet soft-looking curls. Her hair styled this way made her mocha-colored face appear rounder, her cheekbones higher and her neck more slender.

She was still wearing her glasses, and like before, he thought the eyes behind the frames were beautiful. Mesmerizing. And those glasses seemed tilted on a cute little nose. Today she was dressed far more casual with a pair of cutoff jeans and a clingy T-shirt. Both showed off luscious curves and a gorgeous pair of legs. With legs that looked like hers, he thought wearing a long skirt to cover them was such a waste.

"Why are you here?" she asked, breaking into his thoughts.

He leaned against the counter, trying for it not to be so obvious that his gaze was raking her up and down to get a good view of her legs and admiring her sexy lips. "I'm here because I own the place."

CHAPTER SIX

IVY STARED AT NOLAN, hoping she hadn't heard him correctly but a part of her knew she had. How in the world had Nana and Ms. Laverne managed to pull this off? She didn't have to ask herself why they'd done such a thing, because she already knew the reason. They assumed she and Nolan were perfect for each other but they were so wrong on that account.

And why did Nolan appear taller than he had that morning at his office? Now she had to tilt her head nearly all the way back to look up at him. And why was she noticing that he was even more handsome than before? Instead of a business suit he was dressed in a pair of well-worn jeans and a pair of roughed boots. And why was his lean waist, firm stomach, perfect tight abs and muscled shoulders showing in a well-defined way through the cotton material of his T-shirt? Her senses felt overloaded.

"I can't believe this," she said, pushing away from the door to cross the room and sit down at the table. All she could do was shake her head at how easily she'd been conned. "I should have known. I never win contests."

"A contest?" Nolan asked.

She nodded, feeling like a fool. "This was Nana and Ms. Laverne's doing."

"That I believe," he said, clearly putting the pieces together.

Ivy was grateful for that. There was no doubt in her mind that he was just as outraged and disgusted as she was. "Thanks."

"How did you get here?" he asked, finally moving from where he was standing to join her at the table.

"I drove."

"Where's your car? I didn't see another vehicle in the yard when I arrived."

"I put it in the garage." She released a frustrated sigh. "I honestly didn't suspect a thing. I got a call early in the week that claimed I had won a week's stay here from a contest run by a dry cleaner that I frequent."

His brow lifted. "What's the name of the cleaners?"

"Altamonte Dry Cleaners."

He nodded slowly and then said, "That part explains things."

"How?" She wanted to know.

He leaned back in the chair and she tried not to notice how good he smelled. He was wearing the same cologne as before. "Altamonte Dry Cleaners is owned my grand-aunt Pearl's side of the family. She was an Altamonte when she married my granduncle Lee."

Ivy's eyes widened. "Her family would help your great-grandmother with her matchmaking scheme?"

He chuckled and she tried to ignore how the sound seemed to vibrate across her skin. "In a heartbeat. For them it would be like history repeating itself. I understand that they conspired with Mama Laverne years ago to marry their only daughter off to Granduncle Lee. So yes, there's no doubt in my mind if Mama Laverne called on them to help carry out her plans, they would have done what she asked them to do."

Ivy found his statement astounding. "But why?"

His lips tightened into a frown. "You know why. Because my great-grandmother has everyone convinced she is an ace at matchmaking with a 100 percent success record that she can't go wrong. But what Mama Laverne and her adoring believers fail to realize and accept is that there's a first time for everything. Even failure. Just because she's had great success in the past doesn't mean anything about the future."

"I agree. That's what makes everything they are doing so annoying. Did you mention to your great-grandmother you were coming here today?"

"No."

"Then how would she know how and when to put her plan into action?" Ivy asked, trying to break eye contact with him. The intensity of the dark eyes staring back at her was unnerving. She'd noticed the anger in his features was slowly easing and she was trying to let hers do the same. Somehow they needed to replace anger with action. There had to be a way to effectively combat Nana's and Ms. Laverne's foolishness. As far as she was concerned, they had gone too far this time, involving others to participate in their nonsense.

He shrugged those massive shoulders and she found that unnerving as well. "I mentioned my plans to several family members," he said. "I can only assume she got wind of it and came up with a plan."

"Did you not get a chance to talk to her since we last saw each other?"

Frustration appeared in his features. "I talked to her. That same day. But it was like what I was saying was going through one ear and going out the other. Did you talk to your grandmother?"

"Yes. I asked her to stay out of my affairs, but it's obvious my request went in one ear and out the other, also." She released a frustrated breath. "I can't believe after our conversation that she went along with setting us up like this. And what angers me more than anything is knowing it might not be their last time."

"Make no mistake. It won't be their last time. It might be your grandmother's first time trying her hand at matchmaking, but my great-grandmother considers herself an old pro with years of experience. She's not about to let up. It doesn't matter what we tell them, they're determined to have it their way."

After taking a deep breath, Ivy stood. "Well, I refuse to be a pawn in their foolishness. I'll start packing to leave and will be out of your way. Again, I am so sorry for the intrusion. I would not have come here if for one minute I'd thought winning that contest was a sham."

He stood as well, and again she had to tilt her head back to look up at him. "There's no need to apologize since it wasn't your fault."

"Doesn't matter. I'm invading your privacy," she said, moving from around the table.

"I guess you're the reason my refrigerator is stocked and why there's a welcome basket on my living room table."

She nodded. "Afraid so. I stopped by that market a few miles up the road and picked up a few things."

He nodded. "And here I thought that perhaps my property manager was bucking for a raise. Two percent milk should have tipped me off."

She arched a brow. "And what's wrong with 2 percent milk?"

"Nothing, if that's what you like to drink. I prefer whole milk. I grew up on it. The Madaris family used to run a dairy back in the day in addition to raising cattle."

Good Lord, she hoped he hadn't noticed how she was hanging on to his every word. She loved the sound of his voice. It was deep and husky.

"At least let me pay you for those items," he offered.

She waved off his words. "No, I won't accept anything from you. Besides, I got to enjoy the bay for a little while. I just finished a major project and wanted to relax a bit before starting a new one."

"Tell you what, I'll give you my property manager's contact information. Give him a call and let him know what other week you'd be available and I'll make sure you get it, on me."

She was surprised by his offer. "I can't let you do that."

"Sure you can. It's the least I can do. I insist."

"Thanks. I was so excited about winning that I followed the instructions to the letter without getting suspicious about anything." That made her ask, "How did they get the key?"

She watched him stroll to the counter to retrieve the water bottle he'd placed there earlier. "My mom has a spare key," he said.

Why was she noticing how sexy his walk was and how good his backside looked in his jeans? "Your mom? Please don't tell me she was in on it, too."

"She had to be," he said, grabbing the water bottle, turning around and leaning back against the counter. "It makes perfect sense now."

"What does?"

"My gramma Bessie claiming that she needed to be taken to her sister's home in Andrews this morning, which delayed my arrival here by at least eight hours since my great-aunt insisted I stay for lunch. That had to be part of my great-grandmother's plan as well. Had I left Houston when I had originally planned to do so, then we would have arrived here at the same time. They deliberately delayed my arrival, making sure I didn't get here until after you'd arrived and had got settled."

Ivy shook her head. And she thought she had it bad trying to keep Nana in line. "I don't envy you one bit. I only have to put up with my grandmother. However, from the sound of things, your great-grandmother has a legion of conspirators ready to assist her. How can you put up with your family being so…?" Ivy tried her best to come up with a word that would hit the mark but wouldn't offend him.

"Intrusive," he supplied.

"Yes," she said, fighting back a smile as she pushed her eyeglasses up. "Intrusive. I would think that instead of enabling her, at some point someone would have taken your great-grandmother aside and had a little talk with her about…" Again she tried coming up with a word that was noncritical.

"Minding her own business," he said. "You can say it. Trust me, it won't hurt my feelings." He then took a gulp of water from the bottle.

"To mind her own business," she said since he'd invited her to do so. She felt a stirring in her stomach as she watched him when he placed the bottle back down and wiped any lingering liquid from his mouth with the back of his hand. Why did seeing him do something like that affect her?

She pushed back those sensations, refusing to let them overwhelm the feminine side of her. There was no place for them here now, and definitely not with the man standing across the room from her. No matter how handsome he looked, and he did look handsome. "I honestly don't get it. I'm sure you're capable of choosing your own wife."

"Just like I'm sure you can choose a husband."

His words reminded her of Damien. She had honestly thought he was the one, but he had revealed his true self eventually. Considering her parents' marriage, she figured it was best she had learned that before saying "I do."

"I don't plan to marry. Ever," she said, knowing a cutting edge was in her voice.

From the lifting of his brow she knew he'd picked up on it. "Any reason why?"

Strands of curly hair danced in her face and she brushed them back before saying, "My reason doesn't concern you."

SHE WAS RIGHT, Nolan thought. Her reason didn't concern him. "Sorry—it's none of my business." The sooner she left, then the sooner he could begin enjoying his week here. Alone. Without any interruptions. He definitely needed a break from women. All women. Even those in his family who were supporting his great-grandmother in her shenanigans.

But he was forced to admit for the most part, under any other circumstances, he could see himself becoming friends with Ivy. But they weren't. Instead, they were victims of manipulation of the worst kind. He would place the blame where it rightly belonged, and that was at her grandmother's and his great-grandmother's feet.

Giving in to his curiosity, he asked, "Does your grandmother know you're antimarriage?"

"Yes, she knows."

Nolan frowned. "Then why would she waste her time trying to get us together, knowing you feel the way you do?"

She released a frustrated breath. "I guess she's hoping I'll change my mind. I honestly believe your great-grandmother has convinced her that we are supposed to get married and have lots of babies. She's said so many times."

That sounded just like Mama Laverne. "That won't be happening," Nolan said with strong conviction in his voice.

He wasn't antimarriage like she evidently was by any means. He knew for a fact that true love did exist for some people. All he had to do was look around during any Madaris family gathering to see that for himself. Most marriages in the Madaris family were strong, solid and based on love, and lasted a lifetime.

His parents' and grandparents' marriages were good examples, as well as those of his other family members. The only exception had been Jake's first marriage. But from what he'd heard, the marriage had been doomed from the beginning since the woman tried making Jake into something he wasn't.

Nolan's major problem was his great-grandmother trying to shove the woman she'd chosen for him down his throat. When and if he ever married, it would be to a woman he selected and not one who'd been selected for him.

"I can't wait until Nana gets back to town."

He discovered that looking at her chest instead of her legs was just as bad. He liked the way her blouse fitted. "Where is she?"

"She went to Lake Charles for the weekend to attend a gospel revival."

"Umm, so did my great-grandmother. If they're together, then you know what that means. They'll work on the next plan when they get wind that this one didn't work."

"They've got to be stopped," she said, all but stomping her foot. He thought she looked cute when she did that.

"Any ideas on how to do that since talking sensibly with them doesn't seem to work?" he asked her.

"None that I can think of." She checked her watch. "I need to pack up now and leave before it gets dark. I'll be seeing you."

He nodded. "Drive safe."

When she left the kitchen, he drew in a deep breath, refusing to feel bad that she was leaving. He could do the decent thing and leave since she was here first, but he did own the place and there was no reason to give up his week for her. But he could invite her to stay the night and leave in the morning. It was an hour's drive back to Houston and it would be dark before she got there. And he did have two bedrooms.

"I got it!"

He quickly turned around. She had returned to the kitchen and stood there with a huge smile that stretched across those lips he'd been mesmerized by earlier. "You got what?"

"An idea on how to best Nana and Ms. Laverne. And I think it just might work."

She had him curious. "What is it?"

"It means there has to be a lot of pretending on our part."

He lifted a brow. "Pretending about what?"

"In order for the plan to work we need to pretend to be lovers."

CHAPTER SEVEN

"I THINK YOU need to explain just what you mean, Ivy."

Good Lord, Ivy was certain he thought she'd lost her mind. Maybe she had, but the one certain thing was that something had to be done to stop Nana and Ms. Laverne. While repacking, the idea had come to her as clear as glass. Her grandmother and his great-grandmother wouldn't let up until they thought they'd accomplished their goal. *In that case, let them believe that.*

"Ivy?"

"Yes?" She couldn't help noticing how his voice sounded even deeper and huskier and how nice her name sounded off his lips.

"I think you need to explain what you meant."

Yes, she did need to explain. Otherwise, he would think she was stone crazy. First of all, she knew that she didn't have the look or style of a woman he would take on as a lover. But she would worry about that later. It would be a work in progress. "Okay. But you need to promise you'll keep an open mind."

He didn't reply and the look he gave her at that moment all but said he wouldn't be promising anything but she couldn't let that look deter her. "I suggest that we sit down and share a glass of wine while I tell you. I really could use something to relax me right now."

She really could. Normally she didn't get this excited unless it had to do with a project she'd been working on and had discovered a technological breakthrough.

"Okay. I'll get the glasses," he said, moving toward the kitchen cabinet.

Nerves suddenly tightened her stomach. As far as she was concerned, it wasn't too bad of an idea. At least she'd come up with something. Desperate times called for desperate measures. She hoped that he believed that. "And I'll grab the wine."

She left the kitchen to grab a bottle from the welcome basket. By the time she returned, he had placed two wineglasses on the table. In his hand was the wine opener. "Let me," he said, reaching for the bottle.

She gave it to him and then sat down at the table. She watched as he filled both their glasses. "Not too much," she said when she thought he'd poured enough. "I still need to drive."

He put the wine bottle down before easing into the chair across from her. "So...?"

She took a sip of her wine. He was staring at her expectantly, waiting to hear what she had to say. What if he thought her idea was the stupidest, most insane thing he'd ever heard? "We already know that once Nana and Ms. Laverne get wind their plot failed again, they'll put their heads together to come up with another plan, right?"

"Yes."

"Then I suggest we be one step ahead of them. Let them assume their plan worked. That when we got here, although we were upset about it, we discovered we'd give it a try anyway. Trust their judgment so to speak."

He kept staring at her and she wondered what he was thinking. "Go on," he finally said.

"Our job is to do everything in our power to convince them their plan worked for this week and we decided to begin dating. That means that we will need to do what regular people who are dating do while getting to know each other. Going to dinner. A movie. Walks in the park. Those sorts of things."

He didn't say anything and the room got quiet. He just sat there and stared into his drink. She wondered if already he saw her plan as a failure because it was quite obvious she wasn't the type of woman he dated and no one would believe that he would. He liked flashy women and she didn't have a flashy bone in her body.

Men found her too techie to be desirable. Even Damien had admitted that. Most men saw her brain and passion for her work as turnoffs rather than turnons. Boring instead of interesting.

"And how exactly is that besting them? Sounds like we'll be giving in to them," he said, lifting his gaze to stare over at her.

"We won't be giving in to them. We'll just let them assume that we are and that's the beauty of the idea. Let them think what they want, but we will know the truth. Then when they think we should be planning for a wedding, we will tell them we tried to develop a relationship but discovered we weren't compatible."

She paused to give her words time to sink in before saying, "What we're dealing with are two women determined to marry us off. As long as we fight them on that, they will continue to come up with these crazy ideas to get us together. And from what I can see they will stop at nothing. However, if they think we gave in to what they see as their best-laid plans, and then ultimately reached the conclusion that there's no way we can spend the rest of our lives together, then I think they will accept our decision."

When he didn't say anything, Ivy asked, "So, what do you think?"

IN TRUTH, NOLAN didn't know what to think. He knew any further talks with Mama Laverne were out of the question. He'd tried it and she had completely ignored what he'd said. He'd thought about calling a family meeting when he discovered her matchmaking schemes that involved Victoria. However, after talking with his sister, who welcomed their great-grandmother's interference into her life, he knew calling such a meeting was pointless. He had to figure out a way to handle her himself. Fight his own battles. He was on his own. He looked at Ivy. Or was he?

He knew Ivy was waiting for him to say something, so he told her the truth. "I'm thinking."

And he was thinking, considering her plan. At least it was a plan, something he had refused to implement himself. Instead he had dated a lot of women to give Ivy the impression that he wasn't husband material. That ploy had worked at least, but from what Ivy had shared with him, she didn't intend to get married. Ever. So unbeknownst to him, the strategy hadn't been needed.

"Tell me again what we have to do," he said. Already he could see problems arising. Mama Laverne could see through mud, so there was a good chance she would see through this ploy.

"We'll hang out together on occasion. Pretend we're dating. And to make things believable you'll have to stop dating other women for a while."

She'd spoken as if she assumed him doing so would

be a hardship. Little did she know how wrong she was about that. "For how long?" he wanted to know.

"It will depend on us and when we think we've had enough time to convince them. This is the end of March, so I think breaking up before the summer would work. By then they should be convinced that we really gave a relationship between us a try and things didn't work out the way they'd expected."

Nolan wished it could be that easy. "I know my great-grandmother. She would expect us to hang in longer than that. Otherwise, she'll think it's something she could fix."

He could tell from the frown on Ivy's face that wasn't what she wanted to hear. He had to be up-front with her. She wasn't dealing with just anyone, but with a ninety-something-year-old woman who was determined to see each of her great-grands married before she took her last breath.

"Trust me, it's going to be hard to convince Mama Laverne that she made a mistake about us."

Ivy threw up her hands in frustration. "So what are we supposed to do? Give in and let them control our lives? I refuse to do that, Nolan."

She stood and he watched her pace. He tried to keep his gaze from roaming over her and found it difficult to do so. It was also difficult to think about how she was wearing the hell out of those cutoffs. Way too sexy for his peace of mind. It was obvious that she was agitated and he understood the feeling. Under any other circumstances her plan would be doable. But they were dealing with Felicia Laverne Madaris who couldn't easily be outsmarted. He and his cousins had learned that the hard way over the years.

She stopped pacing and turned to him. "Are you saying there's nothing we can do but continue to allow ourselves to be manipulated?"

"Pretty much."

"And you're going to settle for that?" she snapped. "Why don't you just be honest and admit that you don't like my plan and the reason you don't like it."

Nolan frowned. Had he missed something? Why was her anger now directed at him? And what was she talking about, all but accusing him of having an ulterior motive for not wanting to go along with her plan?

"Would you like to explain what you're accusing me of?" he said tightly.

She came back to the table and placed her hands palms down and leaned closer to him as if she demanded his attention. She didn't have to demand it because she had it. He noticed the way the mass of curly hair on her head was sliding over her shoulders. Her glasses seemed off center on her nose and he was tempted to reach out and straighten them. But she was already fired up and there was no need to add kerosene to the fire.

"I read the papers. I see photographs of the kind of women you date. The women constantly on your arm," she said. "I'm well aware of the type of women that claim your attention. And it's quite obvious I'm not like them. I don't even come close. I know that. But can't you put those types of women aside for less than eight weeks and pretend you could settle on someone like me?"

Settle on someone like her? Nolan was stunned into silence. As far as he was concerned, any woman she had read about or seen him with was all flash and no substance. Although he didn't know everything there was to know about Ivy, he believed she was right in saying that she was not like them. Personally, he saw that as a good thing.

"The type of women I date have nothing to do with why I have doubts about your plan working. I know my great-grandmother. The only way we can pull it off is if we're totally convincing. And the only way to do that is for us to pretend we've fallen hard for each other."

He paused for a moment and then added, "But then on the other hand she could use that same premise against us. If she thinks we fell hard for each other in the beginning that would make her more determined to save our relationship when we decide to go our separate ways."

Ivy came to sit back down at the table. "Unless you did something I would consider unforgivable."

He raised a brow. "Like what?"

"Like if I was to find you in a compromising position with a woman."

Her suggestion made him angry. "You want people to believe I betrayed you?"

"Why not? It wouldn't bother me if you did."

He leaned toward her over the table. "But it would bother me. It will bother my family. It will bother anyone who knows me. What you're suggesting will be a direct hit on my character."

"You, a man who doesn't believe in getting serious with any one woman. Who is known around town as Mr. One-Night Stand? A bona fide womanizer? Are you saying you don't play women?"

"That's exactly what I am saying. I don't play women. I date them. And when I do, I make it clear where I stand. I don't do serious relationships nor am I looking for one. I make that understood up front. If there's a communication problem, it's not on my end, so there shouldn't be a woman out there who has the right to feel cheated on by whatever I do."

He stood and leaned over the table, wanting to make sure he had Ivy's absolute attention. "Your plan calls for me to engage in what will appear to be a very serious relationship with you, and then you want to end things when you catch me cheating. That won't work because if and when I ever decide to get involved in a serious relationship with a woman I would never betray her."

"It will only be pretense, Nolan. You and I will know the truth."

He glared at her. Did she not understand the lasting effect of what doing something like that, pretense or otherwise, could do to his character? Did she think most men wouldn't have a problem doing something like that? He wondered what type of men she associated with.

"It doesn't matter," he said in a tight voice. "Come up with another unforgivable act. Infidelity is off the table."

She crossed her arms over her chest and glared back at him. "Fine. I'll come up with something else."

"You do that."

As they continued to glare at each other, he wondered if she understood what he'd told her about his great-grandmother's expectations. Just saying they were involved wouldn't be good enough to appease Felicia Laverne Madaris. She was a "show me" person and was used to displays of open affection, something that was in abundance in the Madaris family. There was no faking that. Could she handle it?

He sat down and leaned back in his chair, still holding her gaze. "So, if I agree to go along with your plan, assuming you come up with an acceptable reason for breaking up, how far are you willing to go to be convincing?"

She lifted a brow. "What do you mean? We won't be sleeping together if that's what you're getting at," she said in a firm tone.

A smile touched his lips. "I didn't think we would be. But we need to give the impression we are."

She frowned. "Why? Your family doesn't know me. For all they know I might be someone who plans to save myself for marriage."

"They might not know you, but they do know me, and my family wouldn't believe I'd be serious about a woman and not sharing her bed."

"Which means?"

"Which means to make things look real, whenever we're out in public there needs to be hand-holding, touching, whispering sweet nothings in your ear and kissing." Heat invaded his midsection at the mention of them kissing. At that moment her tongue swiped across her bottom lip.

"Kissing?" she asked in a low voice, like it had taken everything within her to say the word.

He looked into the eyes staring back at him and took note of their color. They had darkened. But then he was certain his had as well. "Yes, kissing."

She lifted her chin. "I don't kiss in public."

"I do. So I guess that's something you'll need to take into consideration, Ivy Chapman. In fact, just short of making love, kissing is one of my favorite things."

Nolan thought the scowl on her face was priceless. "Sorry if that's not what you wanted to hear but now is the time to be honest. And since I'm in such an honest state, I might as well come clean and say that regardless of what you might think, Ivy, I think you are sexy as hell."

CHAPTER EIGHT

IVY NEEDED TO take a drink of her wine. Not a sip, a full gulp, but she took just a sip instead. This idea of pretending to be lovers was hers, but it seemed she hadn't thought through all the ramifications. Maybe he was just messing with her.

"I take it you don't believe me," Nolan said.

Of course she didn't believe him. Sexy? Her? Please. It wasn't that she thought poorly of herself but she knew most men didn't see her that way. They couldn't get beyond the fact that in most cases, she found computers more fascinating than men. If he thought she would fall for the kinds of lines he fed the women he normally dated, well, she had news for him. She wasn't that hungry. "You don't believe yourself, Nolan, so can we get serious and decide what we plan to do?"

He took a sip of his drink, and continued to stare at her. "I'm being honest with you, Ivy. I can only give your plan real consideration if I think it will work. Like I told you, I have my doubts."

"Just because you don't think we can make it look real enough."

"Yes." A smile touched his lips. "But only on your part."

"My part?"

"Yes. There's no doubt in my mind I will be able to

make it look real. But the question of the hour is will you go along with me whenever I do so?"

Ivy frowned. "There will have to be limitations on any public displays of affection," she said, negotiating. She didn't like how he was complicating things.

"Look, Ivy, I believe your plan has merit but it has to be our best-laid plan."

"Our? Does that mean you're going to do it?"

"Only if I think we can get a sure win out of it. Otherwise, we'll be wasting our time. Are you willing to do whatever needs to be done to convince everyone we are truly serious about each other? And before you answer, I know about your limitations. To rest your mind, we won't be sleeping together. We'll just give the impression that we are. The only persons who will know that we aren't are you and me."

Why did he make it sound like they would have a little secret? And why did the thought of sharing a secret with him suddenly make her feel giddy inside? *Snap out of it*, her brain admonished. *Remember, this is not the man for you, no matter what Nana thinks*. Didn't Damien prove that she was better off without a man? *They deliver fake love before the very real heartbreak.* But she would admit it was hard to remember the bad Damien while sitting across from a man who looked so darn good. Billboard model, tall, dark and handsome personified.

Nolan waved a hand in front of her face and she nearly jumped out of her skin. "Now that I have your attention," he said, looking at her with an intense expression on his face, "will you answer my question?"

Ivy hoped the reason she had his rapt attention wasn't

because she'd been caught drooling. She swallowed deeply before asking, "What was your question?"

"When do we start?"

Suddenly she felt like she was on the edge of her seat. Was that excitement? Or was it anxiety? There was no room for either. They were on a mission to free themselves of the interference of two people who thought they had some God-given right to run their lives under the pretense of knowing what they needed and what was best for them.

"I guess now is as good a time as any," she heard herself say. "Nana and Mama Laverne know because of their manipulations that we're here together." She couldn't believe what she was about to suggest. "It might look suspicious if I go back to the city right away." He took another sip of his wine. She watched him, thinking how perfectly his mouth fitted the rim of the glass. She'd been drawn to his mouth a lot tonight; especially when the subject of kissing had come up.

"I agree. Hand me your phone."

"Why?"

"Because it would look rather odd if we didn't have each other's phone numbers. Don't you think?"

Yes, he was right. She stood and pulled her phone out of her pocket to hand to him. "Here." Moments later his phone rang.

"Now I have your mobile number and you have mine. And to make our affair believable, especially since there's no doubt in my mind there are allies out there who will report to Miss Chapman and Mama Laverne of our activities, I think it would be best if you stayed here."

"Just for the night, though," she clarified.

"No, for the week."

The bunched nerves inside Ivy's stomach kicked. "For a week?"

"Yes, a week. You had originally planned to do that anyway, before you discovered we'd been set up, right?"

"Yes, that's right." She nervously licked her bottom lip. "But…"

"But what?"

"Where will you be?" she felt the need to ask.

"I'll be right here with you."

NOLAN THOUGHT THAT if the situation wasn't so serious, he would find the look on her face downright amusing. In just the short time he'd been with her, he had noticed several things. Like how her brows would bunch tight when she was annoyed by something, how she would push curls away from her face when she wasn't sure about something, how she would lick her bottom lip with the tip of her tongue when she became nervous. Then there were the times she would push her eyeglasses back on her face whenever they slipped down that cute little nose of hers. The gesture usually preceded a strong rebuttal. He didn't mind. Women who thought it would be in their best interests to agree with anything he said irritated him. It was as if they couldn't speak or think for themselves. Obviously Ivy had no such hang-ups.

"Mama Laverne will expect it. Trust me. I know how her mind works. We mustn't forget that our goal is to make her assume her plan is working, right?"

"Yes."

"Then sharing this place for a week is what we'll need to do. The sooner we can convince her we fell in love, the sooner we can convince her we've fallen out of love."

He saw the uncertain look on her face and on cue she pushed a few wayward curls back from her face. He'd been tempted to do it. "I promise not to bite, Ivy. This plan that we pretend to be lovers was your idea. I agreed with the stipulations you put in place. But I've stated more times than I cared to that in order to make it work we have to make our fake relationship appear believable."

He scrubbed the back of his neck, trying to keep his frustration with her at bay. She couldn't have things both ways. "In case you haven't noticed, this place has two bedrooms, split concept with each suite having its own bath. You will have your space and I'll have mine."

"I know that, Nolan, but what will we do together for a week?"

"Whatever you had planned to do without me being here and I will do likewise. But at some point we need to set aside time to get to know each other."

"Why?"

He was surprised she would ask that. "Because after a week everyone would expect us to know something about each other and, trust me, Mama Laverne will grill me and there's no doubt in my mind your grandmother will do the same."

She nodded. "I guess you're right."

"You know I'm right." He stood and stretched his limbs, suddenly feeling exhausted. He wasn't sure whether the cause was from taking time out to play tennis with his cousins earlier today or from verbally sparring with her. "I need a good night's sleep, so I'm going to bed."

"To bed? But it's only seven and it's still daylight outside."

"Not for long. Besides, I think my body is still on Paris time. I had just got back the day before you came to my office."

"What about dinner? Aren't you hungry?"

"No. I'm still stuffed from when my great-aunt fed me earlier today. I assume you will be here in the morning when I wake up."

"Yes, I'll be here."

He nodded. Before heading out of the kitchen, he glanced over at her and said, "Good night, Ivy. See you in the morning."

"Good night."

As Nolan strolled out of the kitchen toward the bedroom he would be using, he hoped like hell that their plan worked. He was tempted to look back at her before opening the door to his bedroom, but he fought the temptation. His only involvement with Ivy would be of the pretend kind and it was best that he remembered that.

CHAPTER NINE

THE SOUND OF someone humming brought Ivy awake. She glanced at her clock and saw the time was just a little past seven. It took her a minute to remember where she was and why. Tiki Island. Pretend lover of Nolan Madaris.

The week vacation she thought she'd won had been nothing more than a setup thanks to her grandmother. Frowning, she pulled herself up in bed and grabbed for her phone to call her grandmother. It was time to put her and Nolan's plan into action, and Helen Chapman was about to get an earful from her.

After Nolan went to bed it was as if she was alone in the cottage and she appreciated that. She had needed that time to reflect on all that had been said since she'd returned from her walk on the bay to find Nolan in her kitchen. It was really his kitchen, she reminded herself.

As soon as the bedroom door had closed behind him last night, she had grabbed a bag of chips and an apple from the welcome basket. She had heard his shower going while making a ham sandwich and a glass of iced tea.

The breeze off the Galveston Bay had relaxed her while she sat outside on the patio to eat. The quiet peacefulness gave her an opportunity to mentally rehash her conversations with Nolan. He had been right. Pretending to be lovers had been her idea and she needed to own it. It had taken another walk on the bay after her meal to finally accept that the plan she'd come up with would work if, like Nolan said, it was believable. More than anything she was determined that it would be.

"Hello?"

Her grandmother's voice sounded soft, almost like a whisper in her ear. "Nana, this is Ivy."

"I know, dear. I recognize your voice."

"Then you know why I'm calling." Ivy paused for a minute and then asked, "Nana, how could you? Why on earth would you and Ms. Laverne set me and Nolan up again?"

"You're calling him by his first name. That's good."

"Excuse me?"

"The last time we talked about him, he was Mr. Madaris. Now he's Nolan and I think that's a good sign."

Ivy shook her head. "There is no sign. Nana, we need to talk about this."

"We talked already, dear. Remember?"

"Yes, I remember but you didn't listen."

"You're right. I didn't listen because I know what's best. Where are you, by the way?"

"I'm still on Tiki Island. Nolan was kind enough to allow me to stay a couple of days. I appreciate him for not blaming me for what happened."

"Of course he wouldn't blame you. And where is he?"

"Not sure. He's around here somewhere. I'm just waking up. Luckily, this place is plenty big enough for the both of us with the two bedrooms and private baths. Split concept. I doubt if we'll run into each other much while I'm here." She figured her grandmother was frowning about now. That's probably not what she wanted to hear.

"Who's doing the cooking? Not you I hope."

Her grandmother knew of her dislike of kitchen duties that required more than putting cold cuts between two slices of bread. "We're on our own."

"What a pity. Nolan is a great cook. He's also a nice man."

"Whatever. We will talk again when I get back, Nana. If you keep this up, I'm going to think you're not in your right mind."

"I'm in my right mind," her grandmother assured her. "In the end you are going to thank me."

Ivy doubted that. "We'll talk, Nana." She heard the sound of humming again and realized the noise was from the television mounted on the wall in the living room.

"We'll see. Enjoy your time on the bay."

And then her grandmother hung up on her. "Oh, you are so wrong for that, Nana. You are wrong for all of this," Ivy muttered, easing out of the bed. She thought about what Nolan said regarding them getting to know each other. That meant spending time with him and she'd rather not do that. She didn't like admitting it but heat would curl in her stomach whenever she was around him. She smiled when an idea came into her head. Instead of spending time with him, she would text information to him. All he needed to know was stuff like her favorite foods, music, movie, color and pertinent facts like that. She would suggest that he did the same. Ivy smiled, convinced that would work.

NOLAN USED THE outside shower to rinse sand from his body. There was nothing like an early-morning swim in the bay. After a good night's sleep, he had awakened at the crack of dawn ready for a hot cup of coffee to get his day started. He had walked through the house toward the kitchen in the nude before remembering he had a houseguest. Rushing back to his bedroom, he had quickly donned a pair of swimming shorts.

Now two hours later, after his coffee, he had taken a leisurely swim and was ready to start his day. And do what? Nothing. He had come here to do nothing but knew with Ivy Chapman under his roof that was no longer an option.

As he dried off and slid into a pair of shorts, he thought about the agreement they'd made last night and the terms that had come with it. He'd been too tired to think about them last night and after his shower he had gone to bed, falling into a deep sleep the moment his head hit the pillow.

Hearing the ring of his cell phone, he picked it up off the patio table. He recognized the ringtone and knew the identity of the caller. Apparently, Mama Laverne couldn't wait for him to call her so she was calling him. He eased down into a patio chair and clicked on his phone. "Good morning."

"Glad to know you're in a good mood, Nolan."

He raised his eyes toward the sky. "I'm not in a good mood, thanks to you. How can I be when my great-grandmother is trying to manipulate my life?"

"Is that what you think I'm doing?"

"That's the way it looks to me," he said, leaning back in his seat.

"Then we need to get you a new pair of eyes."

Nolan fought back a grin. Although this certainly wasn't a laughing matter by any means, you just had to love her. And he did. But he would not allow that love to control his personal life.

"I understand you still have a houseguest."

He lifted a brow. "And how do you know that?"

"I have my ways."

He figured she did. It was his guess that Ivy had spoken to her grandmother either last night or this morning. That meant their plan was in process. "The only reason she's still here is because I felt it was the least I could do. You and your cohorts had her believing she'd won some contest. Imagine how she felt to discover it was a lie just to get her here with me."

"You will thank me one day, Nolan."

"It won't work, Mama Laverne." He knew to make their plan believable, it was important that he and Ivy show resistance. They would expect that.

"It will work. I suggest you show her how good you are in the kitchen."

"She won't be staying that long. Like I said, the only reason she's here is because I felt bad for her. You set her up. You set me up. We aren't happy about that. The least I could do is let her stay a few days."

"That was kind of you."

"I'm a nice person."

"Of course you are. That's the reason you were chosen for her."

Nolan took note of what his grandmother had implied. He was chosen for Ivy and not the other way around where she was chosen for him? "I prefer not being chosen for anyone."

"Too late now."

We'll see about that, he thought, deciding it was time to end the call. But not before saying, "I will be paying you a visit when I return to Houston." He knew another meeting with her would serve no purpose but he had to put up a front.

"It always brings me joy to see you, Nolan. I look forward to your visit. Have a good day, and prepare your crab cakes. Ivy will love them. Goodbye."

"Goodbye, Mama Laverne." He clicked off the phone. Shaking his head, he grabbed the wet items and headed toward the house.

He heard the sound the moment he walked through the back door. Ivy was laughing, and the rich, jubilant sound soaked into his skin, making goose bumps appear on his arms. He wondered what on earth was going on. He paused long enough to toss the wet clothes into the washing machine and followed the sound of her voice.

He found her standing in front of the television. She was watching cartoons. He glanced at the television screen but only for a second. His main focus was on her and those sinful-looking shorts she had on. They weren't Daisy Dukes by any means, but on her they so adequately revealed she had the body of a goddess. Curves in all the right places. Femininity to the core.

Her hair was back to that severe-looking knot on her head but that was fine. He'd seen her hair down yesterday and liked it, but he was noticing things about this particular style as well. How it outlined the contours of her face, making sharp angles appear soft and delicate. She wasn't a big woman. Nor was she small. Instead she fell somewhere in the middle. He also noted she wasn't wearing any jewelry. Not even a pair of earrings. But she did have a watch on her wrist. And it wasn't one of those that resembled a bracelet. It looked to be just what it was—a watch with a black leather band. He knew he shouldn't be standing there ogling her like this but at the present, he was too captivated not to. His gaze roamed all over her again, and this time it zeroed in on her perfectly shaped backside. Not in a thousand years would he have guessed such a well-developed body had been hidden beneath that business suit she'd worn to his office the day they'd met.

She laughed again and the sound flowed through him. Her amusement was contagious and he couldn't help the smile that touched his lips. She hadn't detected his presence and he moved to stand directly behind her. He leaned forward and whispered, "A woman who enjoys watching cartoons is a woman after my own heart."

IVY JERKED AROUND so fast she nearly lost her balance. To keep herself from falling, she reached out and grabbed hold of Nolan. Namely his naked chest. His very naked, hairy chest. Did she include muscular? If not, in that case, his very naked, hairy, muscular chest. She glanced down and saw not only was he shirtless, but a line of hair trailed downward to be hidden by an indecent-looking pair of athletic shorts.

She jerked her gaze back up to his and at that moment noticed how hot his skin felt beneath her fingers. So hot she snatched her hand away, which made her lose her balance and tilt forward, right into his arms.

Again she was touching him and what was doubly bad was that he was touching her. His arms were wrapped around her. Tight. Frowning, she stared up at him. "Have you lost your mind? You scared me."

In addition to that, she was convinced that him touching her was causing irreversible damage to her skin. There was no way she would not remember him touching her arms. OMG! He was still touching her arms. She tried to jerk away from him and he held on tight. Her frown deepened. "You can let me go, Nolan."

He stared down at her with those penetrating dark eyes. "You sure? I wouldn't want you to fall."

"I wouldn't have lost my balance if you hadn't sneaked up on me," she snapped. "You could have let me know you were in the house."

"Maybe I should wear a bell around my neck so you will hear me whenever I approach," he said, speaking through clenched teeth.

"Or you can do the decent thing and announce your presence."

"Or maybe you shouldn't be so clumsy," he said, releasing her and then fencing his arms around her as a shield just in case she tumbled over again. Seeing him do that annoyed her. But at least they were no longer touching.

Ivy pressed down on her lips, refusing to go tit for tat with him. It was barely eight in the morning. The one thing she liked about being self-employed was she got to make her own work hours. Thank God for that because she was definitely not a morning person. Getting up at noon was fine with her, even if it meant her workday extended to midnight. She could deal with that. She rarely got up before noon and seldom went to bed before midnight.

"You're right, I should have alerted you of my presence. I apologize."

His apology took some heat out of her fire. It changed the mood. "I should apologize as well. I should not have snapped at you, but one of my major faults is that I'm not a morning person."

He raised a brow. "You couldn't convince me of that. You were laughing. Almost hysterically."

Yes, she had been but there was a good reason for that. "I love watching cartoons."

"Umm, I gathered as much."

"And Sylvester and Tweety are my favorites. They'll get a laugh out of me no matter what time of day it is."

"That's good to know."

"What is?"

"That you enjoy watching cartoons and Sylvester and Tweety are your favorites. And just so you know, I love watching cartoons as well."

She raised a brow. Very few macho men would admit to such a thing. They would put cartoons on the same shelf as romance novels. "Do you?"

"Yes. And my favorite is *Tom Slick*. I never got into Sylvester and Tweety. But I did enjoy *The Jetsons*."

She smiled. "So did I." In fact they were on her top ten list.

The room got quiet when conversation between them ceased. Unfortunately that was when she remembered what he was wearing…or wasn't wearing. But then this was his house and if he was used to walking around half-naked, then so be it. However, she knew that meant she needed to put as much distance between them as reasonably possible while they were under the same roof. She might be a techie but she was also a woman who could appreciate a good-looking male body when she saw one. It was bad enough seeing him in those jeans and T-shirt yesterday. But to see him like this was a little too much.

"I take it you're an early riser," she said, to get the

conversation started again. She began moving toward the kitchen and unfortunately for her, he followed.

"Yes. Normally, I'm up by the crack of dawn. I believe in that saying 'Early to bed, early to rise, make a man healthy, wealthy and wise.'"

She chuckled. "I believe in that saying 'The best time to get any work done is late at night when all the world is sleeping.'"

He nodded. "And whose quote is that?"

"Mine. Made it up myself and I swear by it."

"I guess we can't have all things in common," he said.

"By the way, I came up with an idea."

"Another one?" he asked, moving toward the refrigerator.

"Yes."

"Let's hear it."

"I figured instead of us having to spend time together to get to know each other, we can exchange text messages with information."

He looked at her and shook his head. "I doubt it will work. To really get to know each other will require personal interaction."

"I disagree. Let's try it and see what happens."

"Suit yourself but don't say I didn't warn you that it won't work." He opened the refrigerator and pulled out eggs, cheese and bread.

She watched him. "You're cooking?" she asked.

"Yes." He moved to a cabinet and pulled out a frying pan.

"Do you plan to share?"

He glanced over his shoulder at her and gave her a look as if she'd asked a silly question. "Of course."

"I'll make the coffee. How do you take yours?"

"Black and light on the sugar."

So did she. Another thing they had in common. "No problem." She moved to the opposite counter where the coffeepot was. After grabbing two mugs from the cabinet, she began making their coffee.

"I understand you talked to your grandmother already."

She glanced over at him. He was standing at the stove. Did he not worry about popping grease? Evidently he felt comfortable being shirtless and wearing just his shorts. Was she a prude for thinking he was barely dressed? Outside the bedroom, Damien had always worn a shirt and the bottom part of him had always been covered in jeans or pants. Come to think of it, she'd never seen Damien in shorts. The most logical reason could be because they'd dated during the winter months.

"Yes. This morning. How did you know that?"

"Mama Laverne."

"She called you?"

"Yes. And I assume it was after you spoke with your grandmother. She knew you were still here and since I hadn't sent you packing, she saw that as an ace in the hole. I'm sure that she, along with your grandmother, assume they got us where they want us."

Ivy leaned against the counter while the coffee brewed. "I'm going to have to agree with you. Even when I played the resistance game, she sounded victorious."

"That doesn't surprise me."

Ivy watched Nolan easily handle the frying pan and gasped when he flipped an egg like a pro. "I thought you were going to make a mess I was going to have to clean up."

Again, he gave her a strange look. "If I make the mess, I clean it up. But rest assured there will not be a mess. I've been flipping over easy eggs for years. By the way, how do you like yours?"

"Not over easy that's for sure. I like mine fried. Well-done. If they look burned around the edges you won't hurt my feelings."

He chuckled. "What about cheese?"

"Definitely. If I end up with more cheese than egg, it won't hurt my feelings either."

He chuckled again and she thought it sounded husky and deep. Even earlier in the living room, it was a deep, masculine baritone murmuring close to her ear that had frightened her.

"You have something against pigs."

She slanted a brow. "No, why do you ask?"

"You didn't purchase any bacon or sausage."

"Oh." Now it was her time to chuckle. "I don't have a thing against pigs but I do have something against pots and pans. If I bought either of them I would have to cook it and I detest cooking." She watched as he flipped her egg. "Fried eggs I can handle, but that's as far as it goes. But I definitely can't handle them the way you do, flipping them all over the place. I heard you can cook."

"Who told you that?"

"Nana."

"Yes, I can cook. In fact I enjoy doing so."

She placed the coffee cups on the table. "Really?" She didn't know of any man who liked to cook. Not her grandfather, her father and definitely not Damien. They'd always gone out to dinner or did fast foods.

"I had a great teacher."

"Your mom?" she asked him.

"No, Mama Laverne. Cooking lessons were required of all her kids, grands and great-grands. And there's no doubt in my mind that if she's still around, when the time comes, her great-great-grands as well. She's the best cook in Houston, hands down."

He slid her plate in front of her before sitting down across from her. Her eggs were just the way she liked. They were pretty. The yolk had been broken evenly. She wondered how he'd done that. After they said grace she dug in. "Mmm. Perfect," she said and meant it. Nothing half-cooked. It was well-done just like she wanted. "Thanks."

"You're welcome and thanks for making the coffee."

"No problem. That's the one thing I can do in the kitchen." She glanced over at his plate, wondering how anyone could eat a half-cooked yolk but decided to keep her opinion to herself.

"Want some of my eggs?"

She glanced over at him. He was smiling. She liked it when he smiled. "No, thanks."

"You might like it."

"There's a bigger chance I might not. I rank half-cooked eggs right up there with oatmeal. They are both on my never-to-do list." She took a sip of her coffee.

"You don't know what you're missing."

"And I hope to never find out."

They continued to eat, for the most part in silence but more than once she found herself staring at his bare chest. Why was she tempted to reach across the table and spear her fingers into all the hair? If he had that much hair covering his chest, then chances were he had just as much covering his—

"Does my being shirtless bother you? If so, I can remedy that."

For him to ask meant he'd noticed her staring. "No, it doesn't bother me," she said. "It's your house."

"And you're my guest. I don't want to make you feel uncomfortable."

"You don't." That was partly true. Seeing him shirtless didn't make her feel uncomfortable. What it was doing was forming crazy ideas in her head. "Do you normally walk around shirtless?"

"Depends on where I am. Whenever I'm here, yes. And if you like, I have no problem with you walking around here shirtless as well."

She couldn't help but laugh and wagged her finger at him. "Don't hold your breath for that to happen."

She took another sip of her coffee. She didn't want to admit she enjoyed his company. She enjoyed his playful side. And she liked his thoughtfulness. He didn't have to invite her to join him for breakfast. He could have reminded her of their agreement to do their own thing.

Her grandmother had been right, Nolan was a nice man. But she'd dated nice men before. They were nice in the beginning but eventually proved her wrong. She glanced at her watch, wondering how long would it take for him to go from a prince to an utter toad.

CHAPTER TEN

"ARE YOU SURE you don't need my help cleaning up the kitchen?"

Nolan glanced over at Ivy. "I'm positive."

He tried not to stare at her as she stood in the middle of the kitchen where a beam of sunlight shone directly on her. It made her skin glow and her features that much more vibrant. For the past five minutes or so he had the pleasure of watching her move around the kitchen when she helped him clear off the table. He loved seeing her legs in motion.

"If you're sure you don't need my help, then I'm going to take a walk along the bay," she said, interrupting his thoughts.

"Okay. What are your plans for the day?"

"To start reading a book I brought with me. That means I'll be in my bedroom most of the day. What about you?"

"I think I'll go fishing. However, first thing I plan to do is go to the grocery store and buy some bacon, sausages and more eggs. Anything you need me to get for you while I'm there?"

"No, I'm good. I'll see you later."

"All right."

He stood at the sink by the window and watched her move down the path toward the bay. If anyone would have told him he would become attracted to the one woman he didn't want to become attracted to, the woman his great-grandmother was determined to put in front of him every chance she got, he would not have believed them. But he knew he was definitely attracted to Ivy Chapman.

Damn.

He couldn't look at her without feeling his stomach muscles clench or a rush of desire invade his loins. And his mind was filled with salacious thoughts whenever he was near her. He hadn't expected it, and personally, he didn't want to deal with it. But they had agreed to the week for their plan to work and the last thing he wanted was for their plan to fail.

Earlier when she had fallen into his arms, it had taken every ounce of strength he had not to tighten his hold on her, lower his head and kiss her. While she'd been in his arms there hadn't been a woman whose mouth he had wanted to devour more. In fact, every time he looked at her mouth, studied the shape of her lips, watched her lick those same lips with her tongue, he would fight the urge to kiss her.

Breakfast had started off great, but by the time they'd finished, he hadn't been able to keep his eyes off her. He was discovering there was a lot about Ivy Chapman that revved his testosterone. And that wasn't good. It was downright disastrous. What he needed from her was distance.

He would spend most of the day on the bay fishing and hopefully she would stay in her room reading like she said she would. They hadn't agreed to eat any meals together, which was good. The only problem with that was that he enjoyed cooking and had planned to do a lot of it while he was here. He couldn't cook without asking if she wanted any. He would ask and would hope she refused.

His cell phone dinged, which meant he'd got a text message. He pulled it out of his pocket and saw the message was from Ivy and all it said was: Red. Seafood. Idris. *The Mountain Between Us.* Nolan shook his head and slid his cell phone back into his pocket. Did she seriously think they could get to know each other to the degree they needed to by exchanging text messages?

She wasn't ignorant, she had to have felt the vibes between them. Was that the reason she preferred sending text messages instead of being around him? And a better question to ask: Was that the reason she had shown so much interest in his chest? He should have put on a shirt but he was used to not wearing one while he was here. Maybe he needed to change that. He didn't want her to get the same wanton ideas that he was getting.

He'd never invited a woman to his cottage, except for his sisters. Ivy's presence here would take some getting used to.

As he finished cleaning up the kitchen his cell phone rang. It was Corbin. He pulled it out of his back pocket. "What's up, Corbin?"

"Is it true?"

Nolan raised a brow. "Is what true?"

"Is Ivy Chapman there with you at the cottage?"

News traveled fast in the Madaris family and he wouldn't waste his time trying to figure out who told who. All he was certain of was that the chain of information had started with his great-grandmother. "Yes, she's here."

"Man, are you crazy?"

Nolan had asked himself that same question several times since waking up this morning. "I hope not."

"Then why are you playing right into Mama Laverne's hands? Why didn't you send the woman away the moment the two of you discovered what Mama Laverne and Ivy's grandmother had done?"

Nolan rubbed his hand down his face. He would let Corbin in on Ivy's and his plan, confident his brother would keep his mouth shut.

"The reason Ivy is still here is because she and I have come up with a plan."

He spent the next ten minutes or so outlining Ivy's and his plan. It would not have taken that long if Corbin hadn't asked so many questions. "So there you have it, Corbin. After what Ivy and I think is a suitable amount of time, we will break up."

"And you think Mama Laverne won't try like the dickens to get the two of you back together?"

"She might try but it won't happen. Besides, I'll be spending most of my time in Paris by then with the construction of Lee's hotel. I won't be around for her to harass. And it will be up to Ivy to keep her own grandmother off her back. Either way, it doesn't matter. There will never be anything romantic between us."

"I doubt if she'd want to develop anything between the two of you anyway. She still believes you to be a man whore, right?"

"Yes, she still believes that." It surprised him how much it bothered him that she thought that, considering that's what his aim had been.

After ending the call with Corbin, Nolan released a deep sigh. Talking to his brother had been good. It was always good to get another opinion and Corbin thought the plan he and Ivy had come up with was a good one. But Corbin had stressed the same thing Nolan had stressed to Ivy. In order to pull things off, their performance had to be convincing, or their great-grandmother would see through their ploy and then there would be hell to pay.

"TELL ME YOU'RE KIDDING, Ivy."

Ivy sat on the wooden dock and looked across the bay while her feet slid back and forth in the water. She loved it here and a part of her appreciated Nolan allowing her to stay.

"Ivy?"

For a quick second she'd forgotten she had Tessa on the phone. "No, I'm not kidding, Tessa. Things went down just like I told you. My winning that contest was a plan concocted by Nana and Ms. Laverne. You can't imagine how it felt walking into that kitchen to find Nolan standing there. I don't know who was more surprised— me or him."

"And he didn't get mad?"

"Not at me but at Nana and his great-grandmother. We decided to work together and get even."

"Is that why you're still there?"

"Yes." She then told Tessa about the plan she and Nolan had come up with. Okay, she had come up with it but he had agreed to go along.

"I hope your plan works. You're dealing with what appears to be two very determined women."

Ivy knew that to be true, that's why their plan had to work. The one thing she knew could complicate things was her attraction to Nolan. That was not a part of the plan. She needed to get hold of her overactive hormones, and fast. If Nolan had any idea of what was going on in her head, there was no doubt he would send her packing in a heartbeat. And for their plan to work, she needed to stay put. She hadn't thought so at first, but after talking to Nana this morning it was obvious her grandmother thought she had things figured out. Ivy intended to prove her wrong.

"We need to get together as soon as you get back and go shopping."

Tessa's words invaded her thoughts. "Why?"

"Get real, Ivy. We are talking about Nolan Madaris. He definitely has a type."

Ivy already knew that. "That's not me."

"True. That's why we need to make it you."

Ivy frowned. "Excuse me?"

"You heard what I said. There will be people other than your nana and his great-grandmother who need to believe your story as well. And the first thought that will run through their minds is what about you drew Nolan. I think you're beautiful but you hide it. Time to bring it out and flaunt it."

Ivy shook her head. "I did that once." It had been for Damien. She had tried making herself into the woman she'd thought he had wanted her to be and in the end it still hadn't worked. He had still cheated on her.

"I know, Ivy, but you're going to have to do it again. Not that you're chopped liver or anything—like I said, you're beautiful—but there are those who are going to wonder why Nolan is interested in you since you aren't the type of woman he usually dates."

She knew Tessa was right and had said as much to Nolan. She'd never been one of those women who put a lot of emphasis on her looks. Her mind had always been filled with technology more than makeup or clothes. "I know you're right, but…"

"But what? It's not like you got a thing for Nolan Madaris and are trying to do a makeover for him. You're doing it for others as part of your plan and nothing more. You're there with him now and haven't changed your appearance, right?"

"Right."

"Because you aren't trying to impress him the way you tried to impress Damien."

Ivy nodded. What Tessa said made sense. Nolan hadn't complained about her curly hair, the eyeglasses she wore or the fact that she never wore lipstick. Damien had. Continuously. To keep him from complaining, she'd begun wearing her hair straight instead of curly, had traded her glasses for contacts and had begun wearing lipstick whenever he saw her.

"You're right. I'll be doing this for me as part of the plan and not for Nolan." She had a feeling he couldn't care less. And of course she hadn't believed him when he claimed he thought she was hot. "We'll go shopping when I get back."

"And when will that be?"

"A week."

"You're staying that entire time with him?"

"Yes, that's part of the plan."

When Tessa didn't say anything, Ivy knew there had to be a reason for her best friend's silence. "Okay, Tessa, what is it? What aren't you saying?"

"Nolan Madaris is a hunk."

Ivy chuckled. "Don't you think I know that?"

"And that doesn't bother you?"

Ivy smiled. "If it did, I can't rightly ask him to change his looks just for me."

"You know what I mean."

Yes, she knew exactly what Tessa meant. Any woman would find sharing a roof with a man like Nolan an impossible temptation to resist. And even with her techie mind, she was still a woman. "I will ignore it."

"Can you do that?"

Ivy doubted it, especially when she thought about how she'd ogled him during breakfast. "I will do my best…but there is something I am concerned about, Tessa. Something more troubling than him being eye candy."

"What?"

"Whether or not we'll truly be able to fool anyone. Nolan says he likes to display his affections in public— holding hands, whispering sweet nothings in my ear and even kissing. It's going to be important that when anyone sees us together that they're able to feel a certain degree of…"

"Chemistry?"

"Yes, chemistry between us. Otherwise, I'm not sure our plan will work."

"I agree. Have you discussed this concern with Nolan?"

"I can't do that!"

"Yes, you can and I suggest that you do. After all, this was your idea and he's all in because he believes it can work. The last thing either of you want is to look awkward when you should be portraying a couple falling in love. I think you ought to tell him about your misgivings."

"Nolan believes that once we get to know each

other that will be enough. That's why we're together this week."

"Yes, but didn't you say you're texting him information to avoid spending time with him?"

"Yes."

"And I told you what I thought about that ploy. It's so impersonal, and to accomplish what the two of you need to do requires personal interaction. With that said, getting to know each other is essential, but body language and vibes are, too, especially the vibes. I remember my cousin Martin and his wife, Peggy. Although they had gone through the motions of being happy, the family detected something off between them. Weeks later it didn't come as a surprise to any of us that they'd decided to get a divorce. So, I agree, chemistry between two people is important and is something you can't fake."

After ending her call with Tessa, Ivy knew her best friend was right. Chemistry was something you couldn't fake. So what could she and Nolan do to make it convincing? She looked up at the sky. The forecasters had also been right about the weather. The sun was out and it would be a beautiful day. The water swirling around her feet and legs felt good. She could get used to this place. It was one's private paradise. Nolan's paradise.

She heard the sound of the car's engine and figured Nolan was leaving for the store. When he returned she intended to be in her bedroom reading...and trying to sort out in her mind how to deal with her attraction to him. Checking her phone, she saw he hadn't texted her back with any information about himself. Maybe just as well.

Ivy also knew she needed to talk about their chemistry and what it would take to fool Nana and Ms. Laverne.

CHAPTER ELEVEN

"GOOD MORNING, NOLAN. Thanks for leaving me something to eat for dinner yesterday as well as for breakfast this morning. You didn't have to do that."

Plastering a smile on his face, Nolan entered the kitchen and closed the back door behind him. "It's no longer morning. It's now afternoon. And you don't have to thank me for the food. There's no way I would cook for myself and not share with you."

Ivy leaned against the counter and his gaze took her in from head to toe. Today she was wearing a pair of white shorts and a printed blouse. Like the day before her hair was in curls and hanging around her shoulders. She looked pretty, well rested. How could that be when he'd heard her moving around late through the night? It wasn't that she'd disturbed him since he'd had a hard time getting to sleep anyway.

"I stand corrected since it's after one o'clock, Nolan. Good afternoon. And I do need to thank you because not everyone would be so thoughtful."

He shoved his hands into the pockets of his jeans. "Then that person isn't a Madaris."

He hadn't seen Ivy since breakfast yesterday. He had returned from the grocery store to find her bedroom door closed. He'd figured she was in the room reading like she'd said she would be doing. He hadn't got any more text messages from her and was glad of that. Like he'd told her, they needed personal interaction.

After putting the groceries away, he had grabbed his fishing rod and walked down to the dock Blade and Slade had helped him build when he'd first purchased the cottage. It was thirty feet in length and the perfect spot to cast your line.

It had been a good day to fish and by the time he returned to the cottage later that afternoon he'd caught a cooler full of fish. It hadn't taken long for him to clean them before putting the majority of them in the freezer. He had kept out several and had cooked them outside on the fire pit.

During all that time he hadn't seen Ivy. Not once did she come out to join him. For a minute he had wondered if she was even still there or if she had fled back to Houston. That suspicion was put to rest when he'd seen her bedroom lights go on. Why he had released a sigh of relief, he wasn't sure.

It was only after he'd showered later that night and got into bed had he heard her moving around in the kitchen. Had her book been that good that it had kept her behind closed doors all day, or had her absence been a deliberate ploy on her part to avoid him?

That question had been at the forefront of his mind upon wakening this morning. He'd noted she had eaten the grilled fish, squash and corn he had left warming for her in the oven the night before. But she didn't make an appearance for breakfast like she'd done yesterday.

"You're right, he wasn't a Madaris."

He? That made Nolan wonder who the ingrate was. Not that he needed to know. "Did you finish reading your book?"

"No, not yet. I got a few more pages left. The food was good by the way, and I loved the way you cooked the fish. And the breakfast you left warming in the oven this morning was delicious as well."

"Thanks."

He moved toward the refrigerator to grab a beer. Like usual he'd been up at the crack of dawn. After breakfast he had spent time sanding down several pieces of his patio furniture to repaint later. He'd come inside to grab a beer and there she was, standing in the kitchen. His steps had faltered when he'd seen her. He realized he had missed her. How crazy was that?

He leaned against the counter, popped the tab on his beer and took a swallow. Then he glanced over at her. She was still standing there, across the kitchen floor and leaning against a counter as well. Unlike him with the beer, she had a bottle of water. "What are your plans for today?" he asked her.

"I want to finish that book."

He nodded. "And after that?"

She shrugged her shoulders. He saw her do it but his gaze was mostly on her lips. There was something about the way they were shaped that was a total turn-on for him. "I'm not sure. Why?" she said.

"I was wondering if you'd be interested in playing a couple of games with me later."

Her brow furrowed. "What kind of games?"

"Video games. Some that I created."

Her eyes flashed excitement. "Only on one condition."

"And what condition is that?"

"That we also play a few that I created."

Nolan chuckled. "Lady, you are on."

"HAD ENOUGH YET?"

Ivy gave Nolan a sideways glance and couldn't help but grin. Not only had he trounced her on three of his games but had done so on two of hers. That was a first. No one had ever done that before, especially with one of the games she'd created. She had to grudgingly hand it to him. He was that good and playing against her had definitely exposed his competitive side.

"No. One more game and I want it to be one of yours."

He gave her a huge smile, one that should not set sensations off in her stomach...but it did. "Fine with me if you think you can handle another loss."

"Whatever. So pick one," she said, trying to calm her stomach.

He shook his head. "No, you pick. I don't want to be accused of setting you up or anything. Besides, you have plenty to choose from."

He was telling the truth about that. Nolan had created and designed many games. Some had become quite popular commercially over the years. But then, so had many of hers. Designing video games had been a side gig for her, one she could count on whenever her social life went sour and she needed time to herself...which was the case most of the time. She'd found it easier to curl up with a computer than with a man.

She had known Nolan owned an electronics company, she really hadn't known just how extensive it was. He'd told her about the technology he would be installing into his cousin's hotel in Paris. All state-of-the-art. All of it sounded like technology heaven. It had been good to spend time discussing a topic with him that most men would get bored of discussing with a woman.

"Fine, show me the list of games again," she said.

After perusing the list, she chose one that was a category five. Like her, he rated all his games in categories based on their levels of difficulty, with five being the highest. "I want to try out this one."

He chuckled. "'The Mighty Marauder'? You sure about that?"

"Positive." What she wouldn't tell him was that she'd played this particular game before against Tessa and knew the key to winning.

"Okay. Suit yourself."

Ivy knew the heat was on. She also knew that although Nolan had beaten her playing the last five games, she inwardly admitted that one of the reasons for her losses was a lack of concentration. Sitting close to him had made it nearly impossible. Like she'd told Tessa, the man couldn't do anything about his looks but did he have to smell good all the time as well?

And then there were his hands. Masculine hands. They looked strong. Broad across the palms with long fingers. She couldn't keep her gaze from becoming fixated on how his fingertips meticulously worked the controllers.

There was no time to talk during game time. Just concentration. And this time she concentrated and perfected her timing. She refused to get off-kilter by his scent, his hands or just the fact they were sitting so close together on the sofa. Her chin up, her fingers wrapped around the controller in a way that made maneuvering easy across the console. Wordlessly demanding a victory and in the end, she got one. A big one.

"I won!" she shouted, jumping up and feeling pretty

darn proud of herself. At least she could boast to winning at the hardest game.

"Big deal. I'll give you that one."

Her head whipped around. "Give? Please. I whipped you good, Nolan Madaris, and it was a category five."

"It was also about time, don't you think? I was beginning to wonder if you were a fake techie or the real thing, Chapman."

She couldn't help but laugh at that because the one thing she didn't have to wonder about was what he thought of her skill as a technology expert. More than once during the game he had complimented her about it. Her losing to him didn't take away the fact that she was good at what she did. He was just far more advanced.

Ivy learned a lot about Nolan. Even the fact they shared the same high school and college alums. But what impressed her more than anything was the fact that he used to work for Nicholas Chenault. The Nicholas Chenault, creator of the Mangolid chip. The Mangolid was one of the first things she'd studied in college. After the Mangolid, Chenault had gone on to create the Shayla chip, which some say had been named after his wife. The S-chip had been a breakthrough in the medical arena.

It was Ivy's lifelong dream to one day meet Nicholas Chenault, a man she considered a technology revolutionist way before his time. She would love to sit down with him and pick his brain. And just to think Nolan had not only worked for Chenault for eight years before starting his business, but had worked on the S-chip with him. And knowing that Nolan also considered Nicholas Chenault a personal friend and mentor was way over the top. She had to admit learning things about him while playing their games was more enjoyable than text messages.

"Tell me some more about your time with Chenault," she requested of Nolan as he began putting the games away. While sitting beside him on the sofa playing video games, more than once she'd had to fight the impulse to lean over to inhale more of his manly scent. She realized this was the first time since Damien that she allowed a man to invade her personal space.

Unlike yesterday when Nolan had walked around shirtless, today he was wearing a pair of khaki shorts and a T-shirt that advertised Luke Madaris Rodeo School. "Don't know what more I can tell you without giving trade secrets away," he teased.

"Funny."

"I never thought of myself as a comedian," he said, before reaching out and straightening her glasses on her nose. She wondered if seeing her in glasses bothered him. It had Damien, which was why she'd begun wearing contacts. She had gone back to wearing her glasses after her breakup with Damien as a way to rebel at how he'd treated her and how easily she had allowed him to bend her to his will.

She frowned. "I like my glasses," she blurted out and immediately wondered why she'd done such a thing. Deep down she knew the reason why. It had everything to do with Damien's frequent criticism of them.

He gave her an odd look before saying, "I would hope so since you're wearing them." He stood to put the games away and she watched him walk off, admiring how he looked from the back. It was just as impressive as the front.

"And just for the record, Ivy," he said, turning

around. "I like your glasses, too. They look stylish on you."

Stylish? Her glasses? He had to be kidding. But she appreciated him for saying so. At times even lies were appreciated. When he returned she said, "I got an idea."

"What?"

"You've been doing a lot of the cooking, so how about if we go out tonight? My treat. I noticed this restaurant at the turnoff to this place."

He nodded. "Andre's. It's a great place to eat if you like seafood."

"I do."

"Okay, we can go there, but it doesn't have to be your treat."

"I insist that it be." Besides, she needed to take Tessa's advice and talk to him about their lack of chemistry and felt getting away from here to do so would be better. This cottage seemed far too intimate at times.

"All right, if you're going to insist."

"I do."

He shook his head, chuckling. "I'm beginning to notice your stubborn streak, Ivy." He looked at his watch. "How about if we meet back here in an hour?"

"That sounds good to me." At that moment, her phone rang. The caller ID said Damien.

"Aren't you going to get that?"

"No." Then she said, "See you in an hour." She then walked off to her bedroom.

Once inside the room with the door closed behind her, she tried to slow her heart rate and admonished herself for checking out Nolan every chance she got. She had begun noticing every single thing about him and that wasn't good. Her heart was pounding just thinking about how he stood across the kitchen from her while drinking his beer. She saw men drink beer all the time, but she didn't know anyone who could look so utterly sexy while doing it.

At that moment her cell phone rang again. Why was Damien calling her? What could he possibly want? She had a good mind to answer it and tell him to lose the number since he obviously hadn't got the message when she'd hung up on him the other day. Evidently he didn't quite understand that the relationship they once had was dead and buried and there would never ever be a resurrection. She wasn't the weak, starry-eyed, easily impressed, believe-anything-Damien-Fargo-tells-you sort of woman anymore. So what if he'd apologized? She didn't want his apology. She had defied the odds and had got over Damien. Now she wanted him to stay out of her life.

Her thoughts shifted to Nolan. The very sexy Nolan Madaris whom she had invited to dinner when she thought she needed to return the favor for all the cooking he'd done. Of course there had been that other reason to get him out of the house so they could talk.

How would she broach the subject? It would be awkward, but she had to remember that she and Nolan were in this together. It was them against Nana and Ms. Laverne. Besides, they were supposed to be getting to know each other. What she hadn't told him was in addition to spending all that time in the bedroom reading yesterday, she'd also written a list of questions to ask him. She would bring that list along so they could discuss more than just chemistry.

CHAPTER TWELVE

"Hungry much?"

Nolan glanced up from his menu at Ivy and couldn't stop the smile that tugged at his lips. "What gives you that idea?"

She shrugged what he was beginning to think was a perfect pair of shoulders. She was wearing a sleeveless top with a pair of white capris and he thought she looked cute in both. And her hair was down around her shoulders, the way he liked. He had to stop staring at her so much but didn't know how he would do such a thing without plucking his eyes out.

"Well, for starters," she said, placing her own menu down and grinning over at him, "you mentioned that you might order two entrées off the menu instead of one. I think that might be a dead giveaway."

"I skipped lunch."

"I offered to make you a grilled cheese sandwich."

"That's the best you can do?"

He saw her flinch and wondered why. Had others teased her about her lack of cooking skills? He was pretty good at reading people and had noticed how she'd gone on the defense when she'd spoken up about her eyeglasses earlier today. He of all people knew how cruel some people could be to people who wore glasses. He had worn glasses until college and was used to kids calling him Four-Eyes. And then there were those who thought he was a geek because of his love for science and math. There was no reason not to think she hadn't encountered the same type of ridicule.

He loved computers and technology as much now as he did in the past, which was why he owned an electronics company. He was able to stop wearing glasses after getting LASIK eye surgery.

Nolan reached across the table and took Ivy's hand in his. "Was it something I said? If so, I apologize."

She eased her hand from his and picked her menu back up. "No need. I know you were teasing."

Did she? His heart thudded hard in his chest at the thought he might have hurt her feelings and didn't understand or know why. He thought that needed to be an issue that got cleared up now. He leaned forward. "If we're going to pretend to be lovers, I need to know what I might say that will offend you, Ivy. Spell it out for me, will you?"

"You didn't offend me."

"Are you sure about that?"

She frowned over at him. "Don't push me, Nolan," she chided.

"Umm, I happen to think you're cute when you are pushed. And I love the way you're wearing your hair down. Makes you look even prettier."

He watched as her tensed chin relaxed somewhat and saw that smile he liked on her lips return. "Compliments, compliments, compliments. Can anyone stay mad at you for long, Nolan?"

At that moment the waitress came and took their order and he ordered two entrées, which made her laugh. "What's so funny?" he asked her.

"All that food? Where do you intend to put it?"

"I will eat what I can here and take a doggie bag to eat later. No biggie." When the waitress left, he said, "And since you're springing for dinner, you don't have to pay for but one meal."

"I can handle it, Nolan. Besides, I looked in the fridge and pantry and saw all the groceries you bought. I thought you only went to the store to pick up bacon and sausages."

"That had been the original plan, but I changed my mind." He leaned back in his seat at the booth. Where they sat gave them a beautiful view of the bay. "So, what questions do you have for me?"

On the drive over, she had mentioned jotting down a few on paper instead of texting. He had several questions for her but hadn't felt the need to make a list.

He watched as she opened her purse and pulled out three sheets of paper. He lifted a brow. "Nosy much?"

She laughed and he laughed with her. "Okay, I deserved that," she said, when her laughter subsided. "But I have a lot to learn about you and only a few days to get it all in."

"I don't know if I should feel flattered or insulted that you think you can do a rush job on me."

She waved his words away. "What you should feel... What we should both feel is annoyance at Nana and Ms. Laverne that we have to do this at all."

"True."

He only said that to appease her. He didn't want to admit it but he was enjoying her company. As she scanned the pages of whatever she'd written through her thick-rimmed glasses, he watched her closely. How beautiful he thought her unpolished fingers were. He'd noticed the same thing when they'd played video games earlier.

His phone began ringing and since it wasn't a ringtone he recognized he ignored it. He was annoyed with the number of phone calls he'd got since arriving on Tiki Island. Evidently some of the women he'd dated had heard he'd returned from Paris and were trying to reclaim his interest. He didn't want to be bothered and would start blocking their numbers.

"Okay, first up on my list, tell me about you."

He crossed his arms over his chest. "Are you going to try to convince me that you haven't Googled me like I did you?"

"You Googled me?"

"Damn right. The second you left my office. Needless to say, I was impressed. If I was looking for a wife, and of course you know that I'm not, I'd have to give Mama Laverne an A for her efforts."

She shook her head. "You honestly don't believe that."

"Lord knows I didn't at first—especially when I went to see Mama Laverne that same day. I was madder than hell. I told her we weren't the other's type and that you didn't interest me in the least. But now that I got to spend a couple of days with you, I can see us being friends…once we get those two manipulating women out of our business."

"Friends? Maybe. We will see."

He smiled. "So you aren't going to admit to Googling me."

She leaned over the table. "I won't admit to anything, so be a good sport and tell me about yourself."

"I'll probably bore you to tears," he said, releasing a deep sigh.

She smiled and pulled a couple of napkins out of the holder and waved them in front of him. "And when you do, I have the tissue ready."

Nolan couldn't help but laugh.

IVY TRIED NOT to do so, but she couldn't help hanging on to Nolan's every word. She loved the way he talked— so articulate. Then there was the sound of his voice— deep and husky. She noticed for the first time that she also liked how he expressed himself with his hands, which was all right with her since she loved looking at his hands.

She loved looking at him. Liked his scent. Liked the way he cooked. Liked his consideration of others. She was beginning to like everything about him.

And that knowledge was beginning to bother her.

An attraction to him was not part of the deal. She had accepted it initially but figured she would be over it by now. She wasn't. But then she figured an attraction would help with the chemistry she intended to bring up later. Without attraction there could be no chemistry, right? She didn't know but figured a man with Nolan's vast knowledge of women would.

He had begun telling her about his college days at MIT, their alma mater. Although she would not admit it to him, she had Googled him and had also been impressed with what she'd read. But unlike him, or so he'd claimed, she hadn't thought that Nana had made the right choice with selecting him. Since her grandmother had known of her decision never to marry, she should not have been playing matchmaker period.

"Did you enjoy living in Chicago?" she asked.

"I did once I got used to the cold weather. The first year I was ready to pack up and return to Texas. There is cold and there is freezing cold. Chicago showed me the brutal side of freezing cold."

He then told her about the eight years he'd spent working for Chenault Electronics and how much he'd learned and all the technological advances he'd been exposed to. "But I always knew I would return to Texas and start my own company," he said, dabbing his mouth with a napkin. "I'm surprised I stayed in Chicago that long. But we were halfway into the development of the Shayla chip and I didn't want to leave before completion."

What he'd done with the napkin had made her gaze slide to his mouth. She wondered how his lips tasted. Pushing such a crazy thought from her mind, she asked, "Is it true Nicholas Chenault named the chip after his wife?"

Nolan smiled and as usual his smile set sensations off in her stomach. "Yes, it's true. Nicholas loves his wife very much. He and Shayla are a beautiful couple with three beautiful children."

She asked him several more questions, some more personal than others, such as why he never married.

"Unlike you, I do plan to marry one day. However, when that time comes I will be selecting the woman I want to marry and refuse to let Mama Laverne do the selecting for me."

She nodded. "And speaking of Mama Laverne, there is something I often wondered about."

"What?"

"Why she never goes by Felicia instead of Laverne."

"She did at one point…until she had a granddaughter who was named after her. Felicia Laverne, or Felicia, is my cousin. She's the one married to Trask Maxwell."

And everyone in Texas had heard of Trask Maxwell, retired football legend, Houston's favorite son, who had his own sports show on television. They talked through the waitress clearing the table and the conversation continued over wine. He'd answered all her questions and she found all his answers interesting and enlightening.

"Have I made a dent in your list yet?" he asked, taking another sip of his wine.

"Almost." She folded the list. "I don't want to ask all my questions in one day. Besides there's something I need to talk to you about."

He lifted a brow. "What is it?"

She nervously licked her lips. "Chemistry."

He lifted a brow. "Chemistry?"

She nodded and swallowed deeply. "Yes, chemistry. The sexual kind."

He took a sip of his wine while his gaze held hers. She doubted he knew what those penetrating dark eyes were doing to her when he looked at her like that, nearly making it hard for her to catch her breath. "Sexual chemistry?" he asked, as if to make sure he had heard her correctly.

"Yes."

He placed his wineglass down, letting her know she unequivocally had his full attention. "And what is there about sexual chemistry that we need to be concerned with, Ivy?"

She licked her lips again before adjusting her glasses on her face. "I don't think we have it…at least not enough for anyone to pick up on those vibes we're supposed to emit."

"Vibes?"

"Yes."

"And you don't think we have them?"

"No, and it's something we need to think about. How can we fool anyone when we don't have the vibes? The sexual chemistry? Is there anything we can do about it? To rectify the problem?"

It took Nolan a minute to realize that Ivy wasn't kidding. She was dead serious and honestly thought the stoking of sexual chemistry would be a problem for them.

"It's my fault really."

Her words reclaimed his thoughts. "Your fault?"

"Yes. When I first thought of this plan, I didn't think it would be this complicated. This intense. That we would be dealing with two busybodies who would be noticing everything and anything. Dissecting our words, our actions, our every move." She paused for a minute and said, "Anyway…I've had more than one man tell me this."

"Tell you what?"

"That I don't have a sensuous bone in my body."

He frowned, trying to figure out how to process that. "And just because they said it, does that make it true?" he countered.

She gave him a closer look. "Wouldn't you think so?"

"No. They might not have known what the hell they were talking about," he said, trying to keep his voice calm and wondering just what kind of jackasses could have told her something like that. Probably to shield their own damn inadequacies.

"What exactly did they mean about you not having a sensuous bone in your body?" He needed her to expound.

She began licking her lips again, making it obvious she felt uncomfortable with this topic of conversation, but was having it with him anyway. Because she cared enough to want them to fight her grandmother and his great-grandmother's manipulations together, she was opening herself up, unloading, about what she truly believed was the ugly truth about herself.

"That I'm not a passionate person. I am not romantic or sensual. And it's hard to wow me. Do you get what I'm saying?"

"Kind of. Please go on."

"Most people who know me are well aware that I think most relationships are too much work. Way too much drama. Far too few rewards. However, a couple of years ago I did get involved with a man. I gave it my all and then some."

"Did you?"

"Yes, but I got hurt in the end. It proved I was right all along—relationships aren't for me."

"Is that why you say you'll never marry?"

"Yes." She paused and took a sip of her wine. "So now you know what I mean, right?"

"Yes, I think I follow you."

"Good. The problem is, because of my issue, there won't be any vibes, so what are we going to do? How are we going to make sexual chemistry appear real between us, Nolan, when none exists? Can you tell me that?"

CHAPTER THIRTEEN

FOR THE FIRST time in his life Nolan was rendered speechless. He knew he needed to answer Ivy's question. And within his gut he knew that it was a deeper, more heartfelt question that she'd intended. A part of him wanted to assure her that what she thought of her sexual abilities or lack of them was silly, ridiculous and asinine at best. But knowing Ivy like he was beginning to, he knew the guy or guys who'd convinced her of what she believed about herself had made themselves jury and judge and she undoubtedly believed in their testimony and had accepted the verdict.

This wasn't the first time he'd had to deal with female heartbreak. A few years ago, while in college, Victoria had experienced her first. It had been her big brothers' shoulders she had come home to cry on. He'd been ready to drive her back to her college in Oklahoma to start kicking asses and taking names. But Reese, Corbin and Lee had talked him out of it.

"Nolan? You're not answering. That's not a good sign."

He forced a smile to his lips. "Sorry, I was thinking on how we need to handle this."

"But it is doable, right?"

He heard the hopefulness in her voice. She was worried about them not emitting vibes when they were there. He felt them whenever they were together. How could she not feel them herself? The key to this entire issue was to make sure she felt them, too, and to believe others wouldn't help but feel them as well.

"Anything is doable when it comes to us against them." He leaned forward, over the table and said, "Lean close for a minute."

She leaned in toward him. "Yes?"

Instead of whispering something to her like she probably assumed he would do, he reached up and clamped her face with his hands before capturing her mouth in a kiss. He'd only meant the kiss to last a second but the moment he tasted the sweetness of her mouth it lasted longer than it should have.

It was only when he heard the clearing of a few throats did he drag his mouth away from hers. "That was merely to test the waters. Personally, I think the sexual chemistry between us is real already, Ivy. But if you want to increase what's already there, then I'm game."

It HAD GOT dark by the time they had returned to the cottage. Ivy watched as Nolan moved around the living room turning on the lights while thinking about the kiss they'd shared at the restaurant. Although brief, the kiss had proved there was sexual chemistry between them. She had felt it all the way to her toes. And what had he said about increasing the level already there?

She drew in a deep breath just thinking about how that could be accomplished. As she stood there, watching him in the silvery light, a sliver of warmth spread through her. Tall and overwhelmingly sexy, he could wear a pair of jeans like he owned the company that made them to get such a perfect fit. And the T-shirt that stretched across such wide muscles, broad shoulders and tight chest was enough to make any woman drool. Then those cowboy boots on his feet gave way to such an imposing figure.

She could see why women didn't care that he was tagged Mr. One-Night Stand and still stood in line for their turns. Whether he wore shorts or jeans, a T-shirt or walked around bare chested, Nolan Madaris had to be the sexiest man she'd ever laid eyes on.

He turned and caught her staring and for the life of her, as much as she wanted to do so, she couldn't break eye contact with him. He tipped his head, their gazes still connected. His dark, penetrating gaze was holding her captive. And then he began moving. She watched as he slowly crossed the living room, in a walk that was so hot she suddenly felt infused with heat. He came to a stop an arm's length in front of her and she had to tilt her head back to continue to hold his gaze.

Standing so close to her she could see the perfect angles of his face, every sensuous line, the smooth dark texture of his skin and sharp cheekbones. She was finding it hard to gather her thoughts and keep them together. This man was such a work of impossible masculine beauty that it almost took her breath away.

Somehow she found her voice to ask, "Although I texted you some information, did you have any getting-to-know-you questions for me, Nolan?"

"I will ask my questions tomorrow while you're helping me paint."

She raised a brow. "I'm helping you paint?"

"I hope so. It will go a lot faster if you do. I'm repainting all the patio furniture. I sanded them all down today."

She nodded. "I will be glad to help you."

"Thanks."

He was in her space. A space she'd long ago decided no man could invade again. Her body and mind should be protesting yet they weren't. He wasn't saying anything, just standing there staring at her. Into her eyes. Through her glasses. She didn't know what to think of it and nervously licked her bottom lip before asking, "Is anything wrong, Nolan?"

"No."

He took a step closer. "I was wondering if you enjoyed our kiss," he said in a husky voice that sent her heart pounding.

Although it had been brief, she had enjoyed it more than he would ever know. "Yes, I enjoyed it." There was no way she could lie and say she hadn't.

"I think you're going to enjoy this one even better."

Before she could draw her next breath, his mouth swooped down on hers. The first thought that immediately slammed into her mind was that he was going to kiss her without removing her glasses again. But the moment she felt his tongue invade her mouth any thought of her glasses was eradicated from her mind. Just like in the restaurant, he seemed to be doing just fine even with her wearing them.

Nolan had a robust taste like the wine they'd had at dinner. That, combined with his heat, sent all kinds of sensations surging through Ivy's body. The feeling was outright intoxicating to the brink of making her delirious. On instinct she widened her mouth under his and he accepted the invitation and intensified the kiss, using his tongue as if to possess hers.

He had wrapped his arms around her and she could feel the hard muscles of his body pressed against her. Their tongues began mating rhythmically and her emo-

tions whirled and skidded nearly out of control. Never
had she been kissed with this much passion, this much
greed or desire. She could actually feel his need in the
form of a huge erection that was poking into her stomach and it amazed her that he could need her to the point
of that. Hadn't Damien told her it was hard for any man
to desire her without putting forth an effort?

He slid a hand up her back and she felt heat where
he touched. Desire, hotter than anything she had ever
experienced, was burning her skin, sending bursts of
pleasure through her veins and making her moan. She
could actually hear herself moan from deep in her throat
while his tongue continued to mate furiously with hers
as if it never intended to stop.

But then, suddenly, just as quickly as the kiss had
started, it ended when he snatched his mouth away.
While he drew in a deep breath she did the same. It was
at that moment she realized her hands were clutching
tight to the material of the T-shirt that covered his chest.
And his hands were sliding up and down her back. His
eyes had turned a darker hue and were staring at her
mouth. After she nervously used her tongue to lick her
bottom lip, he leaned in and licked that same bottom
lip with his own tongue.

"If only you knew the things you do to me, Ivy," he
said in a husky whisper.

"Me?" she asked, almost not recognizing the sound
of her own voice.

"Yes, you." He straightened her glasses on her nose
before brushing a kiss across that same nose. "Good
night, Ivy. I'll see you in the morning."

He walked off and left her standing in the middle of
the living room with her lips flaming hot.

CHAPTER FOURTEEN

"I'VE ALREADY MADE the coffee, Nolan."

Ivy watched as he blinked as if he was surprised to see her and she understood. She, a woman who barely got up before noon, had not only awakened before him but had started coffee. What she wouldn't tell him was that she hadn't been able to sleep most of the night. And when dawn had eased over the horizon, she had got up and taken a run on the beach. She had returned, expecting to find him up, and when she hadn't she had showered and dressed for the day.

He rubbed a hand down his face. "Sorry, I overslept."

"No problem."

He went straight to the refrigerator to take out the ingredients he needed to prepare breakfast. He glanced over at her. "How long have you been up?"

"Since before six."

A look of surprise touched his features. "You got up that early?"

"Yes. I even took a run on the beach. Now I'm ready."

His hands stilled from cracking an egg. "You're ready?"

"Yes."

"For what?"

"To help you paint."

A slow smile touched his lips. "I thought you might be a no-show."

She returned his smile. "I proved you wrong, didn't I?"

He chuckled and the sound seemed to brush across her skin. "Yes, you most certainly did."

He didn't say anything else as he went about preparing breakfast. "Need my help?" she asked when the kitchen got too quiet for her.

He glanced over at her before frying the bacon. "No, you're good."

No, she thought, *Nolan Madaris, you are good.* The reason she hadn't been able to sleep was because all during the night and wee hours of the morning, memories had plagued her. Memories of how he had kissed her, especially when they had returned from dinner. How he had parted her lips with his tongue and began mating with it in a way that had her groaning in her bed most of the night. What man kissed a woman that way, so deeply and thoroughly? Even the tester at the restaurant had left her breathless.

And both times he had kissed her without her removing her glasses. It was as if wearing them hadn't hindered him in the least. She couldn't imagine the kiss in the living room last night going any deeper than it had yesterday. Any deeper would have made her pass out.

"You okay over there?" he asked as he prepared the eggs.

She glanced up and saw him watching her. If only he knew. She was great. She felt great. And because of those kisses, she knew there was hope for them and their plan.

"I'm okay. I think those kisses yesterday were what I needed."

He paused, holding a spatula midair, and asked, "How so?"

"I felt something, both times. Especially the last one." It had been right up there with mind-blowing.

He slid a plate of food in front of her. "Have you never felt something before when you kissed a guy?" He sat down across from her.

She shrugged. "Never like that. I know you did that on purpose."

He paused from taking his first sip of coffee. "I did what on purpose?"

"Kiss me the way you did. Both times. I guess you wanted to arrest my fears. I must have sounded like I was freaking out over dinner."

After taking a sip of coffee, she watched as he sprinkled pepper onto his egg. *Never salt, always pepper.* "No, you had some valid concerns that you addressed. And you don't have to ever thank me for kissing you. I enjoy doing it. Immensely."

At that moment her phone rang. She frowned when she recognized the ringtone and decided to ignore it.

"Aren't you going to get that?"

Funny he would ask her that with the number of calls he'd been getting and not answering. "No. I'm hoping if I ignore him, he will stop calling." She hated admitting the caller was a man, but she didn't want him to think she would ignore her grandmother's calls.

"Why don't you just block his calls?"

She shrugged. "He just started calling me last week after two years."

"Why?"

"He said to apologize but I refused to accept his apology. I don't want anything from him. If he calls again, I will block him."

She continued eating. "This food is good, by the way."

"Thanks."

She glanced over at him and wanted to ask something she had wondered about most of the night. It was something most people wouldn't be concerned with but because of her history, she was. "Nolan?"

He glanced over at her. "Yes."

She placed her coffee cup down and looked directly at him. "How did you kiss me like that without taking off my glasses?"

NOLAN FIGURED TO anyone else Ivy's question was probably a real stupid one. But not to him. "From years of practice."

"Practice?"

"Yes."

A confused look covered her face. "Why would you practice kissing females who wore glasses?"

He couldn't help but smile. "I didn't. I was the one wearing the glasses and refused to take them off whenever I kissed someone. My vision was so bad that without them I might have been kissing their nose instead of their lips."

She blinked. "You wore glasses?"

"As thick as they came until my twenty-first birthday. LASIK eye surgery was still new then, but I desperately wanted it. It was a gift from my family."

"That was kind of them."

"Yes, it was."

She didn't say anything else for a minute, but Nolan had a feeling from the way she would glance up at him every so often that his revelation had filled her with more questions. "You want to ask me something else, Ivy?"

She licked her lips before saying, "I just can't imagine you wearing glasses."

"I did and some people weren't nice to me about it, like doing so was my choice. I got bullied quite a bit. My cousins Reese and Lee used to have to fight for me because I refused to fight for myself."

He chuckled. "I convinced myself the reason I didn't fight was because I didn't want to get my glasses broken. It was my great-grandmother who finally made me realize that Reese and Lee wouldn't always be around to fight my battles and that I needed to know how to defend myself."

Ivy's eyes widened. "She encouraged you to fight?"

"No. Mama Laverne encouraged me to defend myself. There's a difference. Whenever I could, I needed to just walk away, ignore the hateful comments and barbs. But if someone put their hands on me, then that was another matter."

She nodded. "That makes sense."

"I thought so, too. And I was lucky when my grandfather Nolan gave me some boxing lessons. He used to box in his younger days. That helped. Word got around school real fast that I was not a guy to mess with."

"How old were you when you began defending yourself?"

"Around twelve."

"You were still just a kid."

"What about you?" he asked after taking a sip of

his coffee. "Did you get picked on for wearing glasses when you were in school?"

She nodded again. "Yes, all the time, but that wasn't the worst of my problems. My love for technology was, so I was called a four-eyed geek."

He burst out laughing and she frowned. "I don't think that's funny, Nolan."

"It is since I was called the same thing."

"You're kidding!"

"I kid you not."

Something dawned on him. Only someone who had a similar issue would fully understand what she'd gone through most of her life or was still going through. Where he could see the vast beauty behind a pair of rim glasses, some people could not. And in regard to her being a techie, as far as he was concerned, techie women were some of the brightest and the smartest. What man wanted an airhead?

"Tessa fought mine."

He glanced over at her. "Excuse me?"

"I said Tessa fought mine. You mentioned your cousins Lee and Reese fought your battles while growing up. Well, my best friend, Tessa Hargrove, was the one who fought my battles. At least she tried. She moved to Houston in our junior year of high school. She was too pretty for the snooty girls at school, so they ostracized her. I was already being ostracized, so Tessa and I became the best of friends. We still are. A very unlikely pair, believe me." She paused for a minute and then said, "Your sister Victoria graduated with us."

He sat down his coffee cup and raised a brow. "Are you going to tell me Victoria was one of those snooty girls?"

She shook her head. "No, she didn't associate with

any of them, although they tried real hard to be her friends. By then most people heard one of your grand-uncles had married actress Diamond Swain, and every-one wanted to be in Victoria's circle of friends. She was smart enough to stick with the ones she'd always had."

He glanced down in his coffee. He then looked up and met Ivy's gaze. "How did Victoria treat you?"

"Your sister was always kind to me and Tessa. She would speak to us and during the one class we had together she didn't have a problem sharing her notes whenever either of us missed school. She even invited us to her senior graduation party."

He nodded. He couldn't imagine Victoria being like those girls who'd treated her badly and was glad to know she hadn't been. "Did you go to Victoria's party?"

"No. Tessa and I had planned to go together, but Tessa had to go out of town at the last minute and I didn't want to go by myself." Ivy stood. "Do you need my help with the dishes?" she asked him.

"No, it won't take me long to wrap things up in here." He glanced at his watch. Because he had overslept this morning, they were getting a late start. It was close to ten o'clock. "I'll be ready to start painting in around twenty minutes."

"Okay. In the meantime I'm going to go sit on the dock."

"All right."

Nolan watched her leave while thinking he was learn-ing more and more about Ivy every single day. But then that's why they were here, right? That should be easy enough.

He rubbed his hand down his face. Then why were things suddenly beginning to feel rather complicated?

CHAPTER FIFTEEN

"Not bad," Nolan said, inspecting the patio chair Ivy had just finished painting. "It gets my stamp of approval."

Ivy glanced up at Nolan and had to force the thought to the back of her mind that she didn't need a man's approval. With Damien, it had felt like without his approval, nothing she did meant anything. "Do you think we'll need to put on another coat of paint?"

"I think one coat will be fine." He checked his watch. "It's almost two now. You want to take a swim before grabbing something for lunch?"

Did she? While painting it had been hard to keep her eyes off him. He'd given her a paintbrush and he had used a sprayer. Just seeing his body constantly in motion had nearly been too much. And even outside in the fresh air, her nostrils still managed to get a whiff of his scent. How would she handle the two of them swimming together?

She glanced over at him and saw he was waiting for her reply. "Yes, I'd love to."

"Okay, let's meet back out here in fifteen minutes."

It didn't take long for Ivy to change clothes and put on the two-piece swimming suit she had brought with her—one she had purchased during a shopping trip last year with Tessa. Her outfit wasn't like most two-pieces that she thought revealed too much. This one revealed just enough for her.

Nolan hadn't asked her any getting-to-know-you questions yet. Instead they had talked about his cousin's hotel that was being built in Paris. It was obvious he was excited that his company had been selected to install all the electronic and technology work for the Grand MD Paris; some of which would be the first of its kind anywhere. It had been nice listening to someone else talk techie stuff for a change.

When she returned to the patio, it was to find Nolan waiting on her. A pair of aviator sunglasses covered his eyes and he looked sexy wearing them. Where she had selected swimwear that wasn't so revealing, he'd done just the opposite. He was obviously a man who didn't mind showing what a great body he had and what great shape he was in. She should have reached that conclusion that first day when he'd walked around shirtless.

"Sorry if I'm late," she said, trying not to stare at his masculine thighs and how the hair of his bare chest tapered down beyond the waistband of his swim shorts.

"You're not." He surprised her by reaching out and taking her hand. "Come on. Let's head for the bay and you can tell me some more about yourself."

She glanced up at him. "I thought you'd forgotten about that."

He chuckled. "And let you off easy after all your grilling yesterday? Not on your life, Ivy Chapman."

"I still have more questions," she told him, while trying to ignore just how close they were walking side by side.

"But not before I get in mine."

She looked over at him. "Your what?"

"My chance to ask you questions today. Are you daydreaming on me, Ivy?"

She had news for him. She was doing more than daydreaming. She was having full-blown fantasy thoughts. "Just so you know, I probably lived a boring life compared to yours," she warned, loving how her small hand felt engulfed in his larger one.

"I understand you're Dr. Ivory Chapman's daughter."

"Yes. You know my dad?"

"He was my pediatrician as a kid. He was nice enough until he had to give me shots. Then he became my worst enemy."

She wanted to laugh. "That's usually how it is."

"Are the two of you close?"

She shrugged. "Close enough. Closer now than we were when I was younger. He and my mom got a divorce when I turned twelve."

"Sorry."

She glanced up at him. "I'm not. I wished it hadn't taken that long. They were making each other miserable and I felt caught in the middle. Then when they finally decided to go their separate ways, they used me to get back at each other."

He lifted a brow. "How?"

"In a custody battle. I would have been perfectly fine to spend the rest of my days not living with either of them, but with my grandparents. No such luck. They ended up with joint custody. So I had to spend six months out of the year with each."

"What about you and your mom? Do the two of you get along?"

"Pretty much. Mom remarried a few years ago and

lives in Florida. She's happy and I'm happy for her. I try to visit at least once a year."

When they reached the water's edge, he released her hand and placed their towels on the branch of a low-hanging tree. She kicked off her sandals and removed her cover-up, sliding it off her shoulders and placing it on one of the branches as well.

When she turned back to face him, she was startled to find Nolan staring at her. She couldn't quite decipher the look on his face, but it was suddenly intense. She needed some space ASAP. "Race you to the water," she said and then took off running.

NOLAN'S GAZE HAD traveled all over Ivy's body, appreciating every single inch, every delectable curve when she'd removed the cover-up. She looked more than just good in her swimming suit. She looked hot and his body's most primal reaction had kicked in with mega force. It was a good thing she had taken off for the water when she had.

It still amazed him that she didn't know how beautiful she was. From their conversation over breakfast, it was obvious some man, possibly more than one, had convinced her that wearing glasses diminished that beauty and that having such a brilliant mind made her less desirable. It was a pity she'd believed them.

Nolan took off racing after her. She'd made it to the water first only because he let her. His long strides would have overtaken her if he had tried hard enough. He was still remembering everything she'd told him during their walk from the cottage. It was obvious she hadn't had a great childhood. Another pity. Was the demise of her parents' marriage another reason she was so against marriage?

By the time he reached the shore she was already in the water and swimming like a fish. And she looked good doing so. Her hands and shoulders were expertly slicing through the waters.

"You're slow, Nolan."

He grinned before diving into the waters and swimming over to her. "And you're good," he said, swiping excess water from his face. "I watched you from the shore. Were you on a swim team?"

"No. My parents had a pool and I like swimming," she said, swiping water from her own face.

"So do I."

"And you're not such a bad swimmer yourself," she said, smiling at him.

"Let's race," he suggested.

She rolled her eyes. "We did that already and you lost, remember?"

Nolan figured it would be a waste of his time if he confessed that he'd let her win. "We'll race just to that marker over there."

Ivy lifted her hand to shelter her eyes from the brightness of the sun. "Where?"

"Over there," he said, pointing to the marker near the dock.

That was his downfall because she pushed against him, making him lose his balance, producing a huge splash. That's when she took off, swimming toward the marker.

"Cheater," he shouted and began swimming after her.

She refused to look back and he figured she was well aware he was gaining speed and not far behind her. Just when she thought she'd made it home free, he grabbed her legs and pulled her under the water. He went under with her and they both came up moments later, laughing and spurting out water. "That's not fair, Nolan," she yelled, swiping water from both her hair and eyes.

"Oh, now you want to call foul play, huh?" he said wrapping his arms around her.

"Whatever."

Despite the sun that had been shining brightly all day, the beach water was somewhat cool. He pulled her closer and wondered if she could feel his hard erection through his swim shorts. Evidence of what she did to him. He twisted her around to face him and their gazes met. At that moment he had to remind himself they were practicing, pretending to be lovers because they were having so much fun. Regardless, nothing between them was real…other than a friendship based on the mutual respect they were developing. And that was all they could and would ever share. A friendship.

Then why did he want to kiss her again? To plunder her mouth and hold her in his arms, regardless of if her clothing was wet or dry?

"Ready to head back?"

Her question interrupted his thoughts. In truth, he wasn't ready. But he knew it was time to leave before he got himself in more trouble than he was ready to deal with. "Yes, but I have more questions to ask you," he said, taking her hand to lead her out of the water. "One in particular."

"Oh, and what question is that?"

"I want to know about the guy who hurt you."

"WHY DO YOU want to know anything about Damien?" she asked, using the towel to dry off before sliding the cover-up over her shoulders. She had told him all he'd needed to know that day when Damien had phoned and she'd refused to take his call.

"My great-grandmother will ask me about him."

She tilted her head. "Why would she do that?"

"Because she will expect me to know the whole story."

She shrugged. "Maybe she won't. Just tell her I didn't want to discuss my old boyfriend with you."

"She won't believe me."

"And why not?" Ivy asked him.

He wrapped the towel around his shoulders and neck and then looked over at her. "Because she knows I'm a stickler for details and I would want to know all there was about my girlfriend."

She considered what he'd said for a moment and knew he was right. They should cover all their bases in case the subject did come up. If he wanted to know about Damien, she could sum him up in one word. "Damien Fargo was an ass."

"I figured that much, Ivy. Tell me something I don't know."

They began walking toward the cottage, and after a moment, she said, "He wanted me to believe that he fell in love with me regardless of what he referred to as my *imperfections*—the glasses, being a techie and the way I dressed. I never was one who placed a lot of emphasis on fashion and style. I guess you can say he wanted to make me his creation."

"Did he?"

"Yes. I thought I loved him and that he loved me and the change would be for the both of us and not just for me. So I ditched the glasses for contacts, got a closet full of new clothes and had a makeover that suited him."

"Did you try to stop being a techie?"

"No. That was my career, but to satisfy him I stopped talking about my work and forced myself to get interested in other stuff like sports and photography."

"Photography?"

"Yes, that was his hobby, so I figured I would get into it as well. I hated it."

She paused for a minute and then said, "It wasn't enough, though, since he cheated on me anyway. I walked in on him and another woman."

"Not in your bed, I hope."

She heard the anger in Nolan's voice. "No. I had a key to his apartment. I was to be out of town and came back a day early. Imagine their surprise when I walked in and caught them."

Ivy couldn't help but remember that day and the humiliation she'd felt. "I ended things between us then and there."

Nolan nodded. "Good for you. I'm sure he tried like hell to get you back, claimed it was a lapse of good judgment. That it was all the other woman's fault, that he was sorry and it wouldn't happen again and all that BS, right?"

"No. I didn't hear from him again until he called me last week. I guess it took him two years to decide he was sorry. Like I told you, it was too late in coming. Besides, I had learned my lesson."

"Is he still living in Houston?"

She shook her head. "No. I heard he took some job in New York last year and lives there now."

"How long were the two of you together?"

"For almost a year."

They had reached the cottage and Nolan turned

to her, staring at her through the lenses of his aviator sunglasses. "You're welcome to share my lunch with me. I'm having leftovers from the restaurant last night. There's plenty."

"No, thanks, but I appreciate the offer. I'm still full from breakfast." What she wouldn't tell him was talking about Damien had reminded her why she'd chosen not to ever get serious about a man again.

"What are your plans for the rest of the day?" Nolan asked, cutting into her thoughts.

"I think I'll start a new book today. I brought plenty with me to read."

"I hope you're not planning to hide out again in your bedroom reading for the rest of the day and most of tomorrow."

She had thought about doing just that. "And if I am?"

"That's not going to work. Need I remind you why we decided to stay here together?"

No, he didn't have to remind her. "Haven't you asked me enough stuff for today?"

"It's not about asking you anything else for now, Ivy."

She frowned. "Then what is it?"

He took a closer step toward her. "Remember our discussion of those vibes yesterday."

Yes, she had remembered that discussion. "What about it?"

"Time to work on increasing the level of sexual chemistry between us."

"I hope you don't think I've changed my mind about sleeping with you, Nolan."

He sighed. "No, I don't think that, Ivy." He took his hand, reached up and gently caressed the side of her face before tracing her lips with the tip of his finger. "Still feel it?"

Yeah, she felt it. How could she not feel it? Way too much. "Yes, I still feel it," she said honestly.

"Good. In order for others to pick up on our vibes, we must first pick up on them ourselves. It's all about physical attraction."

He held her gaze longer that she thought necessary but for the life of her, she couldn't break eye contact with him. And why couldn't she stop thinking about his mouth? She took a step back. "It's time for me to go."

He dropped his hand from her face and she thought that was the end of it. Instead he took hold of her hand and gently tightened his grip on it.

"Not before you promise me that you'll stop holding back."

Holding back? She had no idea what he was talking about. Honestly. "And just what am I holding back on?"

"Passion. At least the degree we need. I could detect it in your kisses yesterday."

Great! Simply great! Was that his way of letting her know she was a lousy kisser on top of everything else? "Well, maybe, Nolan Madaris, that's the best I can do."

"I didn't say you couldn't kiss, Ivy. In fact, like I told you earlier, I enjoyed kissing you immensely. What I'm saying is that I could tell you were holding back. You didn't allow yourself to feel the kiss enough."

Lordy, had she felt it any more she wouldn't have survived it. "I did feel it."

"Not like you should have. And until you do, the people closest to us will be able to tell something's not quite right between us. Close your eyes for a second."

"Why?"

"Just do it."

Releasing a sigh, she closed her eyes. "Now think of something pleasant that's not a place, animal or human. Think of something that's fun to you."

Not a place, animal or human? For crying out loud, what else was there? She drew in a deep breath, closed her eyes and then thought about her next security job with Wonderbelly. The new security software she would be introducing was on an entirely different level than any on the market now.

Suddenly, she felt the heat of a whisper close to her before that same breath lowered close to her lips. She was about to tense up but then she allowed her body to relax. And when she felt the tip of his tongue slide across her bottom lip, she let out a breathy gasp.

She was tempted to open her eyes to see what Nolan was doing but knew if she did, the moment would be gone. And she wanted to experience this, no matter what it was.

"Open your mouth for me, Ivy."

She heard Nolan's husky whisper and complied, easing her mouth open only to have it fill with his oh-so-invigorating tongue. And that same tongue began stroking her mouth in a way that had her panting with whimpers of pleasure. She was feeling this. Definitely feeling this. And it felt good. He began sucking on her tongue and she felt the motion, the pull, the suction, seemingly in the pit of her stomach. It was causing a rush of sensations to spread between her legs.

Her tongue began mating with his and deep in her throat she moaned something, she wasn't sure what. All she knew was that his tongue was busy inside hers in a way that made her want to scream. However, doing so meant disengaging their mouths and she wasn't ready to do that.

Ivy wasn't sure how long they had been standing there feasting greedily off each other's mouths when the sound of his cell phone invaded. Nolan slowly pulled his mouth from hers but continued to lick around the sides of her lips.

Of its own accord, her body began shuddering, and then she all but slumped against him when he wrapped his arms around her. She tilted her head and met his gaze. Saw the wetness around his lips. He had kissed her that hard, that deep and that thorough. "Could you tell the difference?"

She nodded slowly. Yes, she could.

His cell phone started ringing again and she heard him swear. "Go ahead and answer that, Nolan. I'll see you later," she somehow managed to say.

She turned and rushed inside the cottage. When she heard him call after her, she refused to stop and look back.

CHAPTER SIXTEEN

"YEAH, LEE?"

"For a minute I thought I was going to have to call in the cavalry when you didn't answer. You okay?" his cousin Lee Madaris asked him.

Nolan rubbed a hand down his face. "I'm fine." Was he? Hell, he really wasn't sure.

"I understand you have a houseguest."

Nolan shook his head. Good Lord, did the entire family know? If they did he knew the person to blame. According to Corbin, Mama Laverne was all smiles as she spread the word. She was so sure of herself. So certain her matchmaking plan was working. If only she knew how they intended to best her at her own game.

"Yes, Ivy's here."

"You want to tell me what's going on?"

Nolan leaned against a post and stared at the closed door. The same one Ivy had passed through earlier. "What makes you think something's going on?"

"Because I know you and contrary to what Mama Laverne might want to think, there's no way I'll believe that you and Ivy Chapman have decided to demurely go along with Mrs. Chapman and Mama Laverne's plan."

Lee was right, Nolan thought. His cousin did know him. "Then for what other reason would we still be here together?"

Lee chuckled. "I think you have it in your head that you can outsmart the queen."

"Have you given consideration to the possibility that after seeing how your plan to outsmart her failed, that I decided to just take my chances and go along with her matchmaking, knowing there's no way I can win?" Nolan asked.

Lee was quiet for a moment and then he asked, "Have you?"

He hadn't wanted to get Lee or Reese involved by telling them the truth about Ivy's and his plan. But deep down he knew even if they were to share anything with their wives, they would hold their wives to secrecy as well. Their wives would understand because they'd once been victims to the queen's matchmaking schemes as well. "No."

"That means you have a plan. And from the sound of it, Miss Chapman is on board with it."

Nolan released a deep sigh. "Yes, there is a plan. In fact it was her idea, but I think it's a good one." He filled Lee in, then asked, "So what do you think?"

"It will only work if it's believable. Will it be?"

He thought of the kisses they'd shared so far and how high his testosterone level had spiked. "We're working on it."

"There's something else you might want to consider while the two of you *are working on it*."

Nolan's brow furrowed. "What?"

"The possibility of falling into your own trap."

Nolan frowned. He knew exactly what Lee meant because Lee had fallen into his. "Trust me, Lee. That won't be happening."

"You sound certain."

"I am. Ivy has no plans to ever marry and I don't plan on doing so for years to come, and definitely not to any woman Mama Laverne selects."

"Okay then. I wish the both of you the best because, Nolan, you're going to need it. Just remember who you're dealing with. A woman who has more successful marriages under her belt than Muhammad Ali had title fights."

IVY CLOSED HER book and eased up in bed. Glancing at the clock on the nightstand, she saw it was eight in the evening. She switched her gaze to the window and saw it was dark outside. She had read through lunch and dinner. Intentionally. She had needed time for herself to think, which was why she'd only been sort of reading.

Standing, she went to the window and looked out. The view of the bay silhouetted in moonlight looked beautiful. It looked more peaceful and calm than she felt. It was Monday and they had a few more to go. A few more days of him stroking those vibes. The very thought sent sensuous shivers down her spine.

She turned from the window when her phone rang. She recognized that sound. Nana was calling to check in. She could ignore it or she could answer it. Ignoring it might not be such a good idea, so she quickly moved to the dresser and picked it up. "Yes?"

"How are you, dear?"

Trying to sound as upbeat as she could, she said, "I'm fine, Nana, and how are you?"

"I'm fine. Back home from Lake Charles. We all had a wonderful time."

"That's nice."

"So where are you?"

Like you really don't know. "I'm still on Tiki Island. Nolan's place."

"Oh? Any reason you're still there?"

"Yes, there is a reason. Nolan painted his patio furniture today and I volunteered to help. I thought it was the least I could do for his kindness."

"So, you think he's kind?"

"Yes, he's a kind man." *He's also a fantastic kisser, but I refuse to admit that to you.*

"When are you going home?"

Ivy smiled. She shouldn't enjoy stringing her grandmother along this way, but she did. "Not sure. Nolan mentioned other little things I can help him with and I don't mind if I get to stay here on the island."

"I think that's a good idea. I understand the two of you had a nice dinner the other night at a fine restaurant."

Ivy raised a brow, wondering how Nana had known that. "Yes, it was nice. I enjoyed his company. He's easy to talk to."

She figured if her grandmother knew about dinner at the restaurant chances were she also knew about the kiss they'd shared. Nolan's public display of affection. "I'm glad you think so, Ivy. Enjoy the rest of your time with Nolan, sweetie. Goodbye."

Ivy heard a resounding click in her ear. She figured Nana was in a rush to do that happy dance. Afterward, no doubt, Nana would check in with Ms. Laverne so they could compare notes. And how did Nana know about her and Nolan going out to eat last night? The only plausible explanation was that Nolan had spoken with his great-grandmother sometime today and mentioned it to her. And of course Ms. Laverne had passed the information on to Nana.

She glanced over at the clock after her stomach grumbled, protesting the fact it hadn't been fed since breakfast. Sliding into her sandals, Ivy decided she would remedy that now. She just hoped she wouldn't run into Nolan. Right now he was the last person she wanted to see until she could recover from today's kiss.

After using her private bath to freshen up, she left her bedroom and headed straight for the kitchen, humming as she went. When she entered the kitchen, she stopped dead in her tracks. There, leaning against the counter, shirtless with a pair of jeans riding low on his hips and a cup of coffee in his hand was none other than Nolan Madaris.

And to Ivy's dismay, he seemed to have been waiting on her.

CHAPTER SEVENTEEN

NOLAN HAD ALWAYS prided himself on having a logical head when it came to most things, especially women. But he was slowly discovering that when it came to Ivy Chapman there were times when he couldn't very well think straight. Like now.

He figured she would stay in that bedroom until she thought he'd be out of the way. He was proved right and now here she was. Only thing was that here he was as well. Imagine that. And from the frown on her face, she hadn't imagined it.

"Nolan. I thought you would be in bed about now."

Her words, against his most ardent wishes, evoked a vision in his mind of him in bed. Only thing was he wasn't in there alone. He blinked to clear his mind, not liking that vision at all. "I decided to stay up and wait for you. I figured you'd come out of hiding sooner or later."

Her frown deepened and as graceful as any woman could, she slowly walked to the refrigerator, opened it and began taking stuff out to, no doubt, fix herself a sandwich. Didn't she believe in eating a balanced meal once in a while?

"For your information, I wasn't hiding."

"Weren't you?"

She turned when she placed all the stuff for her

sandwich on the table. She glanced up at him. "How did you expect me to react after you kissed me again?"

"Take it like the woman I know that you are. Enjoy it. Lay one back on me, which I might add that you did."

Anger flared in her eyes and she jabbed a finger at him, seemingly pointing it straight at his heart. "You are taking advantage of the situation."

Now that pissed him off. Really pissed him off. He was certain steam was coming out of his ears. Setting his coffee cup down on the counter with a thump, nearly sloshing the hot liquid on his hands, he crossed the floor to where Ivy stood with her chin up, spine straight and as much anger flaring in her eyes as he was certain was in his own.

He came to a stop in front of her, barely an inch from touching her. Leaning down, they were almost nose to nose. "Taking advantage of the situation? Like hell!" he snarled through gritted teeth. "Baby, had I done that, I would have made love to you so many times by now—all over this house, in every room, more than once, and even here on this damn table—that you would be incapable of walking."

"You don't think I would have had anything to say about that?" she said, huffing out the words.

A slow smile eased onto his lips. Corner to corner. "Oh, you would have had a lot to say about it. Mostly your words would have been in moans and groans in between all those orgasms."

She sucked in a sharp breath. "How dare you say something like that to me?"

"I said it and I'm not taking it back. This whole idea of us pretending to be lovers was yours, not mine. Take ownership of it, will you? I'm beginning to wonder just what you thought being my lover—pretend or otherwise—would entail. Not sure what you and your other boyfriends did as lovers but you're in a different league and on a different team. Either stay and play or quit and leave. Your choice. What's it going to be Ivy?"

IVY HAD A good mind to do the latter. Quit and leave. But she was not a quitter. Never had been and wouldn't start being one now. And he was right. This plan was hers and she should take ownership—of it and everything it would entail, including being 100 percent convincing when people saw them in public. Lord knows she wanted to and that she'd tried. But she hadn't counted on a lot of things and Nolan Madaris being such a hot-blooded hunk who could send her hormones into overdrive was one of them.

Nolan was unlike any other man she'd had to deal with and he probably wondered why she refused to even consider them having a fling. After all, they were both adults who knew the score. They might as well enjoy each other while planning to outsmart Nana and his great-grandmother. A part of her wished it could be that easy. But for her, it couldn't be.

First of all, he had a sordid reputation around town and she refused to be another one of those willing women, regardless if she wanted a serious relationship with a man or not. She knew when to draw the line in some things. And then there was the real possibility that if she let Nolan get too close, she could fall for him and find it impossible to resist him.

And now he stood here, in her face, nose to nose, toe-to-toe, breath to breath. Didn't he have any idea what he did to her? How he was making her feel? Obviously not. "I want to stay and play, Nolan. But..."

He frowned and slowly pulled his head back so his face wasn't right in hers. "But what?"

She licked her bottom lip, wondering how she could explain. She honestly thought she had earlier today. She had hoped he understood. Obviously he hadn't. "You aren't like most men."

His frown deepened. "Meaning?"

Good Lord, did she need to spell it out for him? Did the man not have any idea what he did to women? He had to know; otherwise, he wouldn't have the reputation around town that he had. "No matter how convincing we are in public, how convincing our...public displays of affection are—" Just thinking the word *kissing* had her blushing. "Everyone knows you're too hot for me." She wanted to stop looking into his eyes. She much preferred squeezing her eyes closed after having to say something like that. Something that was so blatantly obvious.

She expected him to stick out his chest or something equally egotistical. Nor would she have been surprised had he burst out laughing at the thought she'd just told him something he already knew. Instead the eyes staring down at her seemed to go from ice-cold to burning hot as they slid over her features.

"Then I think we have a problem, Ivy," he said, as he held her gaze. "Because I think it's just the opposite— you're far too good and way too hot for me."

Ivy blinked and then she was the one who burst out laughing.

NOLAN FROWNED AS he placed his arms across his chest. "I'm glad you found what I said so amusing." Ivy had laughed so hard tears were actually streaming down her cheeks. That made his frown deepen even more.

"Not amusing but ridiculous," she said, grabbing a couple of napkins off the table. She took off her glasses to dab at her eyes, then put them back on again.

"I take it that you don't believe me?"

Ivy looked up at him. Her laughter had subsided but a lingering smile touched her lips and her eyes were now dry. "Of course I don't believe you. Look at me."

He was looking. Furthermore, he was damn sick and tired of her believing she wasn't desirable just because some prick had convinced her she wasn't. "I am looking," he said, as his gaze roamed over her from head to toe. "And do you know what I see?"

She pushed her glasses back a bit on her nose. "No, what do you see?"

"A woman I would love to take to bed but, because I promised that I wouldn't, I won't." He took a step closer to her. "But be forewarned, Ivy. If you decide to stay and play, I intend to kiss and touch you as much as I deem it necessary in order to fool your grandmother and Mama Laverne about us. However, don't get things twisted. All of it won't be just for practice. I intended to get enjoyment out of it and intend that you get enjoyment out of it as well. There's no way we will come out victorious if we don't get pleasure out of what we're doing."

He took several steps back and said, "I baked lasagna for dinner. Help yourself. I'm going to bed now. I plan to get up early and go rent a boat. If you're still here when I get back, then I'll assume you're committed to the plan to stay and play. If you're gone, then I know you quit and left."

He then walked out of the kitchen.

"Hey, Ivy, what's up?"

"I got a problem, Tessa."

"What's wrong?"

Ivy sat outside on the front steps as she stared up at the stars. They were bright. So was the full moon. Was there really a man in the moon? If so, she wished she could join him. Her life was so screwed up now, thanks to her grandmother, who for some reason that Ivy didn't understand, honestly thought she had her granddaughter's best interest at heart. Boy, was her nana wrong.

"Ivy?"

Tessa saying her name in a panicky voice reined Ivy's thoughts back in. "Yes?"

"I asked what's wrong? You call me close to midnight to say you have a problem, then go silent on me."

Ivy checked her watch. Oops. It was close to midnight and, like Nolan, Tessa went to bed early. "I would have called you sooner but I was eating the dinner Nolan cooked. It was baked lasagna and it was oh-so-delicious. What man does that? Most don't know how to boil water right."

"Like you," Tessa said, giggling.

"Yes, like me," Ivy said in a quiet tone.

"Are you on Tiki Island having a pity party, Ivy?"

Ivy shrugged. "Pretty much. Things are getting crazy."

"What's wrong? Did Nolan Madaris renege on your agreement and ask you to leave?"

"Not exactly."

"Well, what exactly?"

Ivy began nibbling on her bottom lip. "I'm the one who might be reneging."

"Why?"

Ivy released a deep sigh. "You remember our last conversation?"

"Yes, what part of it?"

"All of it. First there was the part where you mentioned how much of a hunk Nolan was," Ivy said.

"Yes, and you said you could ignore it," Tessa reminded her.

"Well, I discovered it's not that easy."

"Okay, and obviously there is more to your problem, Ivy."

"There is. Do you also recall when I told you there weren't any vibes?"

"Yes, and I told you I thought it was something the two of you should talk about since the main goal was outsmarting the matchmakers."

"Yes, well," Ivy said in frustration, "I did talk to him about it."

"Good."

"Um, not so good."

"So what's not so good about it?"

"The whole thing. He began stirring passion between us to make sure I felt it. We've kissed a few times. I thought they were absolutely, positively off the charts. He even kisses me without removing my glasses and does it perfectly. I don't think I can handle much more."

"Of Nolan Madaris's kisses?"

"Of Nolan's anything."

Tessa got quiet for a second and then she said, "You do know in order for your plan to work you *have* to handle it, right?"

"Yes, but I honestly didn't think things would get this complicated."

"It really isn't, you know," Tessa said. "To you it just seems that way because…"

When Tessa hesitated, Ivy asked, "Because of what?"

"Because you still haven't got over what Damien said about you and what he did."

"I have got over what he said and what he did. I've got over Damien Fargo, period. That's why I'm ignoring his calls."

"Damien's been calling you?"

"Yes."

"You didn't tell me that."

"Wasn't nothing to tell. He called last week to apologize for how he treated me when we were together."

She heard Tessa's snort. "A little too late for that, isn't it?"

"That's what I told him and hung up. He's called a couple of times since but I refused to take the call."

"Block his number."

"I will."

"I hope you do and as far as Nolan Madaris is concerned, sounds like you're getting way too serious over a few kisses."

"That's easy for you to say," Ivy mumbled. "Like I told you, he's an expert kisser."

"That's better than a man who doesn't know how to use his tongue, trust me."

"Tessa!"

"Well, it's true. Why can't you let yourself go and enjoy the moment? I don't understand why you set limitations. Why not have a full-blown affair with him? You have the perfect opportunity to do so at the cottage. Who will it hurt?"

"Possibly me. Nolan is the kind of man who could

wiggle his way into my heart if I were to let my guard down. I can't let that happen, Tessa."

Ivy released another deep sigh. "Tonight he said he thought I was hot and that whenever he looks at me he sees a woman he wants to make love to."

"Wow. And what's wrong with him telling you that?" Tessa asked. "At least he was honest."

"Was he? Men like him have plenty of lines."

"True. But why do you think he was just feeding you a line? Why don't you think you're hot and are a woman a man would want to sleep with?"

Ivy stared up at the stars again. "You know why."

"Yes, because of some BS Damien Fargo told you. Like I said, Ivy, you need to get over him."

"And like I told you, I have," Ivy said. "I just wished I wasn't so inexperienced."

Tessa smiled. "You slept with Damien," she reminded her. "And that guy Fred."

"Yes, but neither compared to Nolan. I've experienced more passion with kissing Nolan than I did when having sex with Damien and Fred combined." Fred Campers, another techie she met in college, hadn't known any more about what to do than she had. "But we know why Nolan is so good at what he does. He's a womanizer. You wouldn't believe how often his phone rings. He ignores the calls, but I can imagine who they are from. What if he can't give all those women up like he says he will?"

"Why wouldn't he? I don't think he would have agreed to do it if he didn't mean it. And as far as Damien is concerned, maybe you are over him—I believe that you don't want him back—but you're obviously still letting his voice fill your head with self-doubt. And you need to decide what you're going to do about Nolan."

"He gave me an ultimatum," Ivy said, choosing to ignore what Tessa had said about Damien being in her head. "I can either stay and play, or quit and leave. If I stay and play, that means he's going to go into full expert mode and do whatever it takes to get me ready for all those sexual vibes we need to be discharging."

"Sexual vibes are what you wanted, need I remind you."

Tessa didn't have to remind her. "I just hadn't figured on those vibes being so intense."

"Now you know. So, which option are you going to take?"

"I don't know, Tessa, I really don't know."

Tessa didn't say anything for a moment and then she said, "I suggest you weigh the pros and cons of both, and then sleep on it. If you think you can handle Nana and his great-grandmother all by yourself, then quit and leave. Just know you'll be on your own. Otherwise, the two of you can work together as a team and implement *your* idea."

CHAPTER EIGHTEEN

THE NEXT MORNING Nolan noticed the smell of coffee the moment he left his bedroom. He hadn't set the timer on the coffee maker, so that could only mean one thing. Ivy had started it.

Ivy was never up this early. Had she had got up to get a head start on her drive back to Houston? If that was her decision, he would accept it. Walking into the kitchen, he found her sitting at the kitchen table. She glanced up when she saw him, her expression unreadable.

"Good morning, Ivy."

She adjusted her glasses on her face. "Good morning, Nolan. I made coffee."

He nodded. "So I see. Thanks." He walked over to the coffeepot to pour a cup. "What time do you plan to get on the road?"

"That depends on you."

He turned around with his coffee cup in his hand and leaned against the counter. "Me? Why?"

"Because you'll be driving."

Nolan lifted a brow. "Something's wrong with your car?"

"Not that I know of."

He frowned thinking her answer didn't make sense. "Then why do you need me to drive you to Houston?"

"I don't because I'm not going to Houston."

He rubbed his hand over his unshaven jaw wondering what was going on. He had absolutely zero idea and knew he had to be missing something. "So where are you going?"

"With you," she said softly. "I thought I'd get up early and ride with you to pick up the boat. That is, if you don't mind."

He held tight to his coffee cup; otherwise it would have slipped from his hand. Did that mean she would stay and play? "Nah, I don't mind."

He took a sip of his coffee and she took sips of hers. Neither said anything. When moments passed he couldn't hold off any longer on asking her the question he was dying to ask. "How did you reach your decision?"

She placed her coffee cup down and held his gaze. "This whole idea of us pretending to be lovers was my idea and I needed to take ownership of it like you said. So I have. No matter what it takes, I'm in."

He lifted a brow. "Are you?"

"Yes, but my earlier restriction stands. I won't go so far as to sleep with you."

He couldn't help the smile that touched his lips. "You won't?"

"No, I won't. No matter what."

"Okay."

Now she was the one who lifted a brow. Probably because of his easy acceptance of what she'd said. "Okay?"

He repeated it for her benefit, "Yes, okay."

As if satisfied, she nodded. "Fine."

"But there is one thing I think we need to clear up now, since you've decided to stay."

"What?"

"You accused me of taking advantage of the situation regarding you and that isn't true. I would never do something like that."

"I know. I said it because I was mad. I regret doing so and apologize."

He nodded. "Apology accepted." He pushed away from the counter. "If you're ready, let's ride."

IVY WAS READY. All she had to do was grab her cross-body purse off the bed. She hurried out of the house to find Nolan standing beside his SUV in jeans and a button-up shirt, with more buttons unbuttoned than were buttoned. And he was waiting for her. There had to be another way to describe how he looked at that moment. The word *sexy* no longer held the power it once had to depict him. Suddenly other words flowed through her mind. *Erotic. Sensual. Stimulating.* And as usual, his scent was too appealing.

"Ready to go?" he asked, opening the passenger door for her.

"Ready."

He took her hand and assisted her inside. She tried to ignore the sensations that flowed through her from his touch. When he reached across her to grab hold of the seat belt to snap it in place for her, she quickly said, "Thanks, I can do it."

He met her gaze. "Just practicing being the doting boyfriend." He winked at her.

He closed the vehicle's door and walked around to the driver's side. She was definitely feeling vibes and reminded herself they were all part of a plan. She wondered if he felt them, too.

He started the ignition and backed out of the yard. When they were headed down the street, he glanced over at her and, almost like he'd read her mind, he said, "Madarises are pretty affectionate, especially the men. And they all married women who love receiving affection. I don't recall a time that I didn't feel the love radiating between them. That's the case even with my own parents and grandparents."

Ivy didn't say anything. Although she recalled feeling the love between her paternal grandparents, she couldn't say the same about her maternal grandparents since they'd both died before she was born. And she definitely didn't feel any love between her parents. The only thing she ever felt was their animosity toward each other.

"So what part of Houston do you live in?"

Since he was her pretend lover he definitely needed to know that. "The Francesca Glen area."

He chuckled. "You're kidding."

"No. I'm not kidding."

"How long have you lived there?" he asked her.

"A little more than a year." No need to mention that after her breakup with Damien, she wanted to move to another place since her old home held too many memories of their time together.

"Would you believe we're neighbors?" he asked. "I live in the condos adjacent to the Madaris Building. Right by Laverne Park. Guess who the park was named after?"

She lifted a brow. "Your great-grandmother?"

"Yes. My cousins Blade and Slade, who own Madaris

Construction, were the builders who helped to develop that entire area. They constructed all the condos. They named that particular area you're living in after their mother, my aunt Fran. Her real name is Francesca." When he came to a traffic light he glanced over at her. "I guess you didn't know any of that."

"No, but I'm sure Nana did. Especially the fact that your condo is within walking distance of mine. And I spend a lot of time at that park. It's a nice place to jog."

"You jog?"

"Not as much as I like. I usually go out in the evenings."

"And I usually jog in the mornings."

She chuckled. "That figures. Just like our bedtimes, we're total opposites."

"Yeah, we're going to have to do something about that."

Ivy knew he didn't mean it the way it sounded, but that didn't stop the feeling of blood thickening in her veins or every hormone in her body sizzling. It was as if now that she'd decided to take full ownership of her idea, no matter what it took, her body had awakened to all sorts of feelings, sensations and impulses. She wasn't sure that was a good thing.

Neither said anything for a while. He was concentrating on his driving and she pretended interest at the scenery they passed. She finally got the nerve to glance over at him, her gaze drifting over his open shirt and thighs in a tight pair of jeans. She didn't recall making a sound but she noticed he'd brought the car to a stop and he glanced over at her, catching her checking him out. Their gazes connected and held, and she could feel her pulse flicker and leap.

She cleared her throat. "Why did we stop?"

He smiled and the way he did so, slow and easy, sent what felt like frissons of fire escalating up her spine. "We're here," he said in his deep, husky voice.

She broke eye contact with him to glance out the windshield and saw the huge sign for Bannister's Boat Rentals. "Oh."

"Stay put. I'll help you out."

"No, I'll be okay," she said, quickly scrambling to undo her seat belt. The last thing she needed was for his hands to touch her right now.

He came around to help her anyway and had opened the door before she had a chance to do so. Then he was reaching his arms out to her. She knew it was just a courtesy to help her down but for all her body cared, it was to carry her off to his bed.

Yikes! How could she think of something like that? She was the one who had put the rule in place that under no circumstances would they sleep together. Ever. That rule was right up there with her not marrying. Ever. So what was her problem?

"Are you okay, Ivy?"

She looked at him, still standing there with out-stretched arms, staring at her and probably wondering the same thing. What was her problem?

Ivy pasted a smile on her face. "Yes, Nolan, I'm fine."

She allowed him to help her down. The moment he touched her, she moaned. She'd heard herself, which meant he probably heard her as well.

Her feet touched the ground but he didn't let her go. Instead his arms slid tighter around her and she was pinned between him and door's opening, her butt pressed against the side of the seat. She stared into his eyes that seemed to have gone from dark to darker and from heated to hot.

Now it was her turn to ask him, "Are you okay, Nolan?"

He didn't say anything for a second. He just stood there and continued to look into her eyes. Then she watched as his gaze shifted lower to her mouth. As if the heat from his gaze was scorching her lips, she stuck out her tongue and licked them, as if she needed moisture there.

Suddenly, the air surrounding them seemed to sizzle and did she just imagine it or did he take a step closer? She couldn't have imagined it when her body was pressed against the hard firmness of his. She could feel the steady thud of his heartbeat against hers and she was not imagining the feel of a hard erection straining against his zipper and pressing into her middle.

"Nolan?"

He shifted his gaze from her lips back to her eyes, and she could see him staring at her through the lenses of her glasses. The look was so hot it made her want to melt right into him. And she must have done that because the next thing she knew, their bodies had got even closer and that's when he lowered his head to hers.

She closed her eyes the moment their mouths touched and suddenly the heat was on. He deepened the pressure of the lips holding her hostage as he devoured her mouth in a way it had never been before. He was kissing her so thoroughly and with a possession that forced reality out of her mind. It was replaced with passion. And it was passion so provocative she moaned again at the pleasure she felt.

This was their fourth kiss and it seemed each one kept getting more toe-curlingly scandalous. Each one consumed with more bone-melting fire than the previous one. She knew she should pull back, break away from this kiss, but at that moment passion overruled her common sense as his mouth became even more demanding and greedy.

The sound of someone clearing their throat intruded and she heard Nolan growl deep in his throat before he finally dragged his mouth away, breaking off the kiss.

She opened her eyes and glanced over his shoulder to find a nice-looking man about her age, or possibly a year or two older with charcoal-gray eyes standing a few feet behind Nolan with a wide silly grin on his face. She could have crawled under the car in embarrassment when he said, "For Pete's sake, Nolan, give the lady's mouth a break. Do you want to rent a boat today or not?"

Instead of answering the man, Nolan leaned in close to her and licked across her bottom lip with his tongue. He whispered, "I've been tempted to do that for a long time now, Ivy."

He backed up and turned to face the man. "Yes, Brent, I want to rent a boat. My usual one."

"Will do. Come to the office when you're ready to handle the paperwork." The man walked off.

Ivy felt she needed to say something. What, she wasn't sure. They were doing what they were supposed to do, right? Stoking their vibes. She wondered if the man named Brent had felt those vibes?

"You okay?"

She met Nolan's gaze. How could he ask her that after kissing her like that? In front of that man named

Brent or anyone else who'd wanted to look since it seemed a number of people wanted to rent a boat today. "Yes. I'm okay. I'm just not used to getting kissed in public and you like making a habit of it."

"It's good practice, plus I wouldn't be surprised if news of this made it back to Mama Laverne. She seems to have eyes everywhere," Nolan said.

Of course. He didn't just kiss her to kiss her. He was thinking about the plan. Good. They'd have to be two steps ahead of her grandmother and his great-grandmother to succeed. She had to remind herself that every kiss had a purpose. It was a performance that was part of their plans.

"Come on," Nolan said, unwrapping his arms from around her and taking her hand. "Let's go get the boat."

CHAPTER NINETEEN

"BRENT SEEMS LIKE a nice person."

Nolan decided to refrain from saying exactly what he thought of his friend Brenton Bannister for now. Brent had deliberately flirted with Ivy just to get a rise out of him. That damn ploy should not have worked but it had. In a way that was good just in case his cousins tried doing the same when they met her. He needed to act possessive and territorial. Only thing about it was that today he hadn't been acting. He had actually wanted to smash Brent's face in. How crazy was that?

"Nolan?"

He then remembered Ivy had made a statement and was waiting for his response. "He's okay."

"Have you known him for long?"

He was wondering why she wanted to know anything about Brent. He knew it was those damn gray eyes. Women would look into them and go crazy. "I guess you can say we've known each other all our lives. We share cousins."

"Share cousins?"

"Yes. My grandaunt Marilyn, who is married to my granduncle Jonathan, was a Bannister before they married."

"Oh."

"And if you're wondering about the color of his eyes,

all Bannisters have gray eyes, including Grandaunt Marilyn. However, only one of Grandaunt Marilyn's kids got her eyes. My cousin Dex. You'll get to meet them at some point."

She didn't say anything for a while and that was fine with him. He needed to regroup and get his mind back in sync. First of all, he was trying to figure out why he'd kissed her when helping her out of his SUV. He hadn't been thinking about Mama Laverne's spies, like he told Ivy. It had been spontaneous—and amazing. When had he been spontaneous about anything? Usually, he thought things through before he acted.

"I guess you mentioned to your great-grandmother that we went out to dinner the other night."

He glanced back over at her when he brought the car to a stop at a traffic light. "What makes you think that?"

"Nana mentioned it when I talked to her yesterday. I figured since she knew about it that you must have mentioned it to Ms. Laverne."

He shook his head. "No, I haven't spoken to Mama Laverne since our second day here when she called me. But I think I know how she found out."

"How?"

"Mrs. Tucker. Her husband is the head cook at Andre's. He must have gone home and mentioned seeing me to his wife. Just so happens that Erma Tucker and Mama Laverne are good friends. If Mama Laverne knows I took you to Andre's, then she also knows we kissed there as well."

"Wow, guess you were right about spying eyes everywhere."

That had been an excuse at the time, but now that he thought about it, it wasn't that off. He put on his

SUV's blinkers to turn the corner and thought about that kiss they'd shared earlier and then added, "And just so you know, of course Mama Laverne would be good friends with the Bannisters as well, since one of her sons married into the family. So, don't be surprised if word gets out about our kiss. I doubt Brent was the only one who saw it."

A minute or two passed and then Ivy asked him, "Is that why you kissed me at the boat rental place? So they could go back and tell her to further validate our plan?"

Nolan thought it would be so easy to say that yes, that was the reason he'd kissed her. That he had deliberately seized an opportunity for them to be seen locking lips. But he knew that would be a lie. He had kissed her for the same reason he had taken his tongue and licked her lips. He had wanted to do it. He had been tempted to do it. So he had done it and didn't have any regrets doing so. "No," he said, refusing to glance over at her but speaking loud enough for her to hear. "The truth is, my kissing you wasn't part of *any* plan."

She didn't say anything but he could feel the intensity of her gaze on him. He couldn't help but wonder if he'd made himself clear and if she understood what he meant.

Minutes passed before she said anything and then she asked, "Is there anybody that your great-grandmother doesn't know?"

Nolan realized she was changing the subject. Sort of. In a way he was glad she was doing so. "I'm sure there are some people, but I understand what you mean. She has allies everywhere. We all discovered that the hard way while growing up. There was nothing we could do behind her or our parents' backs that they didn't find out about."

He continued to drive but for some reason the thought that she might be interested in Brent bothered him. "So what do you think about Brent?" he finally decided to ask her because her possible response was nagging at him.

"He seems nice enough. Why do you ask?"

"Just wondering. Most women find him good-looking with those gray eyes and all."

"He is good-looking, but a person's looks don't tell the whole story about them. I could tell he's a womanizer."

He was glad she'd picked up on that. "Yes, he is."

"But then so are you."

He fought back the urge to tell her just how wrong she was. He'd only stepped into that role with a purpose in mind. Mainly to get her to look the other way.

"Besides, a man should be the last thing on my mind right now. However, necessity dictates I make you an exception."

He came to another traffic light and glanced over at her as she was pushing her glasses back on her nose. He knew it sounded crazy but he thought she looked sexy whenever she did that. When she glanced over at him he knew he had to say something, otherwise she would have caught him staring at her again. "Why should a man be the last thing on your mind?"

"Because when I return to Houston, I'll be too busy with my work to be involved with anyone."

He nodded. That was one thing they hadn't talked a whole lot about in any great detail. Her work. "I understand you contract out to big corporations and government agencies, right?"

"Yes, whenever they feel they have cybersecurity issues."

"That's a unique job. Being a hacker."

"Unique for a woman. At my first job the men I worked with didn't hesitate to let me know it. They acted like they'd cornered the cyberworld and unless you were male you had no right to claim any part of it."

Nolan knew what she meant. Even while at MIT, there were guys who felt threatened by the females in their class. "How did you handle it?"

"By ignoring them when I could. While they were busy trying to sabotage my work and make me look bad, I was busy doing what I was supposed to do, learning as much as I could and perfecting my skills. It pissed some of them off when I got a lot of the big promotions."

"What about the guys you couldn't ignore?"

"I had to report only one. I drew the line when he assumed it was all right to put his hands on me in an inappropriate way."

The thought of someone doing that to her made Nolan's blood boil. "I'm glad you reported him."

"That was after I kicked him in the groin real good."

Nolan laughed. "He got just what he deserved."

She smiled. "I thought so. After that incident most of the guys left me alone."

"What do you like most about your job?" he asked, making the turnoff onto the street where his cottage was located.

"I believe that I perfect my computer and engineering skills with every project I work on. And I love the fact that I can work from anywhere and at any time. And last but not least is the fact my job will never become obsolete. There will be a need for cybersecurity even more in the future."

He had to agree with that. He didn't want to think about the number of times other technology companies tried hacking into Chenault Electronics' software while they were creating the Shayla chip.

"If you're going to be busy, we'll plan how to squeeze me into your schedule to make it seem as if we're in a hot and heavy relationship," he said.

She nibbled on her bottom lip. "We'll think of something. You did say you would be in Paris for a while anyway, right?"

"Yes."

"Well, that will give us a nice break for the both of us, not having to keep up this pretense, without anyone getting suspicious."

For some reason, Nolan didn't like that she was already looking forward to a break from him. He pulled the car into the yard. After leaving Brent's, they had grabbed breakfast at a diner next door. Her phone had rung and when she ignored it, he had a feeling it had been her ex again. It bothered him that she hadn't blocked the number like he'd suggested the other day.

That only made him wonder if she really didn't want to get back with the guy like she claimed. Otherwise, why hadn't she taken steps to permanently cut him out of her life? He recalled the times he'd run into Andrea or had got a call from her over the years. She had apologized as well, but still, he'd had no problem making sure she knew he could never give what they had a second chance. Betrayal was something he just couldn't get over.

"Will you be going out on the boat today?" she asked him.

"Yes. Would you like to join me?"

She smiled over at him. "Yes, I'd love to."

FIVE HOURS LATER Ivy walked beside Nolan as they headed back to the cottage. She couldn't believe the exciting day she'd had. It had been wonderful being on a boat on the bay. And she'd caught her first fish. She was mighty proud of herself since she'd never held a fishing rod in her hand before.

Nolan had been patient while showing her how to use one and even put up with her acting all squeamish when she had to deal with the bait. But all in all, everything had turned out great. Now they were headed back to the cottage and he would be showing her how to clean her catch. Of course he'd caught more fish than she had. Ivy hadn't been surprised after he'd told her how often he fished. In fact he'd share with her stories of his father taking Nolan and his brothers and sisters out on the water whenever he could.

He also shared other interesting tidbits about his family and it was easy to see he enjoyed being part of such a huge family. She envied that since she didn't have any cousins, aunts or uncles. Neither of her parents had siblings and the same held true for her grandparents.

"How good are you with handling a knife?"

Nolan's questions cut into her thoughts and she studied the set of knives he had placed on the table. It was as if the kitchen was about to become an operating room. "I've never handled a knife before." Already her stomach was getting a little queasy at the thought of what he intended to do with them.

He nodded slowly. "How do you feel about gutting anything?"

He would have to ask and she figured her face had suddenly turned green, giving him an answer. She couldn't be too sure, but when he suppressed a cough she had a feeling he was trying to hold back a laugh. "And I've never gutted anything," she said.

He smiled over at her. "I'll tell you what. I'll clean our catch and get it ready for the grill."

Ivy hoped she didn't look as relieved as she felt. Messing with bait earlier had been bad enough. The thought of cutting a fish open was too much to think about. "Is there anything else I can do to help?"

She figured he was too kind to come out and say that what he really wanted her to do was to get out his way. Instead he said, "You can get the veggies started on the grill. That's easy enough. I'll show you how it's done."

A short while later she was sitting on the patio, watching the veggies. He had seasoned slices of white potatoes, onions, corn on the cob, carrots and broccoli before wrapping them in aluminum foil and placing them on the grill. Her job was just to watch them. He was right, doing this was easy enough.

A part of her felt real dumb. She was a woman who knew a computer inside out, she could decode even the most complicated software and hack into the unhackable, yet she couldn't do something as simple as cook a meal. She was certain she could if she took the time to learn, but doing so never appealed to her. Boiling hot dogs and making grilled cheese sandwiches were things she knew how to do. However, once when she had tried baking a potato in the oven, she had forgotten about it until her smoke alarm went off. That had been the last time she'd used her oven. Maybe she ought to sign up for cooking classes. She could even get Tessa to go with her.

"How are things going?"

She glanced up when Nolan walked out on the patio. He had removed his shirt and she tried not to gaze at his chest. Or his mouth for that matter. Every time she did, she remembered that hot and scorching kiss they'd shared earlier that day. She doubted she would ever forget it although she tried forcing it to the back of her mind.

And what had he meant earlier about the kiss not being part of any plan? Then why had he done it? She didn't know the answer to that but knew deep down a part of her was glad he had. Every time he came near her she could feel her pulse kick up a beat and sensations flood her stomach. The man had just finished cleaning fish for heaven's sake, yet to her he smelled sensual and masculine.

Knowing he was waiting on her response, she said, "So far, so good. I haven't burned anything. I don't know what you used to season those veggies, but they smell wonderful."

"It's a secret."

"Like the Madaris family tea?"

"Yes, like the tea."

While out on the boat fishing, Nolan had told her about the Madaris family tea. He claimed its special ingredients of herbs and spices were a secret recipe that could only be shared with the men in the Madaris family, but only after they had reached their thirty-fifth birthdays. Since he would be turning that age in a few months, he said he couldn't wait to get ahold of the secret.

"I've decided to take cooking lessons. I feel awful that I don't know how."

He glanced over at her as he placed the fish on the grill. She couldn't help noticing how neat he was, spacing each fillet to make sure they cooked evenly. "You live alone and you're a busy woman."

"Hey, don't make excuses for me."

"I'm not, just stating the obvious."

She rolled her eyes. "And you live alone and you're a busy man."

He chuckled. "Yes, but I didn't have a choice but to learn to cook. I told you that. I discovered I enjoyed it and that's why I do it so much. And I know how to cook just enough for me. But if I do overdo it, I know my brothers, Corbin and Adam, as well as a few cousins, have no shame in taking any leftovers off my hands."

He sat down in the chair across from her and she wished her gaze wasn't in a direct line to the center of his chest. That hairy and muscular chest. "Take Corbin for instance," he was saying. "He learned to cook just like I did, but I bet he doesn't own a pot or a pan."

Ivy lifted a brow. She owned an entire collection of pots and pans, she just didn't use them. "Then how does he eat?"

"It's not how but where. Mostly at my folks' place. Mom still cooks a meal every day and enjoys it whenever we stop by. But if the folks are out of town or something, there are other family members who Corbin knows will roll out the welcome mat. There are too many Madarises for one to ever think about starving."

"I think it's awesome that you look out for each other that way."

"That's the Madaris way and it's the only way we roll."

A couple of hours later Nolan and Ivy had finished their meal. "That was so good," Ivy said, dabbing her mouth with a napkin.

Nolan chuckled as he finished off the last of his beer. "Just fish and veggies."

"Oh, no, don't even try making light of what you prepared," she said, shaking a finger at him. "Not only was it good but it was also healthy." And she'd meant what she'd said earlier. She wasn't sure what seasoning he had used on the veggies but they were delicious. The grilled fish was delicious as well.

"I try to eat healthy every chance I get." He leaned back in his chair. "If you were serious about wanting to learn how to prepare a few things, then I can teach you while you're here."

His offer made her smile. "You'd do that?"

"Yes, just simple stuff. We can start tomorrow morning with breakfast. That means you'll have to be an early riser again."

"No problem. I'll just go to bed a little early. Thanks."

"You're welcome." He paused for a minute and then said, "Your grandmother…"

Ivy lifted a brow. "What about her?"

"She didn't encourage you to spend time in the kitchen when you were a kid? You didn't get any of those little bake sets for Christmas?"

Ivy chuckled. "No, I got books, digital games and all things technology. Besides, I came to Nana late in life since her son wasn't in a hurry to be a husband or a father. Nana encouraged me to do the things that I enjoyed doing, not the things she might have wanted me to do. It was all about what made me happy." Ivy thought about the latter and shook her head.

"Why are you shaking your head?"

She drew in a deep breath. "It just seems so strange that she would change that way of thinking now. Back then it was all about what made me happy. Now it's about what makes her happy."

"You think so?"

"Yes. If it was about my happiness we wouldn't be hatching a plan to be in a fake relationship. Me getting married will evidently make Nana happy. But what about me? It won't make me happy, Nolan. I just don't understand why they can't see that we don't belong together."

Leaning over the table Nolan said in a rough tone, "Personally, for causing so much trouble, I can't wait for the day we make that fact known to them."

CHAPTER TWENTY

THE NEXT MORNING Nolan stepped out of the shower, dried off and began getting dressed. His cousin Clayton had called to let him know that he and his wife, Syneda, who were both attorneys, would be in the Galveston area today to meet with a client. They'd invited him and Ivy to join them tonight for dinner.

Nolan wasn't stupid. Clayton and Syneda might be in Galveston on business but there was no doubt in Nolan's mind that Mama Laverne had suggested to Syneda that they contact him when they arrived in the area. Everybody knew Syneda was one of his great-grandmother's cronies and would assist in her matchmaking schemes on occasion. He had a feeling this was one of those occasions.

He'd told Clayton he would get back to him after checking with Ivy. He wasn't sure if she would want to go or not since he and Ivy would be leaving the island to return to Houston tomorrow. It was hard to believe their week together was almost over and he would admit he'd enjoyed her company.

Nolan decided that he would tell her about Clayton and Syneda's invitation and would accept her decision. However, he felt dinner with Clayton and Syneda would be a great test run for them as a new "couple." There was no doubt in his mind Syneda would report back to his great-grandmother how they acted together. In other words, if she detected a romance blooming between him and Ivy.

When he left his bedroom he picked up the aroma of coffee and knew Ivy was up for her cooking lesson. He hadn't known if she'd been serious or not about accepting his offer to show her how to make a few dishes in the kitchen. Evidently, she had been.

As far as he was concerned, he felt that she shouldn't beat herself up about the fact she wasn't into cooking. If she preferred eating out, then that was her business. He intended to show her how to prepare a few quick and easy meals and he would try to make cooking them fun.

He walked into the kitchen and stopped dead in his tracks. Ivy had opened the refrigerator and was leaning into it, looking for something. That particular position outlined a curvy backside in a pair of skinny jeans. He nearly groaned in deep male appreciation. At that moment desire, the likes he hadn't felt in a long time, twisted his guts at the same time a hard whir of lust rushed up his spine.

He swallowed twice before he managed to clear his throat. "Looking for something, Ivy?"

She pulled her head from the refrigerator and straightened her body before smiling over at him. "Good morning, Nolan. I was looking for my carton of milk. Have you seen it?"

"Yes, I moved it to the side of the door."

"Oh."

She reached for the carton and chuckled. "If it had been a snake, it would have bit me."

He had news for her. He wasn't a snake but biting her sounded pretty damn good right now. She was wearing one of those blouses that showed the upper part of her arms, arms he would love putting his mouth on. He recalled Victoria had referred to those type blouses as cold-shoulder blouses. There wasn't anything cold about them. On Ivy that blouse looked hot.

"I got coffee going for you."

That wasn't the only thing she had got going for him. It didn't bother him that he wanted her. He should want her. Otherwise, their plans of fooling anyone would mean nothing. He couldn't pretend to desire a woman— he had to truly desire her.

"What are you going to teach me to do today?"

Hell, that question put ideas in his head, and none of them had anything to do with teaching her how to prepare a meal. "An omelet."

She licked her lips and his stomach tightened. "That sounds delicious."

He almost said that she looked rather delicious as well, standing in his kitchen in her bare feet, wearing a pair of jeans and a sexy top. "Since you enjoyed those veggies yesterday, I thought we would have a veggie omelet this morning."

"All right. Did you sleep okay last night?"

"Yes, I slept fine." No need to tell her about the dreams he'd had of her; especially of that kiss yesterday and the one the day before that and the one before that. He liked getting inside her mouth. "What about you?" he asked, moving toward the coffeepot to pour himself a cup.

"I slept like a baby. I was full and content. You fed me well."

If given the chance there were a number of other things he could do to her well that would leave her full

"4 for 4" MINI-SURVEY

We are prepared to **REWARD** you with 2 FREE books and 2 FREE gifts for completing our MINI SURVEY!

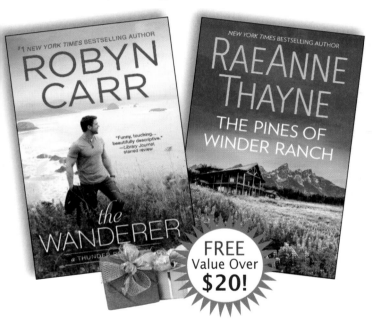

FREE Value Over **$20!**

You'll get...
TWO FREE BOOKS & TWO FREE GIFTS
just for participating in our Mini Survey!

Dear Reader,

IT'S A FACT: if you answer 4 quick questions, we'll send you 4 FREE REWARDS!

I'm not kidding you. As a leading publisher of women's fiction, we value your opinions... and your time. That's why we are prepared to **reward** you handsomely for completing our mini-survey. In fact, we have 4 Free Rewards for you, including 2 free books and 2 free gifts.

As you may have guessed, that's why our mini-survey is called **"4 for 4".** Answer 4 questions and get 4 Free Rewards. It's that simple!

Thank you for participating in our survey,

Pam Powers

To get your 4 FREE REWARDS:
Complete the survey below and return the insert today to receive 2 FREE BOOKS and 2 FREE GIFTS guaranteed!

"4 for 4" MINI-SURVEY

1 Is reading one of your favorite hobbies?
☐ YES ☐ NO

2 Do you prefer to read instead of watch TV?
☐ YES ☐ NO

3 Do you read newspapers and magazines?
☐ YES ☐ NO

4 Do you enjoy trying new book series with FREE BOOKS?
☐ YES ☐ NO

YES! I have completed the above Mini-Survey. Please send me my 4 FREE REWARDS (worth over $20 retail). I understand that I am under no obligation to buy anything, as explained on the back of this card.

194/394 MDL GMYP

FIRST NAME	LAST NAME

ADDRESS

APT.#	CITY

STATE/PROV.	ZIP/POSTAL CODE

ROM-218-MS17

READER SERVICE—Here's how it works:

Accepting your 2 free Romance books and 2 free gifts (gifts valued at approximately $10.00 retail) places you under no obligation to buy anything. You may keep the books and gifts and return the shipping statement marked "cancel." If you do not cancel, about a month later we'll send you 4 additional books and bill you just $6.74 each in the U.S. or $7.24 each in Canada. That is a savings of at least 16% off the cover price. It's quite a bargain! Shipping and handling is just 50¢ per book in the U.S. and 75¢ per book in Canada*. You may cancel at any time, but if you choose to continue, every month we'll send you 4 more books, which you may either purchase at the discount price plus shipping and handling or return to us and cancel your subscription. *Terms and prices subject to change without notice. Prices do not include applicable taxes. Sales tax applicable in N.Y. Canadian residents will be charged applicable taxes. Offer not valid in Quebec. Books received may not be as shown. All orders subject to approval. Credit or debit balances in a customer's account(s) may be offset by any other outstanding balance owed by or to the customer. Please allow 4 to 6 weeks for delivery. Offer available while quantities last.

▲ If offer card is missing write to: Reader Service, P.O. Box 1341, Buffalo, NY 14240-8531 or visit www.ReaderService.com ▲

BUSINESS REPLY MAIL
FIRST-CLASS MAIL   PERMIT NO. 717   BUFFALO, NY

POSTAGE WILL BE PAID BY ADDRESSEE

READER SERVICE
PO BOX 1341
BUFFALO NY 14240-8571

NO POSTAGE
NECESSARY
IF MAILED
IN THE
UNITED STATES

and content. He shook his head while spooning sugar into his coffee cup. Jeez. He blamed this crazy lust on yesterday. They'd spent the entire day together, morning till night. Being around her nonstop was making him notice things like how her lips curved at the ends when she smiled or how sexy she looked while chewing her food.

Nolan took a sip of coffee while thinking that anything to do with her mouth was a total turn-on. That was all well and good when it came to their plans but how in the hell was he to control his desires? Turn them off when they weren't needed?

"How's the coffee?"

He glanced over at her. She was sitting at the table drinking a glass of milk. "Good as usual. You made it just right."

She smiled and his gut tightened. "Thanks."

"You're drinking milk today?"

"Yes. I rarely drink coffee unless I need the caffeine when keeping late hours. I decided to get back on my routine with a glass of milk every morning."

Nolan nodded. "Ready to get started on breakfast?"

"Yes."

"Okay, let's wash up and begin."

IVY HAD NEVER thought this kitchen was super small until now. She tried not to be bothered whenever Nolan came to stand beside her when she was slicing the veggies for the omelet. He'd even had to show her the proper way to hold a knife or she probably would have cut herself. Heck, she hadn't known there was a right way and a wrong way to crack an egg.

As far as she was concerned, Nolan knew everything.

How to test the oil to make sure it was just right to start cooking and exactly what time to start adding the ingredients. For the most part, she was attentive...unless he did something that drew her attention away from the meal being prepared to him. Like when he stood behind her—directly behind her to where their bodies touched—while showing her the proper way to scramble an egg.

"That about does it," she said, sliding both omelets onto their plates. "Let's eat."

When they sat down, he bit into his omelet and smiled over at her. "This tastes fantastic. You did good, Ivy."

His compliment pleased her. "Thanks. You made it easy."

"Cooking is easy. You just need to follow a recipe or directions. You followed my directions and didn't have a problem asking questions when you felt you needed to."

"You had a lot of patience with me. Thank you. I appreciated that."

"You don't have to thank me."

Ivy felt like she did mainly because Damien never had patience with her. He would tell her something once and get upset if she ever asked him to repeat it. He had called her again last night. She didn't answer and had finally done what she should have done long ago, which was to block his number.

"It's hard to believe this big omelet was made with one egg," she finally said.

He chuckled. "Just think of all the ingredients you added to that one egg."

She would admit she'd added quite a bit to hers—spinach, onions, a mixture of peppers and tomatoes.

He'd requested that she add even more ingredients to his. He had wanted to include three kinds of meats where she'd only wanted bacon.

"I got a call from my cousin Clayton this morning. He and his wife, Syneda, are in the area meeting with a client and were wondering if we would have dinner with them this evening. Do you want to?"

She looked up from her meal. "Is Syneda one of your great-grandmother's allies?"

He set his coffee cup down and nodded. "Yes, she's one of her biggest allies."

Instead of saying anything, Ivy stared into her glass of milk for a long moment, considering his words. She then glanced up at him. "Do you think we're ready to…"

"Perform?" he finished for her.

She nodded. "Yes, to perform."

He shrugged. "Yes, I think so. We've only been here together for a few days so there shouldn't be much performing we have to do. I wouldn't think they would expect us to be all hot and heavy already, but they wouldn't expect us to be acting stiff and detached toward each other either. We just need to act like there's a romance blooming between us."

What he said made sense. "Any idea where we'll be eating?"

"Yes, Clayton mentioned the Salamander."

Ivy nodded. She'd patronized the one in Houston before and it wasn't a jeans-and-T-shirt sort of place. "Yes, I'll go but I need to go shopping," she said, quickly finishing off the rest of her food.

"Why?"

"Because I didn't bring a dress with me."

He lifted a brow. "So?"

She glanced over at him. "And I want to wear a dress tonight."

What she didn't add was she was going to try her damnedest to make herself look pretty. She had agreed with Tessa's suggestion of a makeover when she returned to Houston but now it seemed that time was coming sooner than later.

"We passed a strip mall yesterday on our way from renting that boat. If you don't mind moving your SUV, I'll get my car out of the garage and—"

"No need to move your car. I'll drive you."

She stared at him to make sure she had heard him right. "You would take me shopping?"

He chuckled. "Not exactly. I will drive you there but I don't intend to hang around in a dress store. I learned my lesson after going shopping with Victoria once and swore never to do it again. She tried on over fifty dresses and walked out, buying just one. I'll drop you off and then check out the computer store at the mall."

Ivy released a frustrated sigh. "To be honest with you, I'd rather visit that computer store with you but I do need to get a dress." She stood and took her plate and milk glass over to the sink. "It won't take me long to change tops."

He lifted a brow. "Why do you need to change tops?"

"Because I prefer wearing one that will be easy for me to take off while I'm trying on dresses." She threw the words over her shoulders as she hurried out of the kitchen.

CHAPTER TWENTY-ONE

"I'M READY, NOLAN."

Nolan placed the television remote down to turn his attention away from ESPN. *Whoa!* He blinked. Then his gaze roamed all over the woman standing in the middle of the room. "Ivy?"

She gave him a cheeky grin. "Yes, it's me. You like the dress?"

It was more than the dress, he decided, getting to his feet. She looked good. Different. He thought she was beautiful before but even more now. What had she done to herself? She wasn't wearing her glasses but those gorgeous soft brown eyes were the same. And that scent, not too enticing, but a fresh and sweet fragrance that he thought was perfect on her.

He checked out her outfit—a beautiful blue sundress that stopped just above her knees, showing off a pair of great-looking legs in black high-heel sling-back sandals. Her bare arms showed what looked like satin-soft skin, so soft he wanted to reach out and touch it. And she wore matching jewelry. He thought the silver necklace and matching earrings and bracelet looked nice on her and complimented her outfit.

Nolan's gaze moved upward to her hair. She had it pulled together on top of her head but not in that severe-looking bun. She had gathered her hair back in a twist with curls dangling on the side to draw emphasis to what he thought was a very attractive face.

"Well?"

His gaze shifted to her eyes. "Well, what?"

She rolled her eyes. "Do you like the dress?"

He had to be honest. "I love the dress. It looks great on you. You look absolutely stunning." And he meant every word.

"Thanks. I was going to wait until I got back to Houston to do the makeover but decided tonight would be a good time to try."

Her words confused him. "Makeover? Why do you need a makeover?" he asked, shoving his hands into the pockets of his slacks. Otherwise he would be tempted to cross the room and touch her. Never would he have figured himself to be a man that could be tempted to that degree by any woman but he'd discovered around Ivy he was constantly swamped with unfamiliar emotions and reactions. "There was nothing wrong with how you looked before."

He recalled her telling him how that jackass she used to be with wanted her to change her looks to suit him. He meant what he'd just told her. There hadn't been anything wrong with how she looked before. He'd thought she had beautiful features and had looked rather cute in her eyeglasses.

"Thanks, Nolan, that was a sweet thing to say. However, once we get back to Houston and pretend to be a couple, it's important to me that I at least look like a woman you would be interested in. A woman people would believe that you could fall in love with. Otherwise, no one will take our affair seriously."

He frowned. First of all he wasn't sure there was a

woman out there he would fall in love with, regardless of what anyone thought. Second, she was a woman he *would* have shown interest in. "You don't think you're a woman I would be interested in?"

"Of course not. Think about the women you've dated recently and how they looked."

In all honesty, he didn't want to think about them. She had brought this subject up before…on that first day when they were debating the pros and cons of their plan. She honestly didn't think he would have given her a second glance. Okay, he would admit that day she'd come to his office he had immediately ruled she wasn't his type and had even told Mama Laverne so. But he would have claimed that she wasn't his type even if she had been, mainly because she was being forced on him and he hadn't liked it. But he would have to admit that even on that day in his office, he'd noticed her beauty and grace.

Deciding not to get into a discussion about the women in his past, he said, "You would have caught my interest."

Rolling her eyes, she said, "Whatever."

It shouldn't bother him that she didn't believe him, but it did. "You bought all of this while shopping today? The dress? Shoes? Perfume? Jewelry…?"

"Yes, I lucked out. If I'd had time I would have got my nails done and a pedicure at the salon next door. But I didn't want to prolong the time." She then asked, "You haven't noticed anything about my dress?"

He looked at her dress again. What he noticed was just how good she looked in it. "No, is there something I'm missing?"

"Yes. It's blue. Yesterday during dinner I asked what your favorite color was and you said blue. So I bought a blue dress. I figured if your cousins knew blue was your favorite color and I wore blue tonight, they would assume I was trying to impress you. Get it?"

Yeah, he got it. "Smart idea," he heard himself say. He then glanced at his watch. "Ready to go?"

"Yes, I'm ready. I just hope we're able to pull things off."

There was no doubt in Nolan's mind that they would. He knew there was no way Syneda and Clayton wouldn't notice that he couldn't take his eyes off Ivy tonight, and there wouldn't be any pretense about it.

"WELCOME TO THE SALAMANDER," the smiling hostess said, walking over to them when they entered the restaurant. Ivy glanced around, thinking how beautiful the place was. Even more so than the one in Houston because this one was larger and had a gorgeous view of the gulf.

"Thanks."

"Nolan Madaris?"

"Yes, I'm Nolan Madaris."

"The Madaris party is seated this way," the woman informed them. "Please follow me."

Ivy found her hand suddenly tucked into Nolan's as they followed the hostess who led them toward a section with a phenomenal view of the ocean. She had never met Nolan's cousins but was certain they were the couple watching their approach. The first thought that came to her mind was that they were a beautiful, well-dressed couple. The man was dashingly handsome and the first word that came to mind to describe the woman was *radiant*. Then she decided just the word *radiant* wouldn't do her justice. *Gorgeously radiant* would work. Thick and curly golden-bronze hair fell to her shoulders and was perfect for her light brown complexion. When they got closer to the table, the gentleman stood, and the woman's lips formed into a smile that extended to a pair of sea green eyes.

"Clayton and Syneda," Nolan greeted, giving the man a huge bear hug and then leaning down and placing a kiss on the woman's cheek. Ivy thought that up close the woman was even more beautiful.

"I'd like you to meet Ivy Chapman. A friend. And, Ivy, this is my cousin Clayton and his beautiful wife, Syneda."

Handshakes were exchanged and although Nolan had warned her that the woman was one of his great-grandmother's ace allies, Ivy felt the woman's friendliness was genuine.

"Glad you could join us," Clayton Madaris said, grinning brightly. "Are the two of you enjoying the bay?"

Ivy decided to let Nolan answer that. During the drive over, he'd told her to follow his lead. "Yes, we're enjoying the bay, although things didn't work out as we'd planned," Nolan said.

"Oh, what happened?" Syneda asked like she didn't know. Nolan had warned Ivy that she would.

"You tell them, Ivy," Nolan prompted, placing his hand over hers. A gesture she noted Syneda took in. "I get upset every time I think about it."

Ivy smiled over at Syneda and Clayton. "It seems my grandmother and Nolan's great-grandmother are playing matchmakers, although they'd both been told we aren't interested. They duped us and made sure we ended up at the cottage together this week."

Clayton shook his head in a way that had Ivy wondering if he'd truly known about it. More important that he didn't approve. "That's Mama Laverne for you. Always thinking she has to marry people off. Luckily, she was doing a lot of her missionary work out of the country when me and my two older brothers, Justin and Dex, were all still single and dating. But now she's got it in her head that she's a master matchmaker. If you ask me, she ought to stay out of people's business."

"Clayton!" Syneda admonished her husband. Another thing Nolan had warned her about was that this couple usually didn't agree on anything.

"Well, it's true," Clayton said. "She puts people together with no idea just how they will get along."

"But the two of you seem to be getting along," Syneda pointed out, frowning over at her husband before looking at Nolan and Ivy.

"Yes, but only because Nolan felt sorry for me. I was looking forward to spending a week on the beach. Since the cottage can accommodate two, he invited me to stay."

Syneda looked over at Nolan and smiled. Ivy was certain the woman noted that Nolan's hand was still covering hers. "That was so nice of you to do that, Nolan."

He smiled at Syneda before turning his megawatt smile on Ivy. "I would like to think that I'm a nice person."

Ivy gave him a huge smile. "You *are* a nice person. No doubt about it."

"Thanks," he said, lifting her hand to his lips to kiss it.

"I've enjoyed your company."

"And I've enjoyed yours as well. It's hard to believe our week is up, and we'll be returning to Houston tomorrow," he said, looking at Ivy.

"There's no reason the two of you can't continue to see each other, is there?" Syneda asked with obvious hope in her tone.

Nolan didn't respond to Syneda's question right away. Instead he kept looking at her and Ivy couldn't break eye contact with him if she'd wanted to. It was as if his gaze was holding hers captive and there was no pretense about it. She knew Nolan's response to Syneda's would further lay the groundwork for their plan to outwit Nana and Ms. Laverne.

His hesitation in responding would appear that he was giving Syneda's words some serious consideration. Without breaking eye contact with her, he finally said, "As far as I'm concerned, there's no reason. What do you think about that, Ivy?" he asked her.

She swallowed as he continued to hold her gaze, not saying anything at first, as if she was thinking hard about his question. "I think you're right."

There was no telling how long they would have sat there, staring into each other's eyes if Clayton Madaris hadn't cleared his throat. They forced their gazes from each other to look at Clayton. However, it was Syneda, who was bubbling over with smiles, who asked, "So what have the two of you been doing at the cottage?"

Ivy saw a sparkle of amusement in the woman's eyes like she'd understood the moment she and Nolan had just shared and she was privy to Ivy's secret sexual fantasy about Nolan.

Nolan told them about going swimming, her help in repainting his patio furniture, the boat he'd rented and how he'd taught her to fish. They chuckled when he told them about her aversion to baiting her hook and gutting the fish. He even told them that he was teaching her how to prepare a few meals.

"That's wonderful," Syneda said, all but clapping her hands as she continued to smile all over the place. "Nolan is a fantastic cook."

"He most certainly is," Ivy agreed. "I've probably gained five pounds already this week."

"I doubt that you have and even if you did, you look fantastic in that dress," Nolan complimented.

"Thanks," she said, giving him a huge smile. And she noticed, like everyone else at the table, that he was still holding her hand.

At that moment, a waitress came to take their dinner orders.

"I don't care if Syneda is your great-grandmother's biggest ally. I truly do like her," Ivy said, entering the cottage when Nolan opened the door and stepped aside for her to enter. "She is such a sweetheart and it's obvious Clayton adores her."

"Yes, she is a sweetheart. And yes, Clayton adores her," Nolan said, tossing the car keys on a living room table.

Nolan found himself watching Ivy, something he'd been doing all night. She was bending over to remove her sandals, and like earlier that day when he'd caught her bending down inside the refrigerator, he was enjoying the view. It was amazing how the fabric of her dress stretched across her backside like that. And it was even more amazing what a nice and curvaceous backside it was.

She turned to him, twirling her sandals in her hand. "I think tonight went well, don't you?"

"Yes." He couldn't help but agree, but he was hard-pressed to decide which parts of what he said and did were real and which were fake.

"I believe Syneda's report to your great-grandmother will be a favorable one, especially when she tells her of our decision to continue to see each other once we leave here."

He hated to tell her, but at that moment he really didn't give a royal damn about any report Syneda would be giving to Mama Laverne. He wasn't sure of the why but at some point during the night, his pretense had become genuine interest on his part and filled with all kinds of emotions.

It was obvious that Clayton and Syneda were impressed with Ivy. She was nothing like those airheads he'd been dating over the past year. Women who hadn't threatened his bachelor status. Women whose no-boundaries-sex lifestyles had done more to turn him off than to turn him on.

He liked that Ivy was impressed by his cousins ability to work together as partners. And when they'd asked her questions about cybersecurity, she had been in her element. It was quite obvious that Ivy Chapman was a highly intelligent woman. In a way he regretted that Mama Laverne thought she was the ideal woman for him. She *was* the ideal woman for some man but not for him. At that moment a knot formed in his gut at the thought of that nameless man in her life.

"So what do you think?"

Nolan blinked. He had missed her question. "Sorry? What did you ask?"

She smiled at him. "I asked if you wanted to join me in eating that dessert you're holding tight in your hand."

She chuckled. "I'm glad you suggested we got our peach cobbler as takeout. I couldn't believe the hints Clayton was throwing out, clearly letting us know that he was in a rush to get his wife back to their hotel room."

Her observation made Nolan chuckle. "Clayton and Syneda are two of the most sensuous people I know. As far as sexual chemistry and vibes are concerned, they got them hands down, and it's easy for everyone around them to feel it."

"You are right. I felt it."

He nodded, wondering if she felt theirs. Whether she knew it or not, they'd been emitting some pretty strong vibes tonight as well. He knew for a fact Clayton and Syneda had picked up on them because of the stares they'd given them. "At least Clayton gave out hints tonight. Usually they just disappear for a while."

Ivy mouth fell open in shock. "You're kidding, right?"

"Nope. I'm not kidding. The family is used to their overt sexual behavior. They complement each other and keep things exciting. The longer they are married the more adventurous they get. There's never a boring moment with those two."

"I can imagine," Ivy said, shaking her head.

"Have you ever thought about growing your operation into something larger?" he asked, following her into the kitchen. He'd found it impressive that many Fortune 500 companies had sought her out. That meant they had a lot of confidence and respect for her skills and abilities. "You have the clientele to do it. Some very impressive clients I might add."

He watched her grab plates out of the cabinets, going on tiptoe to do it, making the hem of her dress rise. He got a glimpse of her thighs and felt his body get hard. But then he would admit being aroused by her a lot tonight. He slid into a chair at the table, deciding it would be best if he were sitting down when she turned around.

"Yes, I've thought about it," she said, placing plates and forks on the table. "I've even gone so far as to check out office space in various parts of town. But..."

He lifted a brow. "But what?"

She began gnawing on her bottom lip and he tried ignoring the way his pulse flickered watching her do so. "I enjoy being a businesswoman, but I'm doing so at the level that I'm comfortable with as a small business owner. Anything larger would become too overwhelming to me. Right now all I have to concentrate on is the work I do for my clients. If I were to expand, then I would have to think about employees, PR, marketing, rental space and all kinds of stuff."

In a way he understood what she was saying. He employed close to a hundred people and loved taking on huge jobs. And the more challenging the better, which was why he was looking forward to the work he'd be doing for Lee and DeAngelo in Paris. He liked the size of his operations and had good people working for him. His goal was to grow his business even more. He hadn't mentioned it to anyone but Lee, Reese, Corbin and his granduncle Jake, but he and Nicholas had discussed the possibility of combining their companies and becoming partners. Such a move would automatically advance him into a global market.

"You have to do what makes you comfortable," he said, fully understanding her position. "Not everyone wants to be a Fortune 500 company. As long as you're making money and not losing it is what counts." And from his research, he saw her small company was making money. Lots of it. One thing in her favor was that she didn't have the huge overhead since she worked out of her home. And she had only a personal assistant who handled the paperwork she did have.

"Thanks," she said, giving him a radiant smile. "What would you like to drink?"

They'd had wine at dinner but he figured another glass wouldn't hurt. They were in for the night so they didn't have to worry about overindulging. "Sharing another glass of wine would be nice, especially since it's our last night together."

She nodded. "Okay, two glasses of wine coming up."

Nolan watched her walk over to the refrigerator, loving the way her body moved in that dress. He liked the way she looked in her bare feet as well, with those gorgeous legs. And he thought she smelled good. Her scent was invigorating him all over.

Heat flowed through Nolan and he contemplated the moment. His hands itched to touch her, his mouth was burning to taste her. Suddenly, not able to control his desires, he stood and moved toward her, coming to a stop directly behind her. When she closed the refrigerator and turned around he was right there.

"Oops, sorry," she said, nearly bumping into him. "Did you need something out of the refrigerator?"

"No, I don't need anything out of the refrigerator," he said in a voice that was filled with a kind of heat he hadn't experienced in a long time or ever.

He took the wine bottle from her hand and placed it on the counter and then turned back to her. "But I desperately need this, Ivy."

And then he lowered his mouth to hers.

CHAPTER TWENTY-TWO

IVY FELT AS if she was drowning in ecstasy. As profound as it could get. She had been kissed by others and was of the mind that one kiss was the same as another. Nothing unforgettable and nothing to savor. And definitely nothing to constitute any lasting effects. Nolan was knocking all those assumptions down in a way that had her breathless.

She definitely hadn't counted on the heated rush of desire that overtook her senses with every flick of his tongue or her reaction to his entire body when he pressed against her to deepen the kiss and intensify it even more. And she definitely hadn't counted on any kiss keeping her up at night while she relived every tongue-thrusting, teeth-nipping-the-lips moment.

Nolan had once said the one thing he enjoyed doing just short of making love was kissing, and that was becoming quite obvious. It was also quite obvious that she was enjoying going along for the ride.

How could he tap into a part of her she had been satisfied to ignore? A part she had denied wanting or needing? But not only had he tapped into it, he'd place an all-out assault on every erogenous zone on her body just from his heat. Ivy definitely hadn't counted on undergoing a total sexual meltdown in the most intense way.

Ivy was no dummy. She was well aware kisses of

this magnitude and sexual hunger were supposed to lead somewhere. Usually to the nearest bedroom. And at the moment, with her common sense being ripped to shreds, she had no problem being taken there. She needed to experience an end to the sexual hunger invading her body. But then she knew sleeping together was not the answer. It would only complicate things. But she was having a hard time convincing her mind and body of that now.

Suddenly Nolan broke off the kiss and the eyes staring deep into hers were filled with intense heat of the most erotic kind. So much so that Ivy felt a tingling sensation between her legs. Never had she felt such intense desire before. Not even with Damien. Definitely not with Damien.

"I want you."

Nolan had whispered the words low in his throat but she heard them. She felt them. They had oozed all over her skin like rich, warm honey to be licked. Why did she think of that now? As if he had read her mind, he leaned in and began tracing the tip of his tongue across the side of her neck.

She couldn't say anything by way of a response. At the moment she couldn't even think. It was as if her body had a mind of its own, and instead of fighting for control, it wanted to succumb to Nolan's wishes. His every desire, because his desires were becoming hers. He covered her mouth with his again as if he was obsessed with kissing her. And she felt his hands roam over her, touching her in intimate ways that seemed to fuel his fire as well as her own.

Only with Nolan was she experiencing how it felt to get caught up in the depth of a male's yearnings and to be kissed by him in a way that made her feel craved, wanted and longed for in the most salacious way. No man had ever acted like he'd wanted her so much that he would kiss her senseless. Deep down she wanted to be made love to by a man like Nolan to erase her experience with a man who'd thought he was all that but obviously hadn't been.

However all the kisses she'd shared with Nolan were showing her he was definitely all of that and then some. When it came to delivering sexual satisfaction, it was quite obvious no two men were created equal. As far as she was concerned, Nolan Madaris was in a class by himself. He was sexually male on an excruciating level.

And this would be the last night they would spend together like this.

Ivy knew when she returned to Houston and got back to work she would efficiently put her head back on right. They would see each other on occasion for show, but in private there wouldn't be any more kisses. And especially with the heat and greed this one was generating.

He broke off the kiss again and stared down at her while licking his lips, as if to let her know he hadn't finished with her mouth yet. She returned his stare, captivated by his gaze. She could feel her heart beat erratically in her chest and felt a deep ache between her legs.

And she felt the exact moment he lowered his hands and was inching up her dress. It was then she knew she needed to remind him of something. No matter how tempted she was…and Lord knew she was tempted… she refused to become one of his one-night stands, or in this case, his last-night stand.

Ivy reached down and caught hold of Nolan's hand

to stop him from lifting her dress any higher. "Remember our agreement, Nolan. I won't have sex with you."

His dark gaze seemed to burn deep into her. "Define having sex."

She frowned and then narrowed her eyes. "I think you know what it means, Nolan."

He leaned down and licked the side of her face with his tongue before moving to the underside of her ear. "Is this having sex?"

She drew in a sharp breath when he asked the words in a husky voice, close to her ear.

"Part of it."

"And what do you call this part?" he asked in a raspy voice against her throat.

She had to think hard to give him that answer. "Foreplay?"

"You don't sound sure," he said, using the tip of his tongue to lick around her lips from corner to corner.

No, she wasn't sure because she'd never engaged in it. Not really. Damien never got her tuned up, so to speak. He always thought when he was ready that she should be, too. "It's foreplay," she said, with a bit more forcefulness, trying to sound as if she was truly certain about what she was saying.

"What's the difference between foreplay and having sex, Ivy?"

When he began licking around her throat again, she threw her head back, loving the way his heated tongue felt moving along her neck, drawing circles in some areas. "Are you trying to confuse me?" she asked, barely able to get the words out.

"No, I just need clarification."

He smelled good. So good. His scent was overwhelming her senses. And what did he mean he needed clarification? He of all men should know the difference. "Why?"

"To make sure we're on the same page."

On the same page? She was about to ask what he meant when he grabbed hold of her hair, released the band holding the curls on top of her head and grabbed hold of a section of her hair to bring her face closer to his. As soon as his lips touched hers, he greedily captured her mouth and began feasting on it again.

She felt weak in the knees and almost slid to the floor but his hand at her waist held her up. He broke off the kiss and stared down at her. She could see lusty greed in his gaze and it sent her desire skyrocketing through her veins. "Clarify the difference," he said, his breath hot against her ear as he began nibbling on her earlobe.

A throbbing need rushed through her when she felt the hardness of him press against her at the juncture of her thighs. They were standing so close, it seemed her hips flowed into his. Even with clothes on their bodies, they seemed to be intimately and perfectly aligned.

"Tell me, Ivy," he said in a voice so hot it nearly incinerated her. "Tell me the difference. I want you to tell me."

What man wanted things clarified at a time like this? Most would rush through and practically bulldoze you over to get what they wanted. They certainly wouldn't waste time to make sure he and the woman were on the same page. But she was discovering that Nolan wasn't like most men. His focus was intense. Whether it was painting, fishing or cooking.

Knowing how his mind worked, she answered the

best she could. "Sex is intercourse. Penetration. All else is foreplay."

If the smile that suddenly shaped the fullness of his lips was anything to go by, they evidently were on the same page. "Remember your definition, Ivy." He then released her and in a quick movement he ripped off his shirt.

The sound seemed to slash through the air. "What are you doing?" she asked, suddenly feeling light-headed from the manly scent of him. From seeing him standing there, bare chested. Her heart skipped a beat and she fought the low moan that tried slipping past her lips.

"No intercourse and no penetration. But I want a hell of a lot of foreplay with you, Ivy. Are you ready for that?"

For a minute Ivy couldn't reply; she was trying to wrap her head around what he was saying. A part of her wanted to say no, she wasn't ready. But then another part, the part that enjoyed him touching her and all the kisses they'd shared for the past week—even when she didn't want to enjoy them—couldn't help but be curious as to what his brand of foreplay entailed. And what would it hurt for her to find out? At least she would have the knowledge and she would rather share that experience with Nolan than with anyone else.

Over the past days she had got to know him. He was kind, considerate and nice. Definitely nice. And she had enjoyed the time she'd spent with him. He hadn't crowded her space and had made this week fun for her. Even now he wasn't forcing her to do anything she didn't want to do. Tempting her, yes. Forcing her, no.

Making up her mind about how she intended to roll, she took a step closer to him, leaned up on tiptoe and placed the palms of her hands against his bare chest. Loving the feel of the warm flesh beneath her fingers, she said, "Yes, Nolan. I'm ready."

AT THAT MOMENT Nolan was convinced his testosterone levels not only surged through the roof but spiked to the moon. He hadn't wanted to want her so much. But he did. He desired her and every day that yearning had increased the more he'd been around her. And whether she realized it or not, they'd been emitting all kinds of I-want-you vibes all night. There was no doubt in his mind that Syneda and Clayton had picked up on them.

It was nothing she'd done intentionally or unintentionally. He was discovering what set her apart was Ivy being Ivy. He doubted there was a pretentious bone in her body…just a lot of doubting ones. He knew what she could do to a man…to him…with very little effort. Just being herself. Even now the feel of her hands on his chest had his stomach muscles clenching.

In truth, he wanted more than foreplay with her. He wanted to rock her world the way he knew she could rock his. But he would settle for sharing something with her that she would remember for a long time. He pushed from his mind why that was important to him.

He stared down at her. Even standing on tiptoe, she was not tall enough to be eye to eye with him. But that was fine. He loved looking down at such a beautiful face. He missed her eyeglasses but decided whether she wore glasses or not wasn't important. What he loved most were her eyes and how they looked at him with trust—he didn't intend to let her down. On their last night together, he wanted to give them what they both wanted.

He glanced around. *Things could proceed here or elsewhere.* Definitely not in either of the bedrooms. Way too much temptation for intercourse when they'd decided to limit things. Making a decision, he suddenly swept her off her feet and into his arms.

She sucked in a sharp breath. "Where are we going?"

"The living room," he said, taking quick steps to that destination.

Nolan sat down on the sofa and eased Ivy into position on his lap. Then he leaned in and slanted his mouth across hers, needing her taste again. Jets of sensation shot through his body and took over his mind when he intensified the kiss while roaming his hands up and down her thighs. He loved touching her.

But first it was important to him that she understood something. He broke off the kiss and when she stared up at him with a disappointed pout on her moist lips, he knew he had her attention. "What we are about to share, Ivy, is between you and me and is not part of any premade plan. Do you understand what I'm saying?"

She stared at him for a minute before nodding. He wanted to make sure she knew what they were about to share was their own doing, their own decision to fulfill their own needs and desires. Those desires hadn't been orchestrated by her grandmother or his great-grandmother, but were of Ivy's and his doing.

Satisfied that she fully understood, he kissed her again. He was more than ready to give her a night to remember.

CHAPTER TWENTY-THREE

IVY HADN'T KNOWN that kissing a man could be just as intoxicating as overindulging in alcohol. Nolan was mating with her mouth in a way some would consider outrageously indecent. He was sucking on it one minute and licking it all over the next. His tongue was branding her mouth in ways she didn't know was possible until now. He was definitely taking the term *locked lips* to a whole other level.

And she was trying to keep up as need intensified within her—a need he was stroking masterfully. When he suddenly released her mouth, she dropped her head against his bare chest and pulled in a deep breath. "I want to taste you all over, Ivy," he said hotly against the underside of her ear. His words caused a moan to sound in her throat.

He stood with her in his arms, placing her on her feet and before she could draw in a full breath, he pulled her sundress over her head leaving her standing before him in her bra and panties. At that moment she was glad she'd purchased the matching bra and pantie set. But why had he undressed her when they weren't going all the way?

As if he read her thoughts he leaned close, so close the hair on his chest touched the bare parts of hers, and he whispered, "I don't want any clothes to hinder me when I lick you all over."

His words caused every nerve ending in her body to vibrate in a way that rocked her to the core. He intended to lick her all over? And as if to answer that question he used the tip of his tongue to lick the side of her face. And then that same tongue traveled over her collarbone to lap her there. Throwing her head back to give him better access, she moaned deep in her throat, loving the feel of his tongue gliding over her skin.

She felt weak in the knees and grabbed hold of him at the waist as if he were her lifeline. At the moment he was definitely her pleasure-line. His ability to arouse her to such a degree in some ways mystified her because no man had ever done so before. Damien had complained because they'd dated months before she would agree to sleep with him. And when she thought of what they did, she realized he hadn't really tried to arouse her like this. When he was through, regardless of whether he gave her pleasure or not, he fell asleep. She had a feeling that Nolan was more than willing and able to withhold his until the woman he was with got hers. Even now, she wondered what did he get out of licking her all over? What was in it for him? Did he think that driving her to the edge would have her begging for him to go further? For them to engage in intercourse? She hoped that wasn't the case because she had no intention about changing her mind about that.

"Your brow is bunching," he said, using his fingertips to gently caress above her eyes. "You're thinking too much, Ivy."

She loved the feel of his hands on her skin. "Am I?"

"Yes, and I'm about to make sure you're not thinking at all."

SHE MIGHT NOT know it but she was ready for him, Nolan thought. Her scent had begun overtaking his nostrils in the most delectable way. She wanted him just as much as he wanted her.

Reaching around her back, he unlocked her bra, and when it dropped to the floor between them he glanced at her exposed breasts. Beautiful. Full. Plump. Tight. And the darkened nipples resembled hardened pebbles ready for his mouth. Ready to be sucked.

Holding her by the waist, he bent down and eased a nipple into his mouth and began sucking in earnest. The little purr that sounded from her throat made him deepen the suction. He knew she liked it when her hand gripped the back of his head to hold him there to her breast. A needless gesture on her part since he didn't plan on going anywhere. And when he did, it would be to latch onto its twin. But for now he wanted to concentrate on this one, the first one to become victim to his greedy mouth.

When he'd got his fill of nipple number one, he moved to nipple number two, ready to bestow a similar brand of Nolan Madaris torment. He was definitely a breast man and he was enjoying loving on hers. She didn't know it but those purring sounds she was making stirred his libido.

He was very much aware that in the end she would get her pleasure and would assume he wouldn't get his. That was not true. For now his pleasure would be in knowing he had satisfied her. They had agreed to continue to see each other as part of their plan. In the meantime, he wanted to give her time to realize that regardless of their plan to outsmart the two people determined to dominate their lives, she would have to revisit her decision that they not make love. Eventually they would. And when that time came, it would be her decision.

The sexual chemistry they'd intentionally stirred between them was as real as it could get. He looked into her eyes and he wanted her. He touched her and he wanted her. He kissed her and he wanted her. And he wanted it to be the same for her. He wanted her to want him as much as he wanted her. As per their plan they would still break up in the end and go their separate ways, but not before satisfying their sexual hungers to the fullest.

"Nolan…"

He heard her call his name and lifted his mouth from her breast, leaving both nipples wet and swollen. He looked into her eyes and saw how they'd darkened. He saw the need in them. Need that he knew she was beginning to feel. Now to taste another part of her.

Lowering down on his haunches, he licked around her navel before easing her panties down her legs. He drew in sharply, inhaling her luscious scent through his nostrils. He doubted she had any idea how much he wanted to taste her here. And he wanted his tongue to go deep.

Taking her hand he led her back to the sofa. Stretching out on the sofa, he said, "I want you to straddle me." He knew she had no idea what position he intended to put her in, but she would find soon out.

"You're still wearing your pants," she said, looking even more confused.

"I know. This isn't about me. I want to pleasure you, Ivy."

"But what about you?"

"Drowning you in pleasure will give me pleasure as well."

Nolan knew Ivy could feel how aroused he was. There was no way she hadn't noticed the huge erection poking hard against the zipper of his slacks.

"Come here, Ivy," he said in a soft tone, tugging on her hand.

She did and, following his instructions, she straddled his body. She stared down at him when he took a firm grip of her hips. There was something about the way she was looking at him that had desire throbbing through his veins and was nearly pushing him over the edge of madness. But he intended to hang on to his sanity because the woman whose gaze was holding his hostage deserved it.

There was something about Ivy that had got to him, had managed to get under his skin although he never wanted it to happen and had vowed that it wouldn't. She was all wrong for him. She was not his choice. But then no woman was. He would know that woman when he saw her, when he met her. It was his decision to make. His and his alone.

At that moment his great-grandmother's words about his mistake with Andrea came back to haunt him. He pushed thoughts of his past from his mind and went back to concentrating on the present. He didn't want to ponder why it meant so much to him to pleasure Ivy. Why he had to get under her skin like she'd got under his. He wanted her to feel the same rush of desire that was clawing at his insides, even after tomorrow. He wanted to give her something to remember him by. And remember him she would; he intended to make sure of it.

"First, lean down and give me a kiss, baby."

He saw the flash of surprise in her eyes. *Baby?* Why had he called her that? A slip he hadn't meant to make and could only blame it on the moment.

She didn't say anything but leaned down, giving him her mouth. He took it in his and when she released a deep moan, he slid his tongue inside and some serious mating began. She always participated and her doing so sent frissons of intense fire up his spine. Like what was happening to him now.

He released her mouth, drew in a much-needed breath and watched her lick her lips. "Scoot forward."

When she looked at him as if not understanding his meaning, he said, "Scoot up and over my mouth with your vee, Ivy."

When she hesitated he wondered if she'd ever had oral sex performed on her before. If not this would definitely be an experience he couldn't wait to share with her. Using his hands, he urged her hips forward, gliding her body upward. He kissed parts of her, namely her stomach as it passed over his mouth. "Right here is good," he said, planting her knees beside his face. Looking up, he saw what he wanted. "Beautiful," he breathed in a guttural tone, staring at the luscious sight of her right above his face.

He removed his hands from her hips and used his fingers to touch her, tracing a slow trail over her feminine mound and feeling himself getting harder as he did so. He heard her purr and the sound stirred raw carnal energy within him. When he couldn't handle the temptation any longer, he inserted fingers inside her and began stroking her.

"Nolan..."

"Umm."

"I—I never…"

"You never what, Ivy?"

"Did this before."

The words seemed forced from her lips. That made him dislike her ex even more. Did the bastard not try different ways to pleasure her?

"That's okay. You're doing it now." And she was doing it with him and that made it even more special. Stroking her clit was making her wetter, making her heated scent that much more pronounced.

"I can't believe you're doing this," she said in a choppy voice, as if it was hard to get her words out.

He had news for her. She hadn't seen or felt anything yet. This was an appetizer. It was time for the dessert. He slowly removed his fingers from inside her and licked them for a sample of her taste. He growled in response to her delicious flavor.

Not willing to wait any longer, he returned his hands to her hips and spread her thighs. "Ease down to my mouth, Ivy," he said, licking his lips in anticipation. He had his tongue ready and he felt the strength in its need. When her feminine mound was mere inches from touching his tongue, he couldn't wait. He pressed her hips and brought her closer to his mouth and on contact, his tongue pierced inside her.

And then it was on.

"NOLAN!" IVY SCREAMED as she tightly gripped the arm of the sofa. What was he doing to her? How could he make her feel this way? It was as if a million sensations had broken loose right there, where his mouth was devouring her.

His tongue was stroking her sensitive flesh into a

frenzy that she was feeling in every part of her body. He had taken over her clit like he was declaring ownership, making her fully aware she was capable of feeling things she never thought she could. And was it her imagination or was his tongue going deeper inside her with her every moan?

When the sensation bombarding her intensified, she begged, "No more. I can't take any more." Then in the same breath she pleaded, "More. More. Oh, yes, more."

He gave her the more she wanted and he gave it to her in a way that had her bucking against his mouth like that's what she was supposed to do and she was unable to help herself. Breathing hard, she closed her eyes as arousal coiled deep in her core.

Suddenly, sensations of gigantic proportions ripped through her, in every part of her body as an orgasm slammed through her, making her scream at the top of her lungs, bucking farther onto his mouth. That seemed to be what he wanted and his grip tightened on her hips, forcing her thighs even farther apart.

"Nolan!"

Her breath caught on a surge of ecstatic pleasure so intense it seemed her body shattered into a million pieces. Her hands tightened on the arm of the sofa and she held on as if it was her life support. Quivers assaulted her body with a force that had her screaming again.

The tremors began dissipating and she became conscious that he was sliding her down his body. Shifting positions, he had her facing him. Her thigh was thrown on the material of his slacks, her hand on his stomach and her nose buried in the hair on his chest. He smelled good and she was getting used to indulging in the scent of him.

He touched her chin and lifted her face to look into her eyes and she wondered what he was thinking. She was about to ask when he lowered his head to kiss her again. When he finally released her mouth, he tightened his hold on her, cuddled her into his body and held her. Neither of them said anything. It was as if they were incapable of speech at the moment. She lay in his arms, satisfied to be in his embrace and trying to get her breathing under control.

Ivy shifted her leg and the hard erection she felt against his zipper was a stark reminder he had pleasured her but hadn't sought pleasure for himself. She didn't know of too many men with that kind of control. Nor that kind of consideration. She thought about that for a minute before lifting her gaze to find him staring at her.

She swallowed and said, "I—I could..."

As if he knew what she was trying to say, what offer she was about to make, he placed a finger to her lips and said, "I wanted to pleasure you, Ivy. Don't be concerned about me."

And then as if to make sure there would be no further discussion about what he'd said, he lowered his head and slanted his mouth over hers.

NOLAN SIPPED A cup of coffee as he stood at the kitchen windows and watched the sunrise. It would be another beautiful day on Tiki Island, and at some point today, he would be leaving. So would Ivy.

Drawing in a deep breath, he recalled everything that happened last night. In vivid detail. He remembered kissing her. Tasting her. And wanting to keep on kissing and tasting her. He recalled the way his heart kept pounding every time he'd tasted her, and how desire clawed at him the entire time.

Even after they'd parted last night, when he'd gone to his bed and she'd gone to hers, he hadn't been able to sleep. Instead memories had kept him awake. Those same memories had sent spikes of heat bursting inside his gut through most of the night. Desire had somehow become synonymous with Ivy and he didn't want to think what that could mean.

A part of him knew she'd wanted to pleasure him as well, but he'd stopped her from doing so. He had wanted her to so much and would not have been able to stop himself from being pushed over the edge with the intent of taking her with him. Had that happened, there was no way they wouldn't have fallen over the edge and had intercourse. He'd meant what he'd told her a few nights ago. He would not take advantage of the situation that her grandmother and Mama Laverne had placed them in.

So here he was, the morning after, and still nursing a hard-on and a desire for her that went beyond anything he'd ever had to deal with. And knowing her taste wasn't making things easier. It was as if the very essence of her was now branded on his tongue. He hadn't meant for that to happen and a part of him was glad they were going their separate ways. He needed the distance to regroup. He had enjoyed Ivy's company but he needed to pull himself together before they began "seeing" each other again. He caught the scent of her perfume in the air and knew she was headed his way.

"Good morning, Nolan."

He turned and his greeting died on his lips when he saw her. She was standing there looking just like she had that first day when she'd walked through the kitchen door from the bay. Her curly hair was around her shoulders, her glasses were back on her face and she was wearing cutoff jeans and a top. He also saw the packed luggage at her feet.

"Good morning, Ivy," he forced himself to say. "Leaving already?"

"Yes, I thought I'd get an early start."

He nodded. "At least let me fix you breakfast before you go."

"No, thanks," she said quickly. "I'll stop and grab something. Thanks for the offer, though."

"You're welcome. At least let me pour you a cup of coffee."

"Thanks."

He poured the coffee and was aware of the moment she came to stand beside him. When he handed her the cup he couldn't help but stare into her face. A face he now thought of as the most beautiful he'd ever seen. "I enjoyed your company this week, Ivy," he said, really meaning it. He hadn't expected to so much. Had honestly thought she would be a nuisance but she ended up being a good companion. Someone he enjoyed talking to, playing games with, sharing meals with and doing outside activities with.

She looked at him over the rim of her coffee cup and a smile touched her lips. That smile made his stomach clench. She lowered the cup and said, "And I enjoyed yours."

Their gazes held and he could feel those vibes she had doubted they had.

"I better go now," she said.

"I'll walk you out."

"Thanks, but I prefer that you didn't. Too many crazy ideas going through my head right now."

He understood because a lot of crazy ideas were going through his head as well. "I'm going to be busy for a while once I get back to the office. I'll call you but not right away."

She nodded. "No problem because I'll be busy as well."

He took a step closer to her, fighting the temptation to reach out and touch her. To kiss her. "But make no mistake about it, Ivy. I will see you again. I am committed to following through on our plan." There, he'd said it. He'd connected things back to "their plan." Yet he knew what happened last night, what he'd done to her, and what they'd shared, had not been a part of their plan. It was about what they'd wanted, desired and needed.

"Yes, sticking with our plan is important." She placed her coffee cup on the counter. "Thanks for the coffee. Thanks for everything, Nolan. And I mean *everything*."

She swiftly crossed the room to her luggage and, without looking back, rolled it behind her as she quickly left the cottage.

PART TWO

"There's nowhere you can be that isn't where you're meant to be…"

—John Lennon

CHAPTER TWENTY-FOUR

Two weeks later

NOLAN STOOD AT his office window and looked out at Laverne Park. Last week the landscapers had been busy planting a number of flowers, and now it seemed they had multiplied and blossoms were everywhere. They were beautiful but nothing, he decided, was as beautiful as Ivy.

Shoving his hands into his pockets, he couldn't help remembering the week he spent with her. It had been two weeks since they'd returned to Houston and he should have given her a call by now. He hadn't been that busy that he couldn't. Although there had been a few things on this desk that required his attention, his office staff had handled things without him and had done an excellent job.

So why hadn't he called her?

Mama Laverne certainly wanted to know and had contacted him several times asking him why he hadn't invited Ivy to dinner. He told her he'd been busy. He figured she thought he was avoiding Ivy due to feelings he had developed for her during their week together on Tiki Island. In a way that was a good thing. When he began seeing Ivy again and turned up the heat in their romance, his great-grandmother would assume he'd come to his senses. That was a great strategy to strengthen Ivy's and his plan. There was just one problem. He was missing Ivy. Frustrated, he rubbed a hand down his face. It had been a damn long time since any woman had hijacked his mind to the point where he thought of her constantly. And if that wasn't bad enough, there were times he could swear the taste of her was still on his tongue. How crazy was that?

It hadn't helped matters when last week he had received a bill from his aunt Sarah for three months' worth of flowers he hadn't sent to Ivy. But he'd paid it and not as grudgingly as he should have. All he could do was recall that day she walked into his office carrying that huge vase of flowers. That was the day they had officially met. A day he couldn't seem to forget.

Clearly something was wrong with him. The one woman he shouldn't be thinking about this way, he was. And it was because of all those memories that wouldn't go away. Memories that had overtaken his senses.

His cell phone rang and he recognized the ringtone as that of Corbin. It was late afternoon and his brother was probably calling to see if he planned on cooking to invite himself to dinner. Hanging out with Corbin might not be a bad idea. Then he wouldn't have to worry about thinking about Ivy…at least not as much.

He clicked on his phone and, dispensing with a greeting, he said, "Yes, Corbin, I am cooking this evening."

"That's not why I'm calling. You need to get over to Houston General."

He heard the distress in his brother's voice. "Why? Mom? Dad? Mama Laverne? What's wrong—"

"It's Reese. Kenna went into labor."

Nolan frowned. "But she's not due for another couple of months."

"I know and that's what's freaking Reese out. I've never seen him like this before, man. He's driving everyone, especially the doctors, crazy. He thinks they aren't telling him everything and not doing enough."

Nolan could just imagine Reese behaving that way if for one minute he thought Kenna's or his unborn child's lives were in danger. "I'm on my way."

DAMIEN FARGO PACED his office, angrier than he'd been in a long time and all because of Ivy Chapman. It was obvious she had blocked his phone calls. When he couldn't reach her through her personal number, he had tried her business line and he'd been blocked from both. He had called to apologize and that should have been enough. She was trying his patience. After bragging about Ivy's expertise as a hacker, he had promised his boss, Albert Whitfield, he would get her to do the job Whitfield needed done. Now Whitfield was demanding he deliver.

Another thing he'd found out was that she had moved and he'd been unable to obtain a forwarding address. He had sent an arrangement of flowers to her, hoping that would smooth her ruffled feathers, but he'd got word from the florist he'd used that she no longer lived at that residence and had moved over a year ago.

If she wanted to be difficult, then he would show her just how tough he could be in return. Failing Whitfield was not an option. Damien knew what had happened last year to Dan Corley when he had failed Whitfield. Hacking into the government's computer system was vital to what Whitfield needed done and that meant he would go see Ivy himself. Whether she liked it or not, she would do what he wanted her to do. He would not give her a choice.

NOLAN STUDIED REESE. Corbin was right. Reese was a basket case. Right now he was standing in a corner of the waiting room and talking to their cousin Dex, who was trying to calm Reese down. In a way Nolan found that amusing when he remembered how Dex himself had carried on when his wife, Caitlin, had gone into labor.

"Here," Corbin said, handing him a cup of coffee. "Let the caffeine kick in. I don't want you too tired to cook later."

Nolan couldn't help but chuckle. "Thanks. I knew you were good for something."

"So when are you going to pick up with Ivy Chapman?"

Nolan knew Corbin was just trying to take his mind off Kenna and the baby. They were still waiting for an update from the doctor. "I've been busy and so has she. Besides, if we move things too quickly, Mama Laverne will get suspicious. It has to seem natural."

"I heard it seemed pretty natural between you two on the island."

Corbin always got wind of whatever gossip was going around when he had dinner with different family members. "In fact, I heard the two of you were locked in some hot and heavy kiss one day, and that you couldn't keep your hands off her that night the two of you had dinner with Clayton and Syneda."

Nolan took another sip of his coffee. "Is that what you heard?"

"Yes. I also heard the two of you locked lips at a restaurant one night as well."

He wished he could deny what Corbin had heard but couldn't. "Yes, Ivy and I are attracted to each other."

There was no reason to lie about it. "Maybe too attracted."

Corbin eyed him warily. "I hope it doesn't mean what it sounds like it means."

"Which is?"

"That Mama Laverne is winning and that you and Miss Chapman are falling right into her trap."

Nolan was about to assure his brother that wasn't the case when the set of double doors opened and two doctors walked out. The expressions on their faces were so serious that Nolan wondered what news they had for Reese.

IVY GLANCED AROUND SISTERS, the popular restaurant Tessa had dragged her away from work to go to, thinking the place was crowded. It was Friday night, which meant live entertainment and dancing. She couldn't help but think of the intimate meals she and Nolan had shared on Tiki Island. Or the fact that he still hadn't called.

Ivy always came to Sisters for the good food and a chance to spend time with Tessa. The two of them had such busy schedules. As one of Houston's most in-demand property managers, Tessa was worked almost as much as Ivy, so she enjoyed when the two of them got together for girl talk. Her best friend hadn't seriously dated anyone since Harold who'd turned out to be just as much of a toad as Damien. That had been years ago when Tessa had returned to Houston from college.

It had been the last time Tessa had given any man the time of day...at least seriously. Tessa, who Ivy thought had the looks and sophistication to get any man she wanted, dated on occasion but didn't tolerate egotistical men. Men who she said didn't know basic courtesy when dealing with women. Ivy knew that was the reason Tessa found Nolan so intriguing because in Tessa's book, he had gone above and beyond what a normal man would do in a similar sexual situation. A man who would pleasure a woman without seeking pleasure for himself had more than impressed Tessa.

"So, did you like him?" Tessa broke into her thoughts and asked after the waitress took their order.

Ivy didn't pretend to not know who she was asking about. "Yes, Nolan was nice. I liked him."

Tessa grinned. "Go ahead and admit that you didn't think that you would."

To be honest, Ivy hadn't wanted to like Nolan. It would have made rebelling against Nana that much easier if she hadn't. "I admit it. Are you happy?"

"Are you? Seems like you've been wearing a sad face since returning from Tiki Island. Are you disappointed that he hasn't called you?" Ivy had filled Tessa in on her and Nolan's week on the island together.

In a way she was, although he had explained he would be busy for a while. In truth she'd been busy as well. But not too busy to think about him and that's what bothered her. She should not be thinking of Nolan the way she had. "Sort of," she answered.

She had to be truthful with Tessa because that's the only way they rolled. Honesty was important between them. If Tessa ever asked her something that she thought wasn't her business or she hadn't wanted to talk about she wouldn't hesitate to tell her and vice versa. But the one thing she liked about having a best friend, especially one like Tessa, was that she had a confidante, someone she could share her secrets with and know they wouldn't go any further.

"You could have picked up the phone and called him, you know. Had a man done to me what he did to you, I would not have hesitated."

Ivy smiled over the rim of her wineglass. "You would be calling and hoping for a repeat performance."

"Damn right, and the next time I would be showing him what I could do."

Problem was, Ivy thought, she didn't know what she could do and that's what had been plaguing her mind since returning to Houston. Although she'd offered to return the favor to Nolan, she would not have known where to begin. She thought it was pitiful that, at twenty-six, thanks to Nolan she'd finally got her first oral sex experience. She'd heard about how it could be—namely from Tessa—but hadn't thought anything could be that great. Nolan had proved her wrong. Even now, when she remembered what he'd done, how he'd planted that part of her body in his face and all the things that followed, she couldn't help but blush. And she couldn't stop the tingling sensation between her legs.

What if her lack of knowledge in the oral sex department had been a total turnoff for Nolan, to the point where he was ready to end the plan? Maybe she shouldn't constantly dwell on such a thing but she couldn't help it. She would think if their time together on Tiki Island meant as much to him as it did to her, he would not have gone two weeks without contacting her, no matter how busy he was.

"Well, I haven't called him and I won't," Ivy finally said before taking another sip of her wine. "He knows the plan and what we need to do to make it work. The ball is in his court and whenever he gets ready to play it, I'll be ready as well. Nana has stopped asking questions for now and that's a good thing."

"Lordy, don't look now but the owner's husband is here tonight. Be still my heart. Please take a look at him. No man should be that fine."

Unlike the other women in the restaurant who openly stared, Ivy tried to make it not so obvious she was doing so. She'd seen the owner's husband before and thought he was definitely a good-looking man. She'd heard he was half Black and half Cherokee, which was why he wore his hair flowing down his back and around his shoulders. And the man was built for his age. She'd heard…namely from Tessa…that he was a military man, which was why he walked with such sexy precision and stature. The man was definitely good-looking, but she thought Nolan was good-looking as well.

Ivy turned her attention back to Tessa. "Need I remind you he's married?"

"I know. I also understand he's close to fifteen years older than us, the father of four and that he loves his wife to distraction. Lucky woman. I guess that means there's hope for the rest of us."

"Maybe," Ivy said, not really convinced.

"Twins. Can you believe it?"

Nolan glanced over at Corbin. No, he couldn't believe it, and from Reese's expression when the doctors had delivered the news, neither could he. How could a woman carry twins and the doctors not know it? From what the doctors explained to Reese, none of Kenna's ultrasounds had picked up a second baby because one had been hiding behind the other. The movement of the second baby had been done in such a way to bring on premature labor. The doctor felt certain they would have eventually discovered a second baby before delivery. They wanted Reese to suit up if he wanted to be a part of the delivery.

When Reese had emerged from behind the double doors an hour or so later all smiles, everyone had known all was good. Reese had been proud to announce that he had a son and a daughter. His son was the oldest and his daughter had been hiding behind her brother. Kenna and the babies were fine; however, since they were born premature, the preemies would be kept in the neonatal intensive care unit for a while. Reese was now much calmer and believed his family would be getting the best of care.

"I'm happy for Reese and Kenna," Nolan said, smiling. They had called Lee in Paris to tell him and Carly the good news.

"Well, I'm glad we're finally getting something to eat. I'm starving," Corbin said as walked toward the entrance of Sisters.

Coming here had been Corbin's idea after Nolan had told his brother that he was too happy and energized to think about cooking. He'd wanted to go somewhere and celebrate. "You're always starving. I hope the woman Mama Laverne picks out for you to marry knows how to cook."

Corbin frowned over at him. "Don't play like that, Nolan."

Nolan chuckled. Mama Laverne had arrived at the hospital holding firmly on to Jake's arm. She'd looked around at all the Madarises gathered in the waiting room and nodded as if she approved of the show of family who were there to give Reese their support and to welcome two new Madarises. Of course she said she'd tried telling Reese and Kenna they were having more than one baby, but they refused to believe her, saying the doctor had only heard one heartbeat. According to Mama Laverne, she'd believed about the twins because on more than one occasion she'd had dreams of double egg yolks. Go figure. Nolan had been glad Mama Laverne had been so consumed in getting all the details from Reese that she hadn't the time to single him out and ask questions or make any matchmaking comments.

"Welcome to Sisters."

The hostess's words got his attention. "Thanks."

He couldn't help noticing how crowded the place was. At least when women hit on him tonight, he could claim he was in a serious relationship. He thought that sounded pretty good, even if it was stretching it a little. No, that was stretching it a lot.

While Corbin conversed with the hostess he undoubtedly knew personally, Nolan glanced around. He felt a quiver in his midsection when his gaze caught on a table where two women sat. He studied the curly hair that hung to one of the women's shoulders, the tilt of her head and the way the eyeglasses sat on her face…

He had to be imagining things, but what if he wasn't?

IVY SMILED. TESSA was entertaining her with a story about the guy she'd gone out with last week and how he'd tried sticking her with the bill. Suddenly, Tessa stopped talking in midsentence. Ivy lifted a brow. "What's wrong?"

"Lordy, that man is so darn sexy."

Ivy shook her head, grinning. "I refuse to ogle another woman's husband any longer."

Tessa smiled. "Oh, I'm no longer talking about the owner's husband."

"Oh? Then who are you talking about?"

Tessa's smile widened. "I'm talking about the man who'll be *your* husband one day if Nana has anything to do with it."

Ivy's stomach tightened at the same time sensations began moving through her thighs to settle between her legs. She couldn't stop from turning slightly in her chair. When she did so, her gaze connected with Nolan Madaris's.

CHAPTER TWENTY-FIVE

THE SECOND NOLAN'S gaze connected with Ivy's, a spike of heat caught him low in the gut and his breath caught on a degree of yearning that was so immediate it felt like pain.

"Hey, man, you okay?" he heard his brother ask, but at that moment he refused to sever his connection with Ivy.

"I'm okay," he answered, still looking at her.

"Umm, both are good-looking women and both are staring at you. Which one got the stare back?" Corbin asked, having obviously followed Nolan's line of sight.

"The one wearing glasses," Nolan said, moving in that direction as he spoke.

Corbin was right beside him. "Who is she?"

"Ivy Chapman."

He could hear Corbin stumble but he kept walking toward the table where Ivy and a woman sat. In an instant Corbin was back at his side. "Damn, man, the two of you don't have to worry about sexual vibes. If they get any stronger, I'll choke on them."

Nolan said nothing as he kept walking, ignoring the numerous feminine voices calling out for his attention. His concentration was on the woman sitting at the table wearing the red dress. The woman he hadn't seen in two weeks but had thought about every single day, whether he'd wanted to or not.

He'd known he would have to see her sooner or later but he hadn't expected to see her tonight. Now. This very minute. He hadn't been given time to prepare. But there was no hope for that now. At the moment he really didn't care. As he got closer, his nostrils picked up her scent. She was wearing the same perfume she had that night they'd had dinner with Clayton and Syneda. He really liked that fragrance on her. It was hypnotic. Erotic. As seductive as it could get.

Nolan finally arrived at Ivy's table. He broke eye contact for a mere second to nod at the other woman before returning his gaze to Ivy and the beautiful eyes staring at him through her eyeglasses. Corbin was right. There were vibes. Plenty of them. He felt them, and he was certain her friend felt them as well. Hell, he wouldn't be surprised if the entire restaurant felt them.

"Ivy."

"Nolan."

"How are you?" he asked, regretting that they had to make small talk and wishing they were alone somewhere. More than anything, he wanted to kiss her. Taste her again.

"I've been fine. What about you?"

He could say horny as hell since tasting her but instead he said, "I've been fine, too."

She nodded and then broke eye contact and said, "This is my friend Tessa Hargrove. Tessa, this is Nolan Madaris."

He offered Tessa his hand in a handshake as he recalled what she'd told him once. *My best friend, Tessa Hargrove, was the one who fought my battles.* He suddenly felt kindred to Tessa. "And how are you, Tessa?"

She smiled up at him. "I'm fine. Nice meeting you, Nolan."

When Tessa's gaze shifted to beyond his shoulder, he remembered his brother. "And this is my brother Corbin Madaris. Corbin, this is Ivy Chapman and her friend Tessa Hargrove."

Corbin quickly moved forward and offered both women his hand. And when Tessa asked them to join them, Corbin sat down before Nolan could accept her offer. At least he had taken the chair next to Tessa, leaving the chair beside Ivy vacant.

He slid into the chair and immediately gave Ivy his full attention, noticing that Corbin seemed to be giving Tessa his. "Have you ordered yet?" he asked in a low tone, when he really wanted to ask something else, something more personal.

"Yes. I love their crab cakes."

He nodded thinking her voice was a lot softer than he remembered. "So do I."

A waitress came and offered him and Corbin menus. Corbin took his but Nolan declined, smiled at the woman and said, "I'll have whatever she ordered." Glancing at her wineglass, he added, "Including the drink."

The waitress smiled. "Yes, sir."

He turned his attention back to Ivy. Lowering his head to her, he asked, "How is your work coming along?"

"Fine. What about yours?"

"Okay. I've been pretty busy." He felt like he should explain why he hadn't contacted her, when in truth he could have called. He'd deliberately avoided her while trying to get his head screwed back on right. He thought he had made progress and then *bam*! He saw her tonight. A part of him knew that energy had been wasted.

All it had taken was one look and he was a hopeless case again.

"So, Ivy, I understand you're a hacker."

Corbin had spoken, bestowing upon Ivy that Corbin Madaris smile he'd perfected over the years, making Nolan do something totally unexpected—he reached across the table and took Ivy's hand in his.

CORBIN MADARIS AND Tessa had carried most of the conversation during dinner and she'd discovered Nolan's brother was a great conversationalist. He shared with them about their cousin Reese and his wife's early delivery of twins, and that the doctor felt the twins and mom would be okay. The babies would have to stay in the hospital for another month or so.

She noticed Nolan wasn't talking much and wondered why. She hadn't bought his excuse that he'd been too busy to call. There had been something in his eyes to let her know he hadn't been completely truthful about that.

He had kept a hold on her hand until dinner had been served. Was it just for show, for Corbin? Ivy had told Tessa about their plan, but she didn't know if Nolan had confided in anyone. If so, he was putting on a good show. More than once she felt his gaze on her, and when she glanced over at him she found him staring at her. Like now. The waitress had come to remove their plates, and he was sitting there, sipping wine while leveling his concentrated gaze on her.

She glanced away to break their connection and noticed several women were openly staring across the room at Nolan.

And he was sitting here and staring at her.

"Would you dance with me, Ivy?"

The live band was playing their first number; the dance floor had been cleared and several couples had headed that way. She wondered how she was going to handle him touching her, even for a dance. Knowing Tessa's and Corbin's eyes were on her and, like Nolan, they were probably waiting for her response, she gave him a wry smile and said, "Yes, Nolan. I will dance with you."

Nolan stood and led her toward the dance floor. The feel of her hand encompassed in the warmth of his felt good and a part of her shivered inside. Walking beside him, she was reminded of how tall he was. And when he pulled her into his arms, she tipped her head back to look up at him at the same time a jolt of sexual awareness rocked her to the bone.

As if he felt it, he wrapped his arms around her as they moved to the slow music, looked down at her and smiled. It was as if he was pleased with her obvious reaction to him. "With your mouth tilted up like that, Ivy, I'm tempted to kiss you. Remember, I don't have a problem with public displays of affection."

She remembered and lowered her head.

"Does that mean you don't want me to kiss you?" he asked.

She glanced back up at him and saw the teasing glint in his dark eyes. Did he honestly expect an answer? She was tempted to tell him that yes, she definitely wanted his kiss. Memories of the ones they'd shared on Tiki Island had sustained her over the past two weeks.

She had done a lot of thinking over the last fourteen days. She'd learned a lot about men, the selfish ones, during the months she was with Damien. Then in a week Nolan had shown her that there were some who were decent human beings. Still, she was nervous about letting things get too complicated between them. "Did you go to Paris?" she asked him, deciding to change the subject.

He shook his head. "No. I've been around the city."

"Just busy," she said coolly and regretted it instantly. He wasn't accountable to her.

She knew that agreeing to dance with him had been a mistake. A major mistake. Already she felt every single hormone sizzling in her body. She'd had two weeks to dream about him. Fantasize. Remember what he'd done to her and what she'd romanticized doing to him if he'd given her the chance...although she would have been a novice at it. Ivy wondered if that was why he hadn't wanted her to pleasure him in return because he'd known she would not have known what the hell she was doing.

He tightened his arms around her and she thought, as usual, he smelled good. She rested her head on his chest and remembered that chest bare against her. That made her recall how he'd looked in jeans riding low on his hips. But then he looked pretty darn good now, dressed in a business suit.

"I missed you, Ivy."

His words nearly caused her heart to stop, and after drawing in a deep breath, she raised her eyes to meet his. "No, you didn't."

He frowned down at her. "Why don't you believe me? Because I didn't call?"

When she didn't answer, he stopped dancing. He grabbed hold of her hand and tugged her off the dance floor. "What do you think you're doing?" she asked, trying to pull her hand free. She stopped trying when people sent curious gazes their way.

"I'm taking you to a place we can talk privately."

"We don't need to talk." She tried not to notice the feel of his hand on her and the heat it was causing to curl inside her.

"Yes, we do," he countered.

They went down a long hall where several doors were located. He knocked on one and a deep male voice said, "Come in."

Nolan opened the door. Seated behind a desk was the owner that Ivy knew to be a woman named Nettie Sinclair. Ivy thought she was a beautiful woman who carried herself in a confident and sophisticated way and who was always friendly to everyone.

Seated on the edge of the desk, looking gorgeously handsome was *him*. Netherland Sinclair's husband. The man she and Tessa always drooled over whenever they came to Sisters and he was there. He stood and she saw he was taller than she'd thought. He was dressed in a pair of jeans and a shirt that showed a muscular chest and shoulders. And his hair... All that glorious mass of hair on his head flowed around his shoulders and made him look fierce and powerful. The man looked ready and capable of handling any situation that came his way.

"Hey, Nettie. Ashton. This is Ivy. Ivy, this is Nettie and Ashton Sinclair," Nolan said in a quick introduction.

"Nice meeting you, Ivy," Nettie Sinclair said, smiling.

"Same here," Ashton Sinclair said.

"Nice meeting you two as well," Ivy said while wondering if there was anyone Nolan didn't know.

"Nolan, is anything wrong?" Netherland asked with

concern, probably after seeing the firm grip he had on Ivy's arm.

"I need to use one of your conference rooms for a minute. Ivy and I need to talk privately."

"Sure," Netherland Sinclair said.

"Here you go." Ashton tossed a set of keys to him, which Nolan caught with his free hand. "Room five is available," Ashton said.

"Thanks, guys," Nolan said.

"Again, it was nice meeting you, Ivy," Nettie said.

"Same here."

Nolan pulled the door shut and led her to a room several doors down a separate hall. Using the key, he opened the door. When he closed and locked the door behind them, she glared at him. "Honestly, Nolan, was all this necessary?"

"Yes," he said, glaring back at her. "I take my character seriously and earlier you insinuated I was lying to you about something."

"Weren't you?"

"Why don't you believe that I missed you?" he asked her.

He had to be kidding. "For starters, you had my number and could have easily picked up the phone, even if you were busy."

He came to stand in front of her. "We told each other on the island we would be busy. Did we not?"

"Yes."

"Then what's your problem?"

Her anger snapped. There was no way she would admit that although he'd been busy with work, she had hoped at some point she would have heard from him. Heard his voice. Even if it was just to say hello. "My problem is that I wished you would just tell me the truth. That after what happened between us that last night, you had no intentions of continuing our fake affair. But you didn't know how to tell me. Furthermore, I know the reason you didn't want me to—" she waved in the general vicinity of his crotch "—reciprocate is because you figured I wouldn't know how. So don't tell me that you missed me when you didn't, Nolan Madaris."

A PART OF Nolan was fighting the thought of just walking out of the room and letting Ivy think whatever she wanted to think. However, he refused to do that. He *had* missed her and yet she was right. He hadn't been too busy to call. He'd chosen not to for self-preservation.

For the first time since he entered the room, he took in his surroundings. It looked as if it had been used for a party earlier that day. A bridal shower or something. Some decorations were still up but those taken down were neatly folded on one of the tables.

He leaned against one of the tables and drew in a deep breath. His full attention returned to Ivy. She was upset, and he knew the only way to get her to understand was to be completely honest with her. "I didn't expect to even like you, Ivy," he finally said. "It would have been better all around if I didn't. But that week we spent together showed me that you're a very likable person. Another thing I didn't expect while pretending to be your lover and working on those vibes was that I would end up wanting you for real."

He paused and then continued, "If you recall, I told you what we did that last night was not according to any plan."

"Yes, I remember," she said softly.

"What I don't think you know is just what being intimate with you that way did to me, Ivy. It shook me to the core, left me confused and, in a way, angry that a woman I hadn't intended to ever like was getting under my skin."

He released a frustrated breath. "I needed those two weeks to think, Ivy. I needed those two weeks to be reminded why we made the decision to team up in the first place—that two old ladies got it in their minds we're supposed to be together and how wrong they are."

He rubbed his hands down his face. "But on that last night, for just a little while I wanted it to be true."

He stood and walked over to her. "You were wrong about your inability to pleasure me, Ivy. It had nothing to do with your experience. Had you touched me that way, or in any way, I would have exploded, because it was *you*."

There, he thought, it couldn't get any plainer than that. "And I did miss you, but I needed the space, because I had become attracted to you. I kept thinking how we were being played and for me to like you meant I was falling right in with my great-grandmother's plans. I intended to fight that tooth and nail."

He watched as she drew in a deep breath. "I understand all that," she said in a low tone. "Because I've been going through a similar situation myself. I needed distance to think as well. A part of me wanted you to call but then a part of me was hoping you didn't. I resent what Nana and Ms. Laverne are doing, trying to manipulate our lives, but then I'm glad I got to meet you even if we know things won't ever work out between us."

He was glad she understood. "I intended to call you next week. Mama Laverne called a couple of times asking about you, wondering when I'm going to invite you to dinner or something. I'm hearing from my cousins that she believes you and I are just going through a period of resistance. That we really like each other and are fighting it. What pisses me off more than anything is that what she's saying is true. It's not supposed to be that way. I hadn't calculated on it being that way, Ivy."

He paused for a moment, needing her to understand that nothing had changed regarding their plan. "I figure what we're going through is nothing more than a lust attack and all these emotions are only temporary. In the end, at some point, we will reel in our common sense. Then things will be like before. The plan won't change and in the end we still go our separate ways." He wondered if the spiel he'd just said was for her benefit or for his, and quickly decided it was for the both of them.

Nolan began pacing in agitation for a minute, then stopped. "I walked into Sisters tonight and could actually feel your presence. Then when you turned and looked at me, a degree of need I've never felt before took over my senses." He didn't want to admit such a thing but felt he had to.

"And during dinner I could barely keep my hands off you, which is why I held your hand for a while. I needed the connection." He shoved his hands into the pockets of his slacks and took a step closer to her. "Does that sound crazy?"

She shook her head. "No."

Nolan was glad to hear that. "Do you know what I want to do more than anything now, Ivy?"

He saw the look on her face, as if she was afraid to ask but also curious. "What?"

He couldn't stop his gaze from shifting to her full and inviting lips. "I want to kiss you. To be honest, I want to do more, but I'd give anything for a kiss."

CHAPTER TWENTY-SIX

THERE WAS AN awareness in Ivy as she stared at Nolan.
A cognizance she hadn't expected. As strange as it was,
they connected on so many levels. Even when they didn't
want to. And she felt it now more than before because
by voicing his inner fears, he had also stated her own.

Why were all these emotions they were experiencing coming into play? A better question was why were
they there at all? What he said was true. They were beginning to feel feelings they should be able to control
because they had no place in a pretend relationship. But
they were there, clouding up things, making them react
in ways they shouldn't. Such emotions could become
outright dangerous for the both of them if they weren't
handled the right way. But instead of handling them,
she preferred giving in to them. How crazy was that?

Now he wanted to kiss her and she wanted to be kissed
by him. She didn't fully understand what was happening between them and she wanted to forget what had got
them together in the first place. She didn't want to think
about Nana, Ms. Laverne or the plan she and Nolan had
agreed to implement to beat them at their own game.

Right now, at this very minute, they weren't victims
of the two women trying to control their lives and their
futures. They were victims of their own making in a
war they really didn't want to fight, but were doing so

anyway because they felt not fighting, not resisting it, not counterattacking was a defeat for them. Neither she nor Nolan wanted to be defeated. She had discovered they were both stubborn individuals who did not like giving in to anything. But now they understood that there were some things you couldn't fight and lust was one of them. And this was lust as thick and intense as it could get. She no longer wanted barriers or limitations between them. Namely those she'd erected.

Without thinking any further, figuring she'd been thinking too much, she slowly walked over to Nolan. Tilting her head back, she looked up at him. Her pulse flickered and leaped in her throat and the nerves in her body were somersaulting all over the place.

"If you want to kiss me, Nolan, then do it."

He smiled just moments before lowering his mouth to hers. The moment of contact was electric. He stroked with such greed that she couldn't help groaning in feminine appreciation. Nolan was conjuring up memories of the kisses they'd shared, and how her mouth had feasted off his as much as his had feasted off hers. All those deep-seated, wild fantasies she'd had for the past two weeks came flooding back into her mind.

Nolan had the ability to electrify her cells. Intense heat was rapidly moving up her thighs toward her center, muddling her brain in the process and had her teetering on an orgasmic release. If any man had the ability to make a woman come just from working his tongue in her mouth, it would be Nolan.

He suddenly broke off the kiss and stared down at her before pressing her face against his chest. Ivy heard the force of his breathing and felt the hard erection pressing against her. Her womb contracted from the feel of his hardness pressing against her and she knew she wanted it. She wanted him. This intense need overtaking her wasn't according to plan, but to hell with their plan.

"Nolan?"

He was breathing harder than before.

"Yeah, baby?"

Baby. He'd called her that before on Tiki Island, right before giving her the best orgasm of her life. She wondered if he realized he'd used that term of endearment again. She knew what she was about to say would change their relationship in a way she wasn't sure she was ready for, but there was no way she couldn't take it there and keep her sanity.

"I want to have sex with you."

He went still for a moment. Then he leaned back and stared down at her. "What's your definition of having sex?"

She'd known he would ask and was ready with an answer. "Not just foreplay. I want intercourse. Penetration. I want it all."

He nodded and reached for her hand. "In that case, come on. Let's go."

LESS THAN AN hour later, holding tight to Ivy's hand, Nolan led her into his condo. The details were a blur. He'd returned the door key to Ashton. Nolan had asked Ivy how she'd got to Sisters and she'd told him Tessa had driven them.

They'd told Corbin and Tessa they would be leaving— both had given them knowing looks. Corbin had offered to cover everyone's dinner and since they'd driven different vehicles Nolan hadn't been concerned how his brother would get home.

Ivy hadn't asked where they were going nor had she questioned his decision to bring her here. She lived only a jog away and he could have taken her home, but he wanted her here, a place he'd always considered private.

He closed the door behind them and leaned against it, watching her look around. He was proud of his four-bedroom, three-bath condo. It suited him perfectly. One of the bedrooms was used as a workout room and another as an office. A number of his single cousins also lived in the building. Since his condo was the largest, they would often hang out here.

He couldn't stop his gaze from roaming over Ivy. He thought she looked exquisite in that red dress and matching stilettos. He was surprised she owned a pair, but she did and was wearing the hell out of them. She looked absolutely stunning.

Ivy turned around and smiled. "You have a nice place, Nolan."

"Thanks. I'll give you a tour—"

"No," she said, placing her purse on his sofa table. "I don't want a tour. I want you."

Her words fired his blood. Nolan crossed the room, swept her into his arms and headed toward his bedroom. While carrying her he felt something he'd never felt before. It was a stirring of massive proportion deep within him; one she was responsible for. He didn't have time to process the feeling. At that moment he needed to make love to her as much as he needed to breathe. He already knew one time wouldn't be enough. Not nearly enough.

Upon reaching his bedroom he placed her on his bed, then stepped back to look at her while removing his suit jacket and tie. His body was pulsing with so much sexual energy he fought to get his breathing and libido under control. There shouldn't be any doubt in her mind how much he wanted her. The desire was there for her to see in his eyes, his stance and the huge bulge pressing against his zipper.

It was hard to believe that at one time she was concerned about the lack of chemistry between them. Sexual vibes were pouring off them with the force of a tidal wave. He couldn't do anything but surrender to the intensity of his attraction for her. The depth of which mystified him.

She sat in the middle of his bed saying nothing as she stared at him. He felt her eyes roam all over him and every inch of him heated wherever her gaze touched.

He had envisioned her in his bed a lot over the past two weeks. He'd awaken during the night with a yearning so deep it was as if she was there beside him, only to reach out and find that she wasn't. Now she was here and he intended to fulfill every single fantasy he could think of and some he hadn't thought of yet.

"You look good in my bed, Ivy."

His words made her smile. He was glad although he hadn't said it to elicit brownie points. He'd spoken the truth. No other woman had ever shared this bed with him and now he couldn't imagine another woman in it. He pushed that thought to the back of his mind as he began unbuttoning his shirt.

"Can I help?"

Despite the thought of what could happen if she touched him, he said, "You want to?"

"Yes."

He stretched out his hand to assist her off the bed. The moment he felt her touch the floor seemed to shift beneath his feet. Forcing himself to remain steady and keep his balance, he pulled her to her feet. Standing directly in front of him, she took over and continued unbuttoning his shirt. Occasionally her fingers skimmed against his skin and he would suck in a deep breath.

"You okay, Nolan?"

"Yes, if you call fighting to hold on to my sanity okay."

She lifted a brow. "All I'm doing is removing your shirt."

She was doing a hell of a lot more than that and he honestly didn't think Ivy Chapman had a clue just what she could do to a man. Specifically, what she could do to him. He sighed deeply when she pushed the shirt from his shoulders and assisted by working the sleeves from his arms.

"Now..." she said, eyeing his chest like it deserved the close scrutiny she was giving it. Glancing up at him, she smiled. "I never told you this but I love your chest."

He chuckled. "And what do you love about it?"

"This," she said, running her fingers through the hair that dusted it.

He wondered if she could feel the way his heart was pounding beneath her fingers or hear his erratic breathing. He was positive that she couldn't dismiss the hard erection pressing against her middle. "Ivy?"

"Hmm?"

She was really into his hairy chest and was proving how much it fascinated her by the way her fingers continued to play, causing his skin to sizzle. When he couldn't take it anymore, he grabbed hold of her wrist. "I can't handle too much of you touching me."

She looked at him strangely. "You can't?"

"No."

She searched his eyes as if trying to determine if he was really serious. Then as if determining that he was, a smile spread across her lips. "I never knew I had the ability to do this. Turn a man on."

"Well, you do. I want you so much I ache. Let's get me out of these pants."

Determined to assist him with that, too, she unbuckled his belt and pulled it through the loops. Evidently she couldn't resist rubbing the palms of her hands across his belly. "Having fun?"

"Yes," she said, grinning up at him. Now that she knew the power she had on him, he had a feeling she would use it to her advantage. Maybe he should not have told her. He then dismissed the thought. In fact, the way he saw it, some man should have told her before now. That made him detest that prick she'd been involved with even more.

She got his attention again when she unzipped his pants. "Show-off," she said, laughing. "I should have known."

He shouldn't want her to elaborate, but he did. "You should have known what?"

"You were big."

Nolan was positive, absolutely positive, that Ivy was good for his ego. He didn't want his head to swell, but... "You think so?"

"Seeing is believing."

She hadn't actually seen anything yet. He knew she was basing her opinion on the size of his erection outlined through his briefs, which he would admit did give her a good indication.

He stepped out of his pants when she had slid them down his legs. She handed them to him and he tossed them on a nearby chair. "Now, for your—"

"Not so fast, Mr. Madaris," she said, wagging a finger

at him. "I recall I had to strip naked for you to do what you did to me. Now it's my turn to see you."

"What I did to you? You mean when I tasted you?" He didn't want her to feel reserved about anything they ever did together.

She held his gaze. "Yes, that."

Hooking his hands into his briefs to pull them down, he figured he had work to do about her shyness regarding sex. She then took hold of his hand and said, "I got this."

He cocked a brow. Now that she felt empowered, he wasn't sure that was a good idea. "You sure?"

"Positive," she said, cupping him and stroking him through his briefs like she was a pro at it.

At least she wasn't showing any shyness now, Nolan thought. He found it hard to believe Ivy had been worried about not knowing how to pleasure him. If she did it any better, he would be in trouble.

He didn't say anything as she crouched down to slide her fingers inside his briefs and slowly eased them down over his hips, thighs and legs. She tossed them onto the chair to join his shirt, belt and pants.

"Now."

"Now?" he repeated looking down at the way she was still crouched before him, with her face leveled with his groin as if study him with full intent.

She raised her head to look up at him. Straightening her glasses on her nose, she said, "Now I have living proof of just how big you are."

When she took him into her hands and ran her fingers down his hot, slick shaft, he sucked in his breath and moaned, "Ivy…"

"I can't wait until we mesh," she said.

Mesh? Hell, they would be doing a lot more than meshing. Deciding it was time to prove that point, he bent down and effortlessly lifted her into his arms. "I haven't finished," she protested. "I want to do more."

He had an idea of what that "more" entailed. "Next time." Placing her on her feet, he eased the dress over her head. Tossing it aside, he exposed a black lace bra.

"Had I known beforehand what would be happening tonight, I would have worn my red bra and red panties."

It didn't matter to him what color her underwear was. He told her so as he removed her bra. Immediately, he noticed her nipples were taut and aroused. He leaned down and licked them, loving the sound she made when he did.

Deciding it was time to remove her panties, he crouched down in front of her. Taking his time he rubbed his hands along her hips, thighs and legs, while again thinking of just how curvy she was and how he loved the shape of her legs. His patience was gone and his desire for her had increased tenfold. Standing, he reached for his pants to retrieve a condom packet from his wallet.

"Don't ask to help me do this," he said, ripping the condom packet open. "I wouldn't last if you did." He knew she was watching him as he sheathed himself in a condom.

When he finished and glanced over at her, he saw she'd removed her eyeglasses and placed them on his nightstand. She stood in front of him, naked, and he faced her the same way. His gaze roamed all over her and heated desire raced up his spine. Releasing a fierce growl, he gripped a fistful of her curly hair, slanting his mouth over hers to give her a kiss that was filled with all the emotions he felt.

If the truth be known, they were emotions that he didn't quite understand.

CHAPTER TWENTY-SEVEN

NOLAN'S KISSING SKILLS never ceased to amaze Ivy and she loved mating her tongue with his. Wrapping her arms around his neck, she held on as he gave her yet another kiss to remember. One that sent pleasurable shivers all through her body.

Moments later he broke off the kiss and tumbled them onto the bed. Their naked limbs entangled, he pulled her into his arms as if needing the feel of her there. It seemed the bed was filled with the drugging scent of him.

Then he was straddling her, looming above her. She looked up into the darkness of his eyes and felt something she'd never felt before. It seemed her heart suddenly ceased beating as unexpected emotions overwhelmed her. Emotions she thought she would never feel again. Emotions she didn't want to feel now.

Nolan must have noticed the distressed look in her features. "You okay, Ivy?"

No, she wasn't okay and she wasn't ready to admit why. The problem was hers alone to deal with and she would. Falling in love with Nolan Madaris was not an option. "Yes, I'm fine," she lied, wondering if she would ever be fine again. She was well aware of what he'd said earlier. Basically, this was a temporary situation. Their plans hadn't changed. In the end they would go their separate ways, and he will return to being Mr. One-Night Stand.

A slow, sensual smile touched his lips. "I intend to make you feel better."

"Promise?" she whispered, wrapping her arms around his neck.

"Promise. If you don't believe me, just watch."

And then he was kissing her again and the intensity left her moaning. Each stroke of his tongue had her shaking, filled with urgency and need. He broke off the kiss and whispered against her lips, "Wrap your legs around me."

She did as he instructed and could feel the massive head of his shaft ease inside her, stretching her to accommodate his size. His gaze held hers and something, she wasn't sure what, flickered in the depths of his eyes. She started to ask if anything was wrong, but then he was lifting her hips in his big hands, holding her steady as he continued pushing inside her.

Immediately, torrid sensations from where their bodies were joined made her moan. And when he began moving, stroking her and thrusting in and out, hot fire seemed to spread through her loins, causing contractions in her womb. She closed her eyes, convulsed in pleasure, overtaken with desire, by the way he was making her feel. She could get addicted to this, but only with him. As if it had a mind of its own, her inner muscles began milking him, clenching him tight, and her nails dug deep into his shoulder blades.

"Nolan..." She said his name when she felt a climax building.

In response, she heard a growl of deep male satisfaction in his throat just seconds before his body bucked hard into her, causing her body to splinter into never-ending spasms. "Nolan!"

He began thrusting inside her with increased speed as he continued to ride her mercilessly. Her legs tightened around him. And when he screamed her name she knew he was consumed in as much pleasure as she was.

That thought was short-lived when another orgasm ripped through her body. When he made another growling sound, followed by an increase of thrusts, she knew he'd followed her into yet another orgasm.

NOLAN'S NOSTRILS FLARED as they inhaled Ivy's scent. He shifted in bed, realizing just how good it felt to wake up with her beside him. Their bodies were so close it was a tight fit. Snug. And even in sleep her body was hot.

He didn't want to wake her but he wanted to make love to her again. Glancing at the clock, he saw it was eight in the morning. He would be patient. Then his cell phone rang.

Nolan knew who was calling. The gospel-music ringtone was a dead giveaway. He glanced at Ivy and saw the sound had awakened her. Pushing hair from her face, she pulled herself up in bed before reaching for her eyeglasses to put them on.

"Good morning," he said and leaned over to place a kiss on her lips. "Happy Saturday."

"Good morning and happy Saturday to you, too. Do you need to get that?" she said, referring to the ringing phone he was trying to ignore.

"She'll call back if I don't."

Then he pulled her into his arms, needing her taste this morning. He should think that was odd since he'd consumed a lot of her taste last night, but he was discovering when it came to Ivy, he always wanted more. At some point his phone had stopped ringing and now it was ringing again.

Nolan knew how his great-grandmother operated. If she tried to reach you and couldn't, there was a chance she would get Jake to drive her to your place to make sure you were still alive and of sound mind. The way she saw it, there was no other reason for you not to take her call.

Breaking off the kiss, he said, "I need to answer it this time or she'll be sending out the cavalry."

He reached for his cell phone and clicked it on. "Good morning, Mama Laverne."

"Good morning, Nolan. It took you long enough to answer the phone."

He smiled and glanced over at Ivy. "I was busy. You're up rather early, aren't you?"

"I'm up planning the party for tomorrow."

Nolan raised a brow. "What party?"

"A celebration for the two new Madarises."

"Don't you think it's kind of soon? Kenna isn't out of the hospital yet and it will be a while before the twins come home."

"That's fine. We'll have another party again later. Besides, I want the family to meet Ivy."

Nolan went still. A fierce frown appeared on his face. "What do you mean you want the family to meet Ivy? Why?"

"Nolan, that's a stupid question and you're far too intelligent to ask it. I'll see you tomorrow at five. Whispering Pines. Don't be late."

He held Ivy's gaze. "Does Ivy know about tomorrow?"

"No, but you can tell her. If she's awake, you can tell her now."

Nolan's frown deepened. "Tell her now? What makes you think she's here?"

"*Tsk-tsk.* There you go again, asking stupid questions. Goodbye, Nolan. See you tomorrow." And then she clicked off the phone.

Nolan didn't say anything as he continued looking over at Ivy. Then he placed his cell phone back on the nightstand. "Mama Laverne wants to invite you to a Madaris family gathering tomorrow. She figures now will be a good time for you to meet the family and for the family to meet you."

"And how did she know I was here?"

Nolan shrugged. "Trust me, it wasn't Corbin and it definitely wasn't me. It had to have been her allies."

"Allies at Sisters? You're kidding, right?"

"No. I understand several of the waitresses at Sisters attend her church and she was instrumental in getting them hired there. And I heard she's even played matchmaker for one or two with guys on Granduncle Jake's ranch. She doesn't limit what she perceives as her God-given matchmaking skills to just family members."

Ivy frowned. "Thanks for telling me about the invitation, but I'm not going."

Nolan lifted a brow. "Why not?"

"It's obvious that you prefer I not go."

Did he say that? Granted he'd been annoyed at Mama Laverne, but he should have suspected she would try to do something to maintain an upper hand. "Sorry, if what I said to Mama Laverne has you thinking that I don't want you to go, because that's not the case. It just annoys the hell out of me when she manipulates any situation to suit her purpose. But meeting the family tomorrow will be a good thing. Then we can officially put our plan into motion."

Instead of saying anything to him, Ivy quickly got out of bed and moved to the chair to retrieve her clothes. "Where are you going, Ivy?"

"Home. I'll get dressed, and you can take me there or I can walk. Do you have extra toiletries?"

"Yes. Look in the top-left vanity drawer. Why are you leaving?"

She looked at him as if it was an odd question. He refused to think she might think it was stupid one. According to his great-grandmother, he'd asked a couple of them today.

"Why should I stay?"

He started to say so they could enjoy more great sex but figured that wouldn't be a good idea. It was obvious Mama Laverne's phone call had upset her. "No reason. I brought you here and I'll take you home. I refuse to let you walk."

"Fine." She quickly walked to the bathroom and closed the door behind her.

Nolan rubbed a frustrated hand down his face. Today was not going the way he'd hoped. Ivy was wrong. Nothing was fine.

CHAPTER TWENTY-EIGHT

"YOU'RE NOT TALKING, HMM?"

Ivy rolled her eyes. "There is nothing to talk about. I was ready to leave Sisters anyway and so was Nolan."

"But you didn't go home."

"No, and it's not like you to fish."

"And it's not like you to hold back."

Ivy pushed away from her computer and adjusted her cell phone to the side of her face. Typically she never worked on Saturdays but today hadn't started out as she was used to. For starters, waking up naked in a man's bed was definitely an abnormality.

"Ivy?"

Tessa reminded her they were still engaged in a conversation...or they were supposed to be. "Hey, Tessa, what did you think of Nolan's brother Corbin? Looked like the two of you were getting along okay."

"We were. He's a nice guy. And don't try to change the subject, Ivy. That tactic won't work with me and you know it."

Yes, Ivy did know it.

"Were things that bad last night that you don't want to talk about it? Just what did he do?"

She heard the panic in Tessa's voice and the rising anger. She needed to calm her down before she did something like find Nolan and confront him. Nothing had changed since high school. Tessa was still protective of her.

When Nolan had brought her home she hadn't even invited him inside. In fact, she told him he didn't have to walk her to the entry door, but he'd done so anyway. He'd even caught the elevator up to her floor, trying to get her to talk to him. Tell him what was bothering her. But she couldn't. What was wrong with her was something that only she alone could fix. In the meantime, until she found a solution she would deal with it.

He had asked her to reconsider going to his family gathering with him tomorrow and she'd told him she would let him know. She still wasn't sure it was a good idea.

"Yes, I want to talk about it," Ivy finally said.

"Give me twenty minutes. I'm on my way over."

AFTER TAKING IVY home Nolan wasn't ready to return to his condo. Instead he made a decision to visit his cousin Clayton. He had called Clayton from his car and was glad Syneda, like most of the women in the Madaris family, was at Whispering Pines getting ready for tomorrow's party.

Nolan loved Syneda to death, but he needed to talk to Clayton privately. Just like he'd told Ivy, Syneda was one of his great-grandmother's biggest allies. If he didn't know better, he would think Mama Laverne was grooming Syneda to take over the matchmaking gig after she took her last breath. *Her last breath.* He shuddered at the thought. As annoying as his great-grandmother was at times, he didn't want to think of a life without her.

He pulled into the driveway of Clayton and Syneda's

huge sprawling three-story home. He thought the same thing he thought the first day he'd seen it. The place was beautiful and more than large enough for Clayton, Syneda and their two children—their daughter, Remington, who was fondly called Remi, and their son, Caleb, who everyone called Cal.

For as long as Nolan could remember, he considered three of his older cousins—Justin, Dex and Clayton—as big brothers more than cousins. Of the three, Clayton was the most fun since he was more laid-back than Justin and Dex. Clayton's philosophy was there was nothing wrong with being naughty every once in a while. Justin, the oldest of the three, always gave diplomatic advice. Dex was the serious one. Too serious at times and extremely loyal when it came to family.

At fourteen, Reese, Lee and Nolan had seen their first *Playboy* centerfold, compliments of magazines they'd found in Clayton's apartment. Corbin had missed out on the fun that day due to makeup cooking classes with Mama Laverne. Clayton, whom they thought wouldn't be back home for at least a couple of hours, had walked in and caught them practically drooling over the pics of the naked women.

Instead of getting angry, Clayton had sat them down and gave them his version of the facts of life. Needless to say, Clayton Madaris's rendition had been far more interesting than the ones their parents had given them. Of course they had all known about the case of condoms Clayton kept in his closet. They appreciated that he never kept an accurate count or else he would have noticed a few missing from time to time.

Instead of getting out of the car Nolan sat there for a minute, enjoying the scent Ivy had left behind. It was the same perfume she'd worn the night they'd had dinner with Clayton and Syneda. Now he wanted to know the name of it because he wanted to buy more of it for her. He couldn't imagine any other fragrance on her.

He frowned, wondering why he would do such a thing. It wasn't as if they were involved in a long-term affair. He squinted against the glare of the sun and decided the rays must have momentarily affected his brain cells somehow. He opened the car door to get out, certain his brain was back to functioning normally again.

Nolan walked up the brick walkway to Clayton and Syneda's home. Clayton had also mentioned that Remi and Cal were visiting their maternal grandfather's ranch in Austin this weekend and wouldn't be at home either. That meant Nolan could really unload man-to-man on Clayton. The one thing he knew for certain was that Clayton didn't mind calling Mama Laverne out when he thought she was wrong. More than once Clayton had spoken out against Mama Laverne's matchmaking schemes.

The door was snatched open the minute Nolan rang the bell and Clayton had a furious look on his face. Since Clayton had known he was coming Nolan didn't think that anger was directed at him. "Something's wrong, Clayton?"

"Hell, yeah. Some boy just called here for Remi. The nerve of the dickhead."

Dickhead? "Remi isn't allowed to talk to boys?" Nolan asked, not sure what else to say.

"No. She's only thirteen. This boy who called is fourteen. No fourteen-year-old boy should be thinking about girls at that age."

Nolan decided now was not the time to remind Clayton

that he, Lee and Reese had been fourteen when Clayton had allowed them to check out the centerfolds of grown naked women in Clayton's issues of *Playboy*. Not only that, Clayton had pointed out and named all their body parts. First in the biological terms and then by the street terms.

"So, what do you plan to do?" Nolan asked Clayton as he led him through the immaculate house, toward the kitchen.

"It's done. At least I thought it was until the dickhead said he'd got permission from Remi's mother to call. I just had a little talk with my wife."

In other words, Clayton and Syneda, who rarely agreed on anything, had more than a little talk. From Clayton's present attitude they'd had a full-blown discussion that hadn't gone over well. Nolan wondered who would win this round. "Well, I'm sure you and Syneda will work together and agree on how to handle the situation."

Clayton rolled his eyes. "That's BS and you know it. Syneda and I never agree on anything."

"So why are you still married?" he asked the one question he often wondered about.

Clayton stopped walking and turned to stare at him like he was crazy. Immediately, Nolan realized he'd just asked a stupid question again that day. "The reason we're still married is because I love her more than life itself," Clayton said in a heartfelt tone. "Syneda is my heart, my rock, the very essence of my being. Yes, we don't agree on everything and I'm glad we don't. But she and I are a team and even teammates disagree. But in the end, we come together and agree on those things that matter the most. Syneda isn't just my wife—she is my queen."

They began walking again and Clayton added, "One day you'll meet a woman like that. From what I observed at dinner, you've already met her. I hate to say it, but if Mama Laverne had a hand in getting you and Ivy together, then she really hit the jackpot this time."

Clayton opened the refrigerator and handed him a beer. Nolan pulled the tab. "You think so?"

Clayton hunched his shoulders. "I can only go by what I see."

Nolan took a huge gulp of his beer and then said, "What you saw was an act, which is part of Ivy's and my plan. And if we can fool you and Syneda, then we can fool anybody."

"An act?"

Nolan leaned against the kitchen counter and nodded. "Yep. We came up with this plan to outwit Mrs. Chapman and Mama Laverne. We're going to pretend to be lovers and then in a few weeks we'll deliberately break up just to prove their matchmaking scheme didn't work. Then that should be the end of it."

Clayton took a slow sip of his beer while he stared at Nolan. He was staring so hard that Nolan was beginning to feel uncomfortable. "What's wrong, Clayton?"

Clayton shook his head. "Obviously, you already suspect something is wrong with *that* plan or you wouldn't be here. I think we need to sit down and discuss it because you're about to make the biggest mistake of your life."

"WELL, THERE YOU have it, Tessa. I think I could be falling in love with Nolan Madaris. Isn't that crazy?"

Tessa took a sip of her wine cooler and stared at Ivy. "Umm, not crazy. Just something you need to think about. But then, I heard when it comes to love there's nothing you can do to stop it if it's going to happen."

"But I *have* to stop it. Nolan is totally wrong for me. As far as I'm concerned, any man is. But especially him. He reminded me that regardless of any emotions we're dealing with, the plan is the same. In the end we go our separate ways. That pretty much let me know he can't wait to get back to being Mr. One-Night Stand again. You of all people know what happened when I fell in love with Damien. My confidence took a beating and I refuse to go through something like that again."

"Did you really love Damien or did you just think you did, Ivy?"

Ivy honestly believed she had loved him, but after their breakup she realized that maybe she hadn't. "I thought I did. But now I'm convinced I didn't. He was just a man who gave me the time of day when others didn't. I know that sounds pathetic but it's true. Now Nolan comes along. He claims that he finds me interesting and considers me his type. But for how long? How do I know he wouldn't pull a Dr. Jekyll and Mr. Hyde like Damien, and one day suddenly find me the most undesirable woman on the face of the earth? You and I both know that he's only in my life because Nana and his great-grandmother are convinced we should fall in love, marry and have babies."

Tessa studied her. "And what do you think?"

Ivy pushed the hair back from her face. "That's just it. I don't know what to think. He's done more than show me attention. He's shown me great sex."

"Yet you might be falling in love with him," Tessa pointed out.

Ivy released a deep sigh. "Doesn't matter. I plan to put a stop to it."

Tessa chuckled. "Can you speak something like that into existence? Say you refuse to fall in love with someone and don't? Personally, I think you owe it to yourself to find out what your true feelings are for Nolan Madaris."

"And then what? What about our plan? And we're supposed to break up in the end. And trust me, we *will* break up. If I allow myself to fall in love with Nolan knowing that, how am I to handle things when he walks away?"

Tessa didn't say anything because it was a question she couldn't answer. "So what are you going to do?"

"Cut my losses now before too much of my heart gets involved. That means I won't be going to that Madaris family gathering tomorrow. The idea for us to become pretend lovers was my idea. Now I need to convince Nolan that it was a bad one."

CLAYTON SAT DOWN at the kitchen table, across from Nolan and took a sip of his beer. Nolan leaned over the table toward him. "What do you mean I'm about to make the biggest mistake of my life?"

Clayton leaned back in his chair. "I learned something from that Christy and Alex fiasco."

Nolan recalled that episode. Christy was Justin, Dex and Clayton's baby sister and they'd always been overprotective of her. When Christy finished college and moved to Cincinnati, the brothers got together and asked family friend Alex Maxwell to keep an eye on her, since

Alex had business matters in Cincinnati. Little did the brothers know it was like asking the rooster to watch the henhouse. Everything turned out okay in the end with Christy's subsequent marriage to Alex, but it hadn't been okay at first.

"And what have you learned?" Nolan asked.

"To be more observant. However, I slipped up with Luke and Mac. I really hadn't expected those two to get together. After that, I decided not to slip up again and to keep my eyes open. So I have. I was on top of things with Blade and Sam, Reese and Kenna, and DeAngelo and Peyton. I was at a disadvantage with Lee because he'd fled from Houston to Vegas to avoid Mama Laverne's matchmaking…for all the good it did." Clayton then looked at him pointedly. "And I'm also on top of things with you and Ivy."

Nolan shook his head. "Like I told you, there's nothing between me and Ivy. It's all part of our plan. Since we fooled you and Syneda, then—"

"You didn't fool me and Syneda. In fact, that's the one thing my wife and I have agreed on in a long time."

"What?"

"That you and Ivy are crazy about each other. Madly in love."

"That is simply *not* true."

"Then why are you here?"

Nolan took a sip of his beer. He was here because of all those emotions he felt with Ivy, emotions he didn't understand. However, he was absolutely, positively sure love had nothing to do with it. It was all about lust.

Before he could give Clayton a response, Clayton said, "Let me ask you something. I noticed since Lee's wedding you've become the ultimate player. I understand you were often called Mr. One-Night Stand. Did you enjoy that life?"

Nolan thought he would be totally honest. "No. Most of it was for show anyway."

Clayton lifted a brow. "What do you mean for show?"

"I figured I couldn't stop Mama Laverne, but I could make Ivy Chapman want nothing to do with me. So, I messed around—a lot. But after a while it got damn boring. The sex was unexciting and humdrum. And the women were becoming a damn nuisance when they started acting petty and territorial. Even though I always explained up front the rules of a no-strings affair to them. After six months of that, I couldn't take any more. But I had to keep up the charade and make everyone think I'd become a man whore, I began dating women I hired from a legitimate escort service. All it involved was a flashy public date with no sex."

Clayton sat his beer can down. "You're kidding, right?"

"No. I'm not kidding. Honestly, Clayton, did you actually sleep with all those women back in the day?"

"Of course I did," Clayton said, giving him a look as if he'd asked a downright stupid question. Dang. How many did that make today for him? "However, Syneda took away my desire for other women. Now I only have eyes for her."

Nolan could clearly understand why. Syneda was a beautiful woman.

Clayton picked up his can of beer and took another sip and said, "And did it work?"

"Yes and no. Ivy was definitely turned off by my reputation, but then she couldn't have cared less since she is adamantly against marriage—to anyone. It's just hard to convince her grandmother and Mama Laverne of that. They aren't accepting."

Clayton nodded. "So the two of you came up with this plan?"

"Yes."

"If the two of you think it's such a good plan, then what's the problem?"

Nolan took another sip of his beer. "The problem is Ivy was worried about us not emitting enough sexual chemistry, so we decided to work on it. Hold practice sessions so to speak."

Clayton chuckled. "Umm, let me guess. Those practice sessions are working too much, right?"

"Yes. And I've discovered I want her. For real."

"Tell me something I don't know. Syneda and I had dinner with you two. We observed you. Hell, I think everyone in the restaurant observed the two of you that night. You two have sexual chemistry down pat."

"We got plenty of lust, I know that."

Clayton chuckled again. "You honestly think that's all it is? Lust?"

"What else could it be? And trust me, it's not love."

"Can you honestly say it's not? What if it is?"

Nolan stood and began pacing. Moments later he stopped and looked at Clayton. "Love has nothing to do with it. I refuse to fall in love with a woman Mama Laverne has picked out for me. It's all about manipulation, Clayton. Something I refused to let anyone do to me again, even my great-grandmother. You know how I felt about Andrea Dunmire. She manipulated me into believing she loved me as much as I loved her and everything was perfect between us. For that reason I will never fall in love again."

"Who are you telling? Me or your heart? If you're telling me, then, fine, I hear you although I don't believe you. If you're trying to tell your heart, then don't waste your time. I suggest you talk to Alex, Luke, Blade and Lee. They probably said the same thing or thought the same way. You of all people know how Lee felt about it. He thought he had the perfect plan, and he was still outsmarted by Felicia Laverne Madaris."

"Are you saying I should just go along with whatever Mama Laverne does? Allow myself to be manipulated?"

"No. I still think she should stay out of people's business, namely their love lives. What I think you should do is make sure those emotions you think are lust, really are. If they're not, Nolan, then you need to do something about it."

"What do you mean?"

"Earlier you said something about Ivy's plan to never marry."

"That's right."

"Well, if you determine what you feel for her is love and not lust, then you're going to have your hands full in convincing her not only of the merits of love, namely yours, but also the merits of marriage. I know how that can be because Syneda was totally against falling in love as well."

Clayton paused as if remembering that time in Syneda's and his lives. "It's important that you get her to understand and to believe that you were meant to love her."

Nolan frowned. "I wasn't meant to love her," he said with strong conviction in his voice.

Clayton smiled and tilted his beer can up to Nolan. "Be careful what you say, Nolan. I thought the same thing about Syneda, and look where I am today."

CHAPTER TWENTY-NINE

NOLAN'S CELL PHONE rang the moment he walked into his condo. Pulling it out of his pocket, he saw the caller was Ivy.

"Yes, Ivy?"

"Hi, Nolan, I've decided not to go to your family function tomorrow."

He stopped walking and rubbed a frustrated hand down his face. "Why? And I hope it's not because you still think I don't want you to go. I explained things to you this morning."

"No, that's not it."

"Then what is it?" he asked, tossing his keys on the counter before opening the refrigerator to grab a bottle of water.

"I've been thinking that for us to pretend to be lovers isn't a good idea after all."

"What? I hope you're kidding me, Ivy. How many times are you going to change your mind about this?" he said in an angry tone. "Need I remind you it was *your* idea? And what about that spiel at the cottage about taking ownership of that idea?"

"Well, I've changed my mind. I have a right to do that. I'll let you handle your great-grandmother as you see fit and I'll handle Nana. Goodbye, Nolan. Best of luck."

Nolan heard the click in his ear and his frown deepened. *Best of luck?* What the hell! If Ivy assumed this was the end of it, then she assumed wrong. Grabbing his keys off the counter, he headed for the door.

IVY WAS SITTING on her patio that overlooked Laverne Park when she heard her doorbell. Tessa had left earlier with a list of things she needed to do that day, so Ivy figured it wouldn't be her returning.

By the time Ivy was halfway to the door, she suspected who her unexpected visitor might be. Nolan. A glance out her peephole confirmed her suspicion.

Ivy knew he wasn't happy with her right now, but he had no choice but to accept her decision since her mind was made up. She would let him blow off steam since he had every right to do so. Just like she had every right to change her mind.

She opened the door and he stood there wearing the same outfit he'd put on that morning. A pair of drawstring jogging pants and a muscle shirt. She tried not to notice how good he looked in both. And the dark shadow covering his jaw meant he hadn't shaved yet. Why did that unshaven look make him appear so druggingly hot? "Is there any reason you're here, Nolan?"

He studied her face. "Where are your eyeglasses?"

Did he think she never took them off? "I decided to put in my contacts today." No need to tell him she decided to wear them more. Might as well since she'd paid good money for them. Besides, she would no longer spite Damien about anything. He wasn't worth it. "Why are you here?" she asked him again.

"We need to talk."

"Fine. We'll talk. Just as long as you know I won't be changing my mind." She moved aside for him to come in.

He entered and glanced around. Nolan was seeing

her condo for the first time since she hadn't invited him in that morning. She allowed him time to do that since she'd definitely checked out his place. Hers was a lot smaller than his. Her two-bedroom, two-bath condo could fit in his and he'd still have plenty room to spare.

"Say what you have to say and leave, Nolan."

He slowly turned around to look at her and she felt the heat of his gaze roaming over her. Of course she had changed from this morning. When he'd brought her home, she was wearing the red dress and matching stilettos that she'd worn to Sisters. Since then she'd showered and slipped into a short chiffon caftan. It barely covered her thighs and of all colors, it was blue.

He was staring at her like he had X-ray vision. She hoped not since she didn't have a stitch of clothing on underneath. After Tessa left she hadn't expected any more company.

"I'm listening," she said when he continued to stare at her. Suddenly feeling self-conscious, she crossed her arms over her chest and then dropped her arms when the hem of her caftan rose up her thighs.

She wished he wouldn't look at her like that; especially when she was beginning to feel the ragged heat and sensuous pull of desire between them. She now recognized it for what it was. They'd stirred it up so much in perfecting their plan that now all that sexual chemistry seemed to have a mind of its own.

Even from across the room she could feel herself being overtaken by the scent of him. That only reminded her of how his scent had got entrenched into her skin when he'd made love to her. And it didn't help matters that while he was standing there looking so darn sexy, she was remembering every single detail of the time she'd spent in his bed last night. How his muscular power had surrounded her, invaded her body.

They'd made love nonstop. She hadn't known that any two people had that much stamina or that she could have so many orgasms in a single night. Thinking of all that pleasure was eroding her senses, causing a little purr to sound in her throat.

Ivy drew in a deep breath when Nolan began slowly walking toward her. She felt a keen throb of yearning with every step he took. The man was walking testosterone. She tried to take a step back but couldn't. The need and desire she read in his eyes had her transfixed in place.

He came to a stop directly in front of her and she could feel the air shimmering to life around them. He stood so close his chest nearly touched hers. So close his hard erection was pressing against the juncture of her thighs.

"Ivy."

All it took was that one word from him—her name on his lips. She reached up and hooked her arms around his neck at the same time he reached out and wrapped his around her waist. She moaned deep in her throat the minute he took possession of her mouth and they began feasting greedily off each other. He tasted of the beer he apparently drank at some point earlier. Rich, malty and robust. A surge of pleasure rushed over her with the intensity of how he was using his hot and wet tongue. Seducing her. Savoring her. Sabotaging her chances of ever turning her back on this, the invisible threads binding them together whenever he kissed her like this. And he always did. His kisses were those of a man who knew exactly what he was doing. Who knew exactly what he wanted. And who knew exactly how to get it.

He dived deeper into her mouth. Heated passion

overrode caution, overthrowing her earlier decision to walk away from Nolan and not look back.

Grabbing ahold of her bottom, he pulled her tighter against his fully aroused shaft to fit snugly in the juncture of her thighs. Her hips rocked against him and he seduced her mouth even more. Suddenly she was lifted off her feet, and instinctively she wrapped her legs around him. Her fingers gripped his shoulders and she could feel her nails digging into the material of his shirt.

The next thing she knew, they were tumbling down on her sofa. At some point, when she was certain she could think straight again, she would recall how they managed to undress so quickly. All she'd had to do was whip her caftan over her head, but somehow Nolan finished stripping at the same time she did. She then watched as he prepared himself with a condom.

Before she could blink, he had her above him, straddling a pair of thick masculine thighs with the apex of her legs centered above a ramrod-straight erection. From last night, she knew she could accommodate him; but if she didn't know better she would swear it had grown a lot in size since then.

He looked up at her and then down at their bodies, just inches from connecting. He slid his hand to the nape of her neck and began caressing the spot there. She wasn't sure how, but when he did so, the area between her legs began tingling with a need she'd never felt before. Then he rubbed his open mouth against her throat, making her moan out loud.

"Ride me, Ivy. And ride me like you mean it."

His request made every cell inside her body erupt and a slow burn of desire began lubricating her center. She eased her body down on him and held his gaze while doing so. He was rock solid and as she took him inside her, she felt his heat, the way the veins of his manhood seemed to thicken with blood as if rushing more fire into his loins. The more she took him in, the more she felt her inner muscles pulse around him. Holding him. Clenching him tight.

When Ivy had taken him deep inside her, she began to move, rocking her hips, pulling almost out and then bearing down again. She repeated the motion over and over, loving the feel of being skin to skin, flesh to flesh with him.

He groaned as she kept it up, getting better at it, more at ease with every downward movement. She liked this. Was enjoying the hell out of it. She felt in control. It was as if her body was in demand…at least he made her feel that way by the groans and growls he was making, and the raspy breaths he was taking.

She felt empowered and increased her pace. At least she knew her sofa had good cushions. She loved the feel of his shaft sliding in and out of her wet tunnel. And when he clutched her hips as if to slow her down, she dipped her head and, with the tip of her tongue, traced the fullness of his lips.

Suddenly he was kissing her, taking her mouth with a hunger than made her groan. He began stroking his tongue in and out, between her lips, with the same rhythm and timing that she was doing to their bodies. It was too much. And when his hands clenched her hips tighter, she had a feeling he was about to shift their positions. *No dice, Mr. Madaris*, she thought, refusing to let him take control. She rode him even harder and could actually feel his aroused and rigid flesh expanding inside her even more.

"You're killing me." He breathed the words against her lips.

She was only giving him what he'd asked for.

"Ivy!"

He called out her name just seconds before his body bucked beneath her. He managed to shift their bodies sideways, throwing his legs over her as if to lock their bodies, and he began pounding into her. He drove her body straight into an orgasm that made her body jerk in a way that nearly caused them to fall off the sofa. They didn't fall and he didn't stop. He kept going and going. And groaning roughly with every hard thrust.

"Nolan…"

She was certain she was going to pass out from so much pleasure and was convinced she would have if he hadn't started kissing her again, taking her mouth with a greed that she felt in every part of her body. Never before had she felt so much sexual passion unleashed and then served up so deliciously. Unable to take any more and feeling completely drained, totally spent, she closed her eyes seconds before collapsing on him. Barely able to breathe she couldn't as much as open her eyes or lift her head when he gently said her name.

Ivy wasn't sure how long they lay there, facing each other, not saying anything. She felt the gentle brush of his hand along her back and finally opened her eyes to see him watching her. Was she imagining things or was his sex throbbing to life again inside her? She got her answer when the fullness of his expanding shaft began stretching her again.

"I like your sofa, Ivy."

Undoubtedly, that wasn't all that he liked. "We were supposed to talk," she said, knowing she should be upset with herself for lowering her guard. But there was no way she could be annoyed when her body was pulsing with pleasure from head to toe.

"We'll talk later. Now it's my time to ride."

CHAPTER THIRTY

FOUR HOURS AND SIX condoms later, Ivy had insisted they get dressed and get as far away from her sofa as they could. *Damn, what a pity*, Nolan thought, since he really did like her sofa.

He glanced over at her as he slid into his jogging pants. Never before had he been so pleasured by a woman. She was a quick learner, and today he'd taught her several things and she had pleased him immensely, stroke after every sensuous stroke into her body. In the past Nolan had equated having sex with physical release, but with Ivy it rivaled the kind of passion everyone should experience in their lifetime. The kind that made you want to howl at the moon regardless of whether there was a full one out or not.

"We still need to talk."

He smiled at her. Yeah, they would talk all right. And then after they talked…

"Would you like something to drink?"

"Drink? It's time to eat," he said, glancing out the window and seeing dusk had fallen.

"Sorry, my refrigerator is empty."

"No problem," he pulled his phone out of his pocket and placed an order for delivery.

Ivy glared at him. "I didn't invite you to stay."

He shrugged his shoulders after pulling his shirt over

his head. "We need to talk and I prefer not doing so on an empty stomach."

"If you're going to stay, then I need to change clothes."

He chuckled. "You mean put on *more* clothes, don't you? Not that I'm complaining with your lack of undies and bra under that outfit, mind you."

"You need to shave, Nolan."

He rubbed his chin. Yes, he did. "Sorry, I didn't mean to mark you up." He knew the worse of it was on her inner thighs. "Let me kiss the pain away." He moved toward her and when she darted out of his way, he swept her into his arms.

"Put me down. I don't need you to kiss anything. You've done enough already."

He decided not to tell her how wrong she was about that. "Relax. I promise to keep my tongue inside my mouth and not use it to kiss you. And if it makes you happy, we'll talk now."

She frowned at him. "I thought you preferred not talking on an empty stomach."

"For you I'll make an exception."

He carried her over to the sofa and sat down with her in his lap. "Okay. Talk."

She twisted in his arms to face him. "Excuse me, but you're the one who showed up saying we needed to talk."

"Oh, yeah, that's right. Making love to you for four hours has messed up my mind."

"You shouldn't be so greedy."

He smiled. It was hard using his tongue just for talking when he did want to kiss her. "Your fault. You bring out the greediness in me."

Lowering her head, she didn't say anything for a minute. And then when she raised her head back up, she said, "I never wanted for us to get this involved, Nolan."

He knew that since she'd made it clear from day one she didn't want to have sex with him. "I know you didn't," he said, deciding if he couldn't kiss, the next best thing was to touch her, so he gently stroked his fingertips along her arm.

"Sex causes problems."

He shook his head, not agreeing with that. "Sex with the wrong person causes problems. With the right person it causes pleasure. I gave you pleasure and you gave me pleasure. That means we're the right people for each other."

It quickly dawned on him what he'd said and decided he needed to walk it back. At least he needed her to understand their compatibility between them only extended to the physical. "We're the right people for each other when it comes to sex."

"I knew what you meant. To you, that's all a woman is good for."

Was that what she really thought? What did he expect when he'd deliberately set out to make her think he had a deplorable reputation when it came to women. It would be a waste of his time to deny anything now. "The reason I wanted to talk to you, Ivy, is because you're backing out on me. Now is not the time to do that."

"We were going to pretend to break up later anyway, Nolan. Why can't we do it now?"

"Because."

"Because what?"

He didn't say anything. To state the reason that

he wasn't ready for them to go their separate ways wouldn't make much sense, so he said, "Because it's a plan I think will work, but only if we give it enough time. They won't be satisfied we tried long and hard enough. Plus, we haven't figured out a reason to break up that they won't challenge." He grinned. "I was looking forward to outwitting the old gal. Just think you'll get to do the same with your grandmother. Maybe then she won't try picking a man for you ever again."

She seemed to consider what he'd said. "Will it put a stop to your great-grandmother?"

"I doubt it. Mama Laverne will be playing matchmaker until her dying day. At least she'll move on from me to the next person on her list. It should be Corbin but she's skipping him for now to take on Victoria."

"Why?"

"She thinks Victoria is ready to settle down."

"How does Victoria feel about it?"

Nolan recalled his conversation with his sister. "She honestly doesn't have a problem with it. Victoria's rationale is that she doesn't have time to look for a husband and has no problem letting Mama Laverne vet one for her."

"Wow."

"I know. Crazy, right?"

"I guess."

"There's no 'I guess' about it. It *is* crazy." When she didn't say anything, he said, "I'll tell you what. Let's go the family get-together tomorrow, perform our best act and see what happens. Who knows? We might not be able to fool anyone."

"And if we do?"

"Then that's even better and would fall in line with

our plan. In two weeks I'll be leaving for Paris. I'll be there for a couple of weeks and while I'm gone you can think of a way for us to break up with no chance of getting back together. Then when I get back, we'll stage the big breakup and that will be it. Just like we planned. Piece of cake."

"Piece of cake?"

He smiled. "With cream-cheese icing on top. As delicious as it can get. All we need is four more weeks, and for two of them I won't even be around. Four weeks, Ivy."

IT WAS NEARLY midnight when an exhausted Ivy eased out of bed. Slipping into her caftan, she headed for her kitchen, but not before glancing over her shoulder at the man she'd left sleeping soundly.

Tomorrow she would attend his family function where they would put on a show as starry-eyed lovers. Then for two weeks they would date in full view of his great-grandmother's allies. The following two weeks he would be in Paris, giving her a chance to work on a plan for their breakup.

He honestly thought things would be uncomplicated and simple. That was easy for him to say when his heart wasn't involved. Things weren't supposed to go that way. When he'd arrived earlier that day, she'd made up her mind about him…or so she'd thought. First thing she'd intended to do was put distance between them. *Some distance.* Since walking through her front door, their bodies had been more connected than not connected.

The moment he'd touched her she had recklessly thrown caution to the wind and had allowed him to break down her resolve. *And for what?* She knew the answer without thinking much about it. For the best lovemaking any man could bestow on a woman. Granted she didn't have a lot of experience since there had been only two guys before Nolan. This thing with Nolan was so off the charts she had to pause for a minute just to catch her breath. The man had making love to a woman down to an art form. Her thighs quivered just thinking about it. Then there were those sex games he played with her where he would deliberately push her to the edge then snatch her back and then shove her to the edge all over again. But he made the torture worth it in the end when he would make her climax hard. He'd even taught her some naughty little words to say that turned him on. And she would do so, all from the promise of a clit licking. Just one of the naughty terms she'd learned from him.

Her mind should be filled with worry about another heartbreak, but all she could think about was this sexual empowerment she was feeling. And he'd offered her two more weeks of it. Could she take it knowing what the end result would be? Knowing that in four weeks, he would walk away and not look back? Was the pleasure he was giving, and would give her for another two weeks, worth it?

She needed to analyze her situation. Was it wrong to fantasize about a life she would never have? To be satisfied with a sex-filled but loveless relationship? Why not? Couples did it all the time. She had tried the love-the-person-you-have-sex-with thing and had believed the love was being reciprocated, only to find out that wasn't the case. So was she wrong to accept things as they were and hope for the best?

The next question then was what was the best? What life would she return to after her "breakup" with Nolan? Would her life be better or worse? At the start of this, she would have said better, hands down, confident that a relationship was the last thing she wanted.

A shimmery smile touched her lips as sensations washed over it. Sexwise it would be better. Nolan had the ability to remind her that she was a woman with needs. He had the resilience to show her that he was just the man to fulfill those needs. And he had.

Never in her wildest dreams, and over the years she'd allowed herself to have some pretty wild ones, had she thought any man could keep her in bed for the better part of the day and make almost-nonstop love to her. And the orgasms… OMG! Women didn't have that many in her mother's romance novels that Ivy used to sneak and read, and still read now on occasion. During Nolan's lovemaking, the big O came frequently and effortlessly. He treated her body as something to be cherished and pleasured, sometimes at the expense of his own satisfaction. Very few men would do that.

So how could she not fall in love with him when every time she looked into his eyes, she felt herself doing so? She blew out a frustrated sigh as she walked into the kitchen. At least she knew Nolan's reputation. She was well aware he liked women and was sacrificing his time with them by pretending an affair with her. She would have thought he would have jumped at the chance to end the pretense. Then he could go back to his womanizing ways. He was so determined to best his great-grandmother that he would put up with Ivy for another four weeks.

"I woke up and you were gone, baby."

She swirled around to see a shirtless Nolan leaning in the kitchen's doorway with his jogging pants riding low on his hips. He had that sleepy-sexy look in his eyes. It was after midnight and he didn't look like a man who intended to go home. She hadn't invited him to stay. Did she want him to go?

Judging by how her body was responding to him again, no, she didn't. It didn't help that he'd called her baby again. He'd done it a couple of times before. Was he practicing for his family? Yes, that had to be it.

"You were asleep and I didn't want to wake you," she said.

A smile touched those gorgeous lips. "Now I am awake."

He straightened and began walking toward her in that slow, sexy strut that he should patent. Goose bumps began forming on her arms with every step he took. His dark penetrating gaze held her in place as she watched him, feeling sensations swirling around in her stomach the closer he got.

And when he was close enough, he pulled her into his arms and held her. The warm heat of his body pressed against hers felt good and she buried her face in his bare chest. She loved the feel of his chest hair against her skin.

"You smell good, Ivy," he leaned in and whispered close to her ear. "I love the cologne you're wearing. What is it?"

"Forever You by Wingate."

"I will commend James the next time I see him."

She pulled back and looked up at him, her brows scrunching. "James?"

"Yes, James Wingate, CEO of Wingate Cosmetics. He's a family friend."

She shook her head. "Is there anyone you or your family doesn't know?"

He chuckled. "I'm sure there are, but get prepared to meet those who we do know tomorrow. More than likely they will be there, since it's being held at Whispering Pines. Although this whole thing might have been Mama Laverne's idea, Jake will invite his close friends."

"Won't that upset your great-grandmother that non-family members will be there?"

"Heck, no. A friend of a Madaris is family, indirectly or directly. Take James Wingate for instance. His sister, Colby, is married to movie actor Sterling Hamilton. Since Sterling and Colby are considered family, so are James and his wife, Cynthia."

"So you think there's a chance Sterling Hamilton might be there tomorrow?" She couldn't imagine going anyplace where the famous movie star turned director would be in attendance. She'd crushed on him hard when she was a teenager, like practically every other female in the country.

"Sterling and my granduncle Jake are the best of friends so he will get an invite. Whether he's there will depend on his schedule."

He tightened his arms around her. "Enough talk. There're other things we can spend our time doing."

And with that said, he whipped her off her feet into his arms and headed for the bedroom.

CHAPTER THIRTY-ONE

IVY FITTED RIGHT IN, Nolan thought, tipping his head to the side as he watched the "under-thirty group" game of tug-of-war that was going on. Not that he'd had any doubts that she would. After all, she'd been his great-grandmother's pick. As expected, everyone loved her. Also as expected, everyone had heard about them. When he'd taken her around to meet everyone, he thought she was going to faint when he'd introduced her to Sterling Hamilton and Jake's wife, Diamond.

When he'd introduced her to his family, they'd given them *knowing* looks. A part of him was glad everyone seemed to have fallen for their plan, but then, at the same time, it annoyed him that some thought he'd so easily fallen in line with Mama Laverne's matchmaking shenanigans.

His brother Adam, who was three and a half years younger than him and who hadn't a clue about Ivy's and his plan, had pulled him to the side and blasted him up and down. So had his cousins Emerson, Kane and Quantum, who like Nolan, Reese, Lee and Corbin, had only eighteen months separating them in age and hung together, usually like glue. They had also pulled him aside to blister his ear. He'd been tempted to tell them the truth but figured the fewer people who knew of the plan, the more chances it had of going off without a hitch.

His cousin Chancellor hadn't said anything. He'd only looked over at Nolan and chuckled. But that was Chance for you. He pretty much stayed to himself out on his ranch and was the last one to hear family gossip.

Chance had joined the military right out of high school and had been an army ranger when an injury in Iraq left him in a wheelchair. He returned home after being told that he would never walk again. Those army doctors hadn't discussed that prognosis with Mama Laverne, who intended to prove them wrong. She had refused to give up on Chance and wouldn't let him give up on himself. Within a year Chance was out of the wheelchair and riding horses again. Now he owned a two-hundred-acre ranch and, like Jake, raised some of the best cattle in Texas.

Chance credited Mama Laverne with his desire to live again. For that reason Chance would never question anything she did. Like Victoria, he was probably of the mind that whatever woman Mama Laverne picked out for him was fine and dandy. Nolan didn't envy that woman. Chance was a loner and wasn't the easiest person to get along with.

"No need to stand here looking all smug."

He glanced over at his cousin Lee. He and his wife, Carly, had arrived that morning from Paris. Nolan figured you could roll that way when you owned a private jet. "Am I?"

Lee smiled. "Yes. I guess you know that Ivy's and your plan is working."

"Is it?" Nolan asked, returning his gaze to Ivy.

Lee gave him a surprised look. "You don't sound pleased."

He wasn't. Something was bothering him and it shouldn't. Lee was right. He should feel smug. "I guess I am. But..."

"But what?"

Nolan shrugged massive shoulders. "I don't know. It's just strange the way everyone has taken to her and she's taken to them. Too bad that she's..."

When he trailed off, Lee picked up his thoughts and finished by saying, "That she's Mama Laverne's pick and not yours, because she's perfect for you?"

Nolan shoved his hands into his jeans pockets. "Is she perfect for me?"

"If she's not, then the two of you are putting on one hell of an act."

He switched his gaze from Ivy to Lee. "That's the plan."

"Maybe. But..."

"But what?"

"I might be wrong but I believe she's come to mean a lot to you, Nolan. More than you thought possible. More than you want to admit. Will admit."

Nolan broke eye contact with Lee to glance back over to where Ivy and her team were hard at work, trying to tug the opposing team over the line. She looked good in a pair of denim capri pants and a printed blouse. Without taking his eyes off Ivy, he said, "You're wrong. She hasn't come to mean a lot to me."

"So you say."

"So I know." And because he didn't want to entertain such thoughts from Lee anymore, he said, "It seems that she and Carly are getting along great."

Lee chuckled. "You know why, right?"

Nolan looked back at Lee. "No, why?"

"Because I understand that, like Carly, Ivy was a loner while growing up. No cousins or siblings. Carly loves being a part of the Madaris family. More siblings and cousins to go around."

Nolan decided he wouldn't waste his time reminding Lee that Ivy was not a part of the Madaris family and if anyone was waiting for him to make her one, they would have a long wait.

When cheers went up he broke eye contact with Lee to glance back over at the group. Ivy's team was jumping up and down, giving each other high fives and doing a victory dance. They had won. Nolan couldn't help but smile. He was proud of them. He was proud of her. The smile on her face was so radiant it seemed to light up everything around her.

"Remember when we used to be part of the under-thirty group?" Lee asked.

Nolan's gaze remained on Ivy. "Yes, I remember."

"Now we're too old to play but our women are the ripe age."

Our women? Nolan switched his gaze to Lee. "Ivy is not my woman and you know it."

Lee chuckled. "You better not say that too loud. Look who just showed up."

Nolan shifted his gaze from Lee to the newcomers who'd arrived. Wyatt Bannister and Tanner Jamison. The two were very good friends of their cousin Blade and took being bachelors to a whole new level. Both had a lifetime membership in the notorious Gentlemen's Club, and everyone in Houston knew that its members were far from being gentlemen.

Without saying anything to Lee, Nolan moved away and began walking to where Ivy, Carly and Victoria were standing together, chatting with Justin, Dex and Clayton's mother, his grandaunt Marilyn. It just so happened that Marilyn Bannister Madaris was also Wyatt Bannister's aunt. Not surprisingly, Wyatt and Tanner were headed in her direction.

Nolan decided he might was well stake his claim on Ivy before either Wyatt or Tanner could get any crazy ideas. He reached the group and stood in front of Ivy. She looked up at him and gave him a huge smile.

"Did you see us? My team won!"

He smiled down at her and reached out to push a mass of curls back from her face. "I saw you, baby. Congratulations." And then he leaned down to brush a kiss across her lips.

That's all he intended to do to mark a claim. But the moment his mouth touched hers he couldn't resist temptation and in front of everyone he crushed his mouth to hers and gave her an openmouthed, tongue-sucking, tonsil-probing kiss.

IT WAS AFTER midnight when Nolan walked Ivy to her condo. She'd really enjoyed herself and it hadn't even bothered her when Nana had arrived, wearing a huge smile as if the marital union between her and Nolan was a foregone conclusion. Some in the Madaris family had even gone so far to ask if they'd set a date as if assuming they were engaged. Several of the ladies had asked about her wedding dress and offered her help to look. Diamond had mentioned some friend of hers in Los Angeles, who'd made Carly's wedding dress, would love to create another masterpiece for a Madaris wedding.

Although she had enjoyed herself immensely with Nolan's family, a part of her couldn't help but feel bad that they were deceiving everyone. His family truly believed she and Nolan had fallen in love and had easily accepted her into the family. She wondered what they would think when that never happened.

"So how do you think today went?" She glanced over her shoulder to ask Nolan. Ivy noticed he'd been quiet on the drive back from Whispering Pines.

He stood in the middle of her living room with his hands shoved in his pockets and an unreadable expression on his face. "I don't know. You tell me how you think it went. From what I see, you fitted right in."

Was that resentment she heard in his voice? She must be mistaken because things were going according to plan. At least as far as he knew. The fact that she had fallen in love with him wasn't something she planned on sharing. And there was no doubt about it. She hadn't been sure before but was certain now—she was in love with Nolan Madaris. It hit home at Whispering Pines, when she'd been standing with his mother and grandmother while watching one of the younger Madarises—Jake's son, Granite—show off his skill as a horseman. She looked across the way to see Nolan staring at her. Even from across the yard his look had had the ability to send a throb of desire through her veins. She'd returned the stare while her heart had beaten voraciously in her chest. And she'd known at that moment each beat had been for him. Had been her love for him.

"My fitting right in is a good thing, right?" she asked him in a quiet tone.

"Yes," he said, nodding, while still staring at her. "All according to plan and that's what's most important."

He wouldn't know how much his words, although true, had hurt. But then it wasn't his fault that she had lowered her guard and was sacrificing her heart. But at this point Ivy no longer worried about what tomorrow would bring for them. She knew the score. Was fully aware that in four weeks they would be going their separate ways. Yet she had fallen in love with him anyway. Considering everything, she could not have fallen in love with him even if she'd tried. And God knew she *had* tried.

Now he was here, standing in the middle of her living room. Would he stay the night? He had stayed last night, only leaving this morning after breakfast. Then he had returned hours later to pick her up to take her to his family's event. It had felt strange to wake up in the arms of a man two mornings straight. Namely the very handsome man who was still standing there looking at her.

"Yes, according to plan," she finally said. "I have a question for you."

"What is it?"

"Why did you kiss me like you did today? In front of everyone?"

He didn't say anything at first and then said, "You ought to know by now that I have no problem with public displays of affection. And that kiss was for Wyatt Bannister and Tanner Jamison's benefit. They are always looking for conquests and I wanted it known that you weren't available. Again, everything today was according to plan."

Everything today was according to plan. Ivy nodded. A reminder that all their hand-holding, smiles they'd given each other, tasting each other's food—at one point he'd even fork-fed her some of his grandmother's delicious peach cobbler—and all had been done according to plan to give everyone the impression they were a couple in love. Sad thing was that one of them was. "Yes, all according to plan." She'd been delusional to think otherwise.

He broke eye contact with her to glance at his watch. "It's late. I need to go."

It was on the tip of her tongue to tell him that he hadn't worried about how late it had been last night. Why was he in such a hurry to leave now? But considering everything, especially how she was feeling at the moment when she really had no right to, she said, "Yes, it is late. I will walk you to the door."

She walked past him, fully expecting him to pull her into his arms, but he didn't.

"I'll call you this week. We can go out to dinner again. Sisters."

She nodded again. Of course he would be dismissing her until then. And of course he would suggest Sisters. A guarantee they would be seen together. All according to plan. A plan that had been her idea. A plan she was now regretting.

"Dinner at Sisters this week will be fine." She would enjoy whatever time she could spend with him over the next two weeks and while he was in Paris she would come up with a reason for their breakup. But at least she would have her two weeks to make memories.

"Good night, Ivy," he said low, in that voice that could make sensations curl her stomach.

"Good night, Nolan."

He stood there for a moment, his dark eyes probing hers and then he leaned down and brushed his

lips against hers in a chaste kiss. She fought back the
thought that he'd never given her a chaste kiss before.
There hadn't been a Nolan Madaris kiss that hadn't
been one to ravish her mouth.

And then he was gone, heading toward the elevator.
Drawing in a deep sigh, she closed the door behind him.

NOLAN HAD MADE it to the parking lot when he stopped
walking. What in the hell was wrong with him? Why
did the thought of leaving Ivy tonight bother the hell
out of him? He glanced around, noticing the people,
namely couples, who were coming home. Some were
holding hands and beaming at each other with love.
He wondered if what he was seeing was the real thing
or just plans like the one he and Ivy had implemented.

Hell, he knew the couples were real. Nobody had a
great-grandmother like the one he had who would drive
someone to resort to such a thing. He hadn't truly enjoyed a woman's company…hadn't allowed himself to
do so since Andrea. Damn, had it been close to fifteen
years? He'd run into her a few years ago at Sisters. He
had looked at her and felt nothing. Not like, not dislike.
He'd felt nothing. On the other hand, he would look at
Ivy and feel everything. Emotions he'd never felt before. Sensations that had the ability to overwhelm him.

He pushed the thoughts from his mind and forced
himself to keep walking. When he reached his car, he
was about to open the door and get inside when he felt
someone watching him. He glanced up to where he
knew Ivy's condo was located. He saw her standing at
the window and she was watching him do something
he truly didn't want to do. Leave.

He stood there and held her gaze and felt it, all that

sexual chemistry they had perfected so well. At that moment he felt something else, something he wasn't ready to admit to. Something he refused to admit to. But he knew he couldn't leave.

Nolan headed back into the building. Too anxious to wait for the elevator, he decided to take the stairs, not caring he had ten flights of them. Not breaking a sweat, he moved quickly to her door and knocked.

She opened it immediately. "Did you leave something, Nolan?"

"I left *someone*. You." And then he slanted his mouth over hers.

IVY WAS CERTAIN she would remember every single minute of what happened after Nolan returned. *I left* someone. *You.*

His words would forever be etched on her brain as well as how he swept her into his arms and, with the toe of his shoe, closed the door behind them. She would recall how he had taken her into the bedroom and quickly undressed her before undressing himself and putting on a condom. How he had licked her all over before driving her to the edge over and over again before his body had finally straddled hers and entered her in one hard thrust. And she would remember every stroke he made into her body and how she'd reciprocated, lifting her hips up to meet his every thrust.

This was what she wanted, what she needed and damn the consequences. All she wanted to concentrate on was the man whose body was above hers and giving her intense pleasure. Over and over again. This was lovemaking that should be savored, and every ounce of desire surrendered to. When he hollered her name and bucked his body, she followed in hot pursuit as spasms sprinted all through her.

"Nolan!"

"I'm here, baby. Let it rip," he said in a choppy breath.

And she did. More spasms tore through her and she screamed his name yet again while he slowly rocked her body against his. It was as if he wanted to make sure she received the most powerful effect. And she did. The parts where their bodies were connected throbbed in what seemed like never-ending pleasure.

At some point in time, Ivy's body slowly stopped humming and all those spasms ceased. Nolan shifted their bodies in the bed to where they lay, facing each other. Her eyes were still closed as she tried to get her breathing under control. That wasn't easy with the feel of Nolan's tongue licking traces of sweat from her face.

When she finally opened her eyes, he leaned in and brushed his lips back and forth over hers. She wondered if he knew what he was doing, and then quickly decided that, yes, he knew. He'd had sex with her too many times not to know. As if to prove her point, his fingers went to the nape of her neck and she could feel herself getting aroused all over again. And when he slid his tongue between her lips to seduce her with hot, deep glides of his tongue, she knew they were about to do it all over again.

"TELL ME ABOUT Andrea Dunmire, Nolan."

Ivy's request surprised Nolan. They'd made love again and now they were lying in each other's arms, tired and depleted of energy, with their limbs connected. An earlier glance at the clock indicated it was close to two in the morning. He loved being here with her like this.

While glancing down at her and holding her gaze, he asked, "How do you know about Andrea?"

"Your mother mentioned her. She assumed I knew the story and I let her think that. From what she said, I gather Andrea is someone who had hurt you at one time. You never mentioned her. Was she supposed to be a secret?"

"No. Andrea was not a secret. She's just someone in my past. I guess to be fair to you, I should have told you about her when you told me about Damien Fargo."

"Yes, you should have. It would have saved me from having to play it off like I did know. I don't think she noticed, but if Andrea's name is brought up again, someone else might."

He saw the logic in what she said. "Andrea was someone I met one summer when I came home from college. Like I told you, I was the quintessential geek with thick-rimmed glasses and a techie mind. She showed me attention and I flipped and thought I fell in love and hard. She seemed proud to be my girl and I was definitely over the moon to be known as her guy."

Nolan paused, remembering that time and how easily he'd allowed himself to be fooled. "Then I overheard her telling her cousin that she owed her big-time since the only reason she was putting up with me was to help give her cousin a clear path to my cousin Blade, who at the time was a heartthrob around town and was sought after by so many women. And what was so sad was she didn't deny anything when I confronted her."

When Ivy didn't say anything, he added, "That was years ago, Ivy. I was nineteen at the time. I've got over her but there are some lessons you don't forget. Like how easily a person can take advantage of you if you let your guard down or allow yourself to be manipulated. But the one thing Andrea didn't do was to color my opinion of marriage. There are too many solid and happy marriages in my family for her to do that. Unlike you, I have no problem with getting married one day when I'm ready and when I meet the woman that I want to marry."

"And not the woman someone picked out for you."

"Right," he said, although now even that was beginning to become cloudy. He had some serious thinking to do and would do so when he got to Paris. Until then they would operate according to plan.

He tightened his arms around her. "Do I get to spend the night, Ivy?"

Ivy shifted their bodies to push him back against the pillows and crawled on top of him. "I never asked you to leave, Nolan."

She leaned in and the moment she took his mouth, he felt an invisible thread binding them tighter together, whether he wanted it to or not.

CHAPTER THIRTY-TWO

THE NEXT FEW days flowed smoothly, although Nolan thought time was moving too quickly. With Ivy trying to finish up her current project and with him preparing for his trip to Paris, both of their days were extremely busy. However, they made sure their evenings and nights belonged to each other. When he got off work, he usually cooked dinner and she would arrive at his place around six.

He tried preparing meals at her condo but she didn't have a functional kitchen. Instead of her buying cooking utensils she wouldn't ever use, he decided to cook the meals at his place. The trade-off was that when eating out it would be her treat. Usually their place of choice was Sisters or Xavier's. They'd gone to a movie and he'd taken her dancing a couple of times. When she'd complimented him on his dancing abilities, he'd told her how he and several of his cousins and brothers had taken dance lessons a few years back to keep up with Reese's wife, Kenna, on the dance floor.

Every place they went was strategically chosen to make sure word got back to his great-grandmother. He tried to push to the back of his mind they were just following their plan and nothing more.

They shared a bed every night, either hers or his. Nolan was getting used to waking up with Ivy in his arms every morning and going to bed with her the same way. Her being a night owl and him a morning person seemed to work in their favor. He loved leaving her asleep in his bed and it seemed she didn't have a problem leaving him asleep in hers. At first he kept telling himself they had only two weeks so there was no reason for her toiletries to be in his bathroom or his to be in hers, but it didn't stop it from happening. Nor did it stop him from beginning to see her in a new light.

Last weekend he'd taken her with him to the hospital to visit the twins and unsurprisingly, found Reese and Kenna there. He knew the hospital was probably their second home since the twins were still confined. Kenna looked good and was anxious for her babies to gain more weight so they could go home. The names they had chosen for the twins were Landon for their son and London for their daughter.

He had introduced Ivy to Reese and Kenna since they had missed the family celebration *supposedly* given in their honor...not that anyone had expected them to show up. He could tell Reese and Kenna liked Ivy, and again he thought how well she fitted in with his family.

The buzzer on his desk went off and he picked up his phone. "Yes, Marlene?"

"Mr. Lee Madaris is on the line."

"Please put him through."

Nolan leaned back in his chair wondering how Ivy was doing and how close she was in finishing up her project. This coming weekend would be their last one together before he left for Paris. He would love it if she was able to get away. Maybe they could go spend a couple of days on Tiki Island. He'd check with his property manager if the place was vacant this weekend.

"Nolan?"

"Yes, Lee. How are things going?"

"Appears there's a mix-up with some of the equipment you ordered. I'm going to need you here sooner than planned to check things out."

Nolan lifted a brow. "How soon?"

"If you can leave in the morning that would be great."

Nolan sat up straight in his chair. "In the morning?"

"Yes. With Peyton pregnant and due to deliver in a few months, DeAngelo is ready to return to New York, but he will delay things to be present at the meetings we need to have with you and Chenault. I'll send my pilot for you. Think you can be ready to fly out around ten, tomorrow morning?"

Yes, he could but that meant leaving Ivy earlier than planned. It also meant he would be in Paris for three weeks instead of two.

"Yes, I'll be ready," he said. Moments later he hung up the phone, missing Ivy already.

He stood and walked over to the window. A part of him truly didn't want to go but he knew he had no choice. He had planned to take Ivy to a movie tonight and he would still do so. And he'd let her know he would be leaving in the morning.

DAMIEN TOSSED HIS luggage on the bed and began unpacking. Before checking into the hotel, he had driven by Ivy's grandmother's house. When he'd seen her outside talking to one of her neighbors, that validated that she was still living in the same place.

He refused to admit to Whitfield there were problems but had a feeling the man suspected something.

That meant Damien had to make certain Ivy didn't give him any problems and he knew just the way to do that.

He pulled his phone out of his jacket pocket and punched a number he'd saved over the years. When the man came on the line, he said, "This is Damien Fargo… Yes, I'm back in town for a while and there's a little job I need done. I want you to hook me up with the right person to do it."

Ivy smiled when she opened the door for Nolan. "I'm ready. I just have to grab my purse and turn off the lights."

He entered and closed the door behind him. "Take your time. The movie doesn't start for a while."

Moments later when she returned, she saw Nolan standing in the middle of her living room with his hands shoved in his pockets. He was staring at her floor with a pensive expression on his face. "Nolan? Is anything wrong?"

He glanced up and she knew he hadn't heard her approach. "I was thinking that maybe we could go somewhere other than a movie. Maybe dancing or something. There's a live band at Sisters. The Roulettes. You enjoy them, don't you?"

"Yes." She studied his features. "Any reason for the change in plans?"

He drew in a deep breath and met her gaze. "Yes. Lee called today. I'm needed in Paris earlier than planned. I will be leaving in the morning."

"In the morning?" She immediately felt her heart begin to ache.

"Yes. So it will be our last night together for a while."

For a while? He really meant to say that tonight

would be their last night together forever. She knew the plan. While he was in Paris she was to come up with a solid reason for them to break up and be ready to execute that plan when he returned.

"Oh." Now she was the one who looked down at the floor when the meaning of his words stung like needles. They wouldn't have another week as they thought. Only tonight. And she didn't want to spend it listening to music or dancing. If tonight was all she would have with him, she wanted to spend it in the arms of the man she loved.

She glanced up and saw him watching her with an odd expression on his face. Was he ready to end things? Probably no reason why he shouldn't be. In that case she intended to leave him with something to remember. She would leave her imprint on him, making sure even after they called it quits that he didn't forget her.

"I got a better idea about tonight, Nolan."

He crossed the room to stand in front of her. "What's your idea, baby?"

"How about if we stay in and enjoy each other's company?" Judging by the way his eyes flared, she knew he understood just what she meant.

"I think that's a great idea." And he swept her off her feet and headed for her bedroom.

HOURS LATER, IVY lay awake in Nolan's arms listening to the sound of his deep and even sleep. Just like all those other times, her body was still reeling from so many pleasurable sensations. They had made love three times already and she knew before he left, they would do it again. From the intensity of their lovemaking, it was as if he was trying to store up as many memories of their time together as she was, but she knew that was just wishful thinking on her part. After making love they had drifted off to sleep.

Now she was wide-awake and thinking about what came next. He would expect her to come up with a plan for their breakup while he was away. He hadn't said the plan regarding that had changed, and she had no reason to think it had. A wave of pain surrounded her heart in knowing that, once again, she loved a man who hadn't loved her back.

Nolan shifted slightly in sleep and tightened his arms around her and muttered something. Her ears perked up. Had he just said her name? She listened and he said nothing again. His breathing returned to deep and even. He hadn't said her name. She'd only wished that he had.

CHAPTER THIRTY-THREE

"I'M GLAD EVERYTHING worked out and we were only missing part of our shipment," Lee Madaris said, entering Nolan's office. Trailers were set up on the job site and Nolan and his staff had their own.

"So am I." They had been quick to rectify the problem so they could remain on schedule.

Lee eased into a chair across from Nolan's desk. "Sorry I had to get you here quick. I hope I didn't mess up your plans with Ivy."

Hearing her name made his heart ache. He missed her so much and would admit she had got under his skin in a way no other woman had before. And that included Andrea. He honestly didn't see that changing and to be quite honest, which he was finally being with himself, he didn't want it to change. He had talked to her several times since arriving in Paris, but every time he heard her voice, it made him regret calling. His heart was actually aching for her. For that reason he'd begun limiting the number of times he called.

There was no doubt in his mind that he had fallen in love with her, although he hadn't wanted to and had fought it like hell. In the end love had won. Just the thought he could love the woman his great-grandmother had selected for him was definitely something he hadn't counted on happening. Honestly, he hadn't believed that it could. He was more than ready to accept in his heart that Ivy was the woman he wanted, needed and couldn't even think of living without.

"Nolan?"

He glanced over at Lee. "Yes?"

Lee smiled. "I said I hope I didn't mess up your plans with Ivy."

Nolan met his cousin's gaze. "There aren't any plans with me and Ivy. Not anymore. At least not on my end." Lee was a smart man and Nolan knew his cousin was catching on to what he was saying.

"So that's how you're going to roll, Nolan?"

Nolan drew in a deep breath. "Yes, that's how I'm going to roll. Now I have to work hard to make sure Ivy wants to roll right along with me."

"I'M GLAD YOU were able to join me for dinner, Tessa," Ivy said after taking a sip of her wine.

"No need to thank me. You miss Nolan. I understand that. Besides, I look for any excuse to come to Sisters. Especially the nights they have a live band. Hope it will cheer you up."

Ivy doubted anything would cheer her up. It had been a week already. Nolan had contacted her to let her know when he'd got to Paris and had called a couple of times since then. Although he hadn't mentioned anything, she wondered if his calls were to remind her she was supposed to be working on a reason for their breakup.

"Hello, Ivy. I thought I might find you here."

Ivy stiffened at the unexpected—but immediately recognizable—voice. Damien Fargo. What on earth was he doing back in Houston?

"Damien? You remember Tessa."

He glanced over at Tessa like it was bothersome to do so. "Yes. How are you, Tessa?"

"Fine."

Ivy wasn't surprised Tessa hadn't asked how he was doing. She had never liked Damien. "What are you doing in Houston, Damien?"

"I came to see you. Can we talk privately?"

A frown covered Ivy's face. There was no reason for him to come to Houston to see her. "We have nothing to talk about. Privately or publicly."

Ignoring what Ivy said, Damien Fargo said, in a voice that was a little demanding. "We need to talk, Ivy."

Ivy's frown turned to a look of anger. "I said we have nothing to talk about, Damien."

"Is everything okay, Miss Chapman?"

Ivy glanced up and saw Ashton Sinclair had approached their table. Evidently he had observed the encounter, saw her frown and figured Damien was being a nuisance. "Yes, everything is okay, Mr. Sinclair. Mr. Fargo was just leaving."

Damien Fargo glanced at Ashton and, as if deciding the man was not one he would want to tangle with, he said, "Yes, I was just leaving."

Ashton nodded with a stern face. "In that case, I'll escort you out."

AN ANGRY DAMIEN entered his hotel room. The nerve of Ivy, embarrassing him that way in the restaurant. Not only had the man escorted him out, he had stood in the parking lot and made sure he left.

At that moment his phone rang and he didn't have to wonder who was calling him. Whitfield had tried reaching him twice today already. Damien knew it would be wise to take this call.

He pulled the phone out of his jacket, answered and said, "Yes, Whitfield?"

"I assume things are moving as planned, right? You've got that woman to go along with our arrangements."

"Yes," he lied. "I told you I had things under control. She was happy to see me tonight and within minutes I had her eating out of my hands again."

"Good. Keep me informed. We need to get the job done before the end of the month."

"No problem," he said, rubbing the top of his head, knowing he had to put pressure on Ivy. There was a man on standby, just waiting for his call, and he intended to make it tonight.

Moments later, after ending the call with Whitfield, he made a call to get things rolling. Ivy would regret the day she'd begun giving him a hard time.

CHAPTER THIRTY-FOUR

"I SEE THAT some things never change. Like you showing up at the cleaners every Thursday, Ivy."

Ivy turned around. She had just walked out of Altamonte Dry Cleaners when Damien approached. Where had he come from? "Damien? What are you doing here?"

He gave her a smile she didn't feel was sincere. "I've been waiting for you. I don't know where you live now but I knew your routine and figured I'd hang out here, and sooner or later you'd arrive. I wouldn't have to go to the trouble had you talked to me last night."

"You and I had nothing to say."

"You are wrong about that. We have a lot to discuss. Have dinner with me."

"Sorry, I have other plans."

"Change them."

"I will do no such thing because I don't intend to talk to you."

"I suggest you call your grandmother."

Ivy lifted a brow. "Call my grandmother? Why?"

His smile widened. "Tell her to check under her bed. Someone left her a present."

The hairs on the back of Ivy's neck stood up. "What are you talking about?"

"Call her," he all but snapped.

Not sure what was going on, Ivy nervously took her phone from her purse and quickly called her grandmother.

"Hi, Ivy," her grandmother greeted upon answering her phone. "I was going to call you to see if you'd heard from Nolan since he left for Paris."

What Damien had said was making her feel uneasy. "We'll talk about that later, Nana. What I need you to do is go look under your bed."

"Look under my bed? What on earth for?"

Ivy nervously nibbled on her bottom lip. "I might have left something there."

"Under my bed?" Nana asked as if that didn't make sense.

"Yes. Please look and let me know if I did."

It seemed it took forever before Nana returned to the phone. "Yes, dear, you left it. It's such a pretty wrapped box. Why did you leave it under my bed?"

Fear clutched Ivy. "No reason. I'll get it when I drop by in a few. Goodbye."

She then turned blazing eyes on Damien. "What's going on here? What do you think you're doing? What's in that box? How did it get in my grandmother's house?"

His laugh infuriated her. "I am calling the police, Damien," Ivy said, clicking her phone back on.

He snatched the phone from her hand. She glared at him. "What do you think you're doing?"

"Helping you keep your grandmother alive. Trust me, the people I work for wouldn't hesitate to end her life. You saw how easy it was for them to get inside her house and if I remember correctly, she has an alarm. This time the box was empty. Next time who knows what might be in there. Possibly a bomb."

Ivy swallowed, as more fear gripped her. "A bomb? Who are these people you work for? Why would they want to harm Nana?"

"They don't want to harm her. But they will if you don't cooperate."

"Cooperate how?"

Damien shoved his hands into his pockets as if he was sure he had her just where he wanted her. "There's a hacking job I need you to do. I'll cover things in detail when we talk. Cancel whatever engagement you had and meet me at Brennan's in an hour." Ivy watched as Damien walked off, got into his car and drove away.

IVY ENTERED BRENNAN'S and glanced around. When she saw Damien sitting at a table in the back, she headed in that direction. He was trying to force her to do something illegal. She should have gone to the police but knowing about that box under her grandmother's bed had stopped her.

After leaving the dry cleaner's, she'd driven in record time to Nana's house and opened the box. It had been a tube of lotion. Ivy knew it hadn't been important what was in the box but how it got there and by whom. Evidently, someone had access to her grandmother's home. The thought that someone had invaded her grandmother's personal space like that was nerve-racking and had her deeply agitated. The more she thought about it the angrier she became.

Damien saw her before she reached the table and stood. "Ivy, glad you could make it and you're right on time."

Like he'd given her a choice. She slid onto the seat, ignoring his outstretched hand. "Listen, Damien, I don't know what you're into but I have a mind to go to the police. How dare someone enter my grandmother's home and—"

"Go to the cops if you so desire. If you do, I won't be responsible for what happens to your grandmother. The people I'm dealing with mean business, Ivy. They know of your capabilities and need your help."

"To hack into some company's computer system? That's illegal."

"And who's to know?"

"I'll know."

"That's too bad. When you finish you can forget everything you did. You can pretend it never happened. I need you ready to leave in five days."

"Leave? What are you talking about?"

"You heard me. You're taking a little trip with me."

Had the man gone mad? "I am not going anywhere with you."

A cynical smile touched his lips. "Yes, you are. At this very minute my men have your grandmother under surveillance. I just got word she left home to go to the gym. Smart lady, that Helen, for wanting to stay in shape. It will be a pity if her granddaughter doesn't care enough about her to keep her alive."

Ivy just stared at the man she'd thought she loved at one time. "How did you get mixed up with those people, Damien?"

"That is done of your damn business. Just do what I say and your precious grandmother won't be harmed. If you don't follow my orders, then I can't guarantee that she won't. In fact, I can almost guarantee that she will."

He stood. "I'll call you tomorrow, so unblock me on your phone." Smiling at her, he said, "Don't look so sad, Ivy. Going away with me for a few days won't be so bad. I remember a time you adored the ground I walked on. Maybe we can get back together and—"

"Never!"

"Suit yourself. Remember you're not a beauty queen. I'm probably the best you'll ever do, so we might as well kiss and make up."

When she narrowed her eyes at him, he had the nerve to laugh and then walk off.

CHAPTER THIRTY-FIVE

WITH HANDS SHOVED into the pockets of his slacks, Nolan stood at his office window and looked out. Paris was beautiful this time of year and the land Lee and De-Angelo had chosen for the Grand MD Paris was perfect. He had enjoyed dinner last night with Lee and his wife, Carly, at this restaurant known for its fine cuisine. DeAngelo had joined them and it was quite apparent he was anxious to return to the United States and his pregnant wife, Peyton. There was no doubt in anyone's mind that DeAngelo was looking forward to fatherhood.

Nolan could recall the days when DeAngelo had been quite a ladies' man. Now he had given all that up for the woman he loved. Nolan allowed himself to ruminate over that for a minute. Now that he knew without a doubt that he had fallen in love with Ivy, the thought of his life changing didn't bother him.

He was anticipating the day he returned to Houston. He would let her know that she could forget coming up with a reason for them to break up because it wouldn't be happening.

Memories of their lovemaking the last night they'd been together sent wonderful shivers through his body. Making love to her was always off the charts and that night had been even more so. The intensity of what they'd done was so profound that afterward they had fallen asleep in each other's arms.

The buzzer on his desk claimed his attention and he moved away from the window. "Yes, Delphine?"

"A Joe Altamonte is on the line for you, Mr. Madaris," the woman said in a deep French accent.

Nolan lifted a brow. Joseph Altamonte was actually Lee's grandmother's brother. When Nolan was growing up, he'd been Uncle Joe to everyone and still was. They considered him part of their extended family. Nolan wondered why Uncle Joe would be calling, especially at this hour. Nolan knew with the seven-hour time difference, although it was ten in the morning in Paris, it was around three in the morning in the United States. No doubt Joe and his cronies were ending a card game or something. "Please put him through."

"Uncle Joe?"

"Nolan, how are you?"

"I'm fine. What about you?" Nolan asked, easing down into his chair.

"Doing well. I hear you're in Paris with Lee."

"Yes, and I will be here for another two weeks before returning home." And he couldn't wait.

"Well, I'm glad you're not holding that little incident against me, though."

Nolan knew exactly what "incident" he was referring to. Uncle Joe owned the cleaners that had led Ivy to believe she'd won that week on Tiki Island.

"No, I'm not holding it against you. I'm sure Mama Laverne twisted your arm to get you to go along with it."

He heard his uncle's robust laugh. "You know how much I love Felicia Laverne. Over the years she's been the best mother-in-law my sister could ever have. Even going against Lee Senior and standing up for Bessie in the early years of their marriage whenever he was wrong. Not all mothers-in-law will do that."

"No, they wouldn't."

"I hear everything worked out, though, between you and Miss Chapman. I like her. She's one of my best customers. She always takes the time to hold a conversation with me."

Since Uncle Joe was a talker, Nolan could see why the older man would appreciate that.

"Well, I don't want to take up much of your time but I wanted to tell you about an incident yesterday that concerns me. I called and told Felicia Laverne about it and she suggested I mention it to you."

Nolan lifted a brow. "Mention what?"

"Yesterday around two o'clock I noticed a car parked outside my establishment. What caught my attention was that the driver of the car didn't get out. He just sat there. I got concerned that I was about to get robbed so I got my gun ready."

Nolan didn't doubt that since Uncle Joe was an ex-cop. He'd heard stories about how back in the day when those Madaris brothers—namely the senior Milton, Lee, Nolan and Lucas—got into trouble by causing a ruckus at the local bar in town, Joe would deliver them to Mama Laverne instead of locking them up. "Was it a would-be robber?" he asked, leaning back in his chair.

"No. The guy took the time to stretch his legs, and when he got out of the car I saw he was well dressed in a suit and tie. A businessman. So I relaxed and figured he was just waiting for someone."

Nolan wondered where this was leading. Why would

any of this be of interest to him? "So, was he waiting for anyone?"

"Yes. He was waiting for your Ivy Chapman."

Nolan quickly sat up. "Ivy?"

"Yes. As soon as she came in around four thirty and dropped off her clothes to be cleaned, the guy stopped her before she got back into her car. By then I was on full alert. You know how my mind works. I'm suspicious by nature."

Nolan knew that was true. Although Joe had retired from the police force before Nolan was born, Uncle Joe liked to entertain himself by watching all those criminal and cop shows on television. Claimed he was keeping his mind sharp and staying one step ahead of criminals.

"Did anything happen to cause you concern?"

"Yes. For one, she wasn't happy to see him. That was apparent from the way she looked at him. It was also apparent whatever he was saying to her was upsetting. They talked for fifteen or possibly twenty minutes before he got into his car and left. Then she got into her car and left as well."

Nolan wondered who the man could be. The only person he could imagine upsetting her would be her ex-boyfriend Damien Fargo. He recalled how the man had tried reaching Ivy when they'd been at the cottage. He also recalled Ivy telling him Fargo had moved to New York. What if Nolan was jumping to conclusions and the man wasn't Damien Fargo but someone else? But then, who? "Uncle Joe, you still keep video cameras around your cleaners, right?"

"Yes, I sure do."

"Would it be possible for me to look at that footage from yesterday?"

"Yes. Romeo will be here around noon. He's good with that technology stuff. I'll have him email you a copy." Romeo Altamonte was Uncle Joe's grandson who was in his senior year of high school. And from what Nolan had heard, the kid was living up to his name to the point where Uncle Joe had to call former playboy himself Blade in to council Romeo when girls began fighting over him.

"Thanks, Uncle Joe." Nolan had no idea what Fargo looked like but chances were the man had a photo of himself out there somewhere on social media.

After ending the call, Nolan leaned back in his chair. If the man was Fargo, why had he returned to Houston? More important, why had he upset Ivy?

He could call Ivy and ask her directly. The last time they talked, she'd told him she had finished the Wonderbelly project and was sleeping normal hours for a change. For that reason, he didn't want to wake her. First thing he would do was watch the video to determine if there was reason for concern.

"I THINK YOU should tell Nolan, Ivy."

Ivy drew in a deep breath as she listened to Tessa's words. More than anything she wished that was possible but it was not. Adjusting the cell phone to her ear, she said, "I can't do that, Tessa. You know Nolan's and my agreement. When he returns to Houston, he will expect me to have come up with a plan for us to break up. The last thing he would want is to get involved with my problems with an ex-boyfriend."

"This is about more than problems, Ivy. This is about a crime. What Damien wants you to do is illegal and he is threatening harm to your grandmother to make sure you toe the line. There has to be something that can be done."

Tessa paused for a minute and then added, "You can't convince me that Nolan wouldn't want to help, regardless of any plans he expects you to make."

"Yes, but involving him might place his life in danger as well, and I can't allow it to happen. I shouldn't be telling you about it but I had to tell someone. I haven't slept at all last night."

"You did the right thing by telling me, Ivy. I never liked Damien but I never thought he would end up getting mixed up in something like this."

"Me either."

"What are you going to do?"

"I'll try to stall him and figure out something. There is no way I will go along with what he wants, Tessa. No way."

A short while later after her call with Tessa ended, Ivy was pacing the floor when her phone rang. She hoped it wasn't Damien calling. She crossed the room and picked up her phone off the table, and her heart began pounding when she saw the caller was Nolan.

Of all the times for him to call her, why now? As much as she wanted to hear his voice she knew the last thing she needed was to talk to him. There was no way she could without telling him what was happening and she couldn't do that. She refused to unload her problem with Damien on Nolan. And like she told Tessa, telling Nolan could pull him into Damien's craziness. It was bad enough she had Nana to worry about, she couldn't put Nolan's life in danger as well. There was no doubt in her mind that if Damien knew about Nolan and how

much she cared for him, he would make it his business
to be a threat to him, too.

As much as she hated doing so, she would ignore
any calls from Nolan for a while.

NOLAN GLANCED UP upon hearing the knock on his office door. "Come in."

Lee walked in, smiling. "I'm leaving to grab dinner
at one of those cafés on the corner. Carly is going shopping. You want to join me?"

Nolan shook his head. "I would but I can't. I'm waiting for a copy of a video from Uncle Joe."

Lee raised a brow. "Why would Uncle Joe send you
a video?"

Before Nolan could answer, a ding from his computer alerted him that he'd received incoming mail. He
glanced at his laptop screen. "This is it." He picked up
a remote on his desk to roll down the video screen on
the wall across from where he sat. He then answered
Lee's question.

"Sounds like Uncle Joe is playing cop again," Lee
said. "It was probably nothing."

"I'll see," Nolan said, pressing the start button on
the remote.

Within minutes Nolan's suspicions were confirmed.
The man in the video was Damien Fargo. He recognized
the man from the photo on his Facebook page. Uncle Joe
was right, Ivy seemed pretty upset about something. At
some point she pulled her phone out of her purse and
made a call. To who? Her conversation with the person
lasted a few minutes and when she hung up it was apparent her irritation with Fargo had increased. He also

saw when she was about to make a second call, the man snatched the phone out of her hand.

"I wonder who she called and talked to, and who she was trying to call when he snatched the phone," Lee said.

For a minute Nolan had forgotten Lee was there. "I don't know. The guy is her ex-boyfriend. And from what she told me, he was a real ass."

"Looks like he still is," Lee said. "And Uncle Joe appears to have been right. The guy was harassing her. Have you talked to Ivy?"

Nolan rubbed a frustrated hand down his face. "I tried calling her several times but for some reason she's not answering. I even sent her a couple of text messages and she hasn't responded to them either."

"That doesn't sound good, Nolan."

"I know and it has me worried." He glanced at Lee. "I know there's a lot to be done here but I need to return to Houston to see what's going on for myself."

"And you should," Lee said in understanding. "If something is going on with your woman, then you need to find out what. That should be your first priority. Everything else can wait until you get back. I'll have my pilot get the plane ready."

Your woman. Nolan knew at that moment that yes, Ivy was his woman and before returning to Paris he was going to make sure she knew it, too.

CHAPTER THIRTY-SIX

IF IVY PACED the floor any more, she would wear out the wood grain. There had to be something she could do. If it had not been for Texas's privacy laws, she would have taped her conversations with Damien.

She jumped when she heard her doorbell. As far as she knew, Damien still didn't know where she lived and she wasn't expecting anyone. So who was paying her a visit?

She slowly moved to the door and, looking out the peephole, nearly gasped. It was Nolan. He was supposed to be in Paris so what was he doing back in the United States? Had he been calling to let her know he was back? Was he here to see if she'd come up with a breakup plan yet? All those questions rushed through her head as she opened the door.

"Nolan? When did you get back in town?" she asked stepping aside to let him in and closing the door behind him.

"Just now. I came straight here from the airport."

She lifted a brow. "Why? Is something wrong?"

"You tell me," he said, coming to stand in front of her. "I've been trying to reach you."

"Oh. I've been busy."

He crossed his arms over his chest. "Too busy to

take my calls but not too busy to spend time with your ex-boyfriend Damien Fargo?"

Her heartbeat pounded from unexpected surprise. Damien. How had he known? Before she could question him, he said, "I know he was waiting for you at the cleaners on Thursday."

She stared at him as anger surged through her. "Have you had people spy on me, Nolan?"

"No. I've told you more than once about my great-grandmother's allies, and you and Damien Fargo were captured on the cleaners' security cam."

"How dare you question me about anything? We aren't married and I'm not your girlfriend, at least not a real one, so I don't have to answer any of your questions."

He took a step closer. "Wrong, Ivy. I want an answer."

Her mind was churning as to what she could tell him. No way could she tell him the truth. "Okay, you want an answer, I'll give you one."

"I'm listening."

She nervously licked her bottom lip and then said, "It's my idea for our breakup."

He narrowed his eyes at her. "Excuse me?"

"I was to come up with a reason for us to break up, so Damien is it. You didn't want it to seem you were messing around on me. Fine. Then let people think I was messing around on you."

It occurred to Ivy that people would believe he messed around on her before they would believe she would mess around on him. What woman in her right mind would cheat on a man who looked like Nolan Madaris?

"And you want me to believe that?"

"Yes, why not?"

"Because I know how Fargo treated you when the two of you were together. But more important, I know you. Only a weak-minded woman would go back to a man who treated her so shabbily for any reason. The one thing I know about you, Ivy, is that you're not weak. You're strong. You are a woman to be admired and not pitied."

Why did he have to say something like that? "You don't know me, Nolan. You only think you do."

"I know you, Ivy," he said in a somewhat soft tone. "I know you skin to skin, flesh to flesh. I know your taste in the morning and at night. I also know how your mind works. You are not one to take back up with Fargo for any reason."

"I told you the reason. To break off our relationship."

The fury she saw in Nolan's eyes surprised her. Why should it matter to him? He should be jumping for joy. "I just don't understand this, Nolan. You should be ecstatic. Now you can get back to your women. I've just given you a reason to do so—one that's so unforgivable that no one, including your great-grandmother, would expect you to get back with me."

He didn't say anything, he just stood there, staring at her. She could feel his anger like it was a tangible thing and for the life of her couldn't understand why. "I've given you an out, Nolan. Why can't you take it?"

AN OUT? DID Ivy really think that giving the appearance of becoming involved with Damien Fargo again was an out?

Nolan rubbed his hands down his face to break eye

contact with her as well as to rein in his anger. She was lying. Why? He'd watched that video that Uncle Joe had given him. He'd recognized her body language that he'd come to know so well. He could read her eyes and he knew deep within his gut something was wrong. Why wouldn't she tell him?

"You can leave, Nolan, and go back to Paris."

He turned but not to walk out the door. He went to her sofa and sat down. "I want you to tell me the real reason you're letting Damien Fargo back into your life."

She lifted her chin and stiffened her spine. "What part of everything I told you did you not understand?"

"All of it. Frankly, I refuse to believe any of it."

He could tell that angered her. She left her spot in the middle of the floor to come stand before him. "Why are you being so difficult?"

"Why are you?" he countered. "Why can't you tell me why Fargo upset you so that day?" He saw the flash of something in her eyes. Fear. Why? That made him even more determined to find out what the hell was going on. "Tell me, Ivy."

"There's nothing to tell about my seeing Damien at the cleaners. Why can't you accept what I've said?"

He stood from the sofa. She tried to back up but he reached out and placed his hands at her waist. He needed to touch her, to hold her in his arms. "The reason I can't accept what you've said is because I've fallen in love with you, Ivy."

He saw shock radiate in her face. "No, that's not true. You can't."

"And why can't I? Because some bastard, the same one you were seen with the other day, tried convincing you that you couldn't be loved? In that case, he's a liar because I do love you. These past few weeks have meant everything to me."

He saw the tears spring into her eyes and instinctively, he tightened his grip on her waist, pulling her into his arms fully. "I know you believe you can't and won't ever love again, but I plan to change all that. I can be a very patient man, Ivy."

She was crying in earnest now and he continued to hold her. Rubbed his arms gently up and down her back. Sweeping her up, he sat back down and cradled her in his arms. He knew there was something she wasn't telling him. "What's wrong, baby? Why are you crying?"

She shook her head and lifted tearstained eyes to him. "Because you love me and I love you, too, and everything should be all right, but it's not!"

She loved him, too? His heart jumped in joy. "And why can't everything be fine, Ivy? If I love you and you love me, why can't it?" he asked gently, using his fingertips to wipe tears from her eyes.

"I can't tell you."

"Either you tell me or I'll find Fargo and get answers."

"No! You can't," she said, twisting around in his arms to face him.

The fear he'd seen earlier in her eyes was back. "Why?" When she began nibbling on her bottom lip, he pressed for an answer to his question. "Why, Ivy?"

She didn't say anything for a moment and then she said in a low voice, "Because your life will be in danger."

IVY REGRETTED SAYING the words the moment they'd left her mouth. But when he confessed to loving her, he'd destroyed all her defenses.

"How will my life be in danger, Ivy?"

She shook her head. "If I tell you, then I have to protect the both of you."

"The both of who?"

"You and Nana."

What was she talking about? "No, you don't. What you need to do is to tell me everything so I can put an end to this nonsense."

"It's more than nonsense, Nolan. You don't know Damien."

"No, it's the other way around. Damien Fargo doesn't know me." He took her hand in his. "You're going to have to trust me, Ivy. As the man who loves you. And you were wrong about what you said earlier about me wanting to get back to all those other women. The majority of them were from a legal escort service and were women I didn't sleep with. It was all part of my strategy to get a reputation you wouldn't want in a husband. At the time I had no idea you never intended to marry."

He brought her hand to his lips. "But that's going to change because I intend for us to marry when this matter with Fargo is taken care of, so tell me and trust me to know what to do to make things right."

Ivy stared into his eyes. She loved him so much and the thought that he loved her back sent her emotions soaring. At that moment she wanted to believe he had the ability to slay her dragons and make things right. She had to believe. She had to trust.

She swallowed deeply and began talking, telling Nolan everything.

CHAPTER THIRTY-SEVEN

FROM AN EARLY age one of the first things that had been drilled into Nolan was that a Madaris never fought any battles alone; especially those that might have a major impact on the entire family. As far as he was concerned, this one fell within that category. Ivy was the woman he loved, the one who he intended to be a part of his life forever. His future wife.

While she was in the kitchen making coffee, he was on the phone. The first person he knew to call was Alex Maxwell. Alex's extraordinary skills as a private investigator were known far and wide. A former FBI agent who retained plenty of contacts, he was known to piece together even the most challenging of puzzles. He was also married to Nolan's cousin Christy, which meant that Alex was officially a member of the Madaris family. Alex's brother Trask was also married to Nolan's cousin Felicia Laverne II, which made it a double family affair.

ALEX AGREED WITH Ivy that it was unwise to meet at either of their places in case Ivy was being watched. It was decided for Nolan and Ivy to drive out to Whispering Pines. Hopefully Fargo would assume she was visiting with his family. Alex had also arranged for Ivy's grandmother to be protected by a bodyguard...

without her knowing she had one. Alex intended to find out how that box had got inside Helen Chapman's house. Nolan knew he wouldn't have to call anyone else in the family. Alex would be contacting those who needed to know.

"Here you are." At the sound of Ivy's voice, he turned, after ending his call with Alex, to accept the coffee Ivy had prepared.

"Thanks," he said. He placed both their cups aside and pulled her into his arms. He needed this now more than ever, he thought, slanting his mouth over hers. Just knowing what her ex had planned angered him, but this was what he needed to calm him. It was hard to believe how things had turned out. If anyone would have told him he wouldn't have believed them. But he loved her more than life itself and knowing she loved him, too, was a gift beyond price.

He deepened the kiss when he felt a rush of sexual charge. No other woman could do this to him. Make him feel such pleasure from a kiss. No telling how long their mouths would have continued to mate if his cell phone hadn't rung. He recognized the ringtone and broke off the kiss.

Nolan quickly answered the call. "Granduncle Jake?"

"You and your lady okay?"

Nolan smiled while looking at Ivy. "Yes, Granduncle Jake. Me and my lady are okay."

"Good. And let her know not to worry about anything."

"I will. Thanks for calling." He clicked off the phone and put it back in his jacket. Glancing at Ivy, he smiled. "That was Granduncle Jake checking to make sure we were okay. And he told me to tell you not to worry

about a thing," Nolan said, handing her her coffee cup
and picking up his. "Let's sit down so I can tell you
the plan."

Earlier, he'd told Ivy about Alex's credentials and
why Nolan felt confident if anyone should be worried it
should be Damien Fargo and whomever he was working
for. What Ivy would soon discover was that the arms of
protection for the Madaris family ran deep and crossed
international waters.

They sat together on the sofa. "First of all I want to
assure you that no one will harm a hair on your grandmother's head. Already Alex has put a bodyguard in
place."

"He has?"

He saw the relief in her eyes. "Yes, baby, he has.
Knowing Alex, whoever he's assigned to protect her
was good. He only employs the best. Alex also intends
to find out the person who was able to bypass security
and enter her home illegally."

"You think he will be able to do that?"

"Yes. Don't be surprised if he knows the identity of
the person when we meet with Alex later at Whispering Pines."

Ivy nodded. "Did he say what I should say or do if
Damien calls? He demanded that I unblock his number."

"He said to just go along but still show some resistance so Fargo won't get suspicious about anything.
When does he expect you to leave town with him?"

"He said in five days. Four now."

Nolan took a sip of his coffee while Ivy took a sip of
hers. "And Fargo didn't mention the name of the company he wanted you to hack?"

"No. I have no idea."

"Doesn't matter. Alex will find all that out. Trust me."

Ivy lifted a brow. "You seem pretty confident in Alex's abilities."

"I am. He's good. But he doesn't work alone. There are Madaris loyalists who are close family friends. They won't hesitate to come to our aid if we need them. One is a sheikh."

"A sheikh?"

"Yes, Sheikh Rasheed Valdemon. He saved Christy's life once." Nolan placed his cup down and glanced at his watch. "Time for us to go to Whispering Pines. On the drive there I'll tell you how Alex and the gang rescued Lee's wife, Carly, when she was kidnapped."

Ivy placed her cup aside as well. "Carly? Kidnapped? You're kidding, right?"

Nolan chuckled. "No." He pulled her into his arms. "You're about to discover there's never a dull moment in the Madaris family."

IVY DISCOVERED NOLAN had told her the truth. Alex Maxwell was good. As far as she was concerned, the man was better than good. The father of three and his wife, a former investigative reporter, were waiting for them when they arrived at Whispering Pines.

Ivy was surprised to see Nettie's husband, Ashton Sinclair, and was even more surprised to discover he would be retiring as a colonel in the Marines in a year or so. She also met for the first time another married couple, Drake and Tori Warren, who were not only former marines but former CIA agents as well. They had missed the Madaris family gathering since they were spending time at their other home in the Tennessee mountains.

She thought Tori Warren was beautiful and found it hard to believe a woman who seemed so fun loving could be married to someone as stern and severe as Drake Warren. Ivy thought Drake was handsome but his harsh demeanor shielded it.

Then there was Trevor Grant, also a former marine. She had met Trevor and his beautiful wife, Corinthians, at the family gathering. It amazed her that everyone gathered in Jake Madaris's office seemed normal— with the exception of Drake Warren, whom everyone in the room called Sir Drake. He had a fierce look on his face. Almost too serious. Except for that one moment she caught him smiling at his wife.

Other than Drake Warren, one would never have suspected that any of the others were deadly. From what Nolan had shared with her, Ashton, Drake and Trevor were former members of the Marines' elite Force Recon. In Ivy's book that said a lot.

Nolan had been right about the possibility of Alex having learned the identity of the person who entered Nana's house. The man was Neal Cagney, a technician who worked for the security company that had installed Nana's equipment a few years ago. According to Alex's contact at police headquarters, Cagney had been under suspicion for a number of homes robberies that had used that same security company. To arrest the man now would alert Damien that someone was onto him. They didn't want to risk him fleeing before they got a chance to nail his boss, Albert Whitfield. Damien was a small fish in comparison to the organization he worked for.

Alex also informed them the FBI had an open case on the group. So far neither Damien nor his associates were aware they were under the Bureau's radar. Until now the feds hadn't been able to get anything on them and hoped with Ivy's help that would change.

Nana's bodyguard confirmed she was being watched. The watcher was unaware that he also was being watched. The police had run an ID on the license plate and discovered the car was owned by Cagney. The description Nana's bodyguard had given confirmed the man was Cagney. Evidently he'd been given orders to keep an eye on Nana, and if there was access needed to Nana's home, Cagney would be the one to provide it. Ivy was again assured that Nana would be fine and if anything to pity Cagney if he made a move. The bodyguard was one of TDA Tactical Operations Center men. TDA was owned by Trevor, Sir Drake, Ashton and Tori. The men and women they employed were trained by the four. According to Alex, the man who was the bodyguard to Nana was Jaxon Descheeny and he'd been personally trained by Sir Drake. Ivy figured that must have been a good thing. At least Alex had acted like it was.

After the group grilled her about her conversations with Damien, they told her they would come up with a plan and she and Nolan were free to leave. Diamond invited them to stay for dinner and they accepted her invitation. Corbin arrived and joined them. If Nolan's great-grandmother thought it odd that so many people were present for dinner, she didn't let on.

Nolan had explained to Ivy the day of the family gathering that his great-grandmother lived on Whispering Pines with Jake, Diamond and their family for half the year. The other six months were split between her remaining five sons. The grands and great-grands got pulled into the mix when it was time to transport her to doctor visits, church, Thursday-night bingo and anywhere else she wanted to go.

Ivy thought it was wonderful how everyone pitched in to help. She couldn't see her father pitching in and doing too much of anything when Nana got older. He was too busy chasing younger women.

Damien called while she was at Whispering Pines. She told him that she would call him back since she couldn't talk privately at the moment. When she returned his call a few minutes later, the team recorded the call. Ivy was under the impression that in the state of Texas you couldn't record a call without the other party's consent. Evidently Alex and this group made their own rules.

Ivy was beginning to feel sorry for Damien.

NOLAN EASED OUT of bed, but not before placing a kiss on a sleeping Ivy's lips. He'd practically stripped her of her clothes the moment they'd entered his condo. Then he'd swept her into his arms and carried her to his bed. It had been their first chance to make love since he'd rushed home from Paris and them professing their love for each other. The mating had been the most intense they'd ever shared. He bit back a moan just remembering some of the things they'd done tonight. He recalled how she had bucked hard against his mouth when he'd been devouring her clit. Then when he'd moved upward and straddled her, he had loved fitting snugly between her thighs while going deep within the confines of her more-than-ready body.

Then there was the time he'd knelt behind her, skin to skin and eager to mate with her that way. He had felt her climax building by the trembling of her hips pressed against his groin. He'd been planted deep inside her to the hilt, and just feeling the quake of her body had triggered his own turbulent release. A release that hadn't wanted to end. It was as if his body just couldn't stop exploding inside her, drenching her with his semen.

It was then that he'd realized he hadn't been wearing a condom. She'd realized it, too, and had quickly assured him it was okay since she had an implant. He'd been relieved to hear that, although the thought of a little girl who looked like Ivy actually appealed to him. Being skin to skin with her had kept his body on fire even while he was coming off a tremendous sexual high. Instead of being a greedy ass, he had held her in his arms until she'd drifted off to sleep.

He walked over to the window and glanced out. Nolan felt good that Alex and the gang were on top of things and couldn't wait until they apprised him of the plan. He never liked plans but he knew this one would be essential to keep Ivy and her grandmother safe.

He drew in a deep breath and with it came Ivy's scent. It aroused him from across the room. After all they'd done, how could he still want her again? It was as if Ivy had become an addiction.

"Nolan."

He turned upon hearing his name from Ivy's lips. "You're supposed to be sleeping."

"I was but I woke up when I missed your body next to mine."

"That can be remedied," he said, walking naked back to the bed. He slid under the covers and drew her into his arms. "I love you, Ivy."

The smile that touched her lips shot sexual energy

throughout his body. "And I love you, too, Nolan. Make love to me again."

He held her gaze. "Haven't got enough yet?"

She shook her head. "I doubt I could ever get enough of you."

He felt the same way about her. Even now his erection was throbbing with the need for her. The thought of exploding inside her body again had his groin aching in greedy anticipation. "You sure?"

"Positive."

He leaned up and kissed her while his fingers eased between her legs and began fingering her curls and finding her hot and ready for him. He loved how responsive she was, how her hunger and need could match his own. His kiss was meant to consume, overwhelm and incinerate her further. He wanted the same bone-melting fire that was spreading through him to spread through her as well.

"Nolan..."

He loved hearing her speak his name that way. On a bated breath. And when he felt her insides begin to tremble, he knew he wanted to be inside her for the full effect.

Pulling back from the kiss and withdrawing his fingers from inside her, he eased his body over her. Looking down at her, he whispered, "I love you," as he slowly eased inside her body. He could hear her groan beneath him and wanted to give her something to really groan about.

He changed their rhythm, increased the pace and strengthened his strokes. And if that wasn't enough, he slanted his mouth over hers, giving her a hard and greedy kiss. His hands lifted her hips as he dived even deeper into the core of her, giving her even more hard thrusts.

He could feel a climax coming on to the point his balls ached, but he refused to let go until he knew for certain she was going with him. And when he felt her body beginning to tremble in earnest, he broke off the kiss and threw his head back and hollered her name.

And then he heard his name off her lips in a breathless whisper. When the sensations began receding after such a mind-boggling release, he still held on to her. As usual, their mating had been explosive.

He drew her into his arms and cradled her close to his ear. "Ivy?"

"Hmm?"

"Will you marry me, Ivy?"

She eased on her back to stare up at him. Her cheeks were still flushed with heat and her gaze wide. And then he watched a smile spread across her lips at the same time he saw the tears spring into her eyes. "Yes, Nolan. I will marry you. I love you so much."

"And I love you."

He leaned down and kissed her again, believing everything would be all right. Damien Fargo and his band of crazy men would eventually go to jail and once he and Ivy put it behind them they could concentrate on a wedding. They were happy and he knew two other people who would be happy as well.

Helen Chapman and Felicia Laverne Madaris.

CHAPTER THIRTY-EIGHT

THE NEXT MORNING Nolan and Ivy were awakened by the sound of Nolan's cell phone. Using his hand to wipe sleep from his eyes he reached out with his other hand for the phone, recognizing the ringtone. He glanced at the clock—it was five in the morning.

"Alex?"

"Yes, it's me. Put your phone on speaker so Ivy can also hear. I understand Damien Fargo's plans have changed."

"In what way?" Nolan asked, switching to speaker.

"Whomever he works for doesn't want to wait. They want Ivy in place within twenty-four hours."

"Twenty-four hours!" Ivy said, quickly sitting up in bed.

"Yes. Not sure why their schedule changed but we're checking it out. Expect a call from Fargo, Ivy. He will make threats of what will happen if you don't cooperate."

"The hell she will," Nolan snapped.

"I assure you she's going to be okay," Alex said.

"And how can you assure me of that, Alex? You don't know these people."

"Now we do. Their target is the US government, which is why it's important for Ivy to leave with Fargo."

"No! Absolutely not. I don't want Fargo near her."

"Listen, Nolan, you're going to have to trust me that she will never be alone."

"And how do you plan that?"

"Fargo's people ordered a private plane to fly Ivy to where the others are waiting. We were able to intercept the request and will control the situation by using one of TDA's aircraft. FBI agents will be tracking the plane and a couple of agents will be hiding in the cargo area of our jet. If things go according to plan, Ivy won't even have to get off the plane when it lands. The entire plane will be wired for audio. When Fargo makes contact with his people to verify plans, we'll have it all on tape."

Nolan shook his head. "I still don't like it, Alex."

"Will you feel better if I told you that two of our own will be posing as pilot and copilot?"

"No."

"Let's see about that. It's Sir Drake and Tori."

"Damn," Nolan said, drawing in a deep breath. And for the first time he found a reason to smile. "Okay, I admit that's definitely a game changer."

"ALL YOU HAVE to do is say the word, Ivy, and we can call everything off."

Ivy smiled at Nolan when she rolled her luggage out of her bedroom. "I'm fine. Honest. I just want to get this over with and bring an end to what Damien and those people he works for are doing."

If she didn't allow the FBI to stop Damien and the group he was affiliated with now, no telling what else they might do later. Alex had been right about Damien calling to demand she leave within eight hours. She had argued with him and tried her best at resisting; however, just like Alex had said he would do, Damien made more sinister threats against Nana.

"The only reason I'm going along with Alex's plan is because of Sir Drake and Tori," Nolan said. "Both are kick-ass and they won't hesitate to take Fargo down if they have to. I know you will be safe with them."

Ivy didn't know the Warrens that well. In fact, she'd just met them yesterday. But if Nolan trusted their ability to keep her safe then she would, too.

Alex had also explained to her and Nolan that once Sir Drake notified everyone of the trip's destination, which Fargo was withholding so far, the FBI would have men on the ground as well as in the air to converge on the location.

"I'm ready to leave now, Nolan." Damien had given her instructions to drive her car to the private airstrip and park it. He would be waiting for her there.

"I don't like the fact that you have to be anywhere near Fargo. Letting you walk out that door is going to be hard, Ivy."

It would be hard for her as well. But she knew she had to assure him everything would be fine, even when she wasn't truly confident of that. "I'll be okay, Nolan. You trust Alex and his team, and because you trust them, I trust them as well."

She leaned up on tiptoe to kiss him, but Nolan wasn't going to settle for a chaste kiss. He slanted his mouth over hers, giving her a kiss she would remember for days to come.

It took Ivy less than an hour to drive to the private airstrip. She wasn't surprised to see Damien pacing when she pulled up to park. "It's about time you got here," he snapped at her.

She glared. "I am in the time frame you gave me, Damien, so back off. You just better make sure nothing happens to Nana."

"Whatever."

The pilot was indeed Sir Drake, dressed in a pilot's uniform and looking serious as usual. He was standing next to the plane. "Isn't this a big plane?" Ivy asked Damien. It looked to be one of those private jets that were big enough for at least ten or more couples.

"Yes, but it's the smallest I could get on short notice."

They stopped before boarding the plane and Damien spoke to Sir Drake. "We need to leave on time."

Sir Drake, with an unreadable expression on his face, said, "We will, sir. My copilot has arrived."

Damien glanced to where a woman, also dressed in a pilot uniform was approaching. He frowned and looked over at Sir Drake. "That's your copilot?"

"Yes, sir, that's the copilot."

"She's a woman. Are you sure she knows how to fly this thing if she needs to?"

A slight smile touched Sir Drake's lips and Ivy thought it was too bad Damien didn't notice that it really didn't quite reach his eyes. "Yes, sir. I'm sure. To be honest, she's probably a better pilot than I am."

"I would find that hard to believe," Damien said frowning. "Just make sure that you're the one flying this thing at all times and not her."

He then turned to Ivy. "Let's go."

"WAKE UP, IVY. We're here."

Ivy wasn't sure how long she slept. The brevity of sleep last night from making love with Nolan had tired her out. The last thing she remembered was boarding the plane and putting on her seat belt before drifting off to sleep. That suited her just fine since she didn't want to have to converse with Damien.

She glanced out the window as the plane was landing. "Where are we?"

"El Salvador."

"El Salvador? You didn't say anything about leaving the country."

"Didn't I?"

She glared at him. "No, you didn't."

Ignoring her comment, he said, "It was a great flight. The smoothest two and a half hours I've ever flown. Need to commend the pilot." He then pointed out the window. "See that warehouse? That's where your office will be."

Ivy noticed what appeared to be a huge building in the middle of nowhere with an airstrip on one side of it and a jungle on the other. It appeared so isolated. "Are you sure this is the place?"

He chuckled. "Positive. Don't let the outside fool you. It's all state-of-the-art on the inside. You won't believe what all they have going on. They run a huge operation."

"Who are they?" she asked him.

"You will find out soon enough. We even have a couple of politicians in the group. They pay well. Maybe we'll be able to talk you into coming on board full-time."

"Don't hold your breath, Damien."

Instead of coming to a stop on the runway, the plane kept moving. "What the hell?" Damien said, looking out the window. "What is the pilot doing? He's going to hit the damn building."

Damien quickly unbuckled his seat belt and moved

in the direction of the cockpit. When the pilot finally brought the plane to a stop, Damien lost his balance and tumbled back down in his seat.

Ivy fought back a smile at the look of anger on his face. "Remember what you said, Damien. It was the smoothest two-and-a-half-hour flight you've ever flown."

He glared over at her. "Shut up."

At that moment the cockpit door opened and the two pilots came out. Smiling sweetly, Tori Warren said, "I hope the two of you enjoyed your flight. Personally, I think it was the easiest I've ever piloted."

Pure rage consumed Damien. He pointed at Sir Drake. "I told you not to let her fly this plane."

"What's your complaint?" Tori asked, still smiling. "I believe in door-to-door service. Look how close I got you to the entrance so you wouldn't have far to walk."

The plane door opened and Ivy looked out. OMG! They were definitely close to the door. She was convinced only a very skilled pilot could get this close to the building without hitting it.

"What kind of pilots are you two?" Damien was asking, quickly grabbing his briefcase. "You put people's lives in danger. This plane is not even on the runway. I will notify the owners."

"We are the owners," Sir Drake said, smiling. "And if you ever need to fly anywhere else, just give us a call."

"I'll never use the two of you as pilots again."

"Honestly?" Tori asked, smiling. "I could have sworn I heard you tell Miss Chapman this was the smoothest flight you've ever flown."

Damien eyed Tori suspiciously. "How do you know what I told her when you were in the cockpit?"

Sir Drake chuckled. "She has bionic hearing."

"Stop messing with him like that, Sir Drake," Ashton Sinclair said, coming on board.

Damien stared at Ashton like he was seeing a ghost and took a step back. "Hey, wait a minute. You're that man from Sisters. Where did you come from? Who the hell are you?"

Ashton smiled. "Doesn't matter who I am. The important thing is that I know who you are." He then glanced over at Ivy. "You're okay?"

Ivy nodded and smiled. "Yes, I'm fine."

"Good. Nolan should be arriving any minute. He's flying Clayton's Cessna."

"Who the hell is Nolan? What the hell is going on?" Damien all but roared.

"I'll tell you who Nolan is," Ivy said, glaring at Damien. "Nolan Madaris is the man who loves me. Sorry, but what you said the other day wasn't true. You aren't the best I can do. Not even close."

Damien frowned. "Madaris?"

Ivy knew the Madaris family was widely known in the state of Texas. Damien had clearly made the connection. "Yes, Madaris."

"Go ahead and get off the plane, Mr. Fargo," Tori said. "Looks like there's a welcome party of federal agents here to greet you. I'm sure they will explain everything. Oops, I guess they aren't going to wait for you to get off. They're coming up to you."

At that moment several FBI agents boarded the plane. One of them said, "Damien Fargo, you are under arrest." He then read him the Miranda warning.

"Why? What did I do?" Damien asked as he was being handcuffed.

"You're being arrested for human trafficking, computer espionage, treason against the United States of America and plotting to kill Ms. Ivy Chapman."

"Kill me?" Ivy said, swallowing deeply.

"Yes," Tori said, glaring. "He and his associates never intended for you to return to Houston."

"Lies! All lies," Damien screamed. "You can't prove a thing."

"Sorry, but we can," one of the agents said. "We heard everything. This plane was set up with an audio recorder. Every conversation you had with Albert Whitfield was recorded. Including the one you had while seated in the back of the plane on your phone while Miss Chapman was napping, just in case she woke up and overheard."

"That same conversation where you said you were going to use her for more than one computer hacking job before getting rid of her," Sir Drake said. "Yes, we heard you, too, in the cockpit. Every single word. Every sordid detail. Get him out my sight before I decide to beat the hell out of him."

As if the agents were concerned Sir Drake just might do that very thing, they quickly got Fargo off the plane. Ivy glanced over at Tori. "They really planned to kill me?"

Tori crossed over to her and gave her a hug. "Yes. They couldn't risk you being a liability. But you were never in any immediate danger. Drake and I made sure of it. Once we knew of our destination, we notified Alex. Whitfield and his cohorts were caught red-handed bringing in a load of kidnapped women to be flown to South America. Even those two politicians were here to look over the women to select any they wanted as a playmate before shipping them off."

"How sick," Ivy said, not wanting to believe anyone could be that demented.

"Yes, it was. I understand federal agents were able to raid the place and stumbled on more than they'd bargained for, including weapons and explosives that were being shipped to ISIS," Tori added.

At that moment Nolan rushed on the plane. He immediately went to Ivy and pulled her in his arms. "You're okay, baby?"

She nodded, not believing all the excitement. "Yes, I'm fine."

"Give her a chance to breathe, will you?" Tori teased.

Alex and Trevor then came on board. Trevor shook his head at Tori. "What were you trying to do? Give them front-door service? We were inside the warehouse and saw the plane headed toward us. You wouldn't believe how many agents dived out of the way, convinced the plane was going to hit the building. You scared the shit out of a few people today, Tori."

"She was just being a show-off," Sir Drake said, coming to stand beside his wife and taking off her pilot's cap.

"I never show off," Tori said, running her fingers through her hair and tossing it out of her face.

"Whatever" was Sir Drake's response.

"Thanks to you, Ivy, a lot of arrests have been made today," Alex said, grinning. "The feds were able to bring down the entire operation."

"They can send Ivy a thank-you card in the mail. I'm flying her home now."

"She needs to make a statement first, and then the two of you are free to leave," Alex said.

Nolan nodded as he took Ivy's hand and brought it to his lips to kiss it. Then, as if deciding that wasn't enough, he leaned down and captured her mouth, as usual not caring they had an audience.

"Think they need privacy much?" Ivy heard Sir Drake ask.

"Yes. They deserve it" was Alex's response.

"Then by all means, let's get out now," Tori ordered.

Nolan continued to kiss her and Ivy was getting aroused with every sensuous stroke of his tongue in her mouth. She had to break off the kiss to tame her rapid heartbeat.

"Do you know what we're going to do when we get home?" Nolan asked against her wet lips.

"Umm, I have an idea," Ivy said, smiling.

Nolan chuckled. "Yes, that, too. But I'm also going to go to the jewelry store to get an engagement ring to put on your finger."

"Oh, Nolan…"

And then they were kissing again and Ivy knew that in the end, the best-laid plans were the ones they'd always made together.

CHAPTER THIRTY-NINE

JAKE WAS OUT in the yard when Nolan pulled into Whispering Pines. When Nolan got out of the car, his granduncle shook his head, grinning. "I read the article of your engagement in this morning's paper and figured you would show up sooner or later."

"Yes, and here I am," Nolan said, giving his granduncle a huge bear hug.

Jake stared at him for a minute and then said, "I liked Ivy from the first. So did Diamond. She's a very nice young woman and I wish the two of you a wonderful future together."

"Thanks, Granduncle Jake. That means a lot. Where's Mama Laverne?"

"Mom is sitting in her favorite spot on the patio."

And that's where Nolan found her, doing what seemed to be her favorite pastime—shelling peas. Their gazes met the moment he walked through the French doors.

"Nolan, this is a surprise."

He doubted it was. He had a feeling that she'd expected him. He crossed the brick floor and leaned down and placed a kiss on her cheek. "Mama Laverne."

He slid into the empty chair to face her. Unlike before, when she'd shoved a handful of pea pods into his lap, today she just stared at him expectantly before asking, "You have something to tell me?"

Nolan fought back a smile. How could he have thought that he could best her at her own game? All those before him had tried and ended up in the same boat where he was. Madly in love with the person she'd chosen. "I have nothing to tell you that you probably don't already know. But I do have a question for you."

"And what's your question?"

He leaned forward with his elbows resting on his thighs. "How did you know? How did you know Ivy would be the perfect woman for me? How did you know that in the end, although I intended to fight it like hell, that I would come to love her more than life itself?"

His great-grandmother didn't say anything for a moment and then she answered, "I knew because I knew you. And I knew that you were the man Ivy needed. While growing up she'd faced some of the same challenges you had. Namely, being super smart in all that computer stuff and wearing glasses. It shouldn't matter but it did. Kids can be cruel. It's stupid how people judge others. A real doggone shame. You were lucky to be a part of a large family who made sure you felt love and special. Ivy lacked that. Because of my friendship with Helen, I've known Ivy since the day she was born. I watched her grow up and knew what she needed and who she needed. She deserved a man who would understand her, who wouldn't want to change her. A man who would love and accept her as she was."

"She's beautiful," Nolan said softly.

"Yes, you saw her beauty immediately, even when you didn't want to. I knew once the two of you spent time together at your cottage you would fall in love...no

matter what plan the two of you thought you could con-
coct to do otherwise. Don't think I wasn't onto you two."

Nolan's jaw dropped. "How did you know?"

"Don't worry how I know. And none of your cousins
squealed and I didn't have the cottage bugged. Helen
knew her granddaughter and I knew you. We figured
the two of you would try to outsmart us and we were
ready with a plan C."

He lifted a brow. "And what was plan C?"

Felicia Laverne smiled. "No need for you to know
that now." And then she said, "I read about what Ivy's
ex-boyfriend tried to do. That no-good loser. It made
the front page of this morning's paper."

"I know. Upon Ivy's request she wasn't mentioned.
She didn't want the media camped out on her doorstep.
Her part in cracking the case will come out later."

"Good decision. Now, scat. Unless you plan to help
me shell these peas. I can always use an extra hand."

Nolan stood. "Sorry, don't have the time today. I'm
taking Ivy to dinner to celebrate our engagement."

"Have the two of you set a date?"

Nolan laughed. "Don't you know?"

She frowned up at him. "Do you think I know everything, Nolan?"

Nolan couldn't help but smile as he leaned down and
placed another kiss on his great-grandmother's cheek.
"Honestly? Sometimes I think you really do know everything."

EPILOGUE

Seven months later

IVY TURNED AND tossed the bridal bouquet. No one was surprised when it was caught by Victoria Madaris, who let out a happy squeal and held it to her chest as if it was the world's largest diamond. And no one cheered louder than the single Madaris men who thought they were getting a reprieve for now.

Nolan thought that he and Ivy had had a beautiful wedding but would be the first to admit he was glad it was over. So much planning had gone into this day and the end result was that the most beautiful woman had walked down the aisle on her father's arm to him. They had pledged their love and lives to each other.

He glanced across the ballroom where Ivy was dancing with her father. She looked happy and at that moment he vowed as her husband to make sure that same smile that was on her face now remained there for the rest of her life.

They would live in his condo for a while. Because they loved the area, they had purchased two acres of land in Madaris Lakes Estates, the same subdivision where his granduncle Jonathan and grandaunt Marilyn lived.

"Standing over here, looking all smug."

Nolan couldn't help but turn and grin at his cousin Lee. "Why shouldn't I? I married a beautiful woman today."

Lee nodded. "Yes, you did. Ivy looks absolutely radiant."

He thought the same thing. Momentarily switching his gaze from Ivy and her father, he glanced to where Reese was pushing around a double stroller with the twins. "Fatherhood becomes Reese, don't you think? It looks good on DeAngelo, too." DeAngelo's wife, Peyton, had given birth to a son that they named Dante Antonio Di Meglio.

"I hope that fatherhood becomes me as well, since I'll be wearing it in about eight months."

Nolan turned to stare at Lee. "Carly's pregnant?"

A huge smile touched Lee's lips. "Yes, she's pregnant."

Nolan returned the smile. "Have you told the family?"

"Not yet. Probably won't have to. Word is out that Mama Laverne dreamed about fish a few nights ago."

Everyone in the Madaris family knew when Mama Laverne dreamed about fish that meant someone was pregnant. "Congratulations," Nolan said and truly meant it.

"Thanks. Now I need to go find my wife."

When Lee walked off Nolan glanced over to where the dance between Ivy and her father was ending. He saw one of his cousins headed toward Ivy to claim her for a dance and decided this time the honor would be his. They'd had their first dance together as a married couple, had cut the cake and all that. But he wanted to hold his wife in his arms again before it was time for them to leave on their honeymoon.

They would spend two weeks in Australia and from there head to Paris, where they would live for six months while the hotel was under construction. When they returned home they would begin building their own home.

"Nolan?"

He turned at the sound of the soft voice. His great-grandmother. "Yes, Mama Laverne?"

"I only want the best for my family. I hope you know that."

If he didn't before, Nolan certainly knew it now because he thought Ivy was the best. "Yes, I know it, Mama Laverne. Thanks for bringing us together."

She shook her head. "Ivy thanked her grandmother as well. But we didn't bring you and Ivy together. The two of you did that. We merely made sure you got a chance to spend time together and the two of you took it over from there. You and Ivy proved what Helen and I had known all along—that you and Ivy would make a beautiful couple who will have beautiful babies."

Nolan threw his head back and laughed. Already Mama Laverne had her thoughts on expanding the Madaris family. "Yes, one day we will have beautiful babies."

A short while later he held Ivy in his arms while they danced. She had been tickled seeing how Kenna, Lee, Reese, Nolan and Corbin performed on the dance floor. "I told you we all took dance lessons to keep up with Kenna. She likes to dance."

"And you all did a great job. Maybe I need to take

dance lessons. I'll add it to my list with those cooking lessons."

Nolan pulled Ivy closer into his arms. She didn't know it yet but one of her wedding gifts from him was that he had talked to James Wingate and the cologne Forever You would be exclusively hers. It was being taken off the market and no other woman but Ivy would be wearing it. "Are you happy, baby?"

"Yes, Nolan. I am so happy. Thank you for making this a special day."

"Hey, you're the bride and a beautiful one. Today is all about you." He leaned closer and whispered in her ear. "Tonight it will be about me."

"Oh, yes," Ivy said, grinning. "I got everything all planned. It will definitely be a Nolan Madaris night. One you will always remember."

"I can't wait."

Then, in the middle of the dance floor, he leaned down and kissed his wife, believing in his heart that from this day forward, they would live happily ever after.

* * * * *

PR consultant Penelope Brand vowed to never, ever get involved with a client again. But then her latest client turns out to also be her irresistible one-night stand, and he introduces her as his fiancée. Now she's playing couple, giving in to temptation... and might soon be expecting the billionaire's baby...

Read on for a sneak peek at
LONE STAR LOVERS
By Jessica Lemmon.

One

Texas in the springtime was a sight to behold. The Dallas sunshine warmed the patio of Hip Stir, where Penelope Brand sat across from her most recent client. Blue, cloudless skies stretched over the glass-and-steel city buildings, practically begging the city dwellers to take a deep breath. Given that nearly every table was full, it appeared that most of downtown had obeyed.

Pen adjusted her sunglasses before carefully lifting her filled-to-the-brim café au lait. The mug's contents wobbled but she made that first sip to her lips rather than to her lap. Which was a relief since Pen always wore white. Today she'd chosen her favorite white jacket with black silk piping over a vibrant pink cami. Her pants were white to match, slim fitting and her legs ended in a pair of black five-inch stilettos.

White was her power color. Pen's clients came to her

for crisis control—sometimes for a completely fresh start. As their public relations maven, a crisp, clean do-over had become Pen's specialty.

She'd started her business in the Midwest. Until last year, the Chicago elite had trusted her with their bank accounts, their marriages and their hard-won reputations. When her own reputation took a header, Pen was forced to regroup. That unfortunate circumstance was rapidly gaining ground as her "past." The woman sitting across from her now had laid the foundation for Penelope's future.

"I can't thank you enough." Stefanie Ferguson shook her head, tossing her dark blond ponytail to the side. "Though I suppose I should thank my stupid brother for the introduction." She lifted her espresso and rolled her eyes.

Pen smothered a smile. Stefanie's *stupid brother* was none other than the well-loved mayor of Dallas, and he'd called on Penelope's services to help his younger sister out of a mess that could mar his reputation.

Stef didn't share her brother's reverent love for politics and being careful in the public eye. She flew by the seat of her skinny jeans, the most recent flight landing her in the arms of one of the mayor's most critical opponents, Blake Eastwood.

Blake's development company wanted to break ground for a new civic center that Mayor Ferguson opposed. Critics argued that the mayor was biased, given the civic center was to be built near his family's oil wells, but the mayor's supporters argued the unneeded new build would be a waste of city funds.

Either way, the photograph of Stefanie exiting a hotel, her arm wrapped around Blake's while they both wore wrinkled clothing and sexually satisfied smiles, had caused some unwanted media attention.

The mayor had hired Brand Consulting to smooth out the wrinkles of what could have turned into a PR nightmare. Penelope had done her job and done it well. One week after the snafu, and the media had already moved on to gossiping about someone else.

All in a day's work.

"You're coming to the party tonight, right?" Stef asked. "I was looking forward to you being there so I have a girl to talk to."

"I wouldn't miss it," Pen answered with a smile. Those who gained entry to the mayor's annual soiree, held at his private gated mansion, were the envy of the city. Pen had worked with billionaires, local celebrities and sports stars in her professional past, but she'd never worked directly with a civil servant. Attending the most sought-after party of the year was as good as a gold star on her résumé.

Pen picked up the tab for her client and said her goodbyes to Stefanie before walking two blocks back to her office.

Thank God for the mayor's troublemaking sister.

Stepping in at the pleasure of Mayor Chase Ferguson might have been the best decision Pen had made since moving to Dallas. Her heart thudded heavily against her breastbone as she thought about what this could mean for her growing PR firm. The world of politics teemed with scandal.

After finishing her work for the day, she locked the glass door on her tenth-floor suite and drew the blinds. In her private bathroom, Pen spritzed on a dash of floral perfume and brushed her teeth, swapping out her suit for the white dress she'd chosen to wear to the mayor's party. She'd brought it with her to work since her apartment was on the other side of town and the mayor's mansion was closer to her office.

She smoothed her palms down the skirt and checked the back view in the full-length mirror on the door. *Not bad at all.* After way too much vacillating this morning, she'd opted for hair down versus hair up. Soft waves fell around her shoulders and the color of her pale blue eyes popped beneath a veil of black-mascaraed lashes and smoky, silver-blue shadow.

The dress was doing her several favors, hugging her hips and her derriere in a way that wasn't inappropriate, but showcased her daily efforts at the gym.

I couldn't let you leave without pointing out how well you wear that dress.

Shivers tracked down her arms and she rubbed away the gooseflesh as the silken voice from two weeks ago wound around her brain.

Pen had moved to Dallas thinking she'd sworn off men forever, but after nearly a year of working nonstop to rebuild her business, she'd admitted she was lonely. She'd been at a swanky jazz club enjoying her martini when yet another man had approached to try his luck.

This one had been a tall, muscled, delicious male specimen with a confident walk and a paralyzing green stare that held her fastened in place. He'd introduced himself as "Just Zach," and then asked to sit. She'd surprised herself by saying yes.

Over a drink, she learned they'd crossed paths once before—at a party in Chicago. They knew the same billionaire family who owned Crane Hotels, though she'd never imagined running into Zach again anywhere other than Chicago.

She also never imagined she'd ask him to come home with her...but she did. When one drink led to another, Penelope let him lead her out of the club.

What a night it'd been.

His kisses had seared, branding her his for those stolen few hours. Hotter than his mouth were the acres of golden muscles, and she'd reveled in smoothing her palms over his bulging pecs and the bumps of his abs. Zach had a great ass, a better smile, and when he left in the morning, he'd even kissed her goodbye.

Stay in bed and recover, Penelope Brand.

A dimple had punctuated one of his cheeks, and her laugh had eased into a soft hum as she'd watched Zach's silhouetted masculine form dress in the sunlight pressing through her white bedroom curtains.

Sigh.

It had been the perfect night, curing her of her loneliness and adding a much-needed spring in her step. Pen had felt like she could take over the damn world. Amazing what a few earth-shattering orgasms could do for a girl's morale.

She was still smiling at that memory of "Just Zach" from Chicago when she climbed behind the wheel of her Audi and started toward her destination. One night with Zach had been fun, but Pen wasn't foolish enough to believe it could have been more. As the daughter of entrepreneurs, success had been ingrained in Pen's mind from an early age. She'd taken her eye off the prize in Chicago and look what'd happened.

Never again.

At the gates of the mayor's mansion, Pen presented

the shiny black invitation, personalized with her name in an elegant silver script. The security guard waved her through and she smiled in triumph. She was *in*.

She checked her wrap and tucked her clutch under her arm. When her turn came, an attendant walked her to the mayor for a proper introduction.

Standing before the mayor, was it any wonder the man had earned the hearts of the majority of Dallas's female voters? Chase Ferguson was tall; his dark hair pushed this way and that as if it couldn't be tamed, but the angle of his clean-shaven jaw and the lines on his dark suit showed control where it counted.

"Ms. Brand." Hazel eyes lowered to a respectable survey of her person before Chase offered a hand. She shook it and he released her to signal to a nearby waiter. "Stefanie is around here somewhere," he said of his younger sister. He leaned in. "And thanks to you, on her best behavior."

The mayor straightened as a waiter approached with a tray of champagne.

"Drink?" Chase's Texas accent had all but vanished beneath a perfected veneer, but Pen could hear the slightest drawl when he lowered his voice. "You'll get to meet my brother tonight."

She was embarrassed she didn't know a thing about another Ferguson sibling. She'd only been in Texas for a year, and between juggling her new business, moving into her apartment and handling crises for the Dallas elite, she hadn't climbed the Ferguson family tree any higher than Chase and Stefanie.

"Perfect timing," Chase said, his eyes going over her shoulder to welcome a new arrival.

"Hey, hey, big brother."

Now that. *That* was a drawl.

The back of her neck prickled. She recognized the voice instantly. It sent warmth pooling in her belly and lower. It stood her nipples on end. The Texas accent over her shoulder was a tad thicker than Chase's, but not as lazy as it'd been two weeks ago. Not like it was when she'd invited him home and he'd leaned close, his lips brushing the shell of her ear.

Lead the way, gorgeous.

Squaring her shoulders, Pen prayed Zach had the shortest memory ever and turned to make his acquaintance.

Correction: Reacquaintance.

She was floored by broad shoulders outlined by a sharp black tux, longish dark blond hair smoothed away from his handsome face and the greenest eyes she'd ever seen. Zach had been gorgeous the first time she'd laid eyes on him, but his current look suited the air of control and power swirling around him.

A primal, hidden part of her wanted to lean into his solid form and rest in his capable, strong arms again. As tempting as reaching out to him was, she wouldn't. She'd had her night with him. She was in the process of assembling a solid bedrock for her fragile, rebuilt business and she refused to let her world fall apart because of a sexy man with a dimple.

A dimple that was notably missing since he was gaping at her with shock. His poker face needed work.

"I'll be damned," Zach muttered. "I didn't expect to see you here."

"That makes two of us," Pen said, and then she polished off half her champagne in one long drink.

Two

Zach schooled his expression—albeit a bit late.

Penelope Brand wore a curve-hugging white dress like the night he'd seen her at the club. He'd been there with a friend who had long since left with a woman. Zach hadn't been looking to hook up until he spotted Pen's upswept blond hair and the elegant line from her neck to her bare shoulders.

Seeing her hair down tonight drop-kicked him two weeks into the past. Her apartment. The moment he'd tugged the clip holding her hair back and let those luscious locks down. The way he'd speared his fingers into those silken strands, before kicking her door closed and carrying her to her bedroom.

He'd sampled her mouth before depositing her onto her bed and sampling every other part of her.

And he did mean *every* part.

They hadn't discussed rules, but each had known the score—he wouldn't call and she wouldn't want him to—so they'd made the most of that night. She'd tasted like every debased teenage fantasy he'd ever had, and she'd delivered. He'd left that morning with a smile on his face that matched hers.

When he'd stepped into the shower at home that morning, he'd experienced a brief pinch of regret that he wouldn't see her again.

Though, hell, maybe he *would* see her again given lightning had already stricken them twice. He hadn't wanted to let her get away that night at the bar—not without testing the attraction between them.

He felt a similar pull now.

"If you'll excuse me." His brother Chase moved off, arm extended to shake the palm of a round-bellied man who ruled half of Texas. As one-third owner of Ferguson Oil, it was Zach's job to know the powerful players in his brother's life—in the entire state—but this man was unfamiliar.

"Just Zach," Pen snapped, drawing Zach's attention. Her blue eyes ignited. "I thought you were a contractor in Chicago."

"I used to be."

"And now you're the mayor's brother?"

"I've always been the mayor's brother," he told her with a sideways smile.

He'd also always been an oil tycoon. A brief stint of going out on his own in Chicago hadn't changed his parentage or his inheritance. When Zach had received a call from his mother letting him know his father, Rand Ferguson, had had a heart attack, Zach had left Chicago and never looked back.

He wasn't the black sheep—had never resented working for the family business. He'd simply wanted to do his own thing for a while. He had, and now he was back, and yeah, he was pretty damn good at being the head honcho of Ferguson Oil. It also let his mother breathe a sigh of relief to have Zach in charge.

Penelope's face pinched. "Are you adopted or something?"

He chuckled. Not the first time he'd heard that. "Actually, Chase and I are twins."

"Really?" Her nose scrunched. It was cute.

"No."

She pursed her lips and damn if he didn't want to experience their sweetness all over again. He hadn't dated much over the past year, but the way Penelope smiled at him had towed him in. He hadn't recognized her at first—the briefest of meetings at a Crane Hotel function three years ago hadn't cemented her in his mind—but there was a pull there he couldn't deny.

Pen finished her champagne and rested the flute on a passing waiter's tray. With straight shoulders and the lift of one fair eyebrow, she faced Zach again. "You didn't divulge your family status when I met you on Saturday."

"You didn't divulge yours."

Her eyes coasted over his tuxedo, obviously trying to square the man before her with the slacks and button-down he'd worn to the club.

"It's still me." He gave her a grin, one that popped his dimple. He pointed at it while she frowned. "You liked this a few weeks ago." He gestured to himself generally as he leaned in to murmur, "You liked a lot of this a few weeks ago."

Miffed wasn't a good enough word for the expression that crossed her pretty face. The attraction was still there. The lure that existed as they came together that night in her bed twice—no, wait, *three times*.

Zach decided he'd end tonight with her in his bed. They'd been good together, and while he wasn't one to make a habit of two-night stands, he'd make an exception for Penelope Brand.

Because *damn*.

"I'll escort you to the dining room. You can sit with me." He offered his arm.

Pen sighed, the action lifting her breasts and softening her features. Zach's grin widened.

So close.

She qualified with, "Fine. But only because there are a lot of people here I would like to meet. This is a business function for me, so I'd appreciate—"

The words died on Penelope's lips when a female shriek rose on the air. "Where is he? Where is that son of a bitch who owes me money?"

The crowd gasped and Pen's hand tightened on his forearm.

Zach turned in the direction of the outburst to find a rail-thin redhead in a long black dress waving a rolled-slash-wadded stack of paper in her hand. Her brown eyes snapped around the room, and her upper lip curled in a way that made Zach wonder how he'd ever found her attractive.

Granted she wasn't foaming at the mouth when they'd exchanged their vows.

"You." Her eyes landed on him as the security guards positioned around the house rushed toward her. "Write

me a check for a million dollars and I'll be on my way." Yvonne cocked her head and waved the crumpled stack of papers in front of her. "Or else I'll tear up our annulment."

Tearing it up wouldn't make it go away. What was her angle?

"Marrying you entitled me to at least half your fortune, Zachary Ferguson."

It was laughable that she thought a million was *half*.

Penelope's hand slipped from his forearm and Zach reached over and put it back.

"Ex-wife," he corrected for Penelope's—hell, for everyone's—benefit. "And no, it doesn't."

Yvonne's eyes sliced over to Penelope. "Who is this? Are you *cheating* on me?"

Here they went again. Yvonne had asked that question so many times in the two days they were married, Zach would swear she'd gone to bed sane and woken crazy.

He'd had the good sense to get out of the marriage, which was more than he could say for the sense he'd had going in. The details were fuzzy: Vegas, Elvis, the Chapel of Love, etcetera, etcetera… Getting married had seemed fun at the time, but spontaneity had its downfalls. Within twenty-four hours Yvonne had grown horns and a forked tongue.

"Make it two million dollars," Yvonne hissed, illustrating his point.

Zach had money—plenty of it—but relinquishing it to the crazed redhead wasn't going to make her go away. If anything, she'd be back for more later.

"Get her out of here," Zach told the guard, putting his hand over Pen's. "She's upsetting my fiancée."

"Your what?" Yvonne asked at the same time Penelope stiffened at his side.

"Penelope Brand, my fiancée."

Will Penelope play along as Zach's fiancée?
Find out in
LONE STAR LOVERS
by Jessica Lemmon
available March 2018 wherever
Harlequin Desire books and ebooks are sold.
www.Harlequin.com

HARLEQUIN Desire

Family sagas...scandalous secrets...burning desires.

Save $1.00

on the purchase of ANY Harlequin® Desire book.

Available wherever books are sold, including most bookstores, supermarkets, drugstores and discount stores.

LONE STAR LOVERS

JESSICA LEMMON

Save $1.00

on the purchase of any Harlequin Desire book.

Coupon valid until June 30, 2018.
Redeemable at participating outlets in the U.S. and Canada only.
Not redeemable at Barnes & Noble stores. Limit one coupon per customer.

52615593

Canadian Retailers: Harlequin Enterprises Limited will pay the face value of this coupon plus 10.25¢ if submitted by customer for this product only. Any other use constitutes fraud. Coupon is nonassignable. Void if taxed, prohibited or restricted by law. Consumer must pay any government taxes. Void if copied. Inmar Promotional Services ("IPS") customers submit coupons and proof of sales to Harlequin Enterprises Limited, P.O. Box 31000, Scarborough, ON M1R 0E7, Canada. Non-IPS retailer—for reimbursement submit coupons and proof of sales directly to Harlequin Enterprises Limited, Retail Marketing Department, 225 Duncan Mill Rd., Don Mills, ON M3B 3K9, Canada.

U.S. Retailers: Harlequin Enterprises Limited will pay the face value of this coupon plus 8¢ if submitted by customer for this product only. Any other use constitutes fraud. Coupon is nonassignable. Void if taxed, prohibited or restricted by law. Consumer must pay any government taxes. Void if copied. For reimbursement submit coupons and proof of sales directly to Harlequin Enterprises, Ltd 482, NCH Marketing Services, P.O. Box 880001, El Paso, TX 88588-0001, U.S.A. Cash value 1/100 cents.

5 65373 00076 2 (8100)0 12350

® and ™ are trademarks owned and used by the trademark owner and/or its licensee.

© 2018 Harlequin Enterprises Limited

HDCOUP0318

Get 2 Free Books,
<u>Plus</u> 2 Free Gifts -

just for trying the *Reader Service!*

Get 2 Free Books,
Plus 2 Free Gifts—
just for trying the Reader Service!

Get 2 Free Books,
Plus 2 Free Gifts—
just for trying the Reader Service!